Indelible Love — Emily's Story

ISBN: 1470130106
ISBN-13: 9781470130107

Indelible Love — Emily's Story

D W Cee

To Joyce

For your countless hours of editing, encouraging, and listening

Prologue

"Em?" Max called my name so tentatively, that I figured he was nervous about proposing.

"Yes?" I was so excited. Four years and way too many uncertain days later, he was finally going to ask me to marry him. Giddy…yes, I was incredibly giddy.

"Em…you know how much I've loved you the last four years, right? You were the most important person in my life. Someone I couldn't live without?"

I wondered why he spoke in the past tense. "Of course I know this. I love you just as much, Max."

"Please don't ever forget this, no matter what." I thought I saw tears welling up in his eyes, but suddenly his gentle face turned stoic. It scared me.

"Em. I need my freedom. I want us to break up and experience life without each other." There was no more emotion in his voice.

"What?" Tears automatically fell from my eyes. "What did you say?" Had I heard him correctly? Was he breaking up with me? My head and my heart shook in fear.

"I'm sorry. It's over." Without another word, he went out of my room and out of my life.

My heart stopped beating with those last four words. How could I have believed we were about to get engaged, when he believed it was over? How could I have loved this man with all my heart, when his heart stopped loving me some time ago? How could I have been so wrong about Max?

Four years ago, I met this boy and fell in love instantly. Four days ago, I believed we were getting married as soon as we graduated. Four seconds ago this same boy broke my heart and wanted to move on with his life, without me. Sobbing, I called Sarah.

Chapter 1

Christmas Ball

"What time is Jake picking you up?" Sarah asked, as she sat in the salon chair next to me. "Charlie's coming straight here since we need to get to the Christmas Ball a little earlier to help set up. Emily. Emily Logan. What are you daydreaming about? You haven't answered my question. What time is Jake coming to pick you up?"

Ugh! The Christmas Ball! Why had I agreed to go to this event? All of our college friends would be there. Although it had been eighteen months since the breakup, I dreaded seeing Max and his new girlfriend tonight.

Max Davis. My first love. My world.

We had dated throughout undergrad, and he was the absolute love of my life. He was tall, good looking, and extremely intelligent. His sandy-brown hair and matching brown eyes didn't stand out until he smiled. His tender smile melted my heart and made me smile along with him.

He was probably the smartest in our group of friends, but not as driven as I would have liked. His lack of motivation didn't keep me from being absolutely crazy about him. I thought he was it. I would marry no other but Max…until, he dumped me on graduation night. Sadness filled my heart again.

"Um…I'm not sure." I hesitated with my answer.

"What do you mean you're not sure? You did invite Jake to this ball?"

"Yeah, I did, last night when he came over for dinner." Sarah's eyebrows arched up, which signaled bad things to come. That meant there would be more questions followed by a reprimand. Being the oldest of four siblings, Sarah was a bit motherly toward me, the adult orphan.

"Emily! You asked him to this function last night? What if he had to work? As it is, he's always working. What did he say?"

"Well, he wasn't too happy with me. He accused me of not wanting to go because I wasn't over Max." From the corner of my eyes I saw Sarah's head plop into her hands while she made an ugly groaning sound. "And I was stupid enough to tell him that though I didn't like Max anymore, I still hurt a lot from our breakup." Sarah groaned even louder.

I regretted my honesty last night. Jake and I had been dating six weeks, and from day one, I expounded upon my past more than necessary.

"Then I was an even bigger idiot and called what Jake and I have not a relationship but 'whatever it is that we have.' That's when he got up and left in the middle of dinner."

"Emily!" The groan, the sigh...every exasperated noise came out in a flurry. "I thought everything was going so well with you two. When you and I were in New York over Thanksgiving, Charlie and I had a bet going on about you." She smiled in a weird way.

"What bet was that?"

"Which day you would come crying telling me you had to go home to see Jake. You were miserable without him."

"I was not...well, I guess I kind of was." My lips pursed, apologetically. "So who won?"

"Charlie. He said you'd feel too guilty to confess, but he was sure Jake would fly into New York to see you instead."

"He almost did. I had to hold him back." I laughed. "Anyhow, he texted last night and said he's coming over around 6:00pm. He's going to shower and get ready at my place."

"Isn't that a bit dangerous?" Always on the naughty side, her questions confounded my simple mind.

"Why would it be dangerous?" I asked naively.

"Are you kidding me? I've never met such a gorgeous doctor in my life!"

"Don't be silly. We've done nothing naughty, to your dismay."

"Didn't you practically make out with him the first day you met him? And how old are you?" Sarah questioned. "Aren't you beyond the age of making a boy wait so long before letting him do anything other than kiss you?"

Sarah always poked fun at what she called my "unnecessary modesty."

"I'm twenty-four and he's thirty. Yeah, that first weekend we met was crazy. It was so unlike me. Anyhow, we've only had a handful of dates now. I don't think I'm doing anything wrong. We just haven't gotten to know each other well enough," I retorted with a laugh. "Mind your own business."

"What does your dress look like, Emily?" Jon, my hairdresser, interrupted. "And what shall we do with this long brunette mane of yours today?"

"It's a black low-cut sleeveless dress. It's fitted from top to bottom. I'm going to wear black heels with it. Do what you like with my hair."

"Ok." As soon as Jon answered me, his eyes twinkled. "I think I know what I want to do. How about a sleek tie back? I think that will accentuate your high cheekbones."

"Sure." It didn't really matter. At five feet five inches, I'd always been on the slender side but since the breakup I'd lost a considerable amount of weight. I knew I looked unhealthy, but there wasn't much I could do...not much I wanted to do.

It took forever to get my hair and nails done. I figured while here, a facial would do wonders for my dry skin, and an aesthetician could apply my makeup. She did a great job coloring my eyes a smoky black and brushing my pale cheeks with enough blush to give them a slightly flushed look. The lipstick we picked out was the shade of a perfectly blossomed rose. Why not look good? Whether for the present date, the ex, or his new girlfriend, looking good was definitely the best revenge—though, a part of me felt guilty for thinking this.

"Wow, Emily. You look great!" exclaimed Charlie.

"Hey, what about me?" Sarah pouted. "I'm your girlfriend!"

"You're always gorgeous," he said lightly, kissing her pale pink lips.

"See you two later," I called out as we left the salon. "Are we sitting together? Jake won't know too many people there. Put us at a good table, please."

"Don't worry!" They chuckled. Something about the undercurrent of those two words worried me.

I glanced at my watch. Yikes! Running late, I dashed to my car in four-inch heels and a dress that was a size too big on me.

Jake was already at my door when I pulled into my driveway. My house, a small Craftsman about eighteen hundred square feet, sat on a beautifully tree-lined street. I had saved all my money while working through college, then saved another year's worth of my pitiful teacher's pay to put a down payment on this beautiful old home. Built in 1922, it had good bones. Wood beams ran across the ceilings and crown moldings outlined every room. There was a Batchelder fireplace on one end of the living room and built-in cabinets in each room. The bathrooms needed a bit of updating, but to me this house was perfection. I was proud to be a homeowner every time I drove up my long driveway.

Dr. Jake Reid—another picture of perfection. He was absolutely gorgeous. He was my ideal man at six feet tall, fair skin, jet-black hair, and blue eyes the color of Tahitian water. Women nurses probably swooned at the very sight of this dashing doctor. If they found out, the women at the hospital wouldn't be too happy to know he was dating someone. I literally ran into him at the supermarket while tiptoeing on a shelf, reaching for a box of cereal. With the cereal in hand, my one foot tripped over the other foot and I bumped into him hard enough to knock us both down. Twisting my ankle from this misstep, Jake was kind enough to take me to his hospital's ER where he stayed with me for three hours. That night, he asked for my number, and six weeks and several dates later, I invited him to accompany me to this ball.

The sight of him made me giddy with joy. After last night's argument, I thought he might have had second thoughts about escorting me. My actions probably frustrated him. Unintentional, but aggravating all the same, I played an unfair game of keep away with my heart—almost giving, then taking back at will. Jake was never shy about expressing his feelings for me. Though his job as a doctor kept him working like a madman, he made sure I knew he cared for me. Within a handful of dates, Jake had managed to fill the void left by my parents who had passed away years ago.

Jake showered me with both love and attention from the very night I met him. Whenever we separated, emptiness followed. How odd that a man I met less than two months ago could have such an effect on me.

"Hi, Jake. I'm so happy to see you. Have you been waiting long? I wish you had called me." I rushed out of the car as quickly as possible. Jake walked over to greet me.

"Hi, Beautiful. You look stunning," he murmured, kissing my cheek. "Do you not have your phone on you? I called and texted all day but you never answered. You had me worried."

"Sorry. I guess I forgot my phone at home." I stopped to hug him. "I'm really happy you're here. Let's go in. You can use the guest room to get ready."

"Did you not believe me last night when I said I was coming to pick you up at six?"

In all honesty, I didn't know what to believe. Even with his apology via text late last night, I wasn't convinced that he wanted to attend this ball with me. A teeny tiny part of me also wished to attend alone—though I'd never admit this to Jake or even to Sarah. It had been eighteen months since I'd seen Max. As to how I'd react when I saw him again was anybody's guess.

"Well?" he prodded.

I smiled and answered, "Go in and get dressed."

Fortunately, he didn't push for an answer but he began to take off his scrubs before closing the bathroom door. His body look liked one of the many replica statues of Michelangelo's David that populated the city of Florence. His body and face were close to perfection.

Deep breaths!

I went in my room to look over my dress, added a strand of pearls, and touched up my makeup while Jake got ready.

Jake walked into the living room wearing a black tuxedo, and he looked perfect.

"You look amazing," he exclaimed, putting both arms around my waist. I smiled, embarrassed and guilt-ridden, as I wasn't quite sure who I had gotten this dolled up for—him or the ex.

"You look pretty amazing yourself. I'm going to have to fight off all the ladies in the ballroom," I teased.

Jake shook his head in laughter and reached for my fingers. Hand in hand we walked to his car, and for the first time in a very long time, my heart rejoiced at the longing, the awakening I felt. Like a musician dusting off the cobwebs of a neglected instrument, I wanted to play again. I wanted to excel and perform in the symphony again. My heart wanted to love again.

Yes, I would let go of the pain that had lived in me for so long and tonight, with Jake and Max in the same room, would be the test.

"So what kind of college student were you?" Jake asked even before we got into the car.

"What do you mean?"

"You look like the straight-A sorority girl with lots of friends. Is my assessment correct?" Jake had a know-it-all grin on his face.

"You are so wrong about me." I gave him a don't-think-you-have-me-figured-out-already look. "I did well in English and history but struggled miserably through math and science. Those were probably your best subjects, huh?"

"I had to do well in those subjects. Look at the profession I chose. But weren't you popular in school?" He reached over and held my hand.

"Nope. I had a few close friends, along with Max, and that was it. Can't you tell by my overwhelming enthusiasm to all your advances that

I'm as shy as they come?" I joked with my date. "To your dismay, I'm sure, you're dating an introvert who will frustrate you with her self-doubt and vacillation. I might as well have blinking lights and a hazard sign on me." At this point, I couldn't help but let out a giggle. "Does my testimony scare you?" From what I had seen of Jake, I was confident it wouldn't.

"You have to do a lot more than that to scare me." He leaned over for a kiss. "What I see is a kind and gentle spirit who looks out for others before thinking of herself, and who likes me a lot more than she's willing to admit."

Now we both broke into a chortle. Hard to admit, but he was right. Like was not a strong enough word—adoration, bordering on love? Perhaps love wasn't the right emotion, but whatever I felt, it wasn't public knowledge, yet. Though my heart thumped arrhythmically whenever Jake was around and his presence caused much bliss and anxiety at the same time, I was too afraid to give my heart completely to anyone again. I'd have to profess my heart to him soon—possibly tonight if we got the chance.

After valeting Jake's car and walking into the hotel lobby, a thousand twinkling lights cascaded off the chandelier above us. We marveled at each Christmas tree, meticulously decorated in a multicultural theme. Jake held my hand, and as we strolled into the ballroom, my nerves jingled not much differently than the Christmas bells nearby.

Our ballroom, decorated in a White Christmas theme, rivaled New York City's Rockefeller Plaza. The tree, the ornaments, and decorations perfectly displayed the Christmas spirit.

"Emily!" shouted all my college friends whom I had avoided since the breakup, "it's so good to see you. Where have you been? You've lost so much weight," they all said at once as they veered me away from my date.

"Who is that gorgeous man you are with?" They all whispered not only to me, but also among themselves.

"Jake," I called, pulling him back to my side, "this is Becca, Lizzy, and Christie. We have all been roommates at some point throughout my four years in undergrad."

"Ladies, this is Jake."

"Hello, Jake!" they all sang out at once.

"Hi." He grinned his irresistible smile. Jake was always good at conversation and my college friends looked more than happy to converse.

"Jake, I'm going to go see Sarah and Charlie and get us checked in. Hang here with all the gals, will you?" I walked away amused, knowing Jake was in for a long talk with the girls.

While walking toward my best friend and her boyfriend of almost nine years, I nervously scanned the room for Max and his date. Relief washed over me. Perhaps they would be absent tonight? I could only hope.

"Hey," I called out to the lovebirds. "Where are we sitting?"

"Um…"

Their answer, filled with enough hesitation, made my nerves rattle again. This was not going to be an answer I would like to hear.

"You're with Peter, Will, James, Christie, me, Charlie and Max and Jennifer." Sarah spoke so quickly I had to repeat all the names in my head before everything clicked.

"What?" I bellowed. I could see a few heads turning my way. Anger boiled inside me to a point where I wanted to disown my best friend. "Why, Sarah? Why did you do this to me?"

Sarah looked scared. She could tell by my voice that she and Charlie had just ruined the whole night for me. "I thought you were OK with seeing him again. I also thought it would be sweet revenge for Max to see you with Jake."

"Aw, Sarah…I only came here because of you and Charlie. You know I didn't want to be here." As soon as I finished saying these words, a familiar presence stood close behind me. Even in a crowded room I could pick out his footsteps or the sound of his breath. How much of our conversation had he heard? My body turned in fear and anticipation, and he looked at me surprised, almost shocked. His boyish good looks still moved my heart. I hoped he couldn't read the combined joy and sadness in my eyes. I had missed him.

"Em…ily," Max stuttered. Em was what he called me during our four years of courtship. Em was what he breathed every time we kissed. Nobody dared to call me Em, because it was exclusively his. It was a jolt through my system to hear my nickname again.

"Hi." I managed a whisper.

Right at this moment, almost as though it were timed, Jake walked over, put his arms around me, and forced his lips on mine. My cheeks grew hotter by the length of his kiss. I heard Sarah make some saucy comment about our public display of affection.

"What was that?" I whispered when he finally let go.

"Payback." Minus the smile, it sounded like a threat. "Why did you run away and leave me with those women?"

After the shock of the embrace wore off, I started to laugh. Even with Max and Jennifer standing two footsteps away, my only thoughts were on

Jake and the awkward situation I had created for him with my former roommates.

"You didn't like my friends? I'm sure they liked you." I laughed at him.

"I missed you. Don't leave my side tonight. I don't want to be apart from you, OK?"

I agreed to his request by nodding my head yes.

"I'm sorry," Jake spoke, glancing at our broken conversation. "Was I interrupting something?"

"No...um, this is Max. Max, this is Jake. As I introduced the past to the present, I saw Max's disconcerted face as he greeted Jake. Obviously, none of our friends had mentioned to him I was seeing someone. Funny. No one had any difficulties telling me about Max and Jennifer.

"Hi. It's nice to meet you, Max." As Jake greeted Max, my eyes darted back and forth, stealing glances at both men. I didn't know who I was more nervous for—me, Jake, or Max. Nor, could I figure out what gave away my anxiety more—my twitching body or the hitched breath.

"Nice meeting you too," Max stammered to let out the rest of his sentence. "And this is my girlfriend, Jennifer."

Girlfriend. Max might as well have taken a whack at my heart with a baseball bat. I didn't think such an innocuous word could bruise me so severely. How could he have dated her so quickly after our breakup? I hurt watching Max hold another girl's hand. That was my place and he was my love. All the painful feelings I had worked hard to suppress in the last eighteen months resurfaced.

Jake was quick to understand my distress. He cordially said good-bye for us while I tried to act as normal as possible. After my confession to Jake last night, he knew how hard this was for me. Sensing my withdrawal, he stopped me and held me close to his heart. I was grateful for this understanding man.

"You OK?" He didn't ask in any accusatory way, but I noticed he was holding back his own discomfort. The gentle look, the soothing tone, he calmed me, and I decided to let go of my hurt—at least for now.

"Yes. I'm OK. Are you sorry you came tonight? Isn't this what you didn't want to see—me being rattled by the sight of Max and his new girlfriend?"

"You seemed more rattled by watching the rest of our reactions. Emily, seeing you anxious doesn't make me happy, and I have to apologize to you for my behavior last night. There was no reason for me to be so angry, and I definitely shouldn't have walked out on you and our dinner. I'm all right seeing you and Max together. Can we let this go for now and have a long-overdue talk when this function is over?"

I answered yes with a light kiss to his lips. Jake was an amazing man. Bypassing his own pain of seeing me hurt over Max, he did his best to lessen my discomfiture. Without a doubt, this man cared for me deeply. To show him my appreciation, I chose to put aside my feelings and enjoy the rest of the night with him.

Spotting Peter, I said, "Let's go meet some of my friends. I see them at our table. One more thing…" I had to confess, "Max and Jennifer are at our table. I hope you don't mind. Sarah and Charlie thought it would be funny to have us all together. I'm sorry." I didn't bother hiding my annoyance with the two of them.

"I'll have a talk with them when I run into them later tonight," Jake added in an intimidating way, which made me laugh. "You sure everything is OK?"

"It is now," I answered confidently, knowing Jake would protect me tonight.

"Peter!" The friend I most wanted to see since the breakup jumped out of his seat and hugged me. "I've missed you so much!"

"Where have you been? We see each other every day for four years, and then you go AWOL on me the last year and a half. If I didn't know better, I would have thought that you've been avoiding me and the whole gang."

"Peter, I want you to meet my date. This is Jake."

"Jake, this is Peter, my friend, my quasi brother."

"It's nice meeting you, Jake. When did you and Emily start dating? She never told anyone she was seeing someone." Peter looked at me in an accusing way. I hadn't called Peter in such a long time; of course he'd have no idea I was dating anyone.

"Emily and I started dating a couple of months ago."

"Oh, that's not very long." He sounded strangely relieved.

"No, I wish we could see more of each other, but due to my work schedule we date when possible. If I could, I'd spend every day with her," he replied, sending a wink my way.

Having been stood up so many times due to work, I mouthed, "I don't believe you," and shook my head.

He grabbed me and embraced me in front of everyone, then whispered, "I'd spend every waking and sleeping moment with you if it were possible."

Peter looked uncomfortable and surprised. I probably looked alarmed.

"What do you do?" Peter asked.

"I'm a doctor over at General Hospital."

Peter's face lit up, as he was a second-year med student himself. Both guys talked shop while I untangled myself from Jake's arms and strolled over to the other tables to talk to my friends.

No sooner had I said hello when I saw Jake walking over as the emcee called a first dance before dinner. He led me to the dance floor, and Sarah and Charlie waltzed over to us.

"Hey, Jake."

"I don't know if I should be saying hello to both of you for putting us at the same table as Max and Jennifer. Are you trying to help us or tear us apart?" Jake kidded with Charlie and Sarah. We had double-dated enough for Jake to understand that Sarah and Charlie would never mean any harm to us. They all liked and respected each other.

"We were only trying to show you off to Max," Sarah said to Jake. "I want him to know Emily is doing very well without him."

"Sounds great to me," Jake responded enthusiastically.

"Great...thanks," I answered unenthusiastically.

Pulling me close, Jake and I danced a very slow dance. Our bodies moved to the rhythm of the music and I lost myself in his graceful lead. He began to hum the music in my ear and I could feel his mouth slowly brushing the back of my neck, moving toward my jaw and traveling to my tender lips. I quivered ever so slightly when his lips touched mine. In our handful of dates, we'd only shared a few heated kisses. Our chemistry felt different tonight. I understood his intentions. He wanted to progress in more ways than just emotionally. Right as the kiss deepened, his pager went off and broke our embrace.

With critical eyes, I glared at him. He had done this to me too many times—left me in the middle of dinners, brunches, and weekend trips.

He looked back at me, guilty as charged. "Damn! Not again," he groaned.

I had to laugh. Otherwise, I'd start to cry. Even before he left for his call, I knew the scenario. Some emergency occurred where they needed him. He'd have no choice but to go in, and I'd be alone for the night.

"Don't worry about it. I'll meet you back at the table," I said.

I tried to walk away but Peter came out of nowhere and offered to finish the dance with me.

I nodded a puzzled acceptance.

"Emily, have you seen Max tonight?"

Hesitantly, I nodded my head yes.

"Have you talked to him since last June?"

"No. What would we have to talk about, his new girlfriend?"

Peter heard the anger in my voice, but couldn't help himself.

"I can't believe you two aren't together anymore."

"Peter, it's been over for a year and a half. Why bring this up, now? He...I mean we...have moved on. What part of this confuses you?" Peter, being Max's best friend, should have had better sense than to leave our status as a question mark. Who would understand the situation better than he?

"Emily, it's not as simple as you think. Max didn't just let go of you as easily as you make yourself believe."

"Pete, regardless of what you say to me, the fact remains he broke up with me on graduation night, and then started dating a new girl within a month of our breakup. I don't know how else to decipher what happened last June." As soon as I finished saying this, I saw Peter moving us toward Max and Jennifer. He turned to Max and asked if he could dance with Jennifer and all three of our faces had the same look of panic.

"Peter, what are you doing?" I asked indignantly.

"I think you two should talk. Sorry, Jennifer. They have a few things they need to work out." He said this while handing me over to Max and taking Jennifer's hand.

Frightened, our heartbeats danced much quicker than our feet. Our bodies hadn't been this close in a long time. They seem to have missed each other regardless of our consent. Though I worried about Jake's response if he saw us together, there was no denying I had missed Max. No matter how weak the feeling, it hadn't disappeared. Four years couldn't erase Max's absence despite Jake's presence in my life. Perhaps, it was wiser to admit Max would always be a part of my heart.

The dance continued. Max didn't say a word, but before long I felt his body pull toward mine as I unwittingly pushed toward his. Max's chin leaned oh so slightly on the top of my head and his arms curved around my body and embraced me longingly. I closed my eyes and briefly imagined the sweet times we danced like this.

Suddenly I heard Jake clear his throat, and I panicked. "Ahem. May I cut in?" Max and I instinctively jerked away. Feeling alarmed, I didn't know how to explain what had just happened.

"Of course," Max spoke almost apologetically. He walked away, leaving his girlfriend with his best friend, and not a glance back.

Jake looked hurt, and I stammered to get out an explanation. "Peter danced with me after you left and made me switch partners and told us to talk it out and...and..." Stuttering, I feared Jake's response. Max and I were too close, too intimate with one another. I only corroborated Jake's belief that I wasn't completely over Max. As guilty as I felt, I couldn't get off this emotional roller coaster.

"It's OK, Emily. You don't have to explain," was his strained answer while pulling me into his chest.

"I promise, I wasn't trying ..."

"Shh, Emily, it's all right." His arms encircled me, protectively, possessively.

"Nothing happened, I promise. I'm sorry." I almost started to cry.

"Emily. I wish I didn't make you so anxious. It's OK. I'm OK. You don't need to apologize. Let's go back to the table." He stated everything so matter-of-factly, almost too stoically. My anxiety level climbed up another notch.

Jake did his best to reassure me of his feelings, but I couldn't forget the betrayed look on his face. That momentary reaction explained more than anything he could've said to placate my feelings. Since the dance, I couldn't decipher whether it was Max, himself, or nostalgia that confused my heart. These feelings that lingered didn't pose a threat to my relationship with Jake, but I couldn't deny the hurt that wouldn't go away.

"What will happen if I have to leave you early tonight?"

"Do you have to leave?" My petulant tone turned Jake's visible disappointment into an encouraged smile.

"No, not yet. There's a chance, but I think it will be OK."

We were about to sit down when Jake's pager went off again. Patiently, I waited for Jake to return from his call and politely conversed with Jennifer, who was also waiting for her date to return. I found out she was an orthopedic nurse and two years older than Max. With such an uncomfortable situation, she was a good sport talking with me. I was happy to see Max dating a sweet girl. She seemed good for him.

Jake walked toward me, and I had this nervous feeling I was going to be alone...again.

"Hi. Done with your call?"

"Yeah…" The way he said this made me feel even more uneasy.

"Oh, that doesn't sound good," I whined.

"Well, I've got some good news and some bad news. Which do you want first?"

"The bad." Of course, I was always the pessimist.

"I have to go back to the hospital," he said quickly.

"No!" I protested. "Not again. I thought you had the whole night off! Jake, we hardly ever get to see each other. I think I've seen you once a week in the last couple of months." My protest was a bit unfair, but I really didn't want to be alone tonight, of all nights.

"I know and I'm sorry. I thought we'd be together tonight but my patient came back with complications and I need to go back into surgery now."

What could I say? A possible dying patient sat on the operating table waiting for his doctor, while I fretted over my insecurities of sitting alone at a dinner table with Max and Jennifer. Pathetic. But…how was I going to get through the rest of the evening without him?

I unhappily shrugged my shoulders and let him go. "Save another life tonight, Dr. Reid. I want to stop you but I can't…I won't."

He apologized again with both arms tightly wrapped around my body. "BUT…the good news! Chief gave me the whole weekend off, so I'm taking you on a surprise trip. We're going somewhere far where no one can call me back to the hospital. Can you be ready by 7:00am? I'll pick you up at your house."

"OK." Still sounding glum, I couldn't disguise my disappointment with Jake leaving me stranded at dinner again. "Where are we going?" As much as I tried to like surprises, they made me nervous. I didn't like uncertainty. "How shall I dress? Is it going to be very cold?"

"It's always cold up there," Jake slipped.

"Up there?" I asked curiously. Obviously we were going up north but were we driving…? Flying? Suspense grew.

"When will we be back? I assume we will be back tomorrow night?" I asked with more enthusiasm.

"Do we have options? Can we stay the weekend? Would that be OK?" He sounded hopeful.

I thought about what Jake had asked, all too aware everybody at the table was listening and waiting for my answer. They all knew what my answer would've been if Max had asked me this same question back in college. They were curious to know if I'd changed in the almost two-year absence.

It was a simple answer, but I couldn't immediately speak. A part of me wanted to spend the night with Jake. I felt safe with him. A part of me also wanted to hurt Max and say yes just to spite him. I knew it would be unfair to both men if I gave into my ugly side. Max watched me carefully. Eagerly, both men awaited my answer.

"Um, no. I don't think it's wise for us to spend the night," I said, relieved to speak my mind. Accepting my answer with a more than gentle kiss, he relented to the pager that beeped endlessly.

"OK, OK, I'm coming, people," he answered back at his pager. "Bye," he murmured, stealing one more kiss. "I'll miss you." Before he left, he turned to Peter and asked if he would not mind giving me a ride home.

"Please take care of her for me," he added. "And please," he whispered to me, "don't fall back into your ex's arms after I leave." We both laughed.

"Sure will," Peter obliged.

As soon as Jake left, Peter turned to me. "Jake seems like a good guy. I'm relieved to know you're dating someone who loves you."

It never occurred to me Jake might feel that strongly about me. I knew I couldn't say I loved him yet. After all, we hadn't been dating too long and this was the first time I'd opened my heart in a long time.

"You seem to have a way of wrapping men tightly around your finger," Peter noted.

"Yeah, some good that does me in the end," I retorted. I heard a low chuckle coming from everyone at our table except Max and Jennifer.

Dinner was truly uncomfortable. We sat in a round of ten—Peter, me, an empty seat, Sarah, Charlie, James, Will, Christie, Max, and Jennifer. Dinner was served. The roasted tomato soup went untouched. A cold, crisp beet and apple salad, nibbled. Filet mignon, new potatoes, and sautéed veggies, a waste of money, as I only finished the vegetables before having Peter finish the rest of my plate. I consumed some dessert and coffee, along with two glasses of wine. It was no wonder my system wasn't feeling well.

After dinner, everyone started to mingle and dance again. Jennifer excused herself to use the restroom while the rest of our table, except Max, went to dance. Dreading the alone time, I got up to go anywhere and do anything but talk to Max.

"How come you barely touched your dinner, Em?" Max pulled me back down with a caring yet guarded voice.

"I wasn't very hungry," I answered softly.

"You've lost so much weight. Are you OK? Have you been ill? You still look…beautiful." His voice sounded wistful.

With an intense glare I saw Max read my face. It was hard to hide anything from a man who had known me intimately for four years. *No, I am not OK. You left me eighteen months ago without good reason and now I'm sitting here watching you with another woman. How can I be OK?*

My eyes teared as I saw the sadness in his eyes and I chose to turn away from our silent conversation. Muted, awkward distress, surprisingly couldn't suppress the friendship, fondness, and love that had lived between us for so many years. Even now, my heart felt glad to be here with him. My mind continued to dissect my heart. I couldn't free my mind of the way it felt to be held by Max while we danced. His touch brought back so many wonderful memories. There was a part of me that wanted to be held by him again.

Still, I was angry with Max for kicking me out of his life so unexpectedly. How could a man who dumped me after four years of dating, sit here and feign to care for me? He didn't care anymore, and neither should I. I had Jake, and deep inside, I knew we would make this relationship work.

Chapter 2

The College Years

Hot and humid weather greeted my move into my college dorm. Florida, in the middle of August, had to have been more pleasant than this day. It was never this hot in Los Angeles, especially so close to the ocean. With ten stories and 381 rooms, I lived in one of the oldest dormitories on campus. It even required an old-fashioned key card to open up the heavy doors into this secured building. The usual meeting area and common rooms were all located on the first floor, and the dining hall looked like any other well-stocked cafeteria. It was a glorious first year in college.

My room was all of two hundred square feet. In it were three beds, three desks, three chairs, and three small closets. I couldn't figure out how I was going to get all my clothes in this locker of a closet. Arriving in the dorm room before any of my roommates, I picked the only bed that was the bottom bunk. There was another bed above me and directly across my way, the third bed was perched up high with a desk, chair, and locker-sized closet all neatly positioned underneath it. That was my entire room. Needless to say, there wouldn't be much privacy during my first year.

Max and I met in the cafeteria on the first day of school. Catching him smiling at me from a table nearby, I was quickly smitten. He and his roommates came over to our table and introduced themselves to us. We all took turns at small talk and then paired off to go explore the campus. From day one, our chemistry was undeniable. Max and I were naturally drawn to each other like the south pole of a magnet attracting the north pole. We marveled at how much we had in common and how we felt such a strong connection from the moment we met.

As the days passed us by, our connection only got stronger. We spent every waking moment together when we weren't in class. Picnics on the grass, study sessions in the library—if we could have, we would have stayed up every night catching up on the eighteen years we had missed out on in each other's lives. It was a strange bond that couldn't be denied.

Our physical bond was equally as strong. The urge to touch and explore scared me. Such a strong desire went against the core of my belief. I wanted to stay "pure" till I got married. Max, of course, had other ideas and thought I was crazy. We argued and fought constantly. Being the tearful one in the relationship. I hurt easily and cried readily. Max accused me of being way too sensitive. He was right, of course—though he'd never get an admission from these lips.

Maybe it was our age. Maybe it was because this was the first real relationship for both of us. Whatever the reason, we just couldn't hide our emotions from one another. Every disagreement set us off for days. We'd quarrel, not speak, then go right back to our relationship as if nothing happened. I didn't know if we had ever resolved any issues. In many ways, it didn't matter, because we just wanted to be together.

Our typical date started with a casual meal and then a movie. Some days we'd ride our bikes and picnic on the beach. Many times we cooked dinner together at Max's apartment and studied. On occasion, we'd go watch a musical or go out for a nice dinner. Neither of us had much money so we couldn't do anything extravagant. This didn't bother us as long as we were together.

On winter breaks, our usual group of friends would go skiing. We'd rent a cabin, with all twelve of us cramming into whatever sized cabin we got. The girls took care of the food for the week while the guys were in charge of evening entertainment. We'd get up early, have breakfast, ski all day, come back for dinner then play crazy games till the wee hours of the night. Those were some of the best days of my life.

Sarah and I considered ourselves best friends since the day we met. A tall and pretty brunette, her endearing personality helped me through my most difficult days, post breakup. We met as freshmen in college, assigned to the same study group in calculus, and we struggled. Limits…derivatives…integrals…none of it made sense. Every chance we got, we went to each other's dorm rooms and studied math. Failing out of school our first quarter wasn't an option. We had to make it work.

Charlie Abner, Sarah's boyfriend since high school, was better than your average guy. He stood slightly taller than Sarah at six feet tall and boasted a booming personality. High school sweethearts, they met when they were sixteen and loved each other more with each passing year. Charlie was probably waiting for the perfect moment to propose, though he wouldn't dare tell me when. He knew all too well I couldn't keep a secret from his love and my best friend.

Our gang of friends, Peter, Will, James, Charlie, and Max, roomed together all through their college years. They lived in the same disgusting apartment since sophomore year and in all that time, they'd never cleaned their apartment. The most memorable year starred a two-week-old, half-eaten birthday cake, ants, maggots, cockroaches, and an extermination crew. This event evicted an entire apartment building for two days. It was a wonder they didn't get permanently evicted. Indelible memories were made not only for me and Max, but for all of us as friends and as an extended family.

Very different from Sarah and Charlie's relationship, Max and I survived day by day. Max's awkward expression of love made me question how much he cared. It resembled a dark cloud hovering in the horizon with the sun's attempt at an appearance when all forces in the universe aligned properly. Though I knew he cared and often enough he told me he loved me, I still hated the uncertainty. I wanted more expression! Less ambiguity! An unequivocal exclamation of his love for me! Perhaps in the end, it was my fault for feeling so insecure about us.

As complaints went, Max wasn't a romantic either. My ideal man was one who would surprise me with love notes and flowers. I didn't need anything elaborate or fancy. A simple flower or a cute plant would have sufficed, but none of that ever happened. I was always the one surprising him with notes, or I'd have dinner waiting for him at his apartment when classes ended late.

One year, I surprised Max with daily gifts for a week leading up to Valentine's Day. One of the days, I froze water in a heart-shaped pan with a laminated note inside. After the ice had melted, the note read, "Now that you've melted my heart, will you be my Valentine?" Pretty clever, I thought. Another day, I wrote a love poem on a large poster board with candy bars as key words in the poem. As an ego booster, it started with a Big Hunk bar. Not to sound unappreciative, but all I got in return was a teddy bear wrapped inside a balloon. It was a nice gift, but so typical—not much thought put into it.

Maybe I expected too much out of our relationship. We were barely out of our teenage years, and I knew Max wasn't the type to fuss about anything. His laissez-faire attitude was what attracted me to him in the first place. But I always felt like I was the one who coerced us into this relationship. He definitely didn't return the love I showered—or so I thought.

Sarah and Charlie's undying love for one another never helped our situation. They rarely fought. Charlie never left my best friend questioning who loved who more. They operated as one mind and finished each other's thoughts. There was no doubt that they would get married and live happily together, forever. I never had that assurance with Max. In the end, I got what I expected.

Chapter 3

Closure

"Let's continue this party. We can't separate just because the ball is over," Peter announced.

Everyone loved the idea since many of us hadn't seen each other in years. I tried to bow out with the excuse that I had a 7:00 a.m. date, but my friends wouldn't have it. I hesitantly agreed to meet them at a bar. Searching, Peter's absence was beyond noticeable. In fact, everyone had left except for Max, even Jennifer.

Peter had purposely left me alone with Max so we would ride together to the bar. Jake was wrong to trust him with my well-being. Against all odds—a current girlfriend, an eighteen-month absence, and me dating Jake—Peter seemed to believe that we could still get back together. My head shook thinking about this ridiculous idea.

"Get in," Max told me as the valet brought the car around.

"Where's Jennifer?"

"She left a little while ago. She's working a night shift at the hospital tonight."

"Oh, that's right. She's a nurse. You seem to like girls with homey professions." We both chuckled as I finished this thought.

I led Max toward my house, which was a few miles away from the hotel.

"Can we stop by my house so I can change? I don't want to be in this dress the whole night. Also it's a bit cold."

"Sure," he answered, taking off his jacket. "Here, take this for now."

It felt good to be in his jacket, but the warmth of his scent evoked memories I wasn't ready to face. We got to my house within minutes, and I could tell by Max's face, he wondered where we were.

"Do you live here, Em?" He studied the living room while following me toward the bedroom.

"Uh-huh. This is my house."

Max spun his head around and looked shocked.

"When did this happen? You're not living with Sarah anymore?"

"Has Charlie not told you anything about me the last year and a half? I bought this house in June. I finally left Sarah's lair."

I gave Max a change of clothes and showed him the guest bathroom while I went into my room to change into a pair of jeans and a comfy sweater. Max had another bewildered look, as he had just changed into a tailor-made outfit. It looked nice on him.

"Are these Jake's clothes?" He had a hard time spitting out those four words. I saw what Max was envisioning. Finding this situation highly humorous, I contemplated letting his imagination aggravate him but thought it would be better to clear the air.

"I bought these to give to you before we broke up. I didn't have the receipt to return them and felt silly about giving them to someone else, so they've been sitting in my closet for a while," I confessed.

"Oh..." He sounded relieved as he thanked me for the clothes. "Can you give me a hanger for my tux?"

I reached into my closet for a hanger but noticed something had fallen out of Max's pocket and onto the floor. A small blue felt pouch—something that looked like it belonged in a Tiffany's box with a ring or some small jewelry in it—screamed for me to pick it up. Before my hand got anywhere near the mysterious item, Max swooped in and shoved it back into his pocket. His abruptness startled both of us. What was in this pouch that had made him so jumpy?

Pain and guilt riddled his face, though I couldn't understand why. Before I broached the subject, he interrupted my thought. "Hey, Em? You want to go get something to eat instead of going out for drinks? You didn't eat much tonight."

The growl in my stomach gave me away. "I am hungry. Where shall we go?"

"How about a bowl of noodles? You've always had a weakness for something soupy at a late hour. What time is it? Is the ramen house still open?" he asked.

"I think it's about 11:00p.m., they should still be open." A bowl of noodles sounded delicious right now, especially on an empty stomach. "Great idea. You mind driving? I'm a bit tired."

Before we got into Max's car, he texted Peter our situation, my number, and my home address. He told him if we didn't make it to the bar, they'd meet back at my place and go home together. In the twenty-minute car ride, neither of us uttered a sound. Instead, I looked out the window, wondering what we would talk about during our meal if we couldn't stand a twenty-minute ride together. Max looked over at me, stared briefly and sighed quietly. He was probably regretting the predicament we found ourselves in.

Luckily there was a parking spot right in front of the restaurant, and we sat down immediately at the noodle bar. The server came and welcomed us. "Hey, long time no see! You two haven't been here in a while."

"Great…,"I thought. If this weren't awkward enough, the server recognized that this used to be our late-night food joint back in college. This night wasn't getting any easier. She didn't need to ask us what we wanted. She automatically put in an order for two bowls of ramen and an order of gyoza, along with iced green tea and Sapporo on tap. We both started to laugh, realizing we were so predictable. The server helped lighten the mood and we started feeling comfortable with one another again.

"So, what have you been doing the last year and a half?" Max asked with genuine curiosity.

"Well, let's see. After we separated in June, Sarah and I went to Europe for about a month." I quickly wiped away a tear that trickled down my cheek as I talked about last June. Max seemed oblivious to my pain, but my flushed cheeks signaled my weakness. Regardless, I continued my story. "We started in New York for a few days, then went to Rome, Florence, and Paris. After Paris, we biked through the South of France, and then we sailed to Greece. Sarah and I fell in love with the oceans of Greece, so we stayed there the last week of our trip. Charlie actually met us in Greece. We all had a blast together for a few days, and then I separated from them."

"What did you do when Charlie came? You must have been lonely." His face turned somber. I briefly imagined how fantastic it would have been if Charlie and Max had met us in Greece. The four of us—like it used to be.

"I actually did a lot of sightseeing by myself and gallivanted from island to island. It wasn't too bad. Sarah really needed Charlie there. They'd never been apart for that long. After summer, I returned to school and got to teach fourth grade instead of first, as originally planned. It was challenging coming up with new curriculum at the last minute, but it was a fantastic year. I didn't realize I would enjoy fourth graders so much. They start developing a personality and a sense of humor at that age. But at the same time, they're still innocent and sweet. Life hasn't jaded them yet."

"How did the house happen?" Max sounded impressed that I was on my own and doing so well.

"I randomly found my house while driving around the neighborhood. Between my earnings in college, my pitiful salary, and selling my grandparents' condo, I scrounged up enough money to put in an offer. Luckily, the sellers accepted, and I moved in all summer. It took a little while getting used to living alone, but I have to say I'm enjoying it now."

"It's a great house. I'm really happy for you." Max sweetly smiled. I felt my heart melt, as it always did when he smiled.

Max reproachfully asked about Jake. This shouldn't have been a surprise—but it was still disconcerting to hear Jake's name coming from Max's lips.

"How long have you and Jake been together? I didn't realize you were seeing someone."

"Did you never ask Charlie or Sarah anything about me since our breakup? I can't believe how indifferent you were to my well-being. I kept tabs on you from time to time." My lips surprisingly formed a slight pout. With a new girlfriend, there really was no need to ask about the old one.

"We just started dating a couple of months ago. I met him at the grocery store and we've been seeing each other ever since. He's so busy at the hospital that we only see each other maybe once a week. We try to talk on the phone and text, but for the most part, I barely see him. It will be a real treat to have him all to myself tomorrow." This last statement produced a big smile on my face. Tomorrow would hopefully deepen our relationship and give us more stability. We had had too many misunderstandings on where we stood as a couple, assuming we were a couple. This trip would answer all the questions hovering over us.

Max continued with his twenty questions.

"You seem happy with Jake. What about him do you like?" I never liked this pensive look that registered on Max's face. This look always meant that there was more on his mind than he was willing to share.

His question took me by surprise. I never thought about why I liked Jake. Even if I had thought about it, never did I imagine having to explain it to my ex-boyfriend. While pondering my answer, Max conjured up his own crazy ideas.

"It couldn't just be his good looks or the fact that he's an established doctor. That's not why you're attracted to him, is it? How old is he anyway?"

"Max. You can be so silly at times. He's thirty and you know, you're pretty high up the totem pole in the looks category, yourself."

That brought back his good-looking smile.

"I guess if I had to answer your question, I like the fact that I don't feel the need to take care of him or please him all the time. I feel secure with him. He takes care of me."

"Are you trying to say that I never took care of you? You never felt secure with me?" His defensive and angry tone startled me.

"That's not what I'm saying," I stammered. "When we were dating, I was crazy in love with you."

"And I loved you too," he shouted back.

"I know you did, but I always felt like I loved you more, a lot more. Many times, I thought that my love for you bordered on obsession. My main concern was to make you happy. I wanted always to please you. My world revolved around you and your needs, and I probably choked you by being so needy." Suddenly, I sat back in my stool and stopped my defense. "Wow, I think I just had an epiphany. I see now why you said you needed your freedom on graduation night. I suffocated you." Relieved to finally understand our separation, but aching like I did on our broken night, I quickly changed the subject so I wouldn't hurt so much again.

"So, tell me about Jennifer. She seems like a really nice person. I got to talk to her a bit during dinner."

Max didn't confirm or deny anything I said. He looked visibly upset, but answered my questions.

"After we broke up, I actually ended up in the hospital."

"What! What happened? Are you all right?"

"Yeah," he answered reluctantly. "I got into a car accident and Jen works in orthopedic rehab, and that's where we met. She really helped me through a tough time. I thought I wouldn't be able to use my legs again."

"How did this happen? How did you get so hurt?" Tears started rolling down my cheeks. I hurt knowing that Max hurt. No matter what our relationship, I still saw Max as an extension of myself—even with Jake in my life.

Silently, I chided myself.

Emily, why can't you get a hold of yourself? Why do you have to wear your emotion on your sleeve?

Vulnerable. Transparent. Weak.

That was me in a nutshell.

With a comforting smile, Max placed both hands on my cheeks and wiped away my tears with his thumbs. He then pulled me toward him and held me.

He whispered, "It's OK. I'm fine now. It was a freak accident, and I'm completely rehabilitated." He slowly added, "It feels nice to hold you again, Em" and didn't let go of me.

His words created an unwanted spasm in my heart, making me pull away from him. My eyes were down, embarrassed I was crying.

"Sorry. I didn't mean to get so emotional. I think two glasses of wine and no food are getting to me. I'm glad you're OK. Go on."

"Jen helped me rehab daily and her kindness won me over. I guess you are right. I do like being taken care of by women." He chuckled lightly.

"Max, everybody likes to be taken care of, it's not just you." In my heart I wondered why Max couldn't have taken care of me just a little bit more...

With a look of regret he continued his story. "After the car accident, I finally decided I wanted to go to medical school, and I studied hard for the MCATs, then applied everywhere. Once med school started, I realized this was where I should have been all along. It's been a long time coming for me. My big regret is that I didn't get my act together back in undergrad, but I suppose it's better late than never."

"I'm very happy for you. You finally found what you want to do with your life. I'm sure you will do well in school, since you are the brightest person I know." I was truly thrilled for Max. It made me happy to know he had found a career path and would make something of himself. I always knew he would.

After our meal, we walked a little and continued our conversation. I could tell by his pensive look that he had something else on his mind but was afraid to tell me.

"Em?"

"Yes?" I replied, my eyes staring into his soft brown eyes.

He stopped walking and held both my hands. In all ways, I feared what would come out of Max's mouth, but I also hoped that perhaps I could find closure. I wanted to start again without baggage. My feelings for Jake blossomed with each date, but I couldn't comprehend this last hold Max had on me.

"I know I really hurt you on graduation night. I want to say I'm sorry for messing things up so badly. You believe I loved you with all my heart, don't you?"

Max could be so tenderhearted when he wanted to be. He put both his arms around me and held me against his body. My arms went limp—a dead weight hanging by my side. I bit down on my lips to stop from crying. With resolve, I vowed to end all emotional ties with this man whose chest heaved a large sigh against my heart. There would be no more tears, no more hurt.

"Em, I'm so sorry for hurting you. That was truly not my intention graduation night. Please don't believe that I didn't love you as much as you loved me. I was just too stupid and immature to know what I had. You were my world." His broken face broke my heart.

I stopped him from saying any more.

"Max. Thank you, but your apology is unnecessary. You didn't feel as deeply about me as I'd hoped. That's not a crime. I don't blame you for my pain. It took awhile but I'm OK now. I hope one day we can be friends again. Let's go home. It's late."

The car ride back was a quiet one, though Max looked like he still needed to talk. I thought through what Max finally admitted and how I handled the situation. Was this the closure I needed?

Max apologized, I accepted, end of our story? I was going to accept tonight as closure and move on with life.

Luckily, when we got back to the house, we found a distraction in Peter and James who had passed out at my front door.

"Pete, James, are you guys OK?" Max asked.

"I need to sleep," Peter slurred. "We both drank too much, so Will dropped us off here. Emily, can we spend the night at your house? I'm so tired I don't think we can make it home."

"Um, I suppose you guys can spend the night. You know that I'm leaving early in the morning?"

"Yeah. Can you open the door? It's cold." Peter and James crawled into the house but never made it into the guest bedroom. They both fell asleep on the living room floor.

Max didn't have much of a choice but to settle into the guest bed. It was 3:00 a.m.

Chapter 4

San Francisco Confessional

Ding Dong.

Exactly at 7:00 a.m., Jake was at the door. Looking as amazing as ever in slacks, a button-down, and a blazer, he held a latte and a croissant as I opened the door.

"Good morning. Are you ready to leave?"

"Not quite. Come in."

"Whoa, what happened here?" he asked, surveying the mess all around the house. "A slumber party?"

"There was an after party I didn't attend, and these guys drank too much to drive home. They asked to spend the night here, but never made it into the bedroom." I left out the part about me crying like a fool in my ex's arms again. "I think they're getting up now."

Peter and James stretched their arms and slowly got up from the floor. "Good morning," they muttered with one eye open.

"Hey. Did you sleep well? Are your backs OK? You both fell asleep on the floor the second you walked into the house. I have breakfast ready for you guys. You know I won't be home all day, right?" I asked.

My pedantic rambling, followed by obedient nodding of heads, reminded me of my fourth graders at school. I laughed to myself.

"Jake, do you still have my spare keys? Can I have them back?" He slowly handed them to me. I winked at him, knowing he didn't like giving these up.

For a sleepy guy, Peter's senses were alert enough to catch my fumbled throw.

"Make yourselves at home. Just lock up when you go, and return the keys next time."

Without any warning, Max walked out and I caught a startled glimpse on both Jake's and Max's faces. I looked over at Jake apologetically and hoped I hadn't spoiled his mood for the rest of the day.

"Road trip!" My dear friend Peter yelled out, turning the attention on himself to save me. "We need to support our football team. Emily, are you in? Jake, you want to come too? I have ten tickets to the Las Vegas Bowl."

"When is it?" I asked.

"The day after Christmas," he replied.

"I guess so. You want to go?" I said turning toward Jake. "It would be fun."

"You do know I went to your rival school?"

"Boo!" We all jeered, then laughed like good friends.

"I don't know if I can sit through one of your football games." Sure, rub it in that your school has a better football team. Wait till basketball season. "Plus, I can't take any more time off from the hospital."

I was bummed at the thought of Jake being really busy again, No doubt we'd be back to our once-a-week date night at best.

"Emily, what are you doing next Monday to Thursday? My mom called this morning to tell me that we are all going to Hawaii right before Christmas, and she wants me to bring you along. You know my family's been dying to meet you. She's reserved a seat for you on the plane, and you can room with my sister, Jane."

"With your whole family?" I was a bit flustered at the thought of being with Jake's family for four days. Would they like me? Would I like them? Then it dawned on me. "How did you get four days off?"

"Well...the chief of staff at the hospital is my dad's brother. Mom reminded Uncle Henry that I haven't had a vacation since I got there. It didn't hurt that she promised him four tickets to the New Year's Day football game."

"I see. Are you sure you want me there for four days with your family?"

"I couldn't think of a better Christmas present than to have you spend four days with me and my family!" Jake declared.

"OK, then. Tell your mother I said thank you and that I'd love to go." The thought of being a part of Jake's family on this trip gave me a sense of belonging and a sense of family I so desired.

We headed out the door, and I knew I had some explaining to do so before we reached the car; I pulled Jake's hand to a halt.

"Jake, I'd like to explain about the guys you saw this morning, especially Max. I know that was really uncomfortable and I'm sorry."

"Emily, you don't have to explain anything." Jake's face looked even more uncomfortable, than when he saw Max come out of the guest room.

"I do. Peter and Jeff went out to the bar with our friends and drank enough to where they couldn't drive home. We found them lying on my doorstep, and they asked to spend the night."

"Can I ask where you and Max were at this time? I assume you weren't with them?"

"No. We went out for a bite to eat. I didn't have any dinner, and Max suggested I grab a bite to eat before we met up with the rest of the gang. Our dinner took longer than expected, and when we got back to my house, Peter and Jeff were comatose on my front porch."

Jake's face turned a bit pale. "Dinner?"

"It was literally dinner. We also had a good talk, which I'd like to share with you whenever you'd like to hear about it. Are you OK? Can we go on with this day without us being uncomfortable with one another?"

I gave him a hopeful smile.

"I told Max last night that I was really looking forward to spending a whole day with you. Even though we've been dating a few months, I don't think we know each other very well."

"What do you mean we don't know each other?" he asked while opening the car door for me. "Here, get in. We need to get going, or we're going to miss our flight."

Flight. OK, we were probably headed up to San Francisco. I delighted in the idea of spending this day with him.

"How can you say that we don't really know each other?" I guess he couldn't get over my last statement.

"Jake, when was the last time...better yet, has there ever been a time where we spent an entire date without being interrupted? Our first date at the Mexican restaurant, what happened? You got paged and went in to perform some surgery. Our second date, brunch at the hotel, what happened? The chief called you and told you to attend some conference in Atlanta. That's also when we got into our first argument and couldn't even talk it through because you had to leave."

I could tell by Jake's surly expression, he didn't like where I was taking this conversation. I personally enjoyed it. "Don't get me going on our third date to Santa Barbara that ended before it even started. And last night, you left me stranded before dinner was served. Although I think we did manage to spend an entire three hours together. That's a record, you know."

"What about all the times I come by, call, or text you?"

"Are you kidding me? The last time you came by my house, you got mad at me and left in the middle of dinner."

"I apologized about that," he defended himself.

"You did, but only after you realized you were in trouble because I wouldn't answer your calls or your texts. You can be such a five-year-old at times," I teased him. "And as for your calls and texts, you call from the hospital and have to hang up within minutes. Your texts look like an hour-by-hour hospital itinerary. How did you ever have a relationship with this schedule? Does your hospital have no other doctors but yourself?"

I shook my head and chuckled. Time was a limited and precious commodity with Jake. We had never really spent any quality time together, and we shared very few meals in their entirety. Jake stayed quiet for a while and looked to be thinking over our exchange. He turned his head toward me as if to retort but stopped himself.

"So, you see why I'm so excited to spend this whole day with you?" I put my hand over his sitting on the armrest. He turned his palm up and interlocked our fingers.

"OK. I get your point. I already feel very close to you, but you apparently need more convincing. That will be my mission today. Ask me whatever you like. I'll answer all your questions."

As we drove up the 5 Freeway, I did my best to get some answers. "Burbank airport, huh? Could we be flying to San Francisco? It couldn't be Seattle, that's a bit too far for a day trip. Any hints?" He wouldn't budge. "Aw, come on. I thought you said you would be answering all my questions."

"Not a chance," he said with a sly grin. "You'll have to wait till we get there."

"OK, so here's something about me you don't know. I don't like surprises. I like everything planned out, and I prefer to do the planning."

"Control freak."

Laughing, I answered, "I know, but I can't help it." Slowly I counted to five and then begged, "Please? Just a teeny tiny hint?"

Nothing worked till I started slowly working my lips from his neck up to his ear. "Are you sure you can't give me a hint?" My poor attempt as a seductress worked...well.

"You're not playing fair." His body froze and the car started slowing down. "You need to stop before we get into an accident. I'll tell you once we get to the airport. I promise."

We parked the car in the long-term lot and got on the bus headed toward the terminal.

"So, where are we going? You promised to tell me," I whined.

Jake grabbed me by the waist and pulled me in to him. "Where have all the kisses gone?" he asked while practicing the same moves I played on him in the car. Heading into terminal three bound for San Francisco, he didn't have to answer after all.

As soon as we got on the plane, a nervous thought ran through my mind. "You don't have to go in to work today, do you? They can't make you come back from San Francisco, or worse yet, find you an operation to perform up in San Francisco?"

This time, Jake shook his head and laughed. "Does my job make you that nervous?"

"Yup. I think I'm going to reconsider dating a doctor—or at least I'm going to date a doctor who doesn't ever have any emergencies." I peeked over to see his expression. It didn't change.

"Yeah? What kind of doctor would that be?"

"Maybe a dermatologist or perhaps a podiatrist." I knew this would bother Jake, as a podiatrist was vying for my attention when Jake and I started dating.

"Trust me, after today, you're not going anywhere from me."

"Very confident there, Dr. Reid. We'll see about that."

At SFO, Jake rented a car and we headed north. In a little over an hour, breathtaking scenery filled with rows and rows of grapevines came into view. Our final destination—Napa Valley. Though the calendar read December, Mother Nature still boasted fall with trees full of leaves in gorgeous hues of oranges, reds, golden yellows, and greens. Quaint wineries resembled Hansel and Gretel cottages, and the CIA building looked like the Greystone Mansion. Every building looked inviting.

"Wine country reminds me of Tuscany, only flatter." My thoughts rambled out loud.

"Have you been to Tuscany?"

"Yeah…it was the most beautiful place I've ever visited. I want to go back and hear Andrea Bocelli sing in some open meadow." Feeling so at ease, I rattled off one of my dreams. I looked out the window and fantasized being in such a place with Jake—traveling together…possibly growing old together.

"A kiss for your thoughts?" Jake woke me up from my reverie.

I waited.

"Well?" An uneasy smile tugged at his lips.

"Where's the promised kiss?"

He lifted our interlocking hands and brought them to his lips.

"I was admiring all the unique architecture." Not confident enough to describe my fantasy, I stated a blasé fact.

"That's it?"

"My answer was about as exciting as that kiss you just gave me." I hid my smile by facing the scenery through the passenger window.

Before I knew what was happening, he grabbed me and gave me a full-blown kiss with his eyes on the road. The car swerved a bit. It took me awhile to regain the composure I'd lost after that embrace.

"Well? Shouldn't that kiss elicit a better answer?"

I had to laugh. "I thought it would be nice to go back to Tuscany..." I would see what he'd try next in order to get the rest of my answer.

The next kiss I got off the side of the road was too indecent to put into words. My cheeks stayed blushed for a long while after the kiss was done.

"...with you when I'm old and gray..." Leaving everything hanging, I didn't dare look him in the eye for a while.

The smug look on Jake's face made me uncomfortable, so I changed the subject. "It's so beautiful up here. Are we spending the whole day here?"

"Would you like to?" he asked with a smile.

"Sure. But I don't really care where as long as we're together." This statement erased the insecure look Jake had been wearing since he saw Max appear from my guest bedroom. I took advantage of the stop light and leaned over to return the kiss he bestowed on me just a few minutes ago. "I'm really happy to be here with you," I whispered. A myriad of honking car horns broke our embrace reprimanding us to keep driving.

Our lips unwillingly parted.

Jake eventually parked the car on the side of a beautiful two-story house. I knew exactly where we were.

We were at one of the world's greatest, three Michelin-starred restaurants!

"How did you get us a table here on such short notice?"

"You know where we are?" he asked without a hint of surprise. "I had to pull favors from a few people last night. I didn't know till we landed in SFO that we'd gotten a reservation," he explained as we got seated right away.

My dream restaurant sat on a gracious piece of land. What looked to be a two-story brick house was comprised of offices on the second level and the restaurant on the bottom. There was a small courtyard and an organic garden, which most likely supplied all their greens. It was visually stunning. I assumed it would be no less than a sensory treat for the palate.

"How did you know this was my dream restaurant destination? I can't believe we're here! Thank you, Jake."

"The foodie that you are, how could I not know?" Though he formed it as a question, he meant it as a statement.

This thoughtful man brought me to the one destination I'd been longing to visit. How could I not appreciate the heart behind the action?

Lunch began with an amuse bouche—the legendary salmon tartare cornets, a savory black sesame seeded cone filled with salmon tartare and red onion crème fraîche. Enjoying every bite of this teaser course, the inquisition began.

"Jake, tell me about your family. I can't wait to meet them."

"Well, as you know, I'm the oldest of three kids. My sister below me, Jane, is a senior in law school right now. Nick, the youngest is a senior in undergrad, and the real genius in our family. Most likely med school is in his near future but it's a bit up in the air. He's talented in so many ways, he's torn about what to do with his life. He's also the foodie in the family. You two will get along well."

"Did you all go to the same school?" I asked while slurping my oyster with caviar.

"Jane actually went to undergrad up here. She's the black sheep of the family," he joked.

"Huh? I don't understand."

"My grandfather, my dad, his brothers, most of their wives, and we children all went to the same school. Gramps made a lot of money in real estate and was a generous man, as he donated much of it. My sister liked the convenience of his money, but not the notoriety it sometimes brought. So, she decided to come up here and then go live in New York. The rest of us were not as brave or as creative.

"You're quite the homogenous group."

"Boring is a better definition."

"You must have been a hot commodity at school. The girls must have thrown themselves at you to become a part of your family," a hint of jealousy noted my voice.

"I suppose, but I never met anyone that made me want to settle down..." he trailed off. "After med school, residency was at Valley Hospital, and since then I've been at General Hospital, thanks to the chief selecting his nephew over hundreds of applicants."

"Is the name Reid the reason why we got a table here today as well?"

He seemed abashed as he confessed that one of his uncles was an investor in many restaurant ventures.

"I guess I've had it pretty easy all my life. But, my parents encouraged us to work hard."

"Excellent! Good-looking, hard-working, and great earning potential," I joked. "You're definitely a keeper!"

"OK, now your turn. Tell me everything."

Before giving my autobiography, I quickly savored the third course—cured hamachi belly.

"It's not too exciting. It's probably more tragic than anything else. I was born in Texas and spent most of my childhood there. My dad was a structural engineer, and he died when I was in eighth grade. He was at a job site for the city when a part of the building fell on him. He died instantly," I explained.

"I'm so sorry! I didn't realize that you were that young when your father passed away."

"Well, the story gets worse, so hold that thought." I sighed. "After my dad died, my mom and I came to LA to live with my grandparents. My mom had never worked before so she held odd jobs here and there, and we lived modestly. Mom missed Dad terribly, and she was never truly happy again after his death. This was hard on me because I felt the need to be happy around her, always. It was my job to lift her spirits up. During my senior year in high school, my mom died of a heart attack. That's what the doctor's told me, but I think she died more of a broken heart."

Jake reached out and put his hands over mine when he saw the tears forming. He comforted me with a loving smile. "Oh, Emily...that must have been very painful."

My heart warmed, knowing his thoughts were genuine. I composed myself and finished telling Jake that my grandparents passed away a few years ago from old age, and how I've been on my own pretty much since my senior year in high school.

"How did you pay for college and living expenses? How did you buy a house already?"

Our server filleted a whole-roasted turbot, along with an interesting burnt lemon for squeezing, and placed some on both our plates while I explained a bit more about myself. "I guess underneath this weak frame, I have a survival mentality. Tutoring young kids since my sophomore year in high school brought in decent money to pay for living expenses, and tuition was covered through grants and financial aid. I worked a lot in undergrad and saved all my money. There wasn't much of a need to spend any of it. Plus, when my grandparents passed away, they left me their condo. I sold it and added that money to my already growing pot. One day it occurred to me I could put a down payment on a small house, so I decided to try, and next thing I knew, I was a homeowner. So that's the story of my life till now."

Though my life's story was covered in three courses, there was more that Jake wanted to hear and understand.

"Can I ask you about your relationship with Max? Do you mind telling me?"

Jake's serious face told me that he was wary of my answer, but he also seemed quite intent on knowing everything about me. Hoping for a deeper relationship, I didn't want to keep anything from him. He gave me more peace in my heart than I had felt in a long time. I could tell that this was a man who would complement my life entirely, if I'd allow myself to love him. My heart wanted to give it a try.

"Tell me everything. Don't worry about what I might think or feel. I also would like to know what happened with you and Max last night, if you don't mind."

I hesitated, wondering how much of myself to reveal. Would he want to know the whole truth about Max and me? My answer would hopefully add another dimension to our promising relationship.

"Max and I met our freshman year in college. It was absolute love at first sight for both of us."

"Lucky guy!" Jake interrupted. "So what about him did you like so much?"

I instantly laughed at this question. "You guys are both so funny."

"What do you mean?"

"Max asked me the same question last night. He asked what about you I liked so much."

"So what did you tell him?"

"I think I'll keep you guessing on that one." I winked.

"Max and I met in the cafeteria of our freshmen dormitory and we immediately started hanging out. Because I felt so alone after my mom died, I happily accepted the chemistry between us. There was this crazy bond that formed, and we couldn't stay away from one another. We didn't declare our feelings for one another till after the first month, but it was obvious to everyone around us that we were a couple. We spent our entire college life inseparable. I thought we were going to get married. The only thing that was a hindrance was the fact that Max wasn't the most motivated of students. He was super smart, but he didn't know what he wanted to do with his life and this bothered both of us. Although we had no idea how he would support a family, if it came to that, we were so in love, we didn't care."

With my every sentence, Jake's expression turned from curious to somber. He was hurt by my fervent accounts of our college years.

"I'm sorry, Jake. You didn't need to hear all of that. I got a bit carried away." I apologized repeatedly.

"No, it's all right. I asked for it," he stated with a bit of masochistic chivalry. "Continue…"

At this point, I wavered between taking a bite of steak from Japan or continuing my saga with Max. Seeing Jake's anxious face, the beef needed to wait.

"Well, there's not much more to say. On graduation day, Max appeared nervous all day and tried to avoid me, so I thought he was going to ask me to marry him. Instead, after the ceremony, he broke up with me, giving some excuse about not being ready for a serious commitment. Just like that, he let go of four years and the bond that I thought could never be broken…broke."

Jake could see the pain on my face. I didn't know how to explain to him that this feeling left in my heart was not love, but hurt. I wanted Jake to believe it was over between Max and me, and that I had finally let go of the past—if not entirely, almost entirely.

Jake tried to break up my glum mood and asked me again about Max's question from last night.

"Well, I told Max how comfortable I feel with you. I feel protected and secure, and I can be myself with you. Although I've only known you for a short while, it's like you've been with me my whole life. I don't know. It's a bit strange but you're the only person, aside from my parents, who makes me feel entirely comfortable. I can't quite explain this. Max got very angry with me last night when I told him this."

"You mean you've never felt entirely comfortable with Max?"

"With Max, I was always trying to please him. My whole world revolved around him. I think I was infatuated with him. Max appeared at a time in my life when I had nobody but my grandparents. My parents were gone and I didn't have any siblings. Max not only became my boyfriend, but he also became my only family. I think I smothered him. Maybe I was a borderline stalker. That's probably why he eventually broke up with me."

We both got a good laugh.

"You want to know the hardest part about this breakup?"

Jake appeared wary again.

"I guess I'm going to tell you regardless. All the loves in my life left me without any warning—my dad, my mom, and Max. I don't think I ever loved anyone as much as I loved these three people, and I felt abandoned by all of them." The tears hovered again. "I had a tough year and a half letting go. I had lost four years of my life."

"Are you sure you're over Max?" Jake lamented, "Do I want to know?"

"Last night, Max apologized for hurting me. He reassured me that he loved me as much as I loved him while we were dating, and that I wasn't the only one hurting after the breakup. His apology came off a bit contrived since he started dating Jennifer within a month of our breakup. I accepted his apology and decided that this finally closed the Max and Emily chapter. So to answer your question, yes I am over him, but four years is hard to erase."

Initially, Jake looked wholly tentative. He still didn't quite believe I was over Max. After last night, he had credible reason not trust me. Still, I hoped he would want to give me and us a chance. With Max, as much as I'd hoped, I never truly believed that we would be together till the very end. But with Jake, there was an inexplicable sense of completeness, an unbreakable connection, like he was meant to be in my life—like he would always be a part of my life.

Attempting to take the spotlight off myself, I asked Jake about some of the girls he'd dated. This would also give me a chance to eat my dessert— a hot, creamy chocolate cake sitting atop a pool of bittersweet dark chocolate sauce, and below a house made cinnamon ice cream. What decadence!

"It seems hardly fair that I've given you details of my one love yet I haven't heard any details of the loves in your life. I'm sure there have been many women in your life. Tell me everything."

"I had a few girlfriends, but I haven't dated much since I got to General Hospital."

"Oh, that doesn't surprise me. With your insane schedule, how could you have a life? I'm surprised we've come this far."

"Kelley and I dated on and off for years. Our families knew each other since we were little, because both our dads were doctors at the same hospital. It seemed a bit incestuous since our families were such close friends. I think our parents thought we'd get married."

"So what happened?"

"I went off to med school, she went off to business school, and it was too difficult to have a long-distance relationship. We tried several times to get back together but failed."

"I assume she went to school with you? Did you date her all throughout undergrad?"

"Actually, she didn't, and even during undergrad she and I dated on and off."

"What made your relationship so tentative?"

"I liked her very much and I suppose I loved her at one point but I never thought that she was the one."

"What does she look like?" I immediately regretted asking this, as it seemed like a petty question, but curiosity got the better of me.

"She's not nearly as beautiful as you are," Jake said with the most adoring look. I blushed and changed the subject.

After two amuse bouches, nine courses of gastronomic extravagance, and free-flowing wine, we were done with our meal. Time had sped by. With each course, I fell deeper and deeper for a man whose candor and sincerity proved a reciprocity of feelings. In a matter of three hours there was no doubt we would be in a solid relationship.

To my utter delight, the chef and owner graciously visited our table and talked with us about our meal and his restaurant. Asking what my favorite dish was during lunch, I happily answered, "Moulard duck foie gras, the kuroge sirloin and risotto with white truffles…mmm. Anything with white truffles!"

Both men laughed as Jake was warned, "She's got expensive taste."

"Don't I know it!" he answered with a wink.

We got an inspiring tour of the restaurant. It's all about finesse emblazoned the walls of his spotless kitchen with copper pots hanging from the ceiling. All the chefs and sous chefs worked busily to prepare each course with seamless effort and efficiency. The attention to detail marked this restaurant as the top dining place in the world. Every dish that went out looked spotless. My eyes darted from the salad station to the meat station to the pastry station. I wanted to jump in and work with them but Jake pulled me in his arms and led me out of the kitchen so they could continue working. We thanked the staff for an incredible meal, and Jake mentioned visiting his New York restaurant next time he was there. Secretly, I hoped I would be there as well.

We headed down Highway 29 toward the city for the second half of our day. It was probably 2:00p.m. or so, and I felt this lazy urge to take a nap. Jake pulled into a high rise and parked the car. I wondered where we were, but got no explanation. Staring at him gave no clues, but there was only that knowing and annoying grin. Jake opened the door to a beautiful apartment overlooking the San Francisco Bay, juxtaposed between the Ferry building and AT&T Park. It was furnished in a comfortable shabby chic style. I looked at him again for an explanation.

"This apartment belongs to our family. My parents used to come up to the Bay Area all the time when Jane was at school and hoped that Nick would come to school up here as well. I thought we would rest a little before our dinner and show."

"Dinner? Show? How can you eat again after nine courses?" I asked. "There's no way I can eat again today. I am so full. Besides, I have nothing to wear to attend any shows up here. What are we going to watch?"

"You'll see," he answered with a funny grin. "Don't worry. I've taken care of everything. Let's hang out for a couple of hours. I, too, am stuffed."

Jake grabbed my hands and led me to a large white sofa situated right in front of an even larger plasma TV. He sat down and pulled me right next to him. Every inch of our bodies touched, but that didn't seem to be enough for him. Jake curved his arms around my waist and pulled me even closer to him. Somewhere between the nine courses of food and wine, the comfort of the sofa, and the heat of our bodies, I fell asleep.

What seemed like minutes later, I woke up lying on top of Jake's body. Jake had comfortably sprawled out on the sofa with his head on the armrest and his legs stretched out. My body, wedged between the back of the sofa and Jake's warm body, also stretched out comfortably.

"Oh my gosh. How long have I been asleep?"

"A couple of hours, I think," Jake answered with his left hand stroking my long hair and his right working the remote.

"I'm so sorry, Jake. I can't believe I fell asleep on you. I don't think I've ever fallen asleep on a date before."

"It was nice. I rather liked it. You appeared quite cozy." He smiled and kissed the top of my head.

"Um...I didn't drool on you, did I? I asked while wiping his shirt just in case.

"Do you normally?" He was now chuckling.

"I don't think so, but of course the one time I fall asleep with a man, I would make a fool of myself."

Jake pondered over this statement while I pushed myself up.

"Stay," he whispered. He pulled me up, eye to eye, and before I knew it, our lips joined uncontrollably. Both arms tightened around my body, and his lips made several longing trips down my neck and then back to my lips. His kisses felt like a staccato piano piece. They were short, detached, and all over. He never stayed in one place too long. This made me want him even more.

To our chagrin, a knock on the door stopped our long-overdue embrace. Jake grumbled as he got up to answer it. I also got up and fixed myself for whatever company we were expecting. It was a doorman with a rolling rack full of clothes, shoes, and accessories.

"What's all this?" I questioned.

"Remember I told you I would take care of everything for the show?"

And taken care of everything he had. In the apartment sat half a dozen dresses and pairs of shoes for me to try on. There were even the proper undergarments to match the dresses.

"How did this all get here?"

"Actually, Jane is in San Francisco right now and she helped me. I thought about asking the concierge, but she offered to go out and get all this for you. I hope you don't mind. Jane is the only girl in the family and she's always wanted a sister. She's more than excited to meet you and become your friend. Is that OK?" he asked with more hesitation than necessary.

"Jane, your sister? Oh, I can't wait to meet her!" Being an only child, I craved company constantly. My heart jumped for joy at the thought of having a new friend.

"Jane is quite an opera buff, and I remembered you talking about Carmen. So, Jane helped out again and got us a box at the opera house, and that's the final half of our date. We are meeting her for dinner so you have to eat."

"Jake, this has been one of the most amazing dates. Lunch was a gastronomic feast. Meeting the chef owner was almost as phenomenal as lunch, and I'm really touched you figured out how much I like opera. I guess you do listen during our dates even though they're always cut short. You are an amazing man."

Jake had this exceptional ability to read between the lines. He picked up my nuances and facial expressions and could easily decode answers I didn't realize I was giving. After half a date at a Mexican restaurant, was my food obsession that obvious? He correctly guessed that his brother Nick and I would be great foodie friends. It was also a wonder as to how he knew about my fascination with Carmen. Maybe it was the way I listened to Carmen in his car, or maybe it was from the brief conversation we had about the video I watched in high school. None of this information came directly from me.

In one single date, Jake had crossed off many items high on my "to-do" list. After Julia Roberts in *Pretty Woman*, there wasn't a single girl out there who wouldn't want to be whisked off to San Francisco on a date. Today had been a combination of the surreal and the comical as I too, would be watching an opera, my favorite opera in San Francisco. However, I had one up on Vivian Ward. I had dined at the best restaurant in the world.

Quickly, I picked out a dress and a pair of shoes and went in to one of the rooms to get ready. In the living room, Jake was already waiting for me with one more surprise in his hand.

He held out a little box—the kind a girl received when a man got down on one knee, about to propose to the woman he loved.

"I want ask you something. Please don't be scared by the box. It's not as serious as it looks."

That allowed me to breathe a sigh of relief. Jake grinned at the seriousness of my face. He carefully watched me open the tiny box and intently studied my expression as I wondered what exactly I was looking at.

"Um...it's stunning, but could you explain this ring to me?"

In my hand lay a white gold or platinum band with hundreds of pave diamonds set into the shallow depths of the band. There was no end to the shiny diamonds that encircled the ring. This was without a doubt the kind of ring women generally wore on their fourth finger as a wedding band if they were lucky enough to afford one of this magnitude.

"OK," he breathed aloud, "it's not an engagement ring, nor is it a wedding band, as you might fear. I wanted to give you a ring that symbolized our commitment to one another...no scratch that. That didn't come out right." His hands shook as they reached for mine.

"Emily, we've dated a couple of months now, and I know you're not quite sure where we stand in the formal sense. I actually bought this ring for you after our first date. Even back then, I knew I wanted to be with you. I mean, date only you. I wanted to ask you...geez, I feel like a school boy asking a girl to be his girlfriend," he interjected in the middle of his own explanation, "um...I would like for us to date...exclusively date. What I mean is...will you be my girlfriend?" he finally spit out.

I started with a half smile that led to a giggle. He was unusually insecure for Jake's standards. When I didn't answer immediately, his lips turned into a pouty frown.

"Are you going to answer? You're making me nervous."

"OK, so let me get this straight. You spent thousands of dollars to ask my permission to do what we are already doing now? Dating?"

"Um, yeah. Aren't you the one that called our relationship 'whatever it is that we have'?"

I cringed when he said that. Those were definitely not choice words.

"Jake. Aren't we already exclusively dating? Have you been seeing other girls as well? Is that why it's so hard to spend any time with you?" My lips curled into a teasing smile. Jake didn't find me funny. Trying to give him more assurance I said, "I haven't had a desire or need to see anyone else. I feel blessed to be with you."

"I'm still unsure how you feel about me. I know I haven't said much today, but you must know how much I adore you. You're trusting, yet guarded; you're independent, yet willing to follow; and your heart's been broken, yet you're willing to give love another try. I love all these qualities about you. It doesn't hurt that you're fun, funny, and beautiful as well. I wasn't sure you felt the same way. Especially after seeing you with Max last night, I was afraid you might be reconsidering our relationship," he confessed with some satisfaction, but still much apprehension.

"Jake. I really like you, and I want our relationship to grow. You're right. After Max, I needed to guard my heart more than necessary. But I trust you and feel most secure when we're together. You are the only man I want to be with."

Even with my profession, Jake's expression hardly changed so I felt compelled to continue. "I'm sorry you had to witness my first encounter with Max and his new girlfriend. Being such an awkward moment, I didn't react the way I would have liked. It did affect me. I guess it hurt me more than I thought it would, even with you by my side. But, you and our relationship add so much joy to my life. I wasn't lying when I said that you're the only person who makes me feel entirely comfortable. I'm elated when we're together and lonely when we're apart. Will this answer do? I will wear this very expensive ring as a symbol of my commitment to our relationship. I would be honored to be your girlfriend."

Lovingly, he pulled me to him and held me. He wanted a relation-ship with me despite all my inadequacies. We were content being with one another. I wasn't wrong to anticipate that this trip would bring us closer. Love, hope, and joy—a generic mantra for most—took on a completely new meaning in my heart. My heart felt whole again, emancipated from Max's chains. It was finally free to beat for someone else.

With good foresight, Jake bought a necklace to go with the ring. Knowing that I wouldn't want to wear it on my finger, he hung it as a pen-dant on my neck. It was beautiful—heavy, but beautiful.

Jane was already at the restaurant waiting at the bar for us. Her build was slender and she stood at about five feet seven. Her hair wasn't as dark as Jake's, but her eyes were just as blue. She and Jake shared many of the same facial features. Upon first impression, she was just as beautiful as Jake was handsome. I could imagine how stunning the five of them would look in a family portrait.

"Emily, this is my only sister, Jane."

"Jane, this is my Emily."

"I'm so happy to meet you, Jane. Thank you very much for all your troubles. It was unnecessary but much appreciated," I said, giving her a hug. She hugged me right back like we were old friends.

"Thrilled to do it for you. I don't think I've ever seen my brother this happy. You are actually the first girlfriend he's introduced me to since Kelley, right Jake?"

"I guess. I don't know."

I turned to Jake to tease him. "There were probably so many girls before me, he didn't have the energy to introduce them all to you." Jane and I laughed. Jake pouted.

Our restaurant was located in the business district close to the Embarcadero. The nicely decorated restaurant offered another pre-fixe menu. After lunch, I chose the vegetarian option but couldn't resist the sweetbread appetizer, while Jane and Jake chose a four-course meal, starting with the sweetbread as well. Sipping fizzy water, Jane and I spoke endlessly about our likes and dislikes. We talked as though we were close friends catching up on old times. Jake didn't mind that I paid no attention to him. Content just to hold my hand, he watched us converse.

"What's it like living in New York?" I asked Jane. "I've always wanted to live there. Although, I think I could live up here as well."

"Weren't you just there over Thanksgiving?"

"Yeah, I had so much fun. It could have only been better if your brother had gone with me." I squeezed Jake's hand.

"New York is the most exciting city. My girlfriends and I meet at all hours of the day, and there are so many restaurants and cafés bustling with people. I enjoy how busy the streets are, and how people bump into you on the subway. It feels like you're living among everyone. In LA, you drive everywhere, so you don't really get to know your neighbors. In New York, your neighbors become your commuting buddies. You should come visit me. We'd have a great time."

"I'd love that." Next time, I'll make sure Jake and I go together. "Jane, how old are you? Are we the same age? If you're in your last year of law school, does that make you older? There's a bit of a gap between you and Jake."

"No, I'm also twenty-four. My mom says Jake is spoiled rotten because I came along so late. He was an only child for too long."

"Who says I'm spoiled?" Jake dropped my hand and looked aghast. "Mom says you were always the competitive one trying to outdo me."

"Oh, only everyone! Plus, I didn't try. I outdid you in every category," she retorted.

"Because he was the first grandchild in the Reid family, everyone spoiled him. He loved the attention. To this day, he's still the golden child of this family." There was humor and slight resentment in her tone. It made me laugh.

"So, Emily," she said, turning to me, "what about my brother do you like? Why would you want to date someone who can spend no more than a couple of hours with you at a time? I'm shocked he took an entire weekend off. You must be special. I didn't think he'd ever meet anyone who could tolerate his schedule."

"I have to agree that he is quite the workaholic. We've had only four dates in the last six weeks, and every single date was cut short due to work."

"Hey, no more Jake-bashing." Jake frowned again as he pushed his seat closer to me. "Tell Jane what you like about me," he directed with a childlike eagerness.

"I told you he's an attention monger." Jane rolled her eyes.

Not having grown up with siblings, I enjoyed their banter. It was fun watching Jake and Jane argue and poke fun at one another. I'd never experienced this with anyone. Since Max had only brothers, this brother-sister relationship was an entirely new discovery.

"Tell her, Emi."

"Let's see. It's not a very long list," I answered, laughing with Jane. "I'm kidding." I quickly added before Jake disowned me as a girlfriend. "Jake has this amazing way of making me feel like I'm the only person in this world who matters to him. I feel incredibly special." My eyes glowed as I spoke about my boyfriend. "Not only is he attentive, he's a caring, very loving person. Is that a good enough answer?"

His silly grin shouted to everyone in the restaurant that he liked my answer very much. Passing the test, he leaned over and kissed me—a bit too passionately—in front of his sister. Jane had other ideas.

"Are you talking about my brother? Do you know what Kelley's biggest complaint about him was? She always bemoaned the fact that he didn't pay enough attention to her."

"Now why must you bring Kelley into this story? That's the past. Let's leave it there," Jake warned his sister.

"My mom says that Jake needs a woman with a strong sense of self-esteem, because he never pays much attention to anyone but himself. Have you two gotten into an argument yet? Has he been mad at you?"

I shook my head yes. "I don't know if I'd call them arguments, but we got into a couple of disagreements."

"Wait till you get into an all-out argument with him. I don't know if you're going to think he's so attentive and caring, then. You should see the tantrum he throws."

"I love these new revelations about you. You didn't tell me any of this during lunch." My eyes looked at him in delight. "I can't wait to see you throw a tantrum. Maybe I'll purposely make you angry just to see your reaction."

Jane loved my goading. Jake didn't fall into our trap.

"Don't believe a word she says. I don't know what's gotten into my sister." He turned to his sister and tried to give her a stern look. She wasn't scared.

"So, Jake, what do you like about Emily? Try to keep it to a few sentences, OK? We have an opera to watch."

Just then, servers came with our third course. A sautéed striped bass sat in front of them, while I got a medley of mushrooms.

"If I had to sum up what I love most about Emily, it would be her honesty. Even though she knows it's not to her benefit, she'll still tell you what's in her heart. I know way too much about her last relationship." He lightly shook his head.

"Was my honesty at lunch not to my benefit? Am I in trouble?" My forehead creased with a worried look.

Jake's lips reached over to mine again and eased my concern. "I appreciate your honesty, whether or not I appreciate your answers."

Jane broke our tender moment and continued her question-and-answer session, and Jake happily obliged by giving her a detailed account of our first encounter.

"We met late at night at a supermarket and I had to take her to the hospital after she fell, reaching for a box of cereal. So, I take her to General Hospital, and we're sitting in the examination room, and do you know what she asks me? She had the gall to ask if I was really a doctor at GH and not just some staff member."

In response to Jane's "why" look, I said, "Well, for someone who worked at the hospital, he got no special treatment. I waited there just as long as everyone else to get out of ER. In fact, there were patients who came after me but left earlier. I thought he was lying to me about being a doctor. It took us three hours."

Jane broke into a chortle. "Yeah, he has no power there. You should have called Uncle Henry instead. You would have been in and out with a call from him. By the way, why are you guys going back down tonight? Jake, didn't you ask Emily if she wanted to stay the weekend?" I could tell Jake was happy to hear his sister ask this question. Put on the spot, I didn't know how to answer. "Emily, you should stay with us in the apartment and go down tomorrow night. We could spend another day together. Are you uncomfortable with me being in the apartment? Do you want to be alone with Jake?"

This conversation turned even more awkward.

"Oh, no, Jane...I don't feel uncomfortable with you. Jake didn't fully explain what was happening today."

"Then you'll stay the night? We can get to know each other better."

What could I say? "I'd love that, Jane, but I'm not prepared to spend the night here. I don't have any clothes or toiletries."

"You can borrow all of mine. We can also quickly stop by any of the stores in Union Square if you need to pick up something."

"OK." I was really nervous about spending the night with Jake, even with Jane in tow. I hadn't explained to him about my wishes to stay chaste till marriage. Most likely, he would expect or at least desire to spend the night with me. When and how I would have this conversation stayed with me the rest of dinner as Jane and Jake picked up their unfinished thought.

"So, Jake, anything else you want to tell me about Emily?"

"Let me excuse myself to the ladies' room and you two can talk about me all you like. It's a bit embarrassing hearing about myself."

I walked to the ladies' room, leaving the Reid siblings to talk. Jake and Jane had given me a true taste of family, something that disappeared too early in my life. It was altogether sweet, sour, salty, and a bit bitter at times, but most of all, it had the wonderful flavor of love. This is what I'd missed out on being an only child with parents up in heaven. I was glad to have witnessed a small part of their family.

On my way back, seeing that the Reid siblings hadn't finished their conversation, my pace slowed, allowing Jake to finish. What I'd overheard added another cup to my already overflowing feelings for him.

"And...I love her strength. I've never met any girl who is such a survivor. She's pretty much been alone since high school, put herself through college, and then bought and created a home all by herself. She's worked for everything she has. Nothing has been handed to her. Yet she smiles and enjoys life. Her attitude is amazing. But, as strong as she appears, she's terribly tenderhearted. I think this is what makes me so enamored with her. She hurts easily, cries readily, but loves deeply. She makes me want to care for her and shelter her from anything that may harm her. I've never felt such a strong desire to protect someone as I do for Emily."

As I walked back to my seat, happiness swelled in my heart till it felt like a balloon about to burst. Jake had summed up Emily Logan better than I could have. As happy as I was, there was this nagging insecurity. Could such a perfect man exist in my world? I feared answering this question.

We got back to the apartment around midnight and Jane excused herself to answer a phone call. Here it was, the conversation I dreaded.

"So..." Jake started very casually, "where will you be sleeping tonight?"

I cringed at the thought of having to explain myself to him. I waited for him to finish before going into my tedious explanation.

"Door number one is my room, door number two is Jane's room, or you can sleep alone behind door number three." He pointed to each room with a hopeful and expectant look.

There was an awkward silence.

"Jake...I need to tell you something." I dragged his name a bit but quickly let out the next group of words.

"Uh-oh, did I say something wrong?"

"No, I guess it's time to confess since we're at this juncture. Maybe I should have told you before accepting your ring. You might have had second thoughts about wanting me as your girlfriend."

Jake looked mildly horrified. "You're making me nervous; what's wrong?"

This conversation wasn't nearly as difficult to have the first time with Max at age eighteen but now, I sounded so archaic telling my thirty-year-old boyfriend that I wanted to stay a virgin.

"Nothing is wrong. I should have told you this earlier. I want you to know that I've never, um..." There was no reason to be, but I was embarrassed.

"Well...I've never slept with a man before. You are literally the first man I fell asleep with earlier today, though nothing happened. I'm not planning on being with you or any man till I get married." Incredibly nervous, I found my hands tightly clutching my borrowed robe unable to look at Jake till I finished confessing.

Relief, confusion, happiness, and chagrin all flashed across Jake's face and in that order. "You mean you and Max have never...?"

"No, we've never been together in that sense."

"But how? You dated for four years."

"It was hard but I really wanted to save myself for whomever I might end up marrying. My mom was old fashioned, and she wanted me to wait till I got married. This was a promise I made to her before she died, and I'd like to honor her wishes. Also, watching my parents love each other, I thought it would be most special with the man I'd spend the rest of my life with."

"What if that man isn't as pure as you are?" He looked worried again.

I chuckled, realizing he obviously didn't believe what I believed. "That's all right. It would be most perfect if we were each other's first, but I can't expect everyone to have the same beliefs. Are you OK with my confession? I'm sorry I didn't bring it up earlier. I didn't quite know how to approach this subject. Are you upset?" My head fell back down worried what Jake might think.

"Disappointed, yes; upset, no. I guess this happily speeds up our timetable." Oddly, amusement mirrored his disappointment.

"What does that mean?"

"Oh, that's for me to know and for you to soon find out."

I could hear a quiet sigh as he held me in his arms till Jane walked back into the living room. He gently kissed my lips and I followed Jane to her room.

"Emily," Jane carefully called my name. "You don't have to sleep in my room on my account. You can be with Jake if you like."

"Jane, I want to be here with you if you're OK with it."

"I'd love it but is Jake OK with this?"

"I didn't give him a choice." I giggled. After all was said and done, Jake accepted my revelation without much of a fight. Maybe the physical part of our relationship wouldn't be too much of a struggle—or maybe this was wishful thinking.

"Where shall I sleep?" Jane's room had two twin bunks, reminding me of the summer camp I'd visited back in sixth grade.

"I sleep here on this bottom bunk. Why don't you take the other bottom bunk?"

"Why are there so many beds in here?"

Jane's pretty face broke into a laugh. "There was a time in undergrad when we had so much rain, our sorority house got flooded. My room, endearingly called, 'the jungle,' had twelve girls and twelve beds. When we were all displaced, we brought as many beds into this apartment as possible, and we all lived here for a month until the house got fixed. The other two rooms got rid of the bunk beds, but I kept my room the same. I guess you could call it nostalgia. I feel like I'm back in college whenever I sleep in here."

"How fun! Maybe I should have rushed as a freshman. It would have been the perfect solution to not having any siblings."

"So..." Jane had a devilish look about her.

"Yes..?" Fearful—I was definitely fearful of what was coming next.

"Are we good enough friends for me to ask why you are sleeping here rather than with my brother? I promise, he has a very large bed in his room. You'll be more comfortable there than in here."

"Oh...that. Though she didn't know what she was doing to me at the time, my mom made me promise her—right before she died—that I would stay a virgin maid till I got married. I think she just said that hoping to push off the inevitable for as long as possible, but since that was one of my last promises to her, I feel like I have to keep it."

"Oh. My. Gosh! Seriously? This is so hilarious that Jake has to wait till you guys get married to sleep with you. I bet you he's out there running miles on the treadmill to work off his suppressed expectations or he's scheming to see how he can work around your vow."

"He seemed to take it OK when I told him tonight."

The laughter that ensued could be heard all the way to AT&T Park. Perhaps I was a bit hasty in thinking that Jake would be OK with my chastity agreement.

"Oh, this is his comeuppance!" Jane brushed away the natural tears that came from her guffaw. "He always thought he could get whatever girl he wanted and unfortunately, that was the case. I don't know of too many women who have refused my brother anything...till now. He's finally found the girl and she won't play to his tune. Oh, I love it!"

Jane's rambling roused out of me a new set of insecurities. "Has he been with a lot of women? Kelley was the only girl I heard about but...I guess it's silly of me to think that with his looks and at his age that there weren't many more..."

Jealousy, along with sadness, speared through my heart knowing that there had been copious girls who had been a part of Jake's life. Jane quickly defended her brother and tried to turn me around.

"No, no! Don't get the wrong idea, Emily. Yes, there have been other women, but I promise you this—there has never been a girl like you."

I must not have look convinced.

"Life has always been easy for my brother. He's smart, good looking, charming, and fairly wealthy. He's never had to work very hard for anything—especially women. But, seeing him with you this weekend, and without you Thanksgiving weekend, made me do a double take. Regardless of what he's told you, from what my mom and I can tell, he is madly in love with you. We've never seen him so anxious about pleasing a girl."

Her comment brought forth a weak smile.

"I see you're wearing the ring. Did you know he bought it after just one date with you?"

I nodded yes. "He told me today."

"Did you also know that he was miserable the whole week you and Sarah were gone to New York? He looked like a lost puppy. Every member of the Reid family teased him mercilessly during Thanksgiving dinner. Uncle Henry says he's 'whipped'!"

"Jane, you don't have to say anymore. I understand what you're trying to do. It's not so much Jake that worries me. It's more me. He's so perfect. This whole weekend is like a scene out of a movie—it can't be real in my life. My life hasn't been easy since middle school and I don't want to start believing it's changed for this much the better."

Before she could rebut my statement, I gave Jane the long version of my life and told her about all my insecurities. Deep into the night we spoke about my fears. Jane listened like a sibling and encouraged and admonished all in appropriate ways. Similar to the comfort I found in Jake, his sister was no different. I could picture us being fast friends and sisters.

We talked into the wee hours of the morning, but I still found myself awake before the sun was up. The light outside encouraged me to get up, brush my teeth, put on Jane's borrowed clothes, and step into the living room. Surprisingly Jake was up already, reading the paper.

"Good morning," I whispered.

"Good morning, Beautiful. Why are you up so early?"

"I can't ever sleep well outside of my own bed. Are you going somewhere? Why are you dressed like Lance Armstrong?"

"I thought I'd go cycling this morning to release some of this pent-up energy."

Good thing he kept his head in the newspaper. My lips tightly held together to keep from laughing. Jake apparently hadn't taken the news as well as I thought he had.

"You want to ride with me?" As much as I didn't want to, I thought it would be better for the relationship if I went with him.

"I don't have any clothes. Plus, where are we getting bikes at this hour?"

"All the bikes are downstairs in storage and Jane has plenty of clothes for you to borrow. She used to cycle in undergrad." He walked into Jane's room and blinded her by turning on the light. "Jane, where do you keep your cycling clothes?"

Extremely annoyed, she yelled at her brother. "What is your problem? It's still dark out. Why do you need my cycling clothes?"

"Emi and I are going out for a ride."

"Jake…we got to bed a few hours ago. Leave Emily alone. She and I are both tired."

"Just answer my question."

Jake kept the light on till he found what he was looking for and handed me clothes and shoes to change into. Not having done this since grammar school, I worried about the challenge of riding a bike in this hilly city. Plus, the professional gear looked ridiculous on me.

"Where are we going?"

"Let's go get breakfast. There's nothing to eat here," he answered, handing me Jane's bike and helmet. "You do know how to ride a bike?"

"Yes, but I'm no professional. It's been awhile since I've been on one of these." Hesitation marred my face.

"You'll be fine. What do you want to eat?"

"How about a greasy donut or an almond croissant and a latte? Even after two huge meals yesterday, I'm starving."

"I know just the place. Let's go." He led me out of the Embarcadero and headed south.

"Wait! You're not thinking of riding all the way into the Mission District, are you?" I asked warily.

"Yup. You know this town better than I thought."

"Yeah, I've been around the block a few times in this city."

"Apparently you don't go all the way around the block in any city," he answered sarcastically and rode away.

I cracked up laughing. "Wait for me..."

The ride to breakfast wasn't as bad as I thought it might be. The donut shop smelled heavenly. With so many choices, I asked Jake to buy one of every donut and took a bite of every flavor. I couldn't get enough of the banana de leche and lemon pistachio. Jake favored the maple-glazed bacon apple. I wasn't crazy about the sweet and savory combo of his choice. We took the leftovers for Jane and went to our next destination.

My favorite bakery in the Mission District was located many, many blocks from the donut shop. Once here, there were too many choices, so little room in the stomach—as this was always my dilemma.

"Do I need to buy one of everything here too?" he asked in a sour tone. He was still sore about last night.

"Jake...are you going to be upset with me every time we're in an overnight situation?"

"If I say yes, will you do something about it?"

"Yup, I will."

"You will?" Jake's eyes twinkled again. I so didn't want to crush this glow.

"I'm going to have to make sure we are not in this situation ever again. You'll have to apologize to your parents for me and tell them I can't go to Hawaii with you."

If Jake was sore earlier, he was completely pouting now. "Emily!" He dragged my name in frustration.

I put both my hands on his cheeks and kissed his puckered lips. "Will you be OK with Hawaii or should I stay home?" Jake knew he'd lost this round.

He tried to shake my hands loose but instead, I grabbed him and kissed him longingly in front of a long line of strangers. This did the trick. His dimpled smile reappeared. "Jane was wrong about you," I told him. "I find you adorable when you're mad." I kissed him one more time.

A second breakfast of almond croissants, bread pudding, an utterly tantalizing open-faced sandwich with béchamel, gruyere, ham, and grilled asparagus, and a last bite of coconut crème tart gave both of us the surge of energy needed for the excruciating ride back home. Jake mapped out a long route from the bakery to Dolores Park, up to the War Memorial Opera House, then back to the apartment. I guess I should have been thankful that he didn't choose to take me up and down Lombard "Crooked" Street. While my boyfriend rode with vigor, my sloshy stomach struggled the last mile home. A few times, the contents of my stomach slithered its way up, but in the end, they decided to stay put. Finally back at home, we put our bikes away and walked across the street to the Ferry building. To my chagrin, the farmers' market didn't open on Sundays, so I followed Jake into the myriad of shops instead.

Jake started at a cook shop and purchased an all-inclusive picnic basket.

"Where are we going with this basket?" What fun we would have today!

"Maybe *you* are not a part of the *we*. Didn't you prefer Jane's company last night? I'm taking someone else on a picnic today." He smirked as I pouted. This had gone far enough. I turned the table on him and followed him around the marketplace but stopped talking.

He walked into a French-looking pastry shop, and bought two of every flavor of their Parisian macarons. How did he know macarons were my favorite dessert? We walked into the cheese shop for cheese, wine, and crackers; the salumeria for all things salty and pig; an oyster shop for clam chowder, mignonette, and hot sauce. He also bought caviar, foie gras pate, and we stood in the longest line I'd ever witnessed for coffee. I didn't realize we were hosting a party today with all this food. What looked like a haphazard shopping trip translated into a wonderful picnic lunch. With a satisfied look, he led me back to the apartment, not noticing that I hadn't said a word the entire time. How was I going to stay mad when he picked out only my favorites? His attentiveness might have saved him this time.

When we got back, Jane was grazing on everything we had brought back from our bike ride.

"Why did you guys ride this far? You could've just gone across the street."

"I don't know. Ask your brother." I pretended to sound angry and headed into Jane's room to take a shower.

Jake ran in behind me as I struggled to curb my giggle. He grabbed my hand and stopped me right before I shut the bathroom door on him. I tried my best to put on an angry face.

"Emily..." He dragged my name again. "Are you mad?"

"Yes."

"Sweetheart, I'm sorry." He tried to kiss me, but I purposely moved away and startled him. He never liked it when I turned away his embrace.

"Jake," I paused momentarily to swallow the guffaw that screamed to be let out. "I can't be in this relationship with you if you continue to stay angry at me for not having sex with you. Here, let me give you back this ring." I fumbled at the necklace, hoping that he would stop me before I unclasped it.

Locking my hands behind my back, he brought his lips hard on mine and left me gasping for air. If he knew only in the slightest how much I wanted him, there would be no apology necessary.

"OK, I'm sorry. I won't be upset anymore." His lips came down on mine a few more times. "But I'm still going to try to get you in bed every chance I get."

"I'd be worried if you didn't."

Jake was finishing our basket when I came out ready for the rest of our day.

"Jane, you're joining us, right?"

"No," both Reid siblings answered at the same time. Jane looked offended that Jake had decided for her, even though she gave me the same answer.

"My old roommate, Allison, is coming over and we're going out for lunch."

"Allison?" Jake had a peculiar look on his face. "What's she doing in town, and why's she coming over all of a sudden?"

"I don't know. I was going to ask you the same question. She called out of the blue, asked me where you were, and when I told her you were here, she insisted on coming over right away." Within seconds, Jane shook her head. "Oh, my gosh. You didn't finally succumb to her wiles, did you? Jake! Did you two date? Did you sleep with her? You're such an idiot! No wonder she kept asking about you."

"Who's Allison?" I asked.

Jake ignored both of us and hurried me out the door. Of course his past was not so kind, and Allison—tall, thin, and gorgeous—came running toward Jake wrapping her arms ever so longingly around my boyfriend's neck.

"Jake! I'm so happy to see you." I let go of Jake's hand so he could greet his whomever she is or was.

"Uh, hi, Allison." At this point this woman had the gall to not only hug my boyfriend, but kiss him on the lips. I was floored, Jake looked appalled, and Jane gasped, horrified. Jake quickly pushed her aside and tried to grab my hands again but I didn't give him the pleasure.

"Hello," Allison turned her hand out to me. "I'm Allison, Jake's friend." She giggled.

Ugh!

"Nice to meet you. I'm Emily, Jake's girlfriend," I answered as sweetly as possible. *Take that*! As annoyed as I was with this woman, it didn't rival Jake's terrified look as he kept searching for my perturbed expression.

"Jake. I rushed over here because I need to talk to you. Can you spare a few minutes for an old flame?"

At this point, I felt bad for Jake more than anything else. I decided to bow out and let them finish their conversation.

"I'll see you at the car," I whispered to Jake. "Jane, will I see you before I leave tonight?"

"Probably not. I'll see you in Hawaii." She hugged me and pleaded her brother's case. "Please don't be too upset with him."

Jake tried to hold on to me, but I grabbed our blankets and wine case and went out to the car. I turned on the music and sat patiently waiting for Jake to arrive. He probably only took a few minutes to talk to this person but it felt like hours. A myriad of thoughts ran through my head, but I decided to shut it out and enjoy the rest of our day together.

Jake jumped into the car with a most guilty look. "I'm so sorry about…"

"It's OK," I cut him off.

"Don't you want to know why she was here?"

"I prefer not to know, if that's OK with you. I know you didn't live under a rock before you met me. You're thirty. I'm sure you've dated many girls before I came along. *Though you only told me about Kelley.* I prefer not to know what you did before us, OK?"

Jake started the car and headed north.

"Where are we going? I'm really hungry again, not to mention exhausted, after our marathon biking session." I couldn't tell whether Jake's silence signaled guilt or anger about this morning's ordeal. Not liking the silence, I decided to explain why I didn't want to hear about Allison.

I reached over to hold his hand. "Jake?"

"Hmm?"

"Why are you so quiet? Did I do something wrong again?"

"Emily, why would you think you did anything wrong?"

"Well, generally when someone stops talking to you, it's because they're upset with you. All right…let me explain why I don't want to hear about that vile woman."

This brought a chortle out of Jake.

"When I was waiting in the car for you, I realized you were right when you said it's not good to know too much about each other's past. Watching her kiss you unsettled me to a point where my mind raced in all directions, jumping to conclusions about your relationship with her, past and present. Unpleasant would be a mild way of explaining what I felt."

This explanation only brought on a guiltier look.

"But then I thought about what you had to witness on Friday with me and Max, and I decided whatever I felt this morning couldn't have compared to what you must have felt meeting my only boyfriend of four years. So, I thought it only fair to let everything go and enjoy the rest of the day."

His eyes expressed appreciation and we enjoyed the rest of the day at an oyster farm about an hour north of the city. It never ceased to amaze Jake how much I ate. He watched in amusement as I tried to shuck an oyster with no success. Jake also found no success trying to top oysters with the goodies that we brought. His toppings fell off the shell or slid to the side. We decided he should shuck the oysters while I created my masterpieces of oysters with caviar, oysters with mignonette and hot sauce, and grilled oysters with melted cheeses, hot sauce, and pancetta—that was the winning combination. A bottle of wine later, I needed dessert and coffee to wake me up or I would end up asleep on our picnic blanket among a crowd of people.

"Jake, how did you know Parisian macarons are my favorite dessert? I don't think I ever told you this, did I?"

His lips curled into a most endearing expression. "You have this almost wistful look in your eyes when you talk about or see something you like."

"That's exactly what my mom used to tell me. While you call it wistful, she called it covetous." I laughed. "How boring and predictable am I when you've figured me out this easily and so quickly," I stated with chagrin.

"On the contrary, I find you to be the most interesting and desirable woman I've ever met. I can't get enough of you."

I felt blood rushing to my cheeks. "That's only because I'm the one girl who hasn't jumped into bed with you on the first date." I saw blood rushing to his cheeks as well.

Waiting out a delay on the runway at SFO, I couldn't keep my eyes open. Jake pulled up the armrest, placed his arms around my waist and had me snuggle into his chest. I could never tire of this sense of being desired. Drifting into unconsciousness, Jake kissed the top of my head whispering three words that gave me goose bumps. Perhaps I was only dreaming.

Chapter 5

Max's Regret

The phone rang way too early for my liking.

"Hello?" I answered, annoyed.

"Emily. You're back. Where were you yesterday? I tried calling you all day." It was Sarah, probably calling for a minute-by-minute recap of my date.

"Sarah! It's awfully early to be calling. What time is it?"

"Get up! It's 6:00a.m."

Was she kidding? 6:00a.m? "I just got to bed a few hours ago. Leave me alone."

"I'm coming over right now. I got you some coffee."

Sure enough, the doorbell rang within minutes. Ugh. I pulled on a robe, slowly brushed my teeth, and washed my face before answering the door. Sarah was dressed to go to work and ready to attack if I didn't start talking.

"Tell me everything!"

I tried to be vague, because I was tired and wanted her to leave so I could go back to sleep, but that was wishful thinking. I had to give her every detail of our trip from start to finish.

"All right. We flew out of Burbank airport and landed in SFO. Jake rented a car, and we had lunch at my dream restaurant up in Napa."

"Seriously? How did he do that? Didn't he just dream up this trip three nights ago? He's good! Wait, what's that on your neck? That looks heavy. That's not an engagement ring, is it?"

I started walking toward my bedroom threatening to go back to sleep. "OK, I won't interrupt," begged Sarah. "Continue!"

"We ate lunch, drove to his apartment in the city to rest, and then got ready for dinner and an opera."

"What? He has an apartment up in San Francisco? What did you do there?" Her expression turned suggestive.

"Sarah! You know that I didn't have sex with Max during our entire four-year relationship. You know that I feel strongly about waiting till I get married."

"Yeah, yeah. I know. You and your virtues. I don't know how you can hold back when you have someone as gorgeous as Jake in an empty apartment."

"Anyhow, his sister, Jane, was in town as well, so we got ready and had dinner with her and saw *Carmen*. After a nine-course lunch and a four-course dinner, I think I have officially gained back the weight I lost after my breakup with Max," I kidded.

"So, then where were you yesterday? Did you spend Sunday with Jake as well?"

I paused, knowing that Sarah was about to assume the worst. "I stayed up north all weekend."

"You what?" Her eyes bugged out. She knew I had never spent a night with anyone other than her. "You slept with Jake?"

She would jump to insane conclusions. "Sarah, I stayed in their apartment, but slept in Jane's room with Jane."

"Oh." Her excitement deflated faster than a popped balloon. "So you told Jake about your ridiculous pledge to stay a virgin?"

I nodded my head yes.

"What a buzzkill. He must have loved that piece of information about you."

"Yeah, at first I thought that he was OK with it, but I soon saw a whole other side to Dr. Reid. Inside this well-respected doctor who showers me with attention, lives a five-year-old who pouts when he doesn't get what he wants and gets upset quite easily. I found it adorable."

The conversation that ensued covered why I had a very expensive ring on my neck, and how Jake and I were going to give this relationship a chance at a future.

Sarah looked at me as though she wasn't sure she believed my earnest attempt at a new relationship. "I know you really like Jake, and Charlie and I are happy you've moved on, but can you honestly say that you are over Max and that you can seriously date Jake? Jake obviously thinks a lot more of you than you do of him."

"He told me that he really likes me and I like him just as much. I'm going to try, Sarah, to completely let go of the past and to start loving again. I had such an amazing weekend with him." Without a doubt or any pretense, I believed I could start anew. Sarah didn't buy it.

"Peter told me you and Max never made it to the bar Friday night. What happened to you two? Where were you?"

"We went and had dinner. Thanks to you, I didn't eat that night. I can't believe you did that to me. How can you call yourself my..."

Sarah cut me off. "OK, OK. I'm sorry. Back to dinner, what did you two talk about?"

"Max asked about Jake and I asked about him and Jennifer. He apologized to me for breaking my heart, and reassured me that he loved me very much when we were dating. He said that I was his world or something like that." I spoke with much skepticism.

"Charlie told me yesterday that Max and Jennifer broke up."

My head spun. "What?"

"That's what I heard. He broke it off after being with you on Friday, so we thought maybe you two were back together."

"Sarah! That's crazy. You know that I'm seeing Jake. I have no thoughts of getting back together with Max."

Sarah eyed me curiously. Still she wasn't convinced.

"You're such a liar. I still see the hurt on your face whenever I bring up Max."

"Yeah, it still hurts, but I'm over him. I want to be with Jake. I really like him. I feel so at ease with him. With Max, I was always on edge, you know that."

Ding dong.

We looked at each other, wondering who would come by so early in the morning. We both walked over to the door, and to my delight, it was Jake.

"Good morning, Beautiful." He planted a long kiss on my lips. Sarah tried to make her presence known and break us up, but Jake wouldn't let go.

"Hello?" Sarah protested.

Jake looked up from my face and answered, "Hey, Sarah. What are you doing here so early?"

"I was going to ask you the same thing."

"What are you both doing here at this hour?" I tried to sound annoyed.

"After having spent an entire weekend with you, my girlfriend, I was going through withdrawal." He tried to kiss me again, but the phone rang.

"Goodness, it's Grand Central here today. Sarah, can you answer that for me, please?"

"Hello?" We heard from afar.

I continued my conversation with Jake. "To what do I owe this unexpected but much-appreciated visit? I've never seen you so soon after a date.

I thought maybe I wouldn't see you again till we landed in Hawaii." I laughed, knowing this was our reality.

"I missed you after dropping you off last night. I thought I'd come by and see you before I started my day. What's your schedule like today?"

"Absolutely nothing is on my schedule today. This is the life of a school teacher on vacation."

"You want to come to the hospital and have lunch with me?"

I eyed him suspiciously, knowing that he had no set lunchtime.

"Oh? What time?"

A chuckle ensued with no clear answer for a lunch time, but many more kisses to all parts of my face and neck followed. Sarah halted our embrace as she yelled over, "Max and Peter want to know if you want to have lunch with them around noon today?"

My eyes gleamed with mischief, while his shot daggers at the thought of me being back together with Max.

"Well, Dr. Reid? Lunch today? I've got another offer on the table. Can you match that?" I smiled at his perturbed face.

"No. Go ahead and have lunch with your ex. I don't know when I'll get out of surgery." Even with a churlish demeanor, Jake was still endearing.

I hugged him and said, "I thought I might see another one of your tantrums. Don't worry. I promise I won't allow Max to run over and kiss me like you allowed Allison to do. Go save another life, Dr. Reid. Stop by after work, if you like."

He glowered at my snide remark concerning Allison, then lit up at the prospect of us seeing each other later, but quickly turned glum at the thought of me spending the day with Max. We said good-bye and he left for work.

Sarah had told the guys to meet for lunch near her work so that she and Charlie could join us. Today was shaping up to be a more eventful day than I had planned.

"By the way, Sarah, I'm leaving for Hawaii on Monday. You and Charlie want to house-sit for me? I'll be back Thursday morning." Once again, I went into long details with my best friend about Jake and the Reid family. She seemed quite impressed.

"We'd love to house-sit. It gives me a chance to be with Charlie for four straight days." I didn't want to know what was going on in that mind of hers.

"Use the guest bedroom, OK? No funny stuff on my bed." This provoked a pillow fight I was not ready for so early in the morning.

When Max offered to pick me up and take me out to the Westside to meet Peter, Sarah, and Charlie, I hesitantly agreed. Being with Max made me nervous all over again, but for different reasons. Though I knew Jake was the only man in my life, I was still unsure where Max fit, if he fit at all. I got in the car and Max eyes immediately landed on my new necklace.

"What's with the albatross on your neck?" he rudely referred to my ring.

My face scowled in answer to his obnoxious question. After a bit of silence, Max tried to ask me questions about inconsequential things like what I was doing for Christmas and New Year's, but as soon as I reminded him that I was going to Hawaii with Jake, the awkwardness reappeared. Feeling jittery, the conversation stopped for the rest of the ride.

When we got to the restaurant, our friends were seated already. We all said our hellos, and everyone's eyes locked on to my pendant.

"Did you get married and forget to invite us to the wedding?" Peter questioned.

Max sharply answered, "She won't say. I've asked already."

Charlie too was curious about the necklace. "You going to explain why you're wearing a wedding band on your neck?"

"OK. I'll explain," I answered exasperated. "Jake gave this to me Saturday to make our dating official."

"What does that mean?" Peter asked.

"Jake wanted affirmation that we were boyfriend and girlfriend."

"If he buys you something like that when asking to be your boyfriend, what will he get you if he's asking to be your husband?" Sarah wondered.

I saw a bothered look on Max's face and a worried look on Peter's. The two of them exchanged some message I chose to ignore.

"Let's order," I exclaimed, breaking the mood.

Everyone loosened up once our ring conversation was forgotten. It had been a long time since the five of us had sat down for a casual meal, and Max and I eventually relaxed and started chatting like good friends again. We planned out our trip to Vegas, and Peter told us that he would take care of all the hotel arrangements. We deliberated on whether or not to allow Peter to make the sleeping arrangements but since none of us wanted to do it, we let it be.

In the middle of lunch, I received a text from Jake that made me laugh.

Are you done with lunch yet? You did keep your promise concerning Max?

I understood his text but decided to make his life a bit more difficult.

What promise? I didn't make you or Max any promises, did I?

Yes, you did. You weren't going to allow him anywhere near you.

Well, he picked me up, drove me to lunch, and is now sitting next to me. Does that break my promise to you?

Emily! This isn't funny. You're torturing me.

I'm not the one who kissed another woman in the middle of our weekend together.

I thought you said you're going to let that one go. I promise! I didn't kiss her back.

I laughed again.

When will lunch be over? You want to come visit me at the hospital?

I don't know when lunch will be over and no, I don't want to go to the hospital anymore. After the ER incident, I'm afraid of doctors now. Everyone at my table is giving me an unpleasant look because I'm ignoring them while texting you. Come over tonight. I will consider whether or not I want to kiss you since you've now reminded me of Allison. I have to go. Bye.

"Sorry," I said to all my friends. Sarah rolled her eyes at me.
As the hour was up, Sarah and Charlie both had to get back to work, and Peter left soon after. Max and I decided to walk off our lunch and browse the shops. We had a surprisingly pleasant time together. I shopped for Christmas presents for Jake's family since I would be seeing all of them in Hawaii and for Christmas dinner. I had no idea what they might like so it was like searching for a needle in a haystack.

We stopped for coffee and Max had that look again—the one that made my heart fear.

"Em?"

"Hmm?" I asked looking up from my coffee.

"I need to ask you a question."

"OK. What?" I felt queasy about where this was heading.

"Do you love Jake? Is he the man you see yourself with, for the rest of your life?" Such a matter-of-fact question caused me to burn my lips taking an unintentional gulp of hot coffee.

"What? Where did that come from? Why are you asking?"

"Just answer. Do you love Jake? If he proposed to you today, could you say yes?" He was now demanding an answer from me rather than just asking. His demeanor turned abrasive, and yet there was fear in his eyes.

"Max. I don't know why this concerns you."

Max glared at me, and I hesitated, but answered his question.

"No," I answered softly. "Not yet. I mean...I don't know. We just started dating."

"You've been dating for a while. Didn't you tell me that you loved me from the moment we met?"

My unconvincing first answer obviously gave him courage to move forward with this conversation.

"Yes, but what does that have to do with this situation? Not every love is love at first sight. With us, we spent every waking moment together. With Jake, it's different. He's so busy, I feel like we're just getting to know one another."

"We would've spent every moment together if you weren't so stubborn."

I ignored his last comment.

"Max, I really like Jake. You know how introverted and shy I am. He's the only person I've dated since we broke up. When we're together I feel like...like I'm with my family...like I'm home...he makes me feel..."

"Yeah, yeah. You made yourself clear last time when you told me how he makes you feel comfortable and secure." He imitated my tone. "I can't believe after four years together, you tell me now that you were never comfortable with me, that I never made you feel secure."

"I never said I didn't feel comfortable with you!" I shot back. "I loved you more than anyone in this world. You were the most important person to me." The tears began. "What I said was, I never thought you felt the same way about me. I was never the most important person in your world, and now I understand why. You have your family. I technically was not your family. Why would you put me above the people you grew up with your entire life? I don't fault you for this. I was just stating a fact."

Without much warning, tears spilled over. I hated myself for crying so easily. I remembered our love and the happiness it brought to my life. I also thought about the countless days of misery after our breakup. "Why are you bringing this up now?" I asked him. "Why do you find such satisfaction in hurting me? Wasn't once enough? I finally felt like I was putting all this behind me."

I knew it hurt Max to see me hurt. He was never outwardly expressive but I could see tears of sorrow outlining his eyes as well.

"Em, would you ever want to start over with me? Do you think it would be possible? If I told you that I was an idiot, that I had no idea what I wanted in life till I lost it. I never realized till after we broke up that you meant the world to me. However much you loved me, I loved you just as much, probably more. I was just too stupid to know it back then. Would this be enough for us to try again?"

I was too shocked to cry anymore. These were words I had hoped to hear right after we broke up, not now. Only in my world, would I have to contend with the passion I once felt for Max and the hope I now felt with Jake.

"Max, why now? Why didn't you come to me eighteen months ago when I missed you so terribly? I would've given up everything to be with you again. I don't want to hurt anymore. I can't do this again. I won't give up Jake."

"But you just said you don't love Jake! Can you say the same about me? I know you still love me, Em. Please, Em? I know what I finally want...I want you."

I stopped the conversation and asked Max to drive me home. The ride home was silent till I marched out of the car, straight onto my bed, and wailed like the night we broke up. I didn't understand why I hurt today like graduation night.

A severe headache greeted me as I woke up to the ringing of the doorbell. Glancing at the clock, it was almost midnight. I opened the door and found a warm face that quickly morphed into an alarmed one.

"What's the matter, Emily? Have you been crying?"

"How'd you know?" I asked.

"Your eyes are puffier than a marshmallow. Why were you crying?" Jake walked into the house and sat on the chair.

I looked at myself in the mirror and saw that both my top and bottom lids were puffy. What would I tell Jake? I sat at the table with him and contemplated what to say. He waited patiently.

"Does this have something to do with your lunch with Max today?" It didn't take much intuition to figure that one out. "Do you mind telling me what happened?" His troubled look made me feel terrible.

"Max is having breakup remorse," was how I summed up our afternoon conversation.

Jake looked puzzled. "He and Jennifer broke up and he's upset about it?"

"Um, I'm told he and Jennifer broke up but his breakup remorse is not about Jennifer. He, um…regrets our breakup."

"Oh," was all I got from Jake. "What did you say, or should I ask, how do you feel about his regret?"

Damage control needed to be put into effect immediately, but I didn't know how to put into words what I felt in my heart.

"I told Max that I really like you and that I don't want to be in a relationship with him." Jake looked somewhat relieved but only for a second. He asked the next logical question—the one that truly begged an answer. "Why were you crying, then?"

This one, I really couldn't answer. Why I hurt so much today was beyond my understanding but could I tell Jake that I just didn't know?

"I cried because a lot of the pain I felt after we broke up resurfaced. Those were the words I wanted to hear eighteen months ago, not now. Maybe I was angry with him for…"

"Waiting this long?" He tried to finish my sentence. "Do you want to get back together with him, but can't because of me? Am I in your way?"

I vehemently replied, "No. I want to be with you, Jake. I want to give our relationship a chance. Please don't think that. Please, please believe me when I say how much I cherish our relationship." I wrapped my arms around his neck as insecurity crept back into my heart, scared that I might lose this wonderful man.

Jake held me close and calmed me down. "Emily, explain to me what's on your mind. There must be something lingering in your heart for Max for you to be in such anguish."

"To be honest, I don't exactly know what hold Max still has on me, if any. I know there's no more connection between us, but why I still hurt so much when he brings up the past, I can't explain." Apologetically my head fell down. "I'm sorry I'm such a mess. This is the kind of stuff I don't want you to see. What I do know is that in the short while we've been together, you're the one I want to be with, not Max."

"Emily," he called my name softly, and lifted my chin with the crook of his index finger, "I'm not letting you go anywhere." His lips tenderly traced my own. "We are not separating for any reason. I can't imagine my life without you anymore, and I hope you feel the same way about me. You must know by now how much I love you. I can't believe I've waited this long to tell you." He embraced me intently.

Jake's words stopped my heart. I had heard correctly on the airplane. The optimist in me reveled at the thought of Jake loving me. The pessimist in me wondered what he would think when I couldn't reciprocate. I faced him with a signs of hope, guilt, and confusion.

"And...you don't quite reciprocate, I gather by your look?" Jake asked.

"Jake, I'm not there just yet."

"Emily, are you really not there? I think you're just afraid to admit it."

He was probably right. Somewhere in my heart, I loved this man and would tell him when I worked up the courage to admit that I loved someone with all my heart again.

"To me, when I tell someone I love them, it's a forever kind of word. I can't take it lightly. Forever is not in my vocabulary just yet with us."

Jake looked frustrated again. "Why do you keep saying that? Didn't you tell Max you loved him? Why are you so negative about us all the time? Do you think I take the words 'I love you' lightly? The words 'love' and 'flippant' do not coexist in *my* vocabulary either. This appears to be a weekly argument with us."

"I'm sorry, Jake. Can we not argue about this again? Just give me a little more time? Please?" I placed myself on his lap, put my arms around his neck, and attempted to coax him out of his ire.

"You can't admit you love me, and you refuse to have sex with me. Why am I still here with you?" he asked with an irresistible smile.

"Because *you* love *me*," I answered with kisses.

Max called several times during the week, and I purposely evaded him. Instead, Sarah kept me apprised of his life. She told me he was moping around, trying to rally our friends to help win me back. I, in turn, focused my attention on Jake. He stopped by every morning before work and every night after work. In the short hours we had together, we talked about our lives past, present, and future. When he wasn't with me, he attempted to call, but his patients had other ideas.

Tuesday night Jake came over early, and after dinner, I told him stories about my parents. Happily, I started with their college years where they met and fell in love. I pulled out all my photo albums and Jake repeated the same words I'd heard all my life.

"Your mom was stunning!"

"I know, isn't she beautiful? When I was younger, I used to hate it when people told me how pretty she was. Unfortunately, I didn't appreciate her till I got older." So many years I'd wasted thinking of her as competition rather than a companion.

"Why would you hate someone telling you your mom was beautiful?"

"Because I was jealous. No one ever said anything remotely complimentary about me. The comment I got repeatedly was, 'I hope you grow up to look just like your mom.' It bugged me. Plus, my mom had such a vibrant personality, and I was so shy. She was always the life of the party, and I was the wallflower in the corner."

"Love, girls don't come much prettier than you...even your mom." Jake did his best to reassure me but I wasn't convinced.

"You wouldn't be saying that if you'd seen my mom in person."

"I'd say it regardless. So how'd your dad get so lucky?"

I laughed, thinking about my parents telling me this story back in middle school. Jake was in for a great story. "My dad told me when Mom got to college she was the talk of her Texas campus. Every guy wanted to date her. She was in some sorority and every frat and non-frat guy had visited her house to ask her out."

"So did your parents meet at a frat party?"

"No, my dad was the antithesis of my mom. He was awkward and extremely shy. He was a senior when Mom was a freshman, and they became friends only because she needed help in calculus, and he was her school-appointed tutor. He tutored Mom her entire freshman year."

I kept looking through the photo album. It had been months since I'd visited my parents or really thought about them. Jake had consumed my mind and heart. I felt guilty that I had forgotten what they looked like back in college. My last memory of each of them was their peaceful faces lying in their caskets.

72

"She was really beautiful, huh?" Wistfully, I touched her face in the picture. What I would do to be able to touch their faces or hold their hands one more time.

"So my mom was dating some hotshot guy on campus but spending loads of time with my dad, because her math skills were so pathetic, and they developed a friendship during these tutorial sessions. My dad was probably one of the very few men who was more attracted to my mom's heart than her face. Do you know what he told me he loved most about her?"

"What did he love most about her?" Jake was as into this story as I was into telling it.

"Dad said that Mom was the most caring and attentive person he'd ever met. Every time they were together, she'd bring him a little something to thank him for working with her. She'd bring him lunch if it was lunchtime, or a piece of chocolate she knew he liked, or buy him poetry books. My dad was a bit of a poet. He devoured the attention. Oh my gosh..." I'd just had an epiphany.

"What?"

"I'm dating my mother. You remind me exactly of my mom. You're both attentive and outgoing and exceedingly sure of yourselves. Oh gosh..." I said one more time.

"What?" he asked again.

"Max was the epitome of my dad—shy, reserved, and gentle. How sad. I miss my parents so badly, I need to date people who remind me of them."

I had to laugh at myself. The four years I'd loved Max, never once did I think he reminded me of Dad. But tonight, as I told this story, it was very clear both Max and Jake substituted for my lost loves.

"So all this time, my dad loved my mother, but didn't do anything about it."

"Was your mom into your dad also?"

"I asked that same question and they both said no. She was dating someone else, but she said she always thought of my dad as a dear friend."

"So how did they get together if she was dating someone else?"

"When school ended, Mom was driving home to LA, and about an hour away from school, she got a flat tire. She said the first and only person she thought to call was not her boyfriend, but my dad. She knew then he was the man she loved and trusted to take care of her. Of course my dad came to her immediately upon receiving the call."

"And that's how they got together?"

"Kind of...remember how I told you my dad was terribly shy?"

"Uh-huh."

"Well, Mom knew he liked her, but wouldn't admit it unless something extreme happened. So when he got to my mom, she ran to him and hugged him as if he had rescued her from death." I proceeded to laugh really hard. Jake patiently waited for me to continue the story. "She embraced him dearly and started confessing her feelings. My dad, being in a state of shock, didn't say a word, but tried to pry her body off him."

Jake had a bit of a why look on his face so I explained, "You know, they were in the middle of the 10 freeway and cars were honking everywhere."

"Did she let go of him?"

"Nope. My mom told me she held onto him till he was forced to confess his feelings for her. You want to know what else she forced him to do?"

He nodded yes.

"He was about to go off to grad school, and she didn't want to be separated from him, so she got him to propose to her and tied him down all within the same hug. Isn't that insane?"

"Lucky guy! Could something like that happen with you?"

"I doubt it. I'm not brave like my mom. She always knew what she wanted and she went after it till it was hers. Strong and secure would be the two words that epitomized her personality. She rarely wavered. I, on the other hand, take too much after my dad. I'm introverted and insecure. Even if I wanted something, I probably wouldn't outright tell anyone. It can be a bit of a guessing game with me."

"So when did your parents get married?"

"They got married that summer. Mom transferred schools and finished undergrad while she was married to my dad."

"You mean she got married when she was eighteen?"

"Just about...I think she turned nineteen just before her wedding day. Here are their wedding photos."

Mom looked radiant in her wedding dress. She looked so happy. I wished she could've stayed this happy even after Dad's death. It would have helped me during my difficult days after Dad left us.

"That's a great story. So when were you born?"

"The day after my mom graduated from college. She was a balloon at her graduation. Look at her." I touched my mom's picture again. She looked even more beautiful.

"When I was young, I was painfully shy, just like my dad. My mom thought she could turn me into a mini-me but failed miserably. She couldn't understand why I didn't want people other than my family giving me any attention or why I couldn't speak my mind. The only person who really understood me was my dad. He knew exactly how I felt, because he felt the same way."

"But you're not shy now, although I suppose you get embarrassed easily."

"That only happened after my dad died. My dad and I were really close. When I was younger, I preferred my dad over my mom. Because I was unusually small for my age, Dad carried me around like a little child till I was seven. He understood my need to be alone and my fear of unwanted attention. He showered me with love and affection and protected me from all my fears."

The tears finally appeared. They had been brewing, but for Jake's sake, I held off as long as I could. My story started off so happy, I didn't want it to end on a sad note.

"Then he died when I was in eighth grade, and his death devastated me. My mom and I had both lost the love of our lives and our best friend. This was also when I started to finally grow and develop physically. I was a mess in every way when I got to my grandparents' home in LA."

I held back my tears the best I could in order to finish my story.

"When we got to LA, my mom went through bouts of depression, and it terrified me. I forced myself to come out of my shell and tried to be everything my mom wanted me to be—cheerful, lively, and strong. She did her best to stay content and this was when she and I bonded. Even with my grandparents around, we felt like we only had each other. Rather than spending time with friends after school, I spent all my time with my mom. She told me everything she could about Dad up to when my memory clicked and I shared about all my days with Dad when it was just the two of us. She had become my love and my new best friend. Then she died the end of my junior year, a few days before my birthday."

At this point, I couldn't hold back. Jake held me and let me cry. My body shook as I sobbed uncontrollably thinking about both Mom and Dad. No matter how wonderful Jake was or how much he loved me, or how much I loved him, he could never replace the love my parents gave me while they were alive. I regretted not having appreciated this love and not having spent more time with Mom.

"A year later, Max came into my life and soon became my best friend, my love, and my only family. Four years later, I lost him too. My heart's been severely broken three times. I don't think I can stand another heartbreak. That's why I'm so cautious with us. I'm sorry I frustrate you, but do you think you can be even more understanding of me than you've already been and allow me to move at my own pace? I know I'm being unfair to you, but this is the only way I can be in a relationship right now."

His eyes bore a tender and heartbroken expression.

"Emily, I love you regardless of how fast or slow our relationship has progressed. I am happy to do what you've asked if you will promise to do one thing for me."

I looked up at him, wondering what that one thing would be.

"Promise me you will stop looking at me as the one who will break your heart, but try to accept me as your new best friend, your eternal love, and the one who wants to create a family with you. That's what I want to be for you."

In my mind, it wasn't entirely possible to believe what he'd just confessed, though in my heart I desperately wanted to believe him. Nevertheless, I nodded my head and agreed.

"By, the way," he added, "when's your birthday?"

I guess we had never asked each other this very important question.

"May 20th," I answered.

"No way!" he said in amazement. "My birthday is May 19th. We have almost the same birthday. We'll celebrate our birthdays together and for two full days, OK?"

I nodded my head once again.

Sunday was a precursor to our Hawaii trip. Jake went in early to check on his patients and came over by 7:00. He woke me up, as usual, and milled around the house while I showered and got ready.

"How do you function on so little sleep?" I asked while putting on makeup.

"I've never needed much sleep. Three or four hours a day is sufficient." He sat on my bed flipping channels, waiting for me.

"I need at least eight hours, and I feel like I've been on your schedule this entire week. Good thing I'm on vacation. I've taken a nap almost every day this week. It's pathetic!" I said laughing.

Jake walked over and hugged me from behind. "What do you want to do today? I feel like I'm starting my vacation early. Whatever you want, we'll do."

"Anything?" I asked.

"Anything," he answered. "Speaking of, I have a question for you. What are some things you've always wanted to do?"

"What do you mean?" I was a bit unsure of this open-ended question.

"You know, like if money were no object or in your wildest dreams, you'd like to..."

"You mean like a bucket list? Aren't I a little young for a bucket list?"

"Emily Logan, your list," Jake commanded.

"OK." I thought about it for a minute and came up with a short list.

#1—I want to hear Andrea Bocelli sing in some outdoor stadium in the hills of Tuscany.

#2—I want to take a series of cooking classes in Italy, France, or Japan.

#3—I want to climb all the steps of Machu Picchu

#4—I want to eat a formal *Kaiseki* meal in Japan

#5—I also want to go on a dining spree in Spain

#6—I want to live in New York City for a while

#7—I want to spend a few nights in a hut in the middle of some island—like the ones you see in travel magazines.

#8—I want to learn to ballroom dance.

#9—I want to go on one of those trips with that chef from the *No Reservations* TV show

#10—I also want to be a judge on *Iron Chef*

"That's about all I can think of off the top of my head. Of course, you covered a few of them already with our gastronomic feast in Napa and Carmen. Although, if I had a choice, I'd see *Carmen* performed in Paris. And speaking of Paris, #11—I want to picnic at the Tuileries Garden with someone I'm madly in love with. That's all," I finished with a satisfied smile.

"None of those are too hard to accomplish, except for those two items toward the end."

"I'm a simple girl," I answered. "Can we go shopping today? I still haven't bought your mom a gift. I can't show up to your house for Christmas dinner without a gift for her, especially not after she takes me to Hawaii. You have to help me buy something for her."

We walked through the flea market, attempting to find Sandy a clock. Jake told me his mom collected clocks from around the world. It took many hours to leisurely walk through the entire flea market, but I finally found the perfect gift.

At dinner, Jake continued to ask about my pre-Jake years.

"Emily, what did you and your family do during the holidays? Do you have a lot of family?"

"No. I don't think I have much luck when it comes to family. Both my parents were only children and my paternal grandparents passed away when I was young. They were old when they had my father. We didn't know each other very well," I replied while trying to decide between eating the uni or amaebi sushi.

"When my parents were both alive, we used to spend Thanksgiving and Christmas at home, and my maternal grandparents would visit us. After my dad died, the four of us spent holidays together in LA. It wasn't too festive, as you can imagine, cooking a Thanksgiving meal for four people."

We must have been hungry from the three-mile hike today. We plowed through a dozen orders of sushi and were already on to coffee and dessert.

"Green tea flan and a café con leche, please," I asked the server. Jake just ordered a cup of coffee.

"So after your mom and grandparents died, who did you spend your holidays with?"

I could see where Jake was taking this conversation. That same sadness in his eyes that I had seen during our weekend away, when I told him about my parents dying, made an appearance again. He wanted to share in my sorrow. He felt my every pain. Deep in my heart I knew I loved this man as much as he loved me. How could I not? He was already so much a part of me.

"I spent a few holidays with Max's family, and a few with Sarah's family. One Christmas, both Max and Sarah were out of town visiting relatives so I spent it alone. That was a sad Christmas." I tried to smile, not wanting Jake to feel this loneliness that had suddenly landed back in my heart. "I sound so pathetic, huh?" I grinned and fed him a bite of my dessert.

"Why didn't you go with Max to visit his relatives? Were you not invited?" Empathy caressed his voice.

"Are you seriously asking me why I didn't go on a trip with my boyfriend at the time? Shouldn't you be thrilled that we never went away together? Well, I guess there were a few group trips." I made a concerted effort to lighten this conversation. "To answer your question, Dr. Reid, I didn't go with Max because I never felt completely accepted by his family. They were very nice to me, but I always felt like an outsider. I couldn't break into their family bond. No matter, obviously I was not meant to be a Davis."

Jake reached over and caressed my hand. I didn't think I needed comforting, but I accepted his touch.

"Oh, my sweet Emily...my love..." Jake murmured. "I hate thinking about you being alone. Why couldn't we have met earlier? I would've filled your void. I won't ever let you be alone again."

With all my heart I wanted to believe Jake.

Chapter 6

Paradise

I met Jake's parents for the first time at LAX. Sandy, a fairly tall, slightly round woman in her late fifties, gave me a hug and welcomed me with a warm smile. Bobby, a tall, light-skinned and very handsome man in his midsixties, also greeted me with a family-style bear hug and kiss on the cheek. Nick was also there with a brotherly smile that made me feel very welcomed into the Reid family. Nick took our bags, whispered something in Jake's ear, and checked them in with the rest of the family's. Jake stood just steps away, grinning.

"Where's Jane?" Jake put his arms around my waist and kissed my cheek in the middle of my question.

"She's still in San Francisco. She will meet us in Hawaii around the same time we get in."

Turning to Sandy and Bobby, I expressed my appreciation. "Thank you very much for inviting me on your family trip. I couldn't sleep last night thinking about getting to know all of you."

Sandy beamed a tender look only a mother could give. "I'm so glad we finally get to meet. All Jake does is talk about you."

"I hope he only tells you the nice things about me."

"According to my son, there's nothing bad about you."

My cheeks went red, and Jake led me to the boarding area. The only other time I rode in first class was when Jake upgraded my seat when I flew out to New York to meet Sarah. Because I'd slept the whole way there, I didn't fully appreciate the comfort of the plane ride.

Today, I realized this was way better than my first experience. It almost felt illegal to experience such comfort while others were cramped in coach. The seats were double the size of what I was used to, with one attendant to every five passengers. I was thoroughly spoiled.

"I don't know if I can ever fly again in my usual economy seats," I lamented.

"Stick with me and you'll never sit back there with the masses again." His tone was more arrogant than I'd ever heard, but I knew what he was saying was more for my sake than for his ego.

Laughing, I turned to talk to Jake about Hawaii, when out of nowhere his lips attacked mine. Jake refused to let me pull back, though he saw my extreme discomfort with his family sitting right in front of us.

"Excuse me, Dr. Reid," the flight attendant interrupted apologetically. "We need you and Ms. Logan to return your seats to their upright position, as the plane is about to take off."

Mortified, my face turned bright red as I heard giggles from his parents and brother.

"What are you doing? You can't make out with me on the plane in front of ten people. You have to stop."

Jake laughed at me, rose up the armrest and pulled my body close to his. Separating our two bodies was not an option. To my delight, he showed no mercy.

We landed in Maui at 8:00 a.m. and rented two cars—one for us, and another for the rest of the family. We met Jane at the hotel, got checked in, and left for our first activity. We drove to a helipad where a helicopter waited to take us on a scenic tour. We flew over the Haleakala National Park and Crater, the Hana Rainforest Preserve, the largest rainforest in America, and through countless number of waterfalls.

I wanted to tell Jake how the scenery took my breath away but didn't want everyone to hear through the headsets, so I sat quietly enjoying the view and the warmth of Jake's caresses throughout the ride. After lunch, we met up with a guide and hiked a five-mile trail leading to a dormant volcano. The end of this hike led to snorkeling, which eventually turned into scuba lessons for me, as I hadn't ever been scuba diving. If this weren't enough excitement for one day, Sandy and Jane wanted to go to a late afternoon yoga class to unwind. I honestly just wanted to go to my room and sleep the rest of the night, but of course, there was the luau. Who can come to Hawaii and not attend a luau? One would have thought we were leaving tomorrow with all that was conquered today. After the last hula dance/fire breathing show, I got up to say good night, and Jake walked me back to my room.

"I can go by myself. Why don't you stay with your family a bit longer?" I encouraged.

"Are you kidding? I'm just as wiped out as you are. Nick made me go surfing while you were at yoga."

"Not that I'm complaining, but why does your family feel the need to do everything in one day? I had a wonderful time, but I am so exhausted, I don't know how I'm going to function tomorrow."

Jake started laughing. "That's just how all of our trips are. Go, go, go, go, go!"

As much as I wanted to conk out immediately, I hopped in the shower while Jake stuck around to use Jane's computer. When I got out of the shower, Jake was fast asleep, snoring on my bed. I'd never seen his sleeping face before. He looked so sweet! My heart did revolutions thinking about waking up to this every morning. Then all of a sudden, the insecurities spun out of control.

Sigh...heartbreak...tears...

I sat down on the edge of the bed and wiped away my tears. *Jake. I love you so very much. What am I going to do if you leave me? How will I piece back my broken heart?* It took me a few minutes to talk myself back into reality. I didn't want to get caught up in this made-up heartbreak, nor this happily ever after feeling. No matter the myriad of times Jake mentioned forever with me, I wouldn't go down that road again till I was literally walking down the aisle. It hurt too much when fantasies morphed into an ugly reality. Dry-eyed, I nudged Jake's shoulders to wake him up.

He didn't budge. After a few more tries, I gently placed my lips on his and kissed him many times before he realized what was happening. He jostled awake, grabbed me by my shoulders and pulled me onto the bed with him and continued our kiss—though not as gently. His arms around me were like a steel cage.

"Emi." Jake had a serious expression on his face. "What's the matter?"

"Nothing's the matter—except for the fact that you're sleeping in my bed. Please get up and go to bed." He didn't look convinced till I kissed him some more.

"I am in bed," he murmured between kisses.

"No, your own bed!"

He pretended to snore. I tried to get up but his grip around me got even tighter. With his body holding mine hostage, there wasn't much I could do.

"Love, let's just sleep like this," he coaxed.

"My hair is still wet and your sister will be here any minute now."

"Oh yeah." Without moving, he easily freed one hand to reach in his pocket and began texting.

"What are you doing?"

82

He handed me his phone.

Jane, sleep in my room tonight. I will sleep here with Emi.

He sent the text before anything could be done.

"Too late." He smiled a wicked smile. "It's done. Now sleep here with me just the way you are and let's talk tomorrow morning. I am very tired." He showered fading kisses upon my face, and I knew there was no way out. I fell asleep comfortably in his arms that night.

The next morning, my body froze from the shock of pain. Yesterday's activities had crippled me. Once again, I'd fallen asleep with Jake holding me. I wondered how I could give in so easily to spending the night with him when I wouldn't give in to Max's attempts all those years. The only answer I could come up with was that I was too tired to push him away—but I knew this wasn't the whole truth.

Realizing my robe had unraveled itself in the course of the night, I tried to get up but my aching body wouldn't listen. Eventually I managed to tie the robe around myself, and forced myself out of bed. Jake immediately complained.

"Emi...come back to bed. It was amazing being in bed with you the whole night. Let's stay a little longer."

"Jake, we have to meet your family for breakfast. We might be late already. Oh gosh, what will your family think?"

"They will think nothing of our night, and even if they do think something, who cares?"

"I'm hopping in the shower. My hair is a mess from sleeping with it wet. Go back to your room and get ready," I commanded.

"Can I hop in with you?" he dared to ask.

"No! Go, please," I begged.

Smiling faces greeted us when we got to the breakfast table. Everyone seemed to be quietly laughing at a joke that Jake and I were not privy to. I felt uncomfortable, and Jake looked smug that he had wormed his way into my bed last night.

"What's on the agenda for today?" I asked trying to change the silent subject.

"We're going to the Maui invitational to watch our basketball team play," Sandy told us.

"Mom, I gotta warn you, Emi's not a fan of our school." Jake's remark brought on a round of boos for me.

"Emily, your school's playing here as well. We'll get you tickets to that game. You and Jake can go together," Jake's father offered.

"Thank you, but that's OK. You don't have to bother. I'd like to spend the day with the family, if that's all right with you."

"We would love nothing better!" exclaimed Sandy. I spied an enormous smile on Jake's face that filled my heart with joy.

Tuesday was no different than Monday—breakfast, basketball game, lunch, scuba, followed by surfing. Jake dove with me while I was having my hour lesson, then he and Nick surfed near me while I had another hour lesson. The Reid children seemed competent in just about every water sport.

Jake saw the exhaustion on my face and rented a cabana at the pool for me to a nap. We walked in and he closed the cabana curtains just enough to protect us from any prying eyes. He traipsed over to my lounge chair and gently pushed me far enough to one side so he could lay down with me. It became apparent this cabana was more for his benefit than mine.

"I thought you were going to let me take a nap." An accusation coupled with a giggle sounded more like an invitation.

"I'm helping you take a nap," he grinned, putting his arm under my neck. Within seconds, his free hand cupped my hips and his lips began to travel on my body. He carefully found his way to my lips, and we began to explore each other again. His soft hands refused to listen to my weak complaints as he reached under my cover-up and began caressing my back. I could feel his fingers working around the knot of my bikini. My low moans encouraged his hands, and they soon started sliding down my thigh. He moved my body on top of his and worked on my bikini bottom. I tried to wriggle away and participate at the same time, and he knew that I wanted him as much as he wanted me.

Our acrobatics were too much for the narrow lounge chair and we wound up falling off. I burst into laughter. "Jake, I think this is our signal to stop. Sorry. I don't want to aggravate you anymore, so let's forget the nap and go out and enjoy the rest of the day." I smiled apologetically.

"OK." He huffed and puffed his way out of the cabana and mumbled something about tonight.

Dinner was a long six-course meal. Nick and I talked about how dissatisfied we were with the meal, and decided to drive around town tomorrow to eat at popular local hangouts. We were tired of hotel food.

Thankfully, dinner lasted long enough to curtail any evening activities. I was secretly jumping for joy. My body hadn't been this sore since Sarah and I went on a half day hiking trip. After dessert and coffee, I saw Jake whispering in Jane's ear and she nodded subserviently like a little sister listening to her older, wiser brother. What was my scheming boyfriend up to now?

"You want to go watch a movie tonight?" Jake asked, though it seemed more like a command.

"Um, yeah." I hesitated, afraid of how I was going to fight him off tonight. "Jane, Nick, you want to come with us?"

Both started laughing and refused my offer. "We are...busy...yeah, busy."

"What's going on?" I asked Jake.

"You'll see," was all I got for the time being.

We got back to my room, looked through the DVD collection, and found a movie for the evening. My body leaned on Jake's, half comatose, when I suddenly realized that Jane had not come back to the room. I reached for Jake's cell phone to call her, but he took it out of my hands and turned it off.

"Where's Jane?" I asked innocently.

"She's with Nick. They're at the movies," he answered coyly.

"Why didn't we go with them or why didn't they come here with us?"

"Sweetheart, they're trying to give us some privacy."

As soon as he finished these words, I understood that Jane was not coming back into this room tonight. In fact, I looked around the room and realized that Jane and Jake had switched out their belongings. How had I not noticed this from the moment we walked into the room?

"Why is all your stuff here? And, where are Jane's belongings?"

"Jane and I switched rooms. She is going to stay with Nick the rest of the trip, and I'm going to stay right here," he smiled nervously, showing all of his pearly white teeth.

I tried not to look flustered. "Jake! Do I need to have this talk with you again?"

"Come on, Emi. Wasn't last night wonderful? Let me stay here with you. I promise I won't do anything naughty."

"Jake, I'm not comfortable with you spending the night with me again. Last night, I was so tired, I couldn't fight you off. Tonight, though...

it's not proper for us to be together, especially with your parents right next to us. I'd like to be more respectful than that."

"Emily." He turned into his five-year-old self again. I had to be strong and not give into his darling tirade.

"Just one more night, please? I'll switch back with Jane tomorrow."

"No. Will you please ask Jane to come back into this room?" I gave him a choice that was really not a choice. He'd have to respect my wishes.

"Oh, all right. I'll call her right now." He retracted his arm from my shoulder and moved to the other side of the sofa.

"Thank you. Now where were we?" I inched toward him and laid my head on his lap. He didn't hold his grudge too long this time.

Jane and I walked to the breakfast table early Wednesday morning to join the rest of the family. Bobby and Sandy were a bit surprised to see that Jake and Nick came as a pair as well.

"Did you meet each other in the elevator?" Sandy asked Jane, referring to our entrance together.

"No, we came together," she replied and gave her mother an *I don't know what happened look.*

Sandy threw a worried and puzzled look over at Jake and he explained, "Emi didn't want to sleep with me. She chose Jane's company over mine."

I politely smiled.

Sandy started talking about the day and I realized that we were not going to be bound by any tight schedules. "Your dad and I have to attend three different college alumni activities, so I'm afraid you are all on your own. We tried to get out of it but since your dad is the president of the association, there wasn't any way around it."

I was thrilled not to have any strenuous activities for the day. I could go lay out by the pool or even go back to the room and sleep. The day was looking good.

"What shall we do today, Emily?" Jane asked.

"I don't know. What do you want to do?" I high-fived myself, I was so happy.

"Let's go get a facial and a massage. Maybe even a pedicure. Oh, how about a whole day at the spa?" She was so excited.

I was also getting quite excited thinking about unwinding all day before leaving tomorrow night.

"Jane! What am I to do if you take Emi away from me?" Jake's sour look came back.

"I don't know. You and Nick find something to do. Go watch another basketball game." Jane could be stubborn if she wanted to be, and it was a bit comical watching the two argue like five-year-olds.

"No way, Emi's with me. You find your own friend," he retorted.

Nick jumped into this argument as well. "I thought we were going to go find local food?" he said, turning to me.

"OK. I have a solution. How about if Jane and I do a half day at the spa while you boys go watch the morning matches? We'll meet you for lunch around 1:00 and then we can go into town and find yummy food." I turned to Jake and sweetly requested, "My body hurts badly from all the exercise. I need a massage to unwind me. Would you be OK with that?" I added a few kisses in between the request so he would cave without a fight.

"Sounds good to me," Nick and Jane both said at the same time. Jake was the only one pouting because he didn't get his way. We parted for the morning, and Jane and I spent a glorious morning pampering ourselves. *This* was the Hawaii I had imagined before arriving.

We started with a deep tissue massage, continued with a facial, and then got a manicure and a pedicure.

For lunch, we asked the hotel concierge to point out all the local hot spots. We had small meals at several local joints. My favorite was a little shack that specialized in katsu. We ordered chicken, pork, beef, and fish-fried cutlets. I couldn't possibly leave Hawaii without having eaten something lathered in mayo, so I chose the macaroni salad with the deep fried goodies. Honestly, I felt sick from all the grease.

After the third meal, Jake and Jane begged us not to eat any more. Nick and I acquiesced, but only after visiting Maui's most famous ice cream shop where we treated ourselves to strawberry and pineapple ice cream. Today was an ideal day in Hawaii.

Nick and Jane went surfing to work off our lunches, but Jake and I went back into our cabana. After a massage and thousands of calories, I needed a nap. Jake behaved himself after my speech last night, and brought a book to read while I napped on the lounge chair. His hands ran up and down my arm wanting to explore elsewhere, but for the rest of the day, he was harmless.

Thursday was our last day in Hawaii. Nick and I had so much fun yesterday; we tried to convince everyone to go into town in search of yummy food again. Bobby, Sandy, and Jane decided to go off on their own, and then meet us at the airport. Jake had no choice but to go eat some more if he wanted to be with me. Nick and I were only too happy to go find more treasures. We made one more pit stop at the ice cream shop before heading to the airport.

On our red-eye flight back home I pondered over how much this trip meant to me. Fully laid back, Jake held my hand while he snored away. The correct thing to do would be to join him and the rest of the family but I just couldn't sleep.

"Emily." Surprised, I quickly turned my head to Jane's calling.

"I'm sorry. Am I keeping you awake with my reading light?"

"No. I thought I heard a sigh. Is something the matter?"

"Oh, Jane." I answered with a mixture of dreaminess and dread. "How can anything be wrong? The last four days were heaven."

"Then why do you sound like somebody who's headed for ruins?"

I giggled at her comment. Jane giggled back.

With a heavy heart, my voice whispered, "I'm afraid to like your brother as much as I do." Gently, I placed my free hand on his face and moved the overgrown bangs out of his eyes. His body moved closer toward my seat as he pulled my hand into both his hands, and placed it on his heart.

"He loves you—a lot!" Jane looked happy for us.

"I love him too—a lot!" I sighed again.

"Then why the sigh? I don't get it."

"He's too perfect. You're too perfect. In fact, your whole family is like a dream. And you know…my life has been anything but a dream. In fact, it's been closer to a nightmare. I feel like I'm going to wake up from this dream and go back to my reality—a reality where you and Jake and your family are no longer there."

"Emily." Even a frown couldn't mar her pretty face. "A little melodramatic. I don't see Jake going anywhere, anytime soon. In fact, I'd bet my law degree that you two will be married within a year. No one in my family has seen Jake this in love. You and I are going to be sisters like we promised. I will not accept anything less, you hear me?"

"Emi?" Sleepy-eyed, Jake woke up with a worried gaze. "What's wrong, Sweetheart?"

"Nothing." I put on a smile. "Jane and I were just having a heart to heart."

"Jane. Stop gabbing and let Emi sleep." Always protective of my well-being, I kissed his head to show him my appreciation.

Like a proper sister, Jane rolled her eyes and ignored him.

"You sure you're OK?" he whispered while kissing the hand he was holding.

Nodding yes, I turned the light off and reclined. Part of me wanted to cry from being deliriously happy with this man, and another part of me wanted to cry because I couldn't shake off these unsettled nerves that foreshadowed doom and gloom. Inwardly sighing so no one would hear, I pushed away the dread and welcomed sleep.

Chapter 7

Jake's Proposal

We landed at LAX early Christmas morning, and I said my good-byes to everybody before heading home. Jake's mom and dad hugged and kissed me and made me promise to come over early for Christmas dinner. I nodded and got in the car with Jake.

"I had such a wonderful time with your family, Jake. Thank you! Though I just met them, I cherish them like my own." My lips spanned from one ear to the other. "Your mom and dad did an amazing job raising you three. I see why you turned out to be such a caring person. I'm glad I came on this trip. I feel much closer to you and your family," I gushed.

Jake all of a sudden parked his car on the side of the road and pulled out another jewelry box from his suitcase, just like the one I got in San Francisco—the kind a girl received when a man got down on one knee, about to propose to the woman he loved.

"Merry Christmas, Sweetheart."

"Jake. I left your present at home. Let's exchange gifts when we get back to my house."

"No, I want you to open this now. I have something else for you when you come over tonight to Mom's."

"Jake, you're really spoiling me. Hawaii was enough of a present. You didn't have to get me anything else. By the way, wasn't this my Christmas present?" I asked holding the ring from my neck.

"That was, but when I saw this in Hawaii, I knew I had to get it for you. Please open it."

I slowly began to unwrap the silver bow. I could feel my body tensing up, hoping for and against another ring. As much as I adored this man, thinking beyond our current relationship wasn't a smart choice for me.

When I opened the box, he didn't disappoint my hope and fears. Inside the box was a huge solitaire diamond engagement ring. I looked at him, shocked and dazed.

"Emi, don't be scared. I bought this thinking I could hold off till you were ready, but after this trip I realize I don't want to be without you. Emily Anne Logan, I know it's only been a short two months, but I want to be with you forever. I love you more than any man could love a woman, and I promise to love you this way the rest of my life. Will you marry me?" His most sincere blue eyes looked almost in pain awaiting my response.

I hesitated for a while—a long while. I tried not to think about this intimidating situation. I thought about useless facts like how I was sitting in the passenger seat of a car and how this was not what I'd imagined a proposal to be. My heart fluttered, wildly excited about this proposal, but my mind panicked. Was I ready for this? Would the prospect of marriage to one another be as wonderful to him in a few months as it would be to me? Two months—the entirety of our relationship, of us knowing one another—couldn't be long enough for him to love me that deeply, already. Infatuation would be a better terminology for what he felt for me. But, what would he do if I said no?

Copious thoughts raced through my head.

Before I finished my thoughts, Jake shook my arm. "Emi? Are you OK? I'm sorry. I know I turned too serious too soon for you. But, I love you and want to be with you every day and every night for the rest of my life. Let's get married! Huh?" He leaned over and lightly brushed his lips against mine. I didn't respond, but I also didn't push him away.

"Jake...oh, Jake," I sighed. Jake kissed me again. This time a bit rougher than before, and I gave in to his physical desire and demand. My mind was still trying to sort out my heart.

"You know how much I like you." My head automatically shook 'no' as Jake pulled away. "After meeting your family and spending time with all of you in Hawaii, I know your family is just about as perfect as a family can be. But, I'm not ready for a lifelong commitment. It's too soon. You can't mean this already. I am committed to you as a girlfriend and that's where I'd like to stay for a while. I hope this is OK. I'm sorry but my answer is no."

Could you possibly love me this much already? Enough to want to live with me forever? I want to marry you, love you forever, start a family with you. But, I couldn't stand it if you regretted your decision later on.

He stared at me, and didn't respond at first.

"I'm sorry...are you hurt by my response?" I tried to solicit an answer. "I'm sorry." I repeated myself just in case he didn't hear me the first few times.

Jake didn't look my way. He got back on the road and started driving.

"Jake, we just started dating. Why do we need to move so fast? Can't we just enjoy ourselves?"

"Emily, why can't you even consider this proposal? Why do you need to reject it so quickly? I've known since the first day we met at the grocery store I wanted to marry you. Can't you see how much I love you?" Jake became visibly upset. "Why are you so scared all the time?"

"Jake, it's been two months. How do you know already?" Cautiously, I asked, hoping to discuss rather than to argue. "How do you know a few months down the road you will still desire forever with me? Maybe we were both caught up in the bliss of Hawaii."

"The bliss of Hawaii..? Why do you always doubt my love for you? Is it because of Max? Just because he callously dumped you rather than marry you doesn't mean I'm going to do the same thing to you. Don't compare us!"

Just because he callously dumped you... my heart broke at Jake's callous word.

Before I could recover, Jake's tone elevated to an even angrier pitch. "Are you still not over Max? Is this what your rejection is all about? Would you have said no to him if he'd asked you to marry him?"

"Why are you bringing Max into this?" I yelled back. My anger rose above my pain. I regretted my tone, but couldn't understand why he would bring Max into this conversation. It was unfair of him to ask me about a proposal from Max that never transpired. I didn't know what hurt more right now—the fact that my ex-boyfriend of four years dumped me the night I expected a proposal, or that my current boyfriend so cruelly reminded me that he dumped me before I had any chance at a proposal.

"Forget it, Emily. Forget I just proposed. Let's just forget everything."

My heartbreak multiplied exponentially. *Of course this was too good to be true. Jake, what does it mean to forget everything? Does everything include us?*

Swallowing all of my tears, I took a last glance at Jake then stared out the window.

Jake looked angry and aloof. I knew this—Jake, Jane, the Reid family—was temporary. Happiness appeared to be so commonplace in most people's lives—parents, siblings, extended family, love—where was all this for me? I probably just pushed away the best thing that had happened to me since my parents. Why did he have to move so fast? Couldn't he tell that I'd be too scared to commit so haphazardly? If he loved me so much, couldn't he let me answer him in my own time? Although I was scared beyond belief right now, I knew if given a little time, my fear would subside, and I'd admit that we would be together for a lifetime.

My pain aside, I feared what was on Jake's mind at this moment. I knew he believed I didn't care for him the same way he cared for me. Never once did I explain to him how much he meant to me, just how much I loved him. Every time he professed his love for me, I'd never fully reciprocated. He probably believed I didn't feel as strongly for him as he did for me. How ironic Jake might feel this way when I loathed feeling this way with Max. I hadn't been fair to the man I loved.

"Jake? Please say something. I'm sorry for turning you down. Can't you give me more time? I'm not ready to get married." I kept swallowing back my sniffles.

Silence.

He didn't seem to care.

Jake drove the entire forty minutes without saying a word or breaking his visage. I kept looking at him, wanting to say something to ease this tension, but I decided to leave him to his silence. Sadness surrounded every corner of my being. I had lost another person who felt like family. My face stayed focused on the window to hide my fears. *It's over, already.*

Could there be a second chance for us?

The welcomed sight of my driveway brought with it the inescapable tears.

"Do you want to come in and talk?" My eyes blinked rapidly to hold onto the tears.

"No." He wouldn't look at me. "Let's just forget this whole ordeal… just forget everything. I'll see you later."

That was all he said as the car pulled away.

Some time passed and the doorbell rang. Thinking it was Sarah stopping by before heading up to Oxnard, I opened the door to a face that looked as sullen as my own.

"Hi," he whispered—very penitent, very unsure. "Emily…" We both said nothing for a while. "Can I come in? Can we talk?"

Taking a step back, the door opened wide, and Jake was welcomed in.

"I'm sorry," was all he said as his arms draped around my body. "I'm so sorry! It killed me to see you walk away, so hurt by all the things I said to you."

Speechless, I stood there wondering what my reaction should be to his remorse.

"I knew you'd be hurt, I knew you'd be crying, but my ego got the better of me, and I couldn't stay to work this out. My head needed to be cleared before I could come back and find a resolution."

His body still covered mine and slowly my arms lifted to cover his as well—tentatively.

"I'm sorry I yelled at you. I'm sorry I was so angry with you. And I'm really sorry that I brought up Max and said all those crazy words to you."

Confused about where this was heading, I just stood there with pearl-sized tears hovering. Would the next sorry resemble, "I'm sorry but this isn't working out," or was he trying to make amends?

"Emi?" He kissed the tears from my eyes. "Why are you so quiet? Talk to me." For the first time since we started dating, I heard fear in his voice.

"Where does this leave us now?" Worn out—if he wanted to end our relationship, I wanted it done immediately.

"What do you mean?" Jake looked puzzled.

"You told me twice 'let's just forget everything.' Does everything include us? If so, I'd like for you to be honest with me. Since I turned down your proposal, I get it if you want to break up with me."

"Unbelievable!" Jake shook his head with a look that could be summed up as stupefied.

I felt bare as he dislodged his arms from my body, but to my relief, my cheeks felt the immediate warmth of both hands. Without another word, his lips devoured mine and I was only too happy to allow it—more accurately, I was desperate for it.

When we both needed a breath, his lips let go, but his face stayed inches from mine.

"Does that answer your question?"

I shook my head no.

An even longer and more intense kiss followed.

"I can do this all day until you get it." His head came down again.

"Wait!" The last thing I wanted to do was cut short any embrace, but I needed verbal reinforcements rather than a sensual one. "Let's talk." We sat next to one another but not so close that he could attack my senses and discombobulate my brain.

"What did you mean when you said you wanted to forget everything?"

"Emi...I just wanted to undo the mess I had gotten myself into. I'd said so many careless words to you. I didn't mean to bring up your heart-ache with Max. I know you don't love him anymore. In some ways, I was mad, hurt, jealous—there were so many emotions going through my head, and I said everything that came to mind. There was neither discretion nor discernment, and I'm sorry."

"Why would you be jealous? Of what? Of whom?"

"Of Max, I suppose. There was a time you wanted him to propose to you. I thought maybe you'd want the same from me..."

"Jake. I know I haven't made myself very clear on this subject, but I am absolutely in love with you." The gray skies left his face and he beamed the most heartwarming smile.

"Say that again." He inched closer.

"Which part?" I feigned ignorance. "That I haven't been too clear with you or that..."

It didn't take much for Jake to push me onto the sofa and have his way with me.

"You love me?"

"I am irrevocably in love with you, but I'm not ready to marry you. Are you OK with that?"

"Do I have a choice? This just means I have to work harder to get a yes out of you on both accounts."

"Huh?"

"Sex and marriage—in that order, starting now, if possible."

"Go home. I'll see you in a few hours."

I cleaned myself up the best I could before heading toward Jake's parents' home. After such a crazy morning, I needed this time to gather my wits for tonight. With all the presents for the family in the car, I drove over to their home earlier than expected. Jake's parents lived in a stunning old colonial home that sat on a large parcel of flat land. Their front lawn was so huge their home actually looked normal size from the street. As I got closer, I could see that their home was closer to being a mansion than a normal home like mine. I rang the doorbell, and Sandy greeted me with a huge smile.

"Hi, Emily! I'm glad you came early."

"I thought I'd come and help you get dinner ready."

"I'm so glad to have you here with me. No one else is home so we can get to know each other without any interruptions—from my son especially. He won't give any of us a chance to spend time with you."

We both started to laugh. "I'm sorry we were so exclusive in Hawaii. I wanted to get to know everybody, but since Jake hardly gets any time off from the hospital, I couldn't help but enjoy my four days with him. I hope this hasn't spoiled me for when he goes back to work. It's tough dating a doctor."

"I know, dear. We rarely see him even though he works in town. He's mentioned moving back into this house to be closer to you and work. Has he told you this?"

"No, we haven't had a chance to talk about it. I'm sure he'll let me know when he's ready. What can I help you with? I'm somewhat skilled in the kitchen, as I've been on my own for a while."

"Well, there's not much to do. Bobby went out to pick up the flowers and the caterers and servers will take care of the food. The table is set already. Why don't you just sit and have a cup of tea with me?"

"Oh, I forgot. I have a little something for you and the family. It's not much, but I wanted to thank you for such a special trip and say Merry Christmas."

"You are so sweet," she said as she hugged me like only a mother could.

"Jake told us that your parents have passed away already."

"Yeah..." So many years have passed and yet tears always accompanied any talk about my parents being in heaven.

"Oh, Emily." Sandy hugged me and cried with me. "How lonely you must have been all those years without a mother and father. Holidays could not have been very joyful for you."

I nodded in agreement. "But this Christmas is different. I don't think you'll ever know how much I appreciated the four days I spent with your family. It truly felt like I was a part of a family again, and I thank you for giving me that sense of belonging."

"Emily. Regardless of where you and Jake are now, or where you will be in the future, I want you to come to me when times are tough, or when you think of your mother. I know I can't substitute, but I would like to be there for you if a need should arise, OK?"

"Thank you, Sandy. I'll do that."

We took a few minutes to compose ourselves and then talked about everything from Jake's childhood to mine to details of everyone coming to dinner tonight. Jake had so many family members living nearby. I would meet many aunts and uncles and cousins tonight. An hour had flown by when Jane arrived ecstatic to see me here.

"Emily! Why didn't you tell me you were coming early? Does Jake know you're here?"

"No. I actually don't know where he is. He and I had a big misunderstanding this morning, and I need to work my way back into his good graces," I said kiddingly.

"I can't imagine him being upset with you. I've never seen him so in love with anyone. Right, Mom?"

"I would have to agree. It's unusual the way he looks out for you and loves you. I don't think I've ever seen him so passionate about anyone," Sandy said wistfully. "I think he's forgotten about all the other women in his life—namely, me." She was happily laying on the guilt like a real mother would.

"No. He speaks highly of you all the time. He loves you and Jane very much."

"No, he loves *you* very much." Jane shook her head no. "Emily, come with me. I'll show you around the house and you can see what my room looks like." I followed Jane through a vast hallway and up a grand staircase. All of the bedrooms were on the second floor with the exception of the guest suite up on the third floor. Jane's room was larger than my living room and dining room combined. It was filled with memorabilia from all over the world.

"Jane, have you really been to all these places?" I marveled at a large map with different colored pushpins. Each member of the family had his or her own color displaying all the places they'd visited. There wasn't a continent that didn't have a pushpin. Even Antarctica had Bobby and Sandy's color pushed into it.

"OK, what's going on? You might be able to fool Mom but you can't fool me. You look as though you've been crying all morning."

"Am I that obvious?" Was that the case or was Jane so in tune with me already that she could read my face so readily?

"You didn't go into hysterics by yourself about this whole my life is a dream, when is reality coming crap, did you?"

For the first time today, I laughed. As much as I wanted to bring Jane into my confidence about what happened this morning, it felt a little too raw. Rather than discussing this further, the topic of San Francisco came up.

Jane, too, was curious about how I'd reacted to Allison.

"I didn't get upset with your brother. I told Jake I didn't want to hear anything about her, but I'm dying to know what happened between them. Will you tell me?"

"Ally and I were roommates for two years. She's Jake's age and was up north modeling."

"Yeah, I thought she was unusually tall and gorgeous." I shuddered at how pretty she was. "I felt like Smurfette next to her."

"Emily, you're so funny. Anyhow, she was after Jake since the day they met. She finally told me during lunch that she and Jake hooked up briefly while she worked in LA. She was really upset when I told her how much Jake loves you. I don't think she'll be bothering you anymore."

I felt grateful toward Jane for taking my side over her old roommate's. There was a bond that had been created between us during my weekend up north. This bond was different than the one I had with Sarah. Jane and I felt like true sisters rather than close friends. I wished more than anything we could become sisters one day.

"So, why did she want to talk to Jake?"

"I don't know. She won't tell me. I'll get it out of Jake next time I have a chance."

"Thanks, Jane." I hugged my dear friend.

"So, I want you to know that I booked tickets for you to come visit me in New York over Martin Luther King Jr. weekend. I hope you don't have plans already."

"No way. Jane...you didn't have to do that."

"I told my dad how I wanted you to come see me in New York, and he immediately bought you a ticket."

"Oh, he didn't have to do that. That was so nice of him. I'll have to thank your parents when I see them at dinner." I put my arms around Jane. "I'm excited to be spending time with you."

"So this is what I have planned for us. Saturday, let's go to the flea market, then lunch at Gotham, then maybe spend the afternoon at the Met. We'll have dinner in Brooklyn and go see my friend's art show. Sunday morning I'll take you to the Green market in Union Square, we can have lunch at Lupa or maybe Union Square Café. Let's shop afterward and then for dinner, how about Le Bernardin?"

"I was just there over Thanksgiving. Your generous brother sent me and Sarah on a gastronomic adventure there. It was amazing." Vividly those courses continued to linger on my mind and palate.

"Then how about Masa? Maybe Jake will foot the bill for that meal." Jane looked hopeful. "Of course, you'll have to go up the Empire State Building at night so you can see the city all lit up. On Monday...darn,

I think I hear Jake." Jane spoke with disappointment knowing our time together was over.

"Here you are. I searched all over the house for you," Jake said looking relieved. "We need to talk." Jake grabbed my hand and started leading me out of Jane's room.

"Hey!" Jane protested. "We were planning Emily's trip to New York. You can't just drag her out of here. We're not done yet."

Jake turned to me with a surprised look. "You're going to New York, again? How come you didn't tell me?" He looked hurt.

"Jane and I just made plans about thirty seconds before you came into the room. Your dad bought me a ticket so I can spend some time with her over MLK weekend."

"I'm not letting you go off to New York again without me. Nuh, uh. I'm coming too. Plus, why would Dad buy you a ticket and not me? I'm sure he purchased two seats."

"Jake!" Jane protested. "I'll never see Emily if you're there. Come on!"

I tried to smooth the situation over by reminding Jake that there was no way he would get another three days off from the hospital so soon after his Hawaii vacation.

"I have so much vacation time, I will make sure to take those three days off. So what do you have planned for Emily?" Jake gloated while Jane frowned.

Jane regurgitated all the places that she wanted to take me to when Jake rudely cut her off. "Hey, where do I fit in? I want to take Emi to some of my favorite places. You are taking my girlfriend away from me."

"Maybe, you shouldn't come on this trip, Jake!" Jane was serious. She did not want Jake spoiling it for us.

"Jane, you're being unreasonable. If I'm taking time off to be in New York with my girlfriend, then I'd like to spend some alone time with her. I don't want you tagging along everywhere."

"Whoa," I calmly stated. "Let me break this up. I have a solution for us." I turned to my love. "Jake, why don't you see if Nick wants to come to New York with us?"

"Why would I do that? I don't need to add another wheel."

"You do realize that you are the third wheel on this trip? It was a girls' weekend, remember? You wanted to tag along?"

"That's right," Jane declared. "You're the tag along, not me."

I turned to Jake and lovingly asked, "Will you invite your brother so that you will have a friend when I spend some quality time with my friend? Please?" I did my best to break the stare down between the Reid siblings.

"All right. I'll bring Nick and we'll have some quality brother bonding time. So much for a romantic trip to the city."

"Jake," Jane said. "I have one favor."

"What is it?"

"Can you pay for a meal at Masa? I've always wanted to eat there but can't afford it on my budget. You make a lot of money. Will you treat us to this meal? If not for me, will you do it for Emily?"

Masa could be summed up as the most expensive restaurant in New York, maybe even in the entire United States. Each meal costs somewhere around $400–$600 per person, before drinks, tax and tip. This twenty-six-seat, Zen-like sushi temple has a small pond, bamboo garden, and Japanese Cypress Hinoki wood as the sushi bar. Depending on which pre-fixe menu we chose, we'd eat five appetizers, about fifteen to twenty sushi courses, along with dessert and tea. It was French Laundry—sushi style. My mouth salivated at the thought of this meal.

"Would you like to dine at Masa, Emi?"

I gave him an *are you kidding me* look while answering coyly, "Only if you want to take me there."

"Why did I bother asking? I'll call in a reservation if you'll stop bothering me," he told his sister. "You want to see my room?" He asked, but was already pulling me out of Jane's room.

"Um, OK. I'll see you at dinner," I said, turning to Jane.

"Yeah, I'll save you a seat and Jake can go sit with the aunts and uncles." She turned to stick her tongue out at Jake, but he quickly grabbed my hand and led me out the door.

Jake's room was a palace compared to Jane's. It was so large and filled with so much furniture, the giant king-sized bed looked dwarfed. I never realized anyone could have so much furniture in one room. There was a desk along the west wall as well as rows and rows of shelves filled with books. These were the kinds of shelves one would see in movies, where old men went to retire in their libraries. He had one of these libraries on one wall of his room.

If the west wall was for intellect, the south wall was purely for entertainment. On this wall hung the largest TV I had ever seen. There were probably invisible speakers mounted everywhere. In front of the TV sat sleek couches, chaises and lounge chairs—the kind for video game purposes only. The east wall had two doors. One led to a giant bathroom that looked bigger than my master bedroom. The other door led to a walk-in closet that was definitely twice the size of my master bedroom.

"How do you not get lost in your own room?" I half joked. "Your room is practically the size of my entire house."

"Oh, I don't know about that. It's not that big, is it?" He looked around trying to gauge the dimensions.

"Why would you want to move out and get a place of your own when your room is this palatial? If your room looks like this, what does your house look like in the Valley?" I wondered in amazement.

"My house is small. It's probably smaller than yours. I think I'm going to rent it out and move back into my parents' home to be closer to you and the hospital. Nothing is keeping me in the Valley anymore."

"And, there was somebody keeping you there before?" I tried to ask nonchalantly.

"I'm digging this jealous tone, but it wasn't anybody, just a hospital. Remember how I told you that my residency was at a hospital in the Valley? I hated the commute back home in the wee hours of the morning so I bought a house out there."

"I see."

"So, are we OK?" He sounded so un-Jake-like, so unsure of us.

"Shouldn't I be asking you that? You were the one upset. Here lies a permanent scar etched on my heart because of your meanness!" I pointed to my heart and added an umph for effect. "Jane was right. You can be really nasty when life doesn't go your way." I giggled as he tugged me to him.

"This is going to be another Allison situation, huh? You're going to use my folly against me for the next month."

"A month? Are you kidding me? This is worth at least a year!"

"Is that right?" With speed and determination, he picked me up and threw me on his bed.

His lips came down roughly on mine and it was clear that he was not letting go of me for a while. Knowing he wasn't going to get very far didn't sway his determination to undermine my beliefs. I had to admit, I was the one caving toward his beliefs. His right hand immediately began unbuttoning my dress and his left arrested my protesting hand.

I tried to come up for air but his solid body lay on top of mine and didn't give me any room for escape. He finally moved his lips away from me and I let out a whimper. "Jake...your parents...your entire family is in this house."

In between moving his mouth from my lips down to my exposed chest, he uttered, "I don't care." He knew I wasn't putting up much of a fight. Skillfully, Jake managed to pull off the top half of my dress and his hands reached to take it completely off when there was a knock that saved me from Jake as well as from myself.

"Jake...oh, Jake..." Nick's voice called out.

"Go away!" Jake growled.

"Mom told me to come and get you and Emily. Everybody's waiting. Dinner's about to begin. Come out soon or I'm going to have the chief come up and get you." Nick broke into a guffaw.

"Nick, I'm going to remember this next time you have a girl up in your room," Jake threatened amid a loud bellow from beyond the door.

Jake grudgingly let go of me, and I jumped up out of bed reassembling my dress. I couldn't help but laugh at his surly face. "Jake..." His once complacent look turned into a scowl as we were about to leave his room. "Jake. Can I give you your Christmas present before we go down?"

His face lit up instantly. I walked over to my purse and brought out a journal that wasn't wrapped, but tied together nicely with ribbon and a big bow.

"You have to promise me one thing," I said before giving him the present.

"OK. I promise." So cute, he sounded like a little boy agreeing to anything so he could open his Christmas gift.

"This is a journal I started writing soon after we met. I wrote in it after every date or conversation or even a fight. My initial intention was to journal my feelings and thoughts. This wasn't written for anyone to read but myself. When I thought about what I wanted to give you for Christmas, I knew you would most appreciate my heart. Whatever I felt during our two months together...it's all in here."

My boyfriend looked stunned. He probably never imagined I would give him so much of myself emotionally. Rather than taking the present he came over and held me in his arms instead. I knew this man loved me unendingly. I too loved him just as much.

"I'm sorry I'm so frustrating. You're a patient man to deal with someone so indecisive. This journal will hopefully answer all your questions and take away any doubt you might still have about us."

His arms stayed locked on my body.

"OK, so back to the promise." I pulled myself away from him. "You can't read this till after I leave."

"Why not? If you wrote it you know everything that's in there."

"It's embarrassing. You can enjoy it when I'm not around. I also don't want to see your ego blowing up page by page. Your head may burst."

"Can I take a peak before dinner?"

"No. I'm taking this back if you don't keep your promise."

"All right. I promise. I can't wait to read it." He had an eager smile.

"I'll leave it over here on your bookcase."

We started walking out and I stopped him one more time, wanting to declare what was in my heart. "I love you, Jake, and I'm really happy to be here with you." He swept me off my feet again and tried to take me back to his bed, but I forced him downstairs.

There were twenty-three of us at the regal dining table. I met every aunt, uncle, and cousin who lived within a two-hour radius of Jake's house. Sandy put us at the middle of the table so that I could converse with as many family members as possible. I learned that Bobby was the oldest of five brothers and none of the children were married yet. They ranged from eighteen to thirty, with Jake being the oldest. Jake sat to my right, along with Uncle Roy, Aunt Pattie, and their three grown children. Then there was Uncle Billy and Aunt Sandra with their two college-age children. Sandy, Bobby, Jane, and Nick sat together. Uncle Dave and Aunt Debbie brought only two of their four college kids. Then the chief, Aunt Barbara, and their children, Doug and Lane, sat to my left. The chief kept me entertained with stories of all the nurses, interns, and female doctors who had tried to woo Jake since he got to the hospital.

"So, Emily, are you coming to the pre-party and football game with all of us on New Year's Day?" Chief Reid asked.

"Um, I don't think so. I wasn't invited."

He scolded Jake. "Why haven't you invited this stunning lady to our New Year's party and game day festivities?"

"Well, I haven't asked her because I myself wasn't invited. You have me working that day, remember? Will you give me that day off so I can go see the game?"

"Are you scheduled to work? I could possibly give you the day off and put someone else to work. Do you want to go to the game?"

"Actually, I'd be happy to work on New Year's Day if you are willing to give me MLK weekend off."

"Jake!" Jane complained from across of the table.

"That sounds good to me," the chief answered.

"Fantastic!" Jake glanced over at Jane and gloated.

To my delight, Jake's grandmother called during dinner. He had never spoken of any grandparents so I didn't realize she was still living. Bobby answered the phone and greeted her, but quickly turned the phone over to Jake.

"Son, Gram wants to talk to her favorite grandchild."

"That would be me," Jake announced to the family with a smug look.

"Hi, Gram!" Before he could say much more, he answered, "Uh-huh" and handed the phone over to me. "She wants to talk to you."

"Me?"

"Yup. You."

A bit scared, I started my conversation. "Hello, Gram, this is Emily. It's very nice to meet you."

"Emily, I've been waiting since David's birthday to talk to you. Why haven't you called me?" I took her question as a scolding.

Timidly I answered, "I'm very sorry, Gram, but Jake never told me I was supposed to call you. But I'm thrilled to meet you. I lived with my grandmother since I was thirteen. Talking to you makes me miss her so much."

"Is she still alive?"

"No," I answered tearfully, "she passed away a few years ago. Gram, why aren't you here with the family? I wish I could have met you too."

"I live in London. It's too far for me to travel. Why don't you come see me, Emily? Jakey tells me you're more beautiful than I am, and that he loves you even more than he loves me." She didn't sound too happy about this.

I gave Jake a *how could you* look. His shoulders shrugged into a *what did I do?* look.

"Oh, Gram, Jake can be silly at times. How can he possibly think he loves anyone more than his grandmother? Plus, I'm not that pretty. It's only in Jake's eyes."

"You are too. You're gorgeous!" Jake interjected before my thought was over. I pinched his arm and gave him a *be quiet* look.

"I've never seen such a beautiful family as the Reid family. I'm sure that's all a credit to you. Gram, can you send me a picture of yourself?"

Content with my soothing words, she answered, "I'll have my assistant take a picture of me and e-mail it to Jake. So when can you come see me?"

"Well, my vacation is almost over, but I can come at the end of March during spring break. Would that be OK? Should I bring Jake or come by myself?" I kidded.

"Gram, I want to come too," he whined into the mouthpiece.

"You can bring him if he's good to you. Is my Jakey treating you well?"

"He was treating me very well till this morning, Gram."

Gram sounded aghast. Jake looked horrified.

"What happened, Emily? What did he do to you?"

"He was mean to me and he made me cry." I added melancholy for special effects. I noticed the entire family had stopped eating, talking, and whatever else they were doing, and stared at Jake.

"Oh my gosh, Emily! I can't believe you just told everyone I made you cry this morning." Appalled, he didn't know what to say. All the aunts accepted my accusation and began scolding Jake.

"But you did," I answered in my saddest voice.

Back to my conversation with Gram, I said, "Anyhow, I'm going to come see you soon, and as to whether I will bring Jake, I'll think about it."

"Emily, are you going to marry my grandson?" Wow—like grandma, like grandson. She didn't beat around the bush.

"I hope so, Gram. I'm not sure yet. You'll be the second to know when I decide. Gram, I'll get your phone number from Jake and call you again. I think I have to get off. Jake's a bit upset with me. Thank you for talking to me."

With that, I got off the phone and sat as a spectator watching Jake get himself out of trouble.

"Emily, will you please explain, it was me who should've been crying this morning and not you?"

I shrugged my shoulder, winked, and mouthed, "I love you," then went back to enjoying my meal.

When dinner was over, we all played a mean game of White Elephant. The Reid family was ruthless stealing from each other the few prized items that Sandy added to the pile. The most coveted prize was two floor seats to a Laker game. Doug ended up as the grand prize winner. Most of us got ugly tchotchkes that would quickly be thrown away at home. Jake actually won a great bottle of wine, which he handed over to Chief Reid as a bribe to try to get New Year's Eve off. He gladly took the wine, but not the bribe.

I stayed as long as I could, then hugged Sandy, Bobby, and Nick good-bye as they went up to their rooms for the night. I turned to Jane and promised her quality time in New York even with her brother in tow.

Our dinner conversation with Gram seemed all but forgotten, or so I thought, when I turned to say good-bye to Jake. I took a step forward as he took a step backward dodging my attempted embrace. Confounded, I waited with my arms wide open.

"I can't believe you threw me under the bus today." *Oh so that's what this was all about.* "You're so lucky I didn't tell my whole family how you chopped up my proposal and my heart into pieces."

Cuddling up to him, I used my most alluring voice to appease him. "What can I do to make things better? I'll make it up to you. I'm sorry I got you into trouble, but you were a complete gentleman for not giving me away." I added a few kisses to buffer.

"Stay the night with me." This was more a demand than a request.

During my moment's hesitation, Jake swept me off my feet, carried me up the stairs, and took me to his bed. The words "I can't" and "I have to go" waited for their cue, but stayed frozen on my tongue. In silence, we headed toward a path with no recourse. Until I met Jake, I believed I would stay spotless till I said, "I do." Until now, I had never wanted to change my novice status but at this moment, I wanted nothing more than to be with him. My mind was made up—tonight, we would express our love for one another.

The excitement in Jake's eyes mirrored my own. His caresses began on my face. His mouth was soft. Savoring each kiss, his lips brushed over every part of my face. Hungrily, my mouth reached for his, hoping to kiss him, but he gently grazed my lips and moved on. Gentle. This word best described Jake's every move tonight. In earnest resolve—a synonym if there ever was one—he moved ever so slowly and gently for me.

Repeating his earlier steps of unbuttoning my dress, his lips stopped traveling and my body lay still. His eyes stayed glued on mine. I briefly thought about my mom. What would she have said, if I told her what I wanted to do tonight? I wasn't sure if she would have encouraged me or discouraged me. My mind also drifted to my conscience. As much as my body desired to love and be loved, there was a part of me—unsettled—like I was betraying myself in some way. When my mind came back to the moment at hand, I realized Jake had begun redressing me. He gazed lovingly into my eyes.

"Jake?" I whispered his name. "What's the matter?"

"Emily, I'm content to just be with you tonight. We don't have to do anything else."

"Why? What's wrong?"

"Sweetheart, as difficult as this is for me, I want to keep you as you are until we get married—and trust me, we will get married."

"Jake…I'm OK. I want to do this for you…with you. I'd like to be with you tonight." No matter how much I wanted to sound confused, his intentions were clear.

"Emily, I'm going to honor your wishes. That's how much I love you," he answered with regret written all over his face.

Almost every part of me wanted to be with Jake. He must have somehow read that tiny part of me that regretted saying yes. I loved Jake for knowing me so well. I loved him for wanting to help me keep my promise to myself and to my mom, no matter how difficult it was for him. But most of all, I loved him for loving me so much. Tonight I knew, if ever I were to walk down the aisle, he would be the one at the altar waiting for me. I knew that's how much I loved him.

My eyes opened to a frantic thought. Road trip. Oh my gosh, I wasn't ready to leave, and all my friends would be waiting for me at the house.

"Jake, Jake! I have to go. I haven't packed for my road trip and we're leaving in half an hour."

"What? You're going somewhere?" This was a change. He sounded groggy and I was wide awake at six in the morning.

"I'm going to Vegas to watch the football game with my college friends, remember? I have to leave right now."

"Don't go. Stay with me." He held me prisoner in his arms—a happy prisoner. "How am I to go several days without seeing your beautiful face?"

"Jake, let's be real. You won't see me for three days whether or not I'm in town. I don't think Chief Reid is going to let you leave the hospital for a week at least."

"Stay a little longer. I'll fly you out to Vegas later today."

"No. I have to go. Sarah will be waiting. I'm getting up and leaving, OK?"

"Should I come with you?"

"No. Stay in bed."

"I mean to Vegas."

"Jake. Don't be silly. I'll call you later. I love you." I ran out the door and rushed home.

Chapter 8

Road Trip

Within minutes I was home, showered, and packed in time for my friends to arrive. Though I didn't want to be away from Jake, I looked forward to seeing my friends again.

Ding Dong! Ding Dong! 6:30a.m. Right on time. I was looking forward to spending some time with Sarah and getting her caught up on all the craziness of the last five days. She would be able to help me focus and sort out my feelings. I opened the door and to my surprise, it was Jake.

"Good morning, my love." Jake planted a kiss on my lips. "I wanted to stop by and see your face before you left."

"Didn't you just see my face? Didn't we see each other the whole night?"

"Love, I've never slept as well as I did last night. We're going to have to have more slumber parties." He grinned at me. "Here, I brought you your favorite breakfast." He handed me an almond croissant and a latte. My stomach growling, I was grateful for the food. "How did you sleep last night? You claim you don't sleep too well outside of your own bed." He obviously doubted my original claim.

This was a tough question to answer. In all honesty, last night was the best night's sleep—ever! It felt so right to be with him in his bed, to be held by the man who adored me. But, if I admitted this to him, he would want to sleep together every night, and I didn't think I could resist the temptation. I had fallen once only to be rescued by Jake of all people. Next time he would not be such a Good Samaritan.

"Well? How did you sleep?"

"I'm going to plead the fifth on your question."

"Why? Could it be because you enjoyed it as much as I did?" His lips slowly widened to a grin.

"No comment," I answered with a grin of my own. "Don't you need to get to the hospital early and prep or something?"

"No. The rest of the surgical team does that. I walk in whenever they're done and perform the operation. Today's a routine heart surgery. Nothing too complicated."

Of course it wasn't too complicated for him. He would probably be the one to take over for the chief if he were to step down. Chief Reid had filled me in on Jake's important role at the hospital. Before last night, I wasn't quite aware of what a coveted doctor I was dating. His modesty made me appreciate him even more.

"Hey, Emi? Guess what?"

"What?" I asked.

"The chief just called me with some good news."

"Oh?"

"Well, there's this heart association conference in Paris he wants me to attend. He was going to go himself but has a conflict now with some important hospital board meeting. He called to see if I was available."

"That's wonderful. I'm sure it will be a great experience for you. Though, I'll miss you while you're gone." I hoped I didn't sound too sad at the thought of him leaving me. I didn't want him to miss anything on my account.

"Emily. I'm not going to Paris without you. How could you think I could be apart from you for that long? The chief is quite smitten with you and told me to take you along. He's transferred his ticket and hotel room over to my name. I'll just buy you a ticket. What shall we do about the one room? Can we stay together in the same room?" His eyes were hopeful.

"Jake, I don't know what to say. I don't think I can get a whole week off from work. Besides, it sounds kind of dangerous, the two of us in Paris," I teased. "Who knows what kind of concessions I'll make in such a romantic city, especially if we only have one room?" I flirted with his hope.

"I like the sound of that," he said, hugging me. "Let's go to Paris, then we can go visit Gram in London. She really liked you. Dad told me she called early this morning to tell him how wonderful she thought you were. My whole family loved you."

"Oh, I'm relieved to know I passed the test. I do want to meet Gram. I'll work on getting that week off. I'll let you know as soon as school starts."

"So, I have a question that wasn't answered yesterday while you had us broken up in your own mind." He shook his head, looking at me as though I were crazy.

I shrugged my shoulders and raised my eyebrows as a combined apology and *what else was I to think*, response.

"When did you know you loved me, and why didn't you tell me this monumental information before?"

"I've known for a while, but couldn't admit it to myself till the night before we left for Hawaii. At the sushi restaurant when you were asking me about my family, I appreciated how much you cared for me and how you empathized with my every joy and heartache. I, too, wanted to be there for every part of your life. I knew that I would laugh when you laughed, and cry when you cried. That's when I finally admitted that I had fallen in love with you."

"Why didn't you tell me?"

"Well, I kind of waited for you to say it first so I could reciprocate, but you never told me you loved me in Hawaii." I shrugged my shoulders again. "I felt a bit self-conscious bringing it up out of nowhere."

Jake gave me another disapproving look and came over to hug me. "Please don't ever doubt my love for you, OK?"

"OK," I answered but nudged him away. "I think it's time for you to leave, Dr. Reid."

"All right. Don't forget about getting the second week of February off, OK? If your principal says no, then let me talk to her." As I walked Jake out to his car, he held my hand and noticed the eternity band on my finger. Joy radiated from his eyes.

"You're wearing the ring…on your finger?"

"Oh…you noticed finally? It was so heavy around my neck I was getting a neck cramp," I kidded. "I thought I'd try it on the finger and see if it's any better here. Of course as luck would have it, it only fits on my ring finger." I stretched out my ring finger to show him the perfect fit. "Unless of course you think it looks better on my neck, then I'll put it back on as a necklace." I pretended to take the ring off and Jake immediately stopped me.

I confessed my heart to him. "I am committed to you as your loving girlfriend. When I see us heading toward that last step, you'll be the first to know."

Cars started pulling up in front of the house as we continued saying good-bye. Max was one of the first to get out of the car. He stared at me with a hurt expression. As much as I hated seeing Max upset, I wanted to finish saying good-bye. "I love you, Dr. Reid. Now go. Save lives."

Jake wouldn't let go of me, but I gently nudged him away.

"Hi, Jake," Sarah called out. "Did you have a good Christmas? How was Hawaii?"

"It was fantastic. How was your Christmas? You went up to Oxnard?"

"Yeah. It was great. What did you get for Emily for Christmas?"

"You'll have to ask her. I tried to give it to her, but she wouldn't take it. Though, I got an unbelievable present from Emily last night."

"Oh? What did you get?" Jake had piqued Sarah's curiosity. Once she got curious, there was no stopping her.

"You'll have to ask your best friend." His vainglorious face had *I slept with Emily last night* written all over it. Now everyone wanted to know.

"What did you get him? Why's he so happy?" Charlie asked.

"Go to work, Dr. Reid," I admonished.

"My girlfriend is telling me I have to leave. Have a great trip and take care of her for me, OK?"

"Jake, why don't you come with us?"

"No, Sarah. Jake needs to get back to work. He's going to be jobless if he takes any more time off." I gave Jake a disapproving look while he shrugged his shoulders at Sarah. "Bye. I'll call when I get there" was the last thing I said before we started our road trip.

The ten of us took two cars into Vegas. We crammed all our junk into the cars and hopped in uncomfortably for the next four hours. I felt like I was back in college. This was no first class to Hawaii—back to my reality. Max, Peter, Sarah, Charlie, and I squished into Peter's Honda Accord. I sat in the back with Sarah and Charlie and felt distressed after Max and I had such an awkward ending at lunch the other day.

Sarah and Charlie tried to make eye contact with me but I avoided them. Peter went off babbling about the hotel that he booked for all of us. I vaguely heard him say something about a suite but didn't pay much attention. I could tell Max was concentrating hard not to look back at me too often. I stared out the window at the sights and sounds of the busy freeway.

Haphazardly, I started thinking about Max and our times together in college. We had gotten into horrible fights all the time. Max was always so stubborn and hated admitting to any wrongdoing. Chuckling to myself, I remembered how he was supposed to pick me up from the library at 4:00 one rainy afternoon but didn't show up till 5:00. I was wet and late for my study group, but rather than apologizing and making sure I was OK, he fought with me the whole time, arguing that I had told him the incorrect time. Explaining how improbable his reasoning was since I had a 4:30 study group didn't end the discussion. We didn't speak to each other for almost a week. Ugh! He was always so obstinate. Looking back, we were passionate about everything. Maybe that was how collegians were—eager to jump feetfirst into any situation. We loved passionately and fought just as passionately. We made it through one day at a time.

"Emily, how was Hawaii?" Peter woke me from my memory.

"It was wonderful." I tried not to sound too mushy.

"Details, Emily!" Sarah commanded.

"Well, I met Jake's parents and his brother, Nick, for the first time at the airport, and we instantly bonded like family. They were so warm and loving toward me." My face broke into a deep smile. "We arrived in Maui and met Jane there. Then we did so many activities I couldn't even begin to explain all of them. I probably lost five pounds in the four days we were there because of how active we were."

"What were the sleeping arrangements like?" Charlie asked, guffawing like a teenage boy.

"Charlie." I slapped his arm. "The parents were in one room, Jake and Nick had another room, and Jane and I roomed together." I smiled, remembering how Jake had wormed his way into my bed the first night.

"Activities?" Peter kept pressing for more information.

"The day we landed, we had an early lunch, took a helicopter ride, hiked five miles, snorkeled, I had a scuba diving lesson, did yoga, and went to a luau!" I felt exhausted just remembering all the activities.

"How on earth did you do so much in one day?" Sarah sounded amazed.

"I don't know. The Reids are all active people. I was so exhausted after the scuba lesson, I wanted to collapse. But, I kept up with them somehow and finished the day. The next day brought on more scuba and surfing lessons, and I had to drudge through a basketball game. That was a long two hours pretending to cheer for their team."

"Did you get to relax at all?" Sarah asked.

"Yeah. On Wednesday, his parents had to go to a meeting, so Jane and I relaxed at the spa for half a day. We wanted to go the whole day, but Jake wouldn't have it, so we compromised on a half day. We also hung out in the cabana a couple of afternoons. That was a nice respite from all the activities."

"Was it nice being away with Jake?" Sarah continued to press. It was almost like the two of us were having our own private conversation even though everyone else was listening. I knew Max heard every detail, and I felt bad, but I reveled in the fun I'd had in Hawaii.

"I'll fill you in on all the details later, Sarah. I have so much to tell you," I whispered.

Just then my phone buzzed. It was a text from Jake. Reading it made me blush.

Last night was even more amazing than our first night in Hawaii. Miss you. Love you.

Charlie saw my red cheeks and stole the phone from my hand and he read the text aloud. "Emily! Did you have sex with Jake?"

"Charlie!" Sarah and I both yelled at him. I kept quiet till we got to lunch.

Vegas was no different from the last time I'd come—big buildings filled with lights and giant advertisements of half-naked women. I supposed that could be exciting for some, but the in-your-face advertisement was quite a turnoff for me. We pulled into the Venetian Palazzo Hotel and Peter checked in for us.

Peter, being Peter, got one giant suite for all of us to share. It had three bedrooms and three bathrooms and was luxurious. Sarah and I took one room; Peter, Charlie, James, and Max took the other; and Will, Scott, Dave, and John took the third room. We all unpacked and relaxed. Some of the guys went out to gamble and some stayed to watch an MMA fight on TV. Sarah and I didn't leave our room. Charlie knocked on our door to make sure we were OK as I started to fill Sarah in on all the details of Hawaii.

Sarah began by asking about the text. "OK, so what happened? What's with the Christmas present and the text? Did you actually sleep with Jake? He could not have lured you into bed with him already when Max wasn't able to the entire four years."

"Well..." I had a guilty look.

"Emily!" Sarah begged. "The suspense is killing me!"

"You know how the first day we got to Maui we took the five-mile hike, had scuba lessons, did yoga, and went to a luau, right? So I was really tired! Jake walked me back to my room and he too was tired because he went surfing with Nick while I was at yoga. He fell asleep on my bed while I was showering. I tried to send him away, but he pulled me down on the bed and wouldn't let go of me. Eventually, I was too tired to fight him off. I fell asleep in his arms but nothing happened. We just slept," I confessed.

"Anything else happen?" Sarah pressed.

"Well, I kind of fell asleep on him up in San Francisco as well. I don't know why I keep doing this with Jake. My guard is down and I feel very safe."

"You didn't tell me about this before. What else are you keeping from me?" Sarah eyes squinted. She knew this story was nowhere near being over.

"Well..." I had that same guilty tone.

"You didn't! Does this have something to do with last night?"

"Let me explain yesterday morning first. On the way home from LAX, Jake suddenly pulled out another Christmas present and I about had a heart attack. There was a diamond engagement ring in the box and he proposed to me in the car on the side of the road."

"No!" Sarah gasped. "So what did you say?"

"I told him it was way too early. Sarah, we've only been together for two months."

"Emily, you've been awfully intimate for someone who's been dating such a short time. You've been emotionally, mentally, and physically bewitched."

"I know. But, it's still too early. He is too perfect and I'm scared, Sarah. After four years, Max realized one day he didn't love me anymore. What if Jake thinks the same way a few months down the road?"

This was my a-ha moment. I had told myself and Jake it was too soon and that I wasn't ready for a lifelong commitment with him. In actuality, I would marry him in a heartbeat if I trusted he would love me the rest of my life, like he loves me now. I was scared to let this happen to me again—too scared to be hurt by the man I trusted. Jake was right. I did doubt his love for me.

"But, Emily, you can't fear today because of what happened yesterday. Jake is not Max. If you live your life wondering if every man you love will wake up and leave you one day you'll never be happy. If all that's stopping you from accepting Jake's proposal is your paranoid past, you need to rethink your answer." Sarah was right on all accounts. Maybe during this time away from Jake I would carefully rethink us.

"So what did Jake say when you said no?"

"He accused me of doubting his love and asked me if my answer had anything to do with Max. He was mad because I turned him down without even considering his proposal. I thought he was going to break up with me. Sarah, the thought of letting go of Jake was so difficult. It killed me to think it was over. I do really love him, don't I?"

114

"Honestly, Charlie and I thought you were a goner from the first weekend we saw you together with him. We have never ever seen you so enamored with anyone—not even Max."

I sighed. Perhaps I had made the wrong choice.

"How did you resolve this mess?"

"When I asked him if he was breaking up with me he thought I was crazy. He patiently listened to me, and answered all my questions. He then reassured me that he loved me and that we were not breaking up. Then, I told him that I, too, loved him and we ended our crazy morning."

"So what happened last night?" Sarah wondered.

After an explanation of last night Sarah's face never looked more surprised.

"I don't know whether to be more shocked by your concession or by Jake's self-control. What a Christmas you two had."

"Tell me about it."

Everyone started coming back to the suite, and I noticed that our door had been open the entire time. I didn't know if Max might have heard anything, as he was sitting on a chair near our room. We walked out of our room and I searched Max's face but couldn't read his expression.

We drove to the UNLV stadium to watch our football team. During the ride, my phone went off and my heart raced. It was Jake.

"Hi, Jake. We're on our way to the stadium. Are you done with work already? How did morning surgery go?"

Jake sounded tired. He had ended up assisting with two more surgeries. We weren't at the stadium yet so we continued to talk.

"Where are you off to?"

"My house in the Valley. I'm moving my stuff out tonight."

"You're moving already?"

"When will you be back? I miss you." The feeling was mutual.

"We're here till Monday. I'll be home by the afternoon. Come over after work. I'll make you dinner." I could tell he wasn't thrilled with me being with Max. He really wanted to come join me. I encouraged him to rest and said good-bye.

"What was that all about?" Sarah was always the curious one. "Where is Jake moving tonight?"

"Jake is leasing out his house in the Valley and moving back into his mom's house. He wants to be closer to work and to me, I suppose. She lives about five minutes from me. His room at his mom's is amazing. I don't know why anyone would want to live elsewhere. His room has to be about a thousand square feet, and it has everything."

When we got to the stadium we weren't surprised to discover that Peter got ten tickets all separate from one another. We were separated into groups of three, three, two, and two. Before I could say a word, Peter gave tickets to each of us, and "coincidentally" Max and I got the two seats together quite far from everyone else. I tried to switch seats with Peter, but he ran off with Jeff and Dan before I could finish my sentence. I silently waved good-bye to Sarah and Charlie.

"Em, I guess it's you and me. Let's go," Max said.

I hesitantly followed. What else could I do? On our way to our seats, we stopped by the concession stand and picked up dinner. Fans started packing into the stadium, and Max and I almost lost each other in the rush. He had the tickets so I would've been in big trouble if Max hadn't backtracked and found me. He grabbed me by the hand and pulled me along toward our seats.

Once the game started, we cheered for our team, but couldn't get a conversation going. I could feel the uncomfortable current between us and tried to replace it with excitement for the football team, but it didn't work. About twenty minutes into the game, I attempted to have a normal conversation but my first question didn't come out as casually as expected.

"Hey, Max? Sarah tells me that you and Jennifer broke up. What happened? Was it a mutual parting?" I tried to sound nonchalant. Nonchalant, it wasn't.

Max appeared uncomfortable and stayed silent for a few minutes. I waited patiently for an answer.

"Jennifer wanted more out of the relationship than I was willing to give her. She wanted to get married and I didn't. We both thought it would be best if we went our separate ways," he finally explained.

"Oh," was all I could say. I felt an odd sense of empathy for Jennifer.

Max stared at me. "What? Why are you making that face? You're making me feel very defensive."

"What face?"

"That sad look you have. It's making me feel like I'm the bad guy."

I shook my head and chuckled a bit. "I'm empathizing from one exgirlfriend to another ex-girlfriend."

This made him mad. "What do you mean, Em?"

Uh-oh. I was in trouble now. I knew he would badger me till I gave him an answer.

"Max, forget I said anything. I'm sorry. Let's get back to the game." I tried to divert his anger.

"No, I think we need to talk. Em, I need you to explain yourself to me," he demanded.

I sighed, regretting having said anything. "OK, I'll explain myself, but can we do it after the game? I don't want to bother anyone else around us."

"You promise? After the game?" Three hours coupled with an exciting football game would hopefully get his mind off this topic.

When we got back to the hotel, Max immediately forced me to go with him to nearest coffee shop for an explanation. His face turned a bright hue like it always did before he exploded. I decided to start talking without any coercion.

"Max, when did you become so sensitive?" Laughing at him didn't lighten the situation. "I only said what I said because I know how Jennifer is feeling right now."

"What do you mean?" he asked so innocently.

"What do I mean? Have you forgotten that you dumped me a year and a half ago?"

He lamely defended himself. "We didn't break up because you wanted to get married and I didn't!"

"Really?" I asked, dumbfounded. "Then why did we break up? Didn't you give me some lame excuse about not wanting to be tied down and needing your freedom?" I accused. It felt good to hash out our breakup.

"You never mentioned wanting to get married," he retorted.

"Max, are you blind or stupid?" It was me who started with the tirade. "You were the only boy I ever loved. After four years of dating, did you think there'd be any other boy I wanted to marry but you? Of course I thought we were getting married. After graduation...never mind..."

Emotions overwhelmed us both at the memory of graduation night. Tears glistened in our eyes, but I quickly laughed them off and poked fun at myself instead.

"Boy, was I ever wrong—so much for woman's intuition. I went from being married in my head to being single in reality." Max looked away so I wouldn't notice the pain in his eyes...though I did.

"Max, it's late and I'm tired. Let's go to sleep." He obliged and we went up to our room and got ready for bed.

It was 5:00 a.m. when the phone buzzed with an early greeting from Jake. In agony, I weighed the wisdom of calling him and needing to hear his comforting voice versus having to explain why I was up at this hour and why I felt so down. Against my better judgment, the phone call was placed.

"Hi, Jake. Are you off to work already?" I asked.

"Emi. Why are you up so early? Are you all right?"

"I'm all right." I lied, hoping he wouldn't catch the sadness in my voice. "My back was hurting on this couch so I couldn't get a good night's sleep."

"Why are you sleeping on a couch?" I probably shouldn't have explained that one either. I knew what he would say.

"Peter got a gigantic suite and I was supposed to room with Sarah, but Charlie stayed in our room so I ended up on the couch." Of course, Jake immediately insisted on getting me a separate room. "Jake, no. I don't want you to get me my own room. That's not cool. We came as a group. I need to do everything with them. Please, don't do that."

"All right. Emi? Are you sure you're OK? You sound sad. Did something happen with Max again? Do you want me to fly in today?"

"I'm fine." The flat tone in my voice was an unconvincing reassurance. "I think I miss being in my own bed. Between Hawaii and Vegas, a different bed has greeted me each night—yours having been the most pleasant one. I miss being with you as well." My voice cracked a bit and I knew I needed to get off the phone right away.

"Emily, I'm coming to see you right now! I don't like the way you sound."

"Jake, I'll see you tomorrow. You can*not* abandon your work to come get me. I'm fine. Go to the hospital and focus on your patients. I don't want to be a distraction for you."

While I was saying this, Max stepped into the living room, and I quickly wiped my eyes with the back of my hand.

"Jake, I gotta go. I'm sorry. Have a wonderful day. I love you. Bye."

Max had a worried look on his face. He stared at me with his boyish good looks that reminded me of our better days in college.

"Em, are you OK?" I wiped away a final tear and turned my back toward him.

"I'm fine," I lied.

He sat on the couch and turned me around to face him. He comforted me with a hug and to Max's surprise, I didn't push him away. The love and tenderness we once shared for so many years spoke through our embrace. I stayed in his arms for a while, silently, eventually pulling away. Max let go, unwillingly.

"Thanks. I really needed that. It was hard holding back the tears during our phone call. He would come here immediately if he thought there was something wrong with me."

"He's quite protective of you. Jake seems to love you very much." Max didn't like admitting this.

"Yeah, I feel loved when I'm with him, like there's no one else on earth but me. Maybe it's his age or maybe it's just him. He takes care of me without hovering over me. It's been wonderful."

"Then why are you so weepy this morning if everything is so perfect with him? Why'd you call him this early if you didn't want him to see you like this?" Max's expression hardened.

"Jake actually texted me before leaving for the hospital, and I should have just let it go, but I missed him and wanted to talk to him.

"Is that why you're crying, because you miss him? I'm going to be really mad if I was your shoulder to cry on because you missed your boyfriend." I couldn't tell whether Max was joking or serious. Perhaps it was a bit of both.

I laughed. "No. That's not why I'm crying. I'm just a bit frustrated at the ironies of life."

"What does that mean?"

"After our conversation last night, I realized all throughout undergrad, I wanted nothing more than to marry you, but you never asked. Obviously, that wasn't in your plans. I finally meet a man who wants to marry me, and I don't have that same assurance. Maybe it's just too early. We've known each other for such a brief period, and yet Jake is so sure I'm the one. I believe I feel the same way, but I'm not positive."

Max's nervous expression worried me. To my surprise, he pulled me off the couch and told me to get dressed. "Let's go have breakfast, Em."

Chapter 9

A Second Proposal

We went downstairs and enjoyed each other's company like old times. I had missed his friendship during our time apart.

"How is it that you can eat so much?"

"I know, Jake wonders the same thing. I think I eat as much most men, huh?" After polishing off a breakfast burrito, it was time to dive into my chocolate croissant. "Do you know what we're all doing today?"

"No. I heard some talk about outlet shopping and some want to gamble again. What do you want to do?"

"I don't know. You know I don't like this city. There's not much here for me to do. We should have all gotten tickets to go watch a show or gone out to a nice meal."

"Em, I don't think I've ever taken you anywhere special in all the years we've dated, huh?"

"Of course you have. You've done lots of nice things for me." I was hoping he wouldn't ask me to list them because none came to mind at this instant.

"There's something I've always wanted to do for you. Would you mind spending the day with me?"

This was not the Max I had lunch with a week ago, nor the Max I went to the football game with last night. This was the Max I'd dated all through college. The same boy I had loved with all my heart, wanted to spend time with me today. This was my desire as well.

"OK," I answered with a smile. "What do you want to do today?"

"If you're done, let's go. I think the first flight leaves at 7:00."

He grabbed my hand and rushed me out to the strip and into a taxi. Not far from the Palazzo sat dozens of helicopters ready to take off.

"You haven't been to the Grand Canyon yet, have you?"

"No. It's still on my to-do list. Is that what we're doing? We're flying over the Grand Canyon?"

"Get in. This should be fun."

Max was absolutely right. We took off from Vegas and saw an unobstructed view of Boulder City, Hoover Dam, Lake Mead, and the Colorado

River. During this time, headsets provided interesting facts and stories on these places. Next, we flew over the breathtaking grandeur of one of the Seven Wonders of the World—The Grand Canyon. Words could not describe the awe of taking in the sights of this geographic amazement carved out by the Colorado River.

"Are we also going to walk on the Skywalk?"

"Uh huh," he answered smiling at me.

If our ride wasn't cool enough, the helicopter descended four thousand feet below the canyon along the Colorado River. We were able to land and explore the canyon where the Haulapai Indians guard. The touring company gave us four hours to have lunch and enjoy the surroundings. Max and I decided to take a mule ride during this time.

"Are you enjoying yourself?" Max put his jacket around my shoulders as he noticed me shivering.

"Yeah. This is really cool. Thank you. It was sweet of you to remember all this."

"This mule ride is supposed to take us to a ranch where we can have lunch. I'm sure you're hungry again. Some things don't ever change no matter how much time goes by."

"Hey. We didn't tell anyone where we were going. Can you call Sarah and let her know what we're up to? We left in such a rush I didn't bring anything."

Max took out his cell phone, but realized we didn't get reception. We would call from a payphone when we got to the ranch.

The mule ride wasn't as enjoyable as I'd imagined. We rode on the edge of the canyon overlooking what could be death if the mule took one misstep. I feared for my life while Max laughed at me the whole way.

"You're still such a chicken. There's not one daring bone in that body of yours."

"Knowing this, you shouldn't have suggested a mule ride. It's frightening. What if we die?" The last four words needed to be whispered in order to not freak out the other riders.

"Em, you can be so ridiculous at times."

"I don't consider this being ridiculous!"

We argued, we laughed. It was just like old times. We were both very happy.

"Hey, Em?"

"Yeah?"

"Never mind." Max just shook his head.

"You know I hate it when you do that. Tell me."

"It's nothing."

"Ugh! Whatever." I rolled my eyes at him. It bugged me when he started a conversation that led nowhere.

During this ride, I thought about Jake, and how fun it would have been to have him here. As enjoyable as it was being with Max, I would have preferred riding with, and sharing this time with him. Pathetically, my joy and sadness hinged on Jake's words and actions toward me. Thoughts of my love brought a smile to my face.

"What are you smiling about? You look goofy," Max commented poking his index finger into my cheek.

"Be quiet," I answered swatting away his finger.

We arrived to find an impressive spread at the ranch. There was a barbeque as well as a Native American dance. We got so caught up in the festivities neither one of us kept track of time.

"Max, what time is it? Shouldn't we get going?" He looked at his watch and jumped off the rock we were sitting on.

"Crap! The helicopter just took off."

"What? How did this happen? What are we going to do?" A howl of laughter that escaped my lips couldn't be helped. Max looked at me as though I had gone mad.

"What are you cackling about?"

"Why do these kinds of things always happen to you? You plan a wonderful activity, and somehow it always goes awry. Remember the time you planned a Valentine's picnic, but forgot to bring the address to the park? We searched for hours then picnicked at some random park."

"I planned to go to that park."

"Liar. You still can't admit to any wrongdoings." I shook my head and laughed some more. "So what now?"

"Wait here. Let me go make some calls."

Max left to resolve our mess and a plan B was necessary, as always, when Max made the arrangements.

He came back to our seat and gave me the news.

"OK, so here are our options." His face already told me that these options were really not options.

"Number one—we walk up to the top of the canyon and drive back to Vegas—that would take three hours just to walk up.

Number two—we charter a helicopter to pick us up and fly us back to Vegas—we need permission from the Indians to have a helicopter land near here.

Number three—we spend the night here, then either take a mule back to the original landing point and fly back into Vegas, or ride the mule all the way up to the top and then drive back to Vegas."

"So you're basically telling me that number three is our only option. It's just a matter of three A or three B."

Max nodded his head yes.

"I pick three B. I still want to go on the Skywalk. Then let's rent a car and drive back to LA. What are we going to do about clothes and toiletries? Does the ranch have rooms for us to stay in?"

"This ranch is kind of like a dormitory where all the women stay in one cabin, and all the men stay in another. Front desk says that you're the only female occupant so far and there are a few male occupants in the other cabin. They also provide toothbrushes and stuff at a nominal charge."

"All right, then. There's not much we can do about this situation."

"One more thing…"

"Uh-oh. Now what?"

"Peter tells me you need to call Jake."

"Jake?"

"Yeah. He's in Vegas right now looking for you."

Oh no! How would I explain this situation to my boyfriend?

"Max! You're going to get me into so much trouble. Jake's going to insist on chartering a helicopter to come and get me when I tell him I'm spending a night here with you."

"Cool. Then we can go home tonight."

"No, you're not going anywhere. He'll fly me home and leave you here." We both laughed.

Time to face the music…

"Jake?" The sweetest voice magically appeared. "What are you doing in Vegas?"

"Emi. Where have you been? I got so worried when you didn't answer your phone."

"Well…I'm a bit stuck here in the Grand Canyon right now. A certain ex-boyfriend of mine brought me out to the canyon then got us stranded." Max started tickling me in retaliation.

"Stop!" I whispered to Max. "I'm in a lot of trouble with Jake right now."

Unhappy, Jake came up with the scenario I had pictured earlier. He offered to charter a helicopter to come pick me up.

"It's no use, Jake. They can't come down here without the Haulapai Indians' permission. Plus where we are, you have to walk at least another hour. It will be too dark by then." I could hear Jake's sigh all the way here at the bottom of the Grand Canyon. "Why don't you spend the night in Vegas and come into the Grand Canyon tomorrow morning? I'd love to go to the Skywalk with you. Can you do that or do you have to work tomorrow?"

"Emily. Where will you sleep tonight?"

"Right here on the ranch. We'll stay here then take a mule ride first thing in the morning up to the Skywalk."

"Why are you there with him? Never mind. You don't need to answer that."

"I love you, Jake, and I miss you. I'll see you tomorrow morning?"

"All right. I'll see you then. Sleep well."

"Good night."

"I love you, Jake and I miss you." Max imitated my last line. "When did you become so corny?"

"What do you mean? I've always been like this. There wasn't a day that passed without me telling you how much I loved you."

"Maybe you did, but it was never that lovey-dovey."

"Whatever. Where are we sleeping? Let's go get some rest if we're leaving at the crack of dawn."

Max bought me a toothbrush, soap, and a small towel and took me to my cabin. It was a good-sized room filled with bunk beds. It was like summer camp in junior high all over again. I slowly walked to my bed and sat there feeling fearful about being alone in this room. Max read me immediately.

"You need me to stay here with you?"

"Would you?" My outlook brightened as the prospect of having a roommate. Perhaps the fact that he was my ex should have stopped me from wanting him in the same room with me but fear got the best of me.

"OK. I'll take the bunk next to you if you're sleeping here. You know I'll get kicked out if someone finds me here. And by the way, what will Jake think if he knew I was sleeping in the same room with you?"

"Trust me, this is exactly what Jake's worrying about. It wouldn't surprise me if he got a helicopter to land right outside tonight and took me home." *Jake, I'm really sorry but it scares me to death to sleep in this place by myself. I hope you'll understand.*

Under normal circumstances I wouldn't have gone to bed at 9:00 but there wasn't much else to do. Max and I chatted for a while, then tossed and turned for another hour till we decided to talk again. Our talk turned a lot more serious than it had been all day. The serious Max from our lunch in Santa Monica slowly reemerged.

"Em?"

"Huh?"

" Does it bother you that I still call you Em? Should I stop?"

"No. Why would it? That was your name for me. It'd be weird if you called me anything else."

"Doesn't it take away from Jake creating a nickname for you?"

"Funny thing, he's always called me Emi. Instinctively, he's never called me Em, so that's your name forever if you like."

"You seem to be in love again. Will you tell me about you and Jake?"

"I'll tell you if you'll answer one question for me."

"What's that?"

I didn't know if I was ready to hear this story, but it had been a nagging question the past year and a half. "Why did you break up with me? Did I do something wrong in the end? Did you get tired of me?" Tears began streaming down my face.

"Em, how can you ask that?" He placed his hand on my cheek and wiped away my tear. "I loved you more than life. Breaking up with you was the hardest decision I'd ever made."

"Then why did you break up with me? You were my love, my life, my only family. You broke all of that up."

"Em..." he began to say, "I don't quite know where to begin with this explanation. Graduation day was probably the darkest day of my life. I didn't mean to break up with you but everything went wrong." He rambled incoherently about things that happened that day and all I could give him was a confused stare.

"OK, let me try to start from the beginning. I started the day thinking that I was going to surprise you and propose after graduation."

So he was going to propose.

"I was truly excited about our future. I ran around making sure that all details were set, staying away from you all day knowing I couldn't keep my surprise a secret from you. After the ceremony was over, we were going to go to a nice dinner and a proposal was to happen during dessert. It was all perfectly planned out." He let out a breath and then stalled for a few nerve-wracking minutes.

"What I didn't factor in was the graduation speech we listened to that afternoon. Do you remember it?"

"No. I don't remember much about that day but the end," I said sadly.

"Well, it was a speech about going out into the world after graduation and making something of yourself. During this speech, our so-called future plagued me. There was no job prospect, no plans for more schooling. All I was sure about was my love for you. But then flashbacks of you working so many hours to support yourself and your undertakings to establish a stable life came to mind. Your life had been nothing but struggle the last ten years, and my uncertainty would only add to this struggle. This made me think that we really didn't have a future until I could get my act together. I didn't think it was fair to keep you with me if I wasn't going anywhere."

"Did you ever think to consult me about my feelings rather than break my heart? Didn't you know how much I loved you and how your actions would devastate me?"

"I should have done that. I was stupid for not discussing our future together. To this day, I regret not having worked this through with you. We'd probably be engaged, maybe even married by now if I hadn't let pressure get to me."

"Did you feel that much pressure to figure out what you wanted to do? How come you never told me how stressed you were about your future? You always appeared so relaxed."

"Pressure mounted when I thought of it as our future. What if I never figured out what I wanted to do? What if I worked some nine-to-five job I hated? What if I couldn't support you or a family? I had so many doubts in my head, I kind of went crazy. During the entire ceremony, I wrestled with questions that had no answers."

"Why didn't you talk to me?" I asked, quite frustrated.

"Knowing the pain you'd been through with the loss of your parents, I thought you should be with someone who could provide a stable and secure future for you—emotionally and financially. I didn't ever want you to suffer again. I didn't know it back then, but maybe that someone is Jake. That's when I decided to let you go on with your life, and I went on to figure out what to do with the rest of mine. You have to believe me when I say letting go of you was the hardest thing I've ever done. You were my world. I truly love you more than my own life," he declared sadly.

Odd that he used the word love in the present tense. It was probably a grammatical error.

"OK, assuming I believe everything you just told me, why Jennifer? Our breakup was hard enough without having to hear about you and another girl so soon. Did our four years mean that little to you where you could move on so easily and so quickly? Was I just some girl you had fun with and then tossed by the wayside?"

"No, Em. I'm sorry you believed that. If breaking up with you was my biggest mistake, getting together with Jennifer was my second-biggest mistake." Max gently caressed my head and wiped away more of my tears. "Has Jake seen you this weepy or have you not had any reason to cry in front of him?" This question carried a heavy tone of regret. He knew I had shed far too many tears over him.

"We weren't supposed to be apart this long. Once I figured out what I wanted to do with my life, I was planning to beg you to take me back. This—our separation, Jennifer, Jake—none of it was supposed to happen." Regret, anger, frustration soared to a loud crescendo. "Remember how I told you I was in a car accident? Well, after our breakup, I was so upset I purposely crashed my car into a wall. I really didn't want to go on with my life without you. It was during my rehab sessions where I met Jennifer. She was kind to me, and she filled your void. I know. It was stupid and I feel terrible for having hurt you both for my indiscretion."

My body agonized at the thought of Max being so hurt. I wished I could've known. I would've been there for him. This sympathy didn't last once I envisioned him purposely driving a car into a wall.

"What were you thinking crashing your car? You could've died. That would've sent me to my grave as well." If there was ever a doubt, Max understood tonight how much he was loved.

"You know, I came by your apartment every night after we broke up. I sat outside staring at your window till you fell asleep. More than anything I wanted to get back together with you."

"What stopped you?"

Max hesitated..."My family."

"Your family? Did they not like me?"

"No, they liked you very much but they wanted me to focus on my future and not spend so much time focused on a girlfriend. They didn't empathize with my feelings of wanting to make you my wife one day."

Max's confessions about wanting to make me his bride made my heart ache. I'd had no greater wish than to be Max's wife.

"Thank you for your explanation, Max. I think I understand now. I needed to believe that you loved me during those years. Our four years will always be a beautiful memory for me."

"I should be the one thanking you. You were the best thing that ever happened to me, and I'm sorry I was such an inattentive boyfriend. Jake is good for you. I hope he will be for you what I should have been all those years." With that he kissed my forehead and we turned to our private thoughts away from one another.

For the first time, I felt at peace with our breakup. All my questions were answered and doubts erased. Wonderful memories of Max could live deep within my heart.

Bright and very early the next morning, we got back on the mule and headed up the canyon. Max's solemn mood kept me quiet for most of the ride. I hated that we were back to our awkwardness. Yesterday was so much fun for both of us. After three hours, we finally arrived at the Skywalk.

In awe, but terrified of the glass walkway, I grabbed on to Max's arms. It felt like we were walking on air. This free-fall feeling kept me from looking over the glass to glance into the canyon. Knowing my fears, Max stood behind me and pretended to push me, and I jumped into his arms.

"Stop scaring me! You know this is freaking me out right now."

Max couldn't stop laughing. "I'm right behind you. I'll make sure you don't fall off," he reassured me while his arms encircled me. "By the way, are you cold? You want my jacket?"

"No, I'm OK." While I appreciated his concern, something about it made me feel uncomfortable.

Max turned me around so my back was against the canyon and his face turned serious again. I peeked over his shoulder looking for Jake. It was sometime past 8:00, and I was hoping he would arrive soon. I wanted him to experience this Skywalk with me.

"Em, I've had your graduation present here in my pocket every day since we broke up. Do you think I can give it to you right now?"

His random statement put me at a loss for words.

That same Tiffany blue jewelry pouch that fell on my bedroom floor the night of the Christmas Ball produced a beautiful engagement ring. I gave him a blank stare.

"What is this? Is this an engagement ring for Jennifer?" Perhaps Max was going to propose to Jennifer, but got cold feet. "Why do you still have it? Why haven't you given it to her?"

"Em. It's your engagement ring. I've had it since graduation."

"What do you mean this is my engagement ring?" Sometimes, I got things so wrong. A wave of nausea rolled through my body as I worked to understand this situation.

Suddenly he got down on one knee and held my hand. "Em, I love you. You have been always been the most important person since the day I met you and I want you to complete my life now. Will you marry me?"

Shocked.

Horrified.

Angry.

Confused.

These emotions engulfed my being.

"Max...why are you doing this to me now? We've been separated for two years. Why did you have to wait so long? I was so in love with you. Why are you trying to hurt me again? Was it not enough you hurt me the first time?"

"I know, Em, and I'm so sorry for hurting you. I wish I could take back that night, but I can't. I just want to make things right."

"Em?" His voice was so sweet, I couldn't help but gaze at him. "Do you still love me?"

"I love Jake. He's the one I want to marry," I tried to convince Max.

"I know you turned down his proposal. You might love Jake, but it can't be as strong as what we had. You don't have to answer right away. It took me this long to ask you to spend the rest of your life with me; I don't expect you to give in easily. Please consider it. Give me a reason to hope that there's still a part of you that loves me. This part could grow, and we could get back to where we were in college. It's going to take effort and hard work on my part. I am confident now that I can make this effort. I can't live without you any longer, Em. I love you and would be honored if you would be my bride."

I couldn't answer him.

I drew a blank.

I went mute.

"Emi!" I heard a shout from the other end of the Skywalk. Horrified, I retracted my hand from Max's and wiped my tear-stained cheeks. Thankfully, Max didn't fight me when I pulled him up from the ground and tried to erase the proposal that just happened.

"Sweetheart." Jake ran over and held me. He gave Max an unpleasant look. "Are you all right? What just happened?" This was a question posed more toward Max than me.

I was never more relieved to see Sarah, Charlie, and Peter running toward us. They immediately pulled Max away from me.

"Em…take your time, I'll wait…" His voice trailed, but both Jake and I heard it clearly.

"What happened, Emily? What was that all about?" Jake needed to know, but I wasn't ready to tell him. How could I explain to a man who wanted to marry me that my ex-boyfriend had just proposed? Jake would only jump to the wrong conclusion and get angry with me. I stayed in his arms, quiet.

Sarah walked over to check on me. "Do you want me to stay with you? Are you OK?"

I wanted to ask her to stay so I didn't have to face Jake alone, but I nodded my head and silently told her I was OK. She handed me my belongings and left.

"Emi, please," Jake pleaded. "Can you tell me why I saw Max on his knee?" Frustration mounted as I continued to remain silent. "*EMILY!*"

"Max just proposed to me." My head stayed down. I was even too afraid to cry.

"Why would he do that? What happened between you two yesterday? Did something happen last night?" A sound close to a roar marked his last two questions.

Alarmed, I stared at him. *How could you think such a thing?*

"What happened last night?" he asked again.

"Nothing happened last night, and as for yesterday, it was the most pleasant day we've had since Max and I broke up," I answered in an angry tone.

"Then why would he be encouraged enough to propose to you?"

As angry as I was that Jake would think so lowly of me, I knew I needed to explain everything that had led up to this proposal. Ignorance only encouraged him to jump to wrong conclusions.

"Max told me last night, he was going to propose to me after graduation but got cold feet. Then this morning, he asked if he could give me my graduation present that he'd been holding on to all these years. Well, the ring was the graduation present, and he asked me to marry him."

Jake's tightened visage relaxed in a show of obvious relief that a proposal was all that had happened. He had forgotten what he had accused me of just moments before.

"So, what did you say to him? I assume you said no, but how did you turn him down?" Jake sounded insecure when he asked this question and rightly so. What little trust he had in me right now was about to be shattered once he knew that Max and I had found no resolution. But, I believed Jake would end up listening to reason once his anger subsided, and after I turned down Max's proposal, we could get back to our own proposal. Yes, we'd weather this storm and eventually get married. I just couldn't be sure how long it would take for Jake to calm down.

"Jake...I didn't get a chance to answer Max," I confessed.

"What do you mean you didn't answer him? Emily, I don't understand."

Immediately his eyes shot daggers of pain straight into my heart. *It will be OK. Once he calms down, he'll forgive me and we'll be all right. This is only a misunderstanding. It will clear up soon.* "Jake, I'm sorry. I don't know why but I went mute. I was in such shock when he asked me...and I knew the right answer was no...but it wouldn't come out. Then you came and...I don't know what happened."

"How could you turn down my proposal without a second thought but give his proposal a second chance?" Jake cried in disbelief.

"I'm not giving him another chance. I don't want to marry him."

"Then why didn't you tell him that?" He enunciated each word in a biting tone.

"I don't know...but I will...I will as soon as I see him." The plea came out more despondent than desperate. The bright light in my life grew dim. Judging from all we'd been through in the last two months, a shutdown would be his next course of action. I tried to explain my feelings to him, but Jake ignored me like he had the morning he proposed to me. He wouldn't respond or listen to anything I had to say. He was trying to protect me from his hurtful words, but this lack of communication hurt even more.

I begged, "Please, Jake. Don't shut me out. Talk to me. Yell at me. Do whatever you want, but don't go silent on me. Please...I don't love Max. I love you. As soon as we get home, I'm going to have a talk with Max and tell him the truth. I'll clear everything up."

Nothing worked. Jake's afflicted face made me hold back, and I gave him room to think. Only a few minutes passed before he let go of my hands and walked away. Afraid to be alone I walked toward him and attempted to grab his hand. He gently pushed me away and walked into a crowd of people and out of sight. I crouched down in the middle of the Skywalk, hugging my knees to my chest, and waited for Jake to return. Once he calmed down and gathered his thoughts, I trusted he would come back and talk to me. He would reassure me that he loved me just like he had Christmas morning. *He'll be back. He'll be back soon.*

My phone rang, and I was only too happy to answer it, believing it was Jake.

"Emily, it's me, Sarah. Are you OK?"

Not knowing what to say, "I'm OK," was the lie that came out.

"Do you want us to come and get you?"

"No, I'll go back with Jake. I'll see you at home." I trusted Jake would come back for me.

"OK, call if you need anything."

"Thanks, Sarah."

Visitors came and left, and many were annoyed that I was in their way. My body didn't move. I became a part of the Grand Canyon scenery. As the hours ticked by, I thought about my life. I couldn't believe the hurt both Max and Jake were putting me through. My mind fought with my heart trying to figure out why I couldn't have answered Max's proposal sooner. I knew in my mind I didn't love Max anymore. There were no more desires or fanciful thoughts of marrying Max. We didn't have a future together. I knew in my heart that I loved Jake. Though I had refused his Christmas proposal, I would answer yes to his next proposal and live my happily ever after. All thoughts of my future only included Jake. *Jake will be here. He'll be here any moment now.*

The sun went down sooner than expected. Even my deep sadness couldn't deny Grand Canyon's majestic sunset. Jake never came back for me. Dejected, I couldn't believe he left me waiting for him. *How could he not know I'd wait?* How could he not believe all my declarations this morning? At this very moment, I understood my relationship with Jake was over. A dream, a nightmare—this was not what I had pictured. How would I salvage my relationship with Jake? Would there be a second chance?

Jake's silent walk out of my life signaled his gracious way of letting me go. Whether he was letting me go because he was tired of me and my roller coaster emotion, or so I could have a life with Max, I didn't know. What I knew for sure was that he wouldn't want to see or talk to me. My biggest fear had come true. Today, Jake woke up and realized he didn't want to love me anymore. Yes, it was my fault this time—but the fact still remained, I had been abandoned again.

The ironies of life were unending. My two offers of marriage within a week spoofed a comedy and a tragedy, as neither was viable at this point. Max's love for me destroyed my love for Jake. I could write a Shakespeare play based on my life—only child loses both parents, loses first boyfriend, first boyfriend pushes away second boyfriend, girl ends up alone, again. Almost comical…

Feeling tired and beaten up by life and love, I couldn't cry anymore. I didn't want to fall apart this time. I wanted to be strong, accept the curve ball life had thrown at me again, and move on. Of course, this was easier said than done.

"Miss? Excuse me, Miss?" I awoke to find my body still crouched in the middle of the Skywalk.

"Are you OK?" a park ranger asked. "You've been here a long time. Do you need help?"

"What time is it?" I asked, dazed and a bit confused.

"It's 6:00 p.m. We need to close the Skywalk. Are you with anyone? Do you need a ride somewhere?"

The ranger woke me up to my living nightmare—Jake had never come back for me. I was left stranded in the middle of the Grand Canyon.

"Sir, could you take me to the nearest rental car place?"

"Sure."

During the car ride, I did everything in my power not to break down and sob. I couldn't believe the man who said he wanted to take care of me the rest of my life abandoned me. I was sure he saw my friends leave. Didn't he wonder how I would get home? How could Jake leave me?

"Miss, here you are." The ranger kindly dropped me off. "Take care."

"Thank you."

At the car rental place, the first call went to Sarah.

"Sarah?"

"Emily. Where are you? Did you and Jake go back home?"

I started to cry.

Frantic, Sarah started crying with me. "What's wrong? What happened?"

"Sarah, I'm still in Arizona."

"What? Why are you still there?"

"Oh, Sarah!" My tears continued. "Jake never came back for me. He left me here by myself."

"*WHAT*?" Sarah yelled loudly. "Where exactly are you? Charlie and I will come get you."

"I'll explain it all when I get home. Right now I want to go visit my parents in Texas. Could you book a room for me at that hotel near their gravesite? You remember, the one we stayed at last time?"

"Emily, it's too far for you to drive alone. Let me go with you." Sarah was always a kind soul. She would go to great lengths for me and for that, she would always have my thanks.

"I need to be alone and figure out a few things. I'll call as soon as I get home."

"Why don't I fly out and meet you there? Let's do that."

"Thanks, Sarah but I need to do this on my own."

Chapter 10

Visiting Mom and Dad

Today was New Year's Eve, and having no one to turn to, I wanted to see my parents. As grateful as I was for Sarah's friendship, I needed to be with family. After leaving the rental agency, I drove all night, eager to be with my parents. If timed perfectly I could be there by New Year's Day and spend New Year's with them. That would give me just enough time to get back for school. This would be a great distraction from my sorry life.

Struggling to smile, I tried not to think about the pain that lodged back into my heart. I wondered if Jake was worried about me right now. Would he call soon to reconcile? Or was he so angry he simply stopped caring?

The drive through Arizona was a peaceful one. It was a bit windy at times but the serene setting was much needed and appreciated. To distract myself, I marveled at the beauty and diversity of plant life. One would never find such huge cacti in Southern California, but Arizona was filled with them at every turn. My stomach growled, signaling that it was running on empty—a highly unusual occurrence for me. Jake and Max would have both laughed at this notion.

I forced myself to think about everything but Jake. Unfortunately, when not thinking of Jake, my mind wandered to the confusion I'd caused with Max. What would I tell Max when I turned him down?

Sigh!

Thinking over all the fond memories created during college, there could be no other resolution than to tell Max that I loved him. But, no amorous love existed between us anymore. We loved each other like the five of us, Peter, Charlie, Sarah, Max, and I loved each other—as the best of friends. Max and I would always love each other since we knew no other feeling when it came to one another. A passionate love that bonded a man and a woman to live happily with one another for the rest of their lives, was not a part of us anymore. Ours was the kind of love family members shared. There was no set beginning and no direct course but it would always be there. I would always love Max, but only as a friend.

Hopefully, I could also convey that I had moved on and found a new and deeper love. One that made me feel joyful and content, safe and protected, one that I knew could be there forever. Why couldn't I have mentioned this to Max in the morning? Just a few hours earlier and I could've avoided this chaos. My fiasco with Jake forced me to view life more objectively—finally with clarity.

With Jake, I saw love in the future tense.
With Max, I saw love in the past tense.

I woke up New Year's Day in a hotel in Texas after a long drive. A pinch of hope mixed with a cup of pessimism, I checked my phone to see if I had any missed calls from Jake. There were none. Too afraid to call, I texted Jake before visiting my parents.

Happy New Year, Jake. I'm alone in Texas right now visiting my parents. My parents would have liked meeting you. You three would've gotten along well. I thought this new year would bring us closer together. I guess I botched up my own hope. My new hope is that you find it in your heart to forgive me. I'm so sorry for hurting you. I would like to share with you what's in my heart right now. Please call me.

Soon after I sent the text, my phone rang and I nearly jumped out of bed thinking that Jake was responding.

"Hello?" I answered without checking to see who was calling.

"Hi, Emily," said a cheerful voice. "It's me, Jane."

"Hi, Jane, how are you? Happy New Year." Though it wasn't Jake, my heart thrilled at the possibility of Jane calling on Jake's behalf.

"Happy New Year to you too. Where are you? Aren't you going to the chief's tailgate party? Everyone will be asking for you."

"Um, I'm in Texas right now visiting my parents' grave. Have you talked to Jake?" Would she shed some light on his feelings toward me? I could only hope.

"Yeah, I talked to him, but he wouldn't say much. He's such a grouch and a loner when things don't go his way. He's a bit moody. I figured you two must have had a fight. I warned you he's no fun when he's mad." Her words sounded so innocuous. Little did she know she and I would never become sisters.

"Jane, please tell everyone I wish them a happy New Year and have a great time."

Before visiting my parents, I stopped by the gift shop and purchased a new outfit, as I'd lived in the same clothes for three days. I also picked up a bunch of yellow Gerbera daisies my mom liked. The last time I was here was soon after Max and I broke up. I felt bad only coming to them when I was in need.

With the flowers placed in a vase beside their graves, my fingers quickly cleared away all the dried leaves that had blown onto them. Tears began trickling down my face, and soon I couldn't stop crying. I told them about my life since Max.

"Momma, Daddy. I've missed you! I'm a bit sad right now, and I needed to talk to you, so will you please hear me out for a while? I met a wonderful man two months ago. You both would have loved him. He's been so kind to me. He took me on an amazing date up to San Francisco. Mom, remember how you used to say that I had a certain look on my face when I coveted something? Well, Jake also figured out this look and gave me what I coveted every time. He told me this look was wistful. I felt so loved by him.

His family is also wonderful. Jake has a younger sister and a younger brother. His mom and dad invited me on their family trip and took me to Hawaii. I learned to scuba dive and got up once on a surfboard. They treated me like a member of their family. I hadn't felt like I was a part of any family since Dad died. When we got back from Hawaii Jake proposed to me, and stupidly, I turned him down. I didn't think I was ready.

Yesterday, it all came to a terrible end. You remember Max, don't you? Well, he also proposed to me, but I didn't turn him down even though I don't want to marry him. Jake saw everything that happened with Max, got mad, and left me. Momma, he left me stranded at the Grand Canyon. For eight hours I waited for him. He never came back.

Momma, what do I do when a boy breaks my heart this badly? You never taught me this lesson before you left. Why did you both have to leave me so early? I'm so lonely right now, and there's no one I can turn to. Maybe I was never meant to keep the love I find. Maybe anyone who's ever loved me will leave me, just like you both did. I'm sorry to come all the way over here and blame you for my woes, but I'm really mad at both of you. You're up in heaven happy with one another while I'm down here miserable by myself."

What was I doing? I snapped myself out of my childish tirade.

132

138

"I'm sorry, Mom and Dad. I'll be OK. I'm sad now but don't worry about me too much. You know I'm a survivor."

I cried on them till the sun went down.

Though physically and emotionally exhausted from all the crying, I chose to fly back home tonight. Home provided stability and warmth, and I desperately needed to be back in my own surroundings.

My phone rang many times. No doubt, they were all calls from Sarah.

"Hello?"

"Emily, are you OK? I've been trying to get a hold of you all yesterday and today. Why aren't you picking up your calls? I've been worried about you."

"Hi, Sarah. I'm sorry for worrying you. I saw my parents today, and now I'm at the airport."

"When does your flight land in LA? I'll come get you."

"I get in late. I'll catch a cab home."

"Emily, who catches a cab in LA? Text me your flight information, and I'll pick you up."

"Ok, thanks. I'll do that. See you soon. Bye."

I hung up the phone wondering when this sadness might leave me. Perhaps when I got home, Jake and I could resolve our problem and go back to loving each other again. Sadly, I believed our time was done but with forced optimism I texted him even before sending Sarah my flight information.

Hi, Jake. I'm at the airport coming home after visiting my parents. I'd hoped that you might have called by now—but you haven't. I know I messed up our relationship, but I'd really like to try to work it out with you. Please forgive me. I can't imagine how hurt you must be right now. Believe me when I tell you I love you. Please call me.

Before I hopped on the plane, I had one last call to make.

"Hi, Max."

"Em. Where are you? Sarah told me what happened. I've been worried sick about you. I'm so sorry I left you back in Arizona. Peter forced me back to LA and I had no idea that you were left stranded. What happened to Jake? How could he just leave you there?" Max's caring voice turned to anger. "Emily Anne Logan, why didn't you call me when you needed help?" He got even angrier.

"Max, I'm OK. I'm on my way home right now. I was hoping we could talk sometime soon? You and I need to resolve our issues."

"Sure. I'd like to meet with you too."

"As soon as I get back, I'll call you. Do you have a hectic school schedule this winter?"

"Yeah. School's going to be hard, but I'll make time to talk with you. Em?"

"Yes?"

"I'm sorry. I'm sorry for hurting you, and I'm sorry for taking so long to get my act together."

"I know, Max. I know you're sorry."

"Em?"

"Yes, Max."

"I love you."

"I know that too. Bye."

It felt good to have a conversation without choking up. Letting any emotion overpower common sense would result in disaster for me. From now on, I needed to find strength in myself, and only myself.

Chapter 11

Lost

The flight back was pleasant, and though I was tired, I looked forward to opening up to my best friend. Sarah came over equipped to spend the night and go to work the next morning from my house. Her wrinkled forehead and pronounced frown demonstrated her own heartache and distress for me. Between hearing bits and pieces from Max and Peter it was my turn to fill in the blanks. Whether or not I had the emotional capacity to tell the entire story, Sarah deserved to know the truth.

After a late dinner, Sarah was ready to be my crying shoulder.

"What happened? Start from the beginning when you and Max disappeared Saturday morning."

The entire story spanned from breakfast to Grand Canyon to the night we spent at the ranch.

"Sarah, did you know that Max was going to propose to me?"

"Yeah, I found out after he broke up with you. I figured it would do you no good to know this information since he was dating Jennifer."

"Did you also know that he was going to propose again?"

"No. I think Peter was the only one who knew. Peter told me he tried hard to convince him otherwise, but Max wouldn't listen. Max heard our conversation when we first got to Vegas, and he got nervous when he heard that Jake had proposed."

"I really messed up, Sarah. I don't think Jake will ever speak to me again. He was so angry and hurt when he left."

"Explain to me how he can leave you stranded for eight hours. It doesn't matter how upset he is, his actions were inexcusable." Her clipped tone matched her anger.

"I don't know what happened exactly. I'm sure he wouldn't have left me if he knew I would be alone...would he?" *No, Jake would never do that to me—regardless of the reason.* My chest felt the throbbing again.

"So what are you going to do? How do you feel about both men?"

"Max and I don't have a future together. I'll meet with him soon and let him know. I love him, but not the same way he loves me."

"As for Jake, I've tried to contact him, but he won't respond. I don't know what to do."

Sarah and I talked deep into the night and by the time I got up; she had left me breakfast and a kind note.

Emily, regardless of what happens, I love you!

Ready to start the new school year, I jumped out of bed and mustered up every ounce of excitement. As a New Year's resolution, I decided I would not cry anymore and would work toward being a strong person. It was no man's duty to take care of me. That would be my job alone. I had been on my own before, and it was time to do this again.

I also decided nothing was final with Jake. There was still hope he would come around. He was just taking a bit longer than usual to calm himself down. As soon as my resolution to be a stronger person was set, laughter followed as I texted Jake before leaving for school.

Hi, Jake. School starts for me today. I'm quite relieved to have twenty-four kids clutter my mind from now on. I see that you haven't found it in your heart to forgive me yet. It makes me sad, but I understand. I still have hope that your love for me will win over your anger toward me. I hope you are doing well. I miss you. I love you.

The first day back to school, it rained, the kids acted like goons and I wondered why I became a teacher. For the first time in a week, I didn't check my phone twenty times in the morning to see if Jake had texted back, and my mind was preoccupied with everyone else's problems. My kids at school were the solution to my problems.

Every day I came to school looking forward to new joys, new issues, and a respite from my love life, or a lack thereof. I ignored calls from Jane and Max and concentrated my efforts on my kids. Of course, the call I wouldn't ignore never came. My day started at 6:30 am and didn't end till after sundown. Throwing myself into work helped ease the hurt, somewhat. Sarah called daily to check up on me, but every phone call only acknowledged the call that never came. Neither of us spoke his name. Sarah saw through my pretend bravado and tried to come over as often as possible. Since she lived and worked almost an hour away, the only way to discourage her was for me to stay at work even later. My students were the only beneficiaries of my pathetic life.

My texts to Jake continued. I looked at it as a daily page in the diary. More than anything, I missed talking to him and it made me feel a little less lonely texting him—like I was still a part of his life.

Of course the lack of response mocked my lonely heart.

Hi, Jake. How are you doing? I hope you are not working too hard. What a silly thing to say, of course you are working hard. I, too, have been working hard at school. Today was an ugly day, as my student Jimmy got sick and threw up on me. It's been a while since we last spoke. Wow, you can hold a grudge. I thought you might have responded by now. I know I hurt you and don't have a right to say this, but I hurt, too, as you don't respond to any of my messages. Please call.

Today, I got another phone call from Jane. This time I chose not to ignore it. She had been patient enough. I didn't want to run away from her just like Jake was running away from me.

"Emily! Where have you been?" Jane asked in utter exasperation.

"Jane. I'm sorry. I've been really busy with school," I fibbed. She saw right through me, even though we were on the phone.

"Don't lie to me. It's because of Jake, huh? I finally got Jake to give me some answers, and all I could figure out was that you two weren't seeing each other anymore."

Heaven came crashing down. Tears automatically poured from my eyes. Jake had told his sister we were no longer together. Why hadn't it occurred to me that we had broken up? Simple as that—we were no longer boyfriend and girlfriend. In my optimistic mind, we were still together, just working out a kink in the relationship. The tears continued in response to this truth—Jake no longer wanted me. That was why there had been no response to my texts. I felt stupid for realizing this so late. I sat quiet for a while.

"Emily, I just e-mailed your plane ticket. You're coming to see me this holiday weekend."

"Huh?"

"Remember you promised to come spend the weekend with me? You promised!"

Was it that time already?

"Jane, I don't think it's a good idea. Your brother will be there…"

"No, he won't," she cut me off. "I know for a fact that he's working this weekend and I won't tell him that you're coming. Will you *please* come?"

I did want to spend some time with Jane, as she was my last link to Jake. It was wrong of me to do this, but if Jake wouldn't listen to me, I wanted to at least tell Jane everything that was in my heart.

"Are you still there, Emily?"

"Yeah, I'm here. Jane, I'll go if you promise not to tell your brother that I'll be there, not that he'll care. As soon as I get home, I'll buy a ticket."

"Don't be silly. This is the ticket my dad purchased for you back when you first said you'd visit. It's yours. Only caveat, it's a red-eye early Friday morning."

"All right, I'll see you in a couple of days. Bye."

Excited to see Jane and to get some of this grief off my chest, my mind raced throughout the night wondering what to say first. I know I promised to be strong, and I had been. I hadn't cried...much; nor wallowed in my sorrows...much; nor looked for texts that never came...much. But, I needed to vent. I'd ignored my hurt and frustration too long. Jane would be my shoulder to cry on this weekend and afterward I would start the healing process. If Jake had closed me out of his life, I needed closure as well.

Authoring one last text to Jake, I promised myself not to bother him anymore. Obviously he was either irritated by me, ignoring me, or wasn't receiving my texts because he changed his number to get away from the stalker who was me. It was probably all of the above.

Hi, Jake. I spoke with Jane a few days ago and she told me you said we were no longer seeing each other. I don't know why it never occurred to me you didn't want to be with me anymore. I sent all those texts thinking you still cared for me. I understand, and I don't blame you. I'm sorry I've continually bothered you. This will be my final text. I want to say I'm sorry one last time and ask you to forgive me. You have been nothing but kind and loving, and I've only returned it with pain and uncertainty. I want you to know you are the only man I love. I wish I had figured this out sooner. Be well.

Pain burned in my chest while writing this last text. I sobbed uncontrollably and went into hysterics. It hurt knowing that Jake could let go of me so quickly. Nervously twirling the eternity band around my finger, reality set in that the ring needed to come off. We would not love each other eternally. I guess I didn't mean as much to him as I'd believed. We had both hurt each other badly.

Chapter 12

The End

With no one left to text, my cell phone stayed at home and I boarded the plane bound for JFK. Although my seat was more than comfortable, I couldn't sleep. Part giddy, part scared to see Jane, it was anyone's guess what Jane's reaction would be once she found out about the love triangle that should never have been. Our friendship, our promised sisterhood, was all in jeopardy.

I landed in JFK early Friday morning and found myself in familiar territory, as Jane had sent a car to pick me up. Of course, only a Reid would be so considerate and generous. The driver dropped me off at a beautiful old building in Soho. Jane lived in a two-bedroom spacious apartment—spacious by New York standards. As soon as I arrived, Jane took my bags to the guest room, sat on the sofa, and grilled me about past events. Neither my grogginess from the plane ride nor the nausea from lack of food mattered. She needed to hear my story.

"Emily, my mom and I are going bonkers trying to figure out what happened between you and Jake. He's hardly ever home anymore, and when he is, he will not say a word to Mom. Can you please fill in all the blanks? Please?"

At first I thought it was just curiosity, but I soon realized that Jane and Sandy were desperate to understand Jake. I felt obliged to tell her everything.

"Oh, Jane. Where do I begin?" The well broke immediately. Jane ran over with a box of Kleenex.

I started to babble incoherently. "During my trip to Vegas, my ex-boyfriend, Max, proposed to me. He was my college sweetheart, and I thought that we would get married after graduation. He, too, intended to marry me, but got cold feet on graduation day, and didn't propose as expected. He broke my heart. I was broken for almost two years till I met your brother.

Apparently, Max had this engagement ring since graduation day, and he was tormented about breaking up with me. He decided during our road trip to propose and to try to win me back."

Jane looked thoroughly confused.

I took a deep breath and tried to calm myself down.

"Let me backtrack a little. The morning we came back from Hawaii, before the road trip, your brother proposed to me in his car, on the way home. Did you know this?"

Jane's mouth dropped, and for the first time, I saw her speechless.

She finally asked, "What did you say to him?"

"At that time, I said, no. I thought it was way too early. We had just started dating, and it scared me that your brother was so sure about his commitment toward me. To be honest, I doubted his love. I was scared he would one day wake up and decide he didn't love me anymore—just like what happened with Max."

"Your insecurities again?"

I nodded yes. "Jane, Max pretty much mauled my heart. It was so damaged. I didn't think that I would ever recover. Knowing this, caution was my guide. Possibly, a too eager of a guide, for Jake's liking."

Every time Jake told me he loved me, I was too frugal with my love. Frustration and hurt must have built up inside of him.

"Anyhow, Max and I visited the Grand Canyon, and kind of got stuck there. He used this time to stun me with a proposal and between the confusion of this proposal, and with Jake questioning me about what had just occurred, the answer that should have been no, never came out. I still haven't answered him."

Jane looked at me with sympathetic eyes.

"Jake came at that very moment to the Skywalk to witness Max on his knees proposing to me. He first assumed that something improper happened between Max and me the night before, then he was livid when he saw the proposal. But more than livid, he was hurt when I told him I hadn't given Max an answer yet. Of course, that's when he went into shutdown mode and stopped talking to me." The tears came back like a hurricane. "He left me, Jane. He walked away and never came back. I waited for him for eight hours in the middle of the Skywalk thinking he would return for me. I'm such an idiot, huh? Why am I so naïve all the time? After a couple of hours, I should have known it was over." My face fell into my hands and I cried again for a while. The tears wouldn't abate. "You want to hear what's even more idiotic? I've been texting him every day hoping, believing, trusting his love for me would prove stronger than his anger toward me. He hasn't responded...not once."

Jane looked horrified at my confession. "Even still, I miss him so much, Jane. Why was I so stupid and insecure about us? After all those weeks together, I only got up the courage to confess my love to Jake on Christmas day. He was ecstatic when I told him that I loved him." My own confession tricked me into an aching smile. The image of Jake staring in adoration and amazement at my profession of love brought a split second of happiness.

"To the wrong guy I gave my heart so freely, and yet to the right one, I was so stingy with my heart. What I'd do to talk to him one more time and tell him how I feel." My tears went everywhere. I had been holding back this dam for too long. It didn't take much pressure for it to break. Jane rubbed my back with her hands and tried to console me. It was useless. No one could console me.

Finally, I calmed down enough to answer some of Jane's questions.

"So why could you answer my brother's proposal but not Max's proposal? Do you still love Max and my brother?"

I knew the answer to this but wasn't comfortable admitting this to even myself. Max had been my true love for so long; I didn't want to erase his place in my heart.

"No. I don't love Max anymore. I haven't loved him in a long time. I realized after Jake left me that the way I loved Max was purely platonic. You know, like the love you feel for your family or best friend. I met Max and fell in love with him soon after my mom died. Not having a family, he became my only family for four years. If Max had proposed, I would've said yes and we would be living a happy life right now, I'm sure. But he didn't, and I let go of the physical love a long time ago. Only, I just couldn't let go of the bond that existed between us. However, I only love him like family—no more, no less. And I now understand it's not wrong for me to love him this way. He was my best friend, and in many ways, he still holds a dear place in my heart. That will never change."

It felt good to say this to someone. The truth finally came out.

"That's how I feel about you too. I love you like a sister." Jane hugged me in response to those words.

"Does this make any sense, Jane, or have I gone crazy?"

"I'm still a bit fuzzy on why you couldn't answer Max right away."

"In all honesty, there just wasn't a chance to say no. It all happened so fast. Max proposed; I got angry at him for doing this two years too late; your brother came and pulled me away; we got into an argument; and next thing I knew, I was alone."

"So, if you got a chance to talk to Jake..." Jane shook her head and stopped her train of thought. "...no, let me put it this way...if Jake asks you to marry him again, what will you do?"

That was an easy answer...now. "When I said no to Jake the first time, I knew it was only a matter of time before I accepted his proposal. I *love* your brother but I was scared back then. Now, if I got another chance, there's no way I'd let him go. But, that's just wishful thinking. When you called me about this weekend, I told myself this was my chance to let out all the pain and start letting go."

"Emily!" Jane pleaded. "Don't do this to yourself. We promised to be sisters." She lightly smiled and wiped away my tears. "Jake can be stubborn, but I know he's dying inside right now without you. He'll come around."

"No. He's made himself pretty clear. Since he told you we weren't seeing each other, I don't know what else to think but that he's moved on. All this time, I thought that we were still together, just going through a rough patch. I'm such an idiot. It never occurred to me that in his mind, we had broken up. He's probably so tired of my emotional ups and downs. He probably thinks that I'm a serious nut job."

We both chuckled.

"Emily, Jake didn't say in those words that you guys had broken up. You need to understand something. Jake shuts down completely when he's upset. It drives my mom batty that he stops talking to her when something sets him off. When we were younger, if he thought that he was wronged somehow, he would march up to his room and not talk to anyone for days. I guess old habits die hard. I thought he might have grown out of this by now."

"He might have shut down on me initially, but I really think he's moved on with his life. I've been nothing but heartache to him."

The truth hurt.

"Jane, will you do me a favor?"

"Sure," she answered gladly.

"Please don't repeat any of this to Jake or to any member of your family."

"Why not? Shouldn't Jake know how you feel?"

"Yeah, he should, but evidently he doesn't want to know. If he does have a chance to hear it, I'd like for him to hear it from me. Please?" I begged.

"Oh, all right! I'll keep my mouth shut. By the way, you must be starving. Let's go get something to eat."

We filled the rest of the day with food, sightseeing, food, shopping, and more food. We attempted to go see a show, but my lack of sleep snuck up on me in the cab on the way to the show. Jane turned the cab around and headed back to her apartment. Sleep—which had avoided me since Christmas night—became my best friend tonight.

Early the next morning, the phone rang, and Jane yelled so loudly I quickly ran to her room to see what was going on. She began apologizing as I calmed her down.

"That was Nick on the phone. Jake and Nick are in town and they're on their way here. I'm so sorry, Emily. Please believe me when I say that I didn't know that they were coming. I checked with my mom, and she told me that Jake was scheduled to work all weekend."

My knees buckled at the thought of seeing Jake again. I panicked and ran to the guest room and started packing my belongings.

"Emily, I'm so sorry!" Jane began crying.

I comforted her and told her not to worry. Of course I trusted Jane. I knew that she wouldn't trick me into coming to New York to meet up with her brother.

"Jane, it's OK. I'll leave."

"Emily," she cried some more. "No. Don't go. This is your chance to talk to Jake and resolve your problems. You have nowhere else to go. Please stay!"

She could tell by my doubtful expression that her words were not convincing.

"Where will you go? Don't you want to clear up this misunderstanding?"

"I don't know where I'll go. And yes, I'd like to go back to my life before Christmas, but I think what's between me and Jake is a bit more than a misunderstanding," I answered as curtly but politely as possible, trying to squelch any emotion, lest I cry again. "I'll call you when I figure it out."

I had no idea where I would go. To a hotel? Back home? As much as I wanted to see Jake one more time, I didn't think my feeble heart could handle it. I thought it best to leave before they arrived.

Ding Dong.

Too late. My heart beat a million times a second. I felt faint and nauseous again. My face turned red from the tears I held back and my body began to shake. The moment I had dreamt of for the last three weeks crept up on me in the last thirty minutes. How was I going to handle seeing Jake without crying? I wanted to be strong but didn't know how.

"What are you doing here?" Jane yelled after slamming the door.

"What's gotten into you?" That sounded like Nick fighting back.

"Why didn't you let me know you were coming?"

"We did. That's why we called when we landed at JFK. Why are you so angry we're here? I have some good news. Jake agreed to keep our reservation at Masa so we're basically here to eat dinner. We're both leaving first thing tomorrow morning."

"It might have helped if you had called." Jane was still angry.

"We left at midnight. That's three in the morning your time. I didn't think that you'd appreciate that call. Anyhow, why are you really angry? Are you hiding a boy in the other room? Is that why you're so upset? It's all right. I won't tell Mom."

Nick continued to speak and I didn't hear Jake outside so I thought maybe he hadn't arrived yet. Thinking the coast was clear I got my suitcase and came out of the guest room. Everyone—Jane, Nick, and Jake—stopped talking and stared at me. Though I saw Jake, I didn't look at him. My eyes stayed on the ground until Nick came to give me a hug.

"Emily, when did you get here? It's so great to see you!" His bear hug reminded me of my first encounter with the Reid family. It was so warm and loving.

"Um, I um got here yesterday," I stammered.

"Why do you have your suitcase in your hand? Are you going somewhere?"

"Yeah, I was just leaving. It was nice seeing all of you."

I gave Jane a quick hug and darted for the door. As I opened the door, I could hear Nick calling me back saying, "Emily, don't go. We're going to Masa for dinner. You have to join us."

Jane simultaneously yelled at Jake. "Jake, you're such a jerk! How could you leave Emily stranded in Arizona? Why are you ignoring her when she's been trying to get a hold of you for weeks? How can you be so cold? How do you propose to Emily and then completely disregard her? That's not love."

Not able to endure any more, I shut the door and ran down the hallway, half hoping Jake would follow me, and half scared he wouldn't. I got in the elevator and ran out the front door, walking as fast as I could to the biggest intersection to catch a cab. Nearing the end of the block, I heard the voice that stopped my heart.

"Emily!" Jake yelled out at me.

I stopped in my tracks. His one word paralyzed me. *I have to be strong and not let him break my heart again.* My legs wanted to buckle under and collapse to the ground. *I'm not going to cry, I'm not going to cry.* This was all I could promise while he ran over to me. I flailed my arms, caught a cab, and started putting my suitcase in when Jake caught up with me. He started our conversation with much tenderness in his eyes and love in his voice. I wanted to fall into his arms and tell him how much I loved him...just how terribly I missed him.

"Emily. Please, don't go." He grabbed my hand and tried to get me to take my suitcase out of the taxi.

"I should leave. You three have a great time."

"I feel terrible interrupting you and Jane, but I'm glad you're here. You didn't mention you were coming to see my sister... Regardless, we need to talk." So I guess he did read my texts. He just didn't feel the need to respond. Why would he? Why should he?

"Emily, what was Jane talking about me leaving you in Arizona?"

I didn't answer him because I felt foolish waiting for a man who never returned for me.

"Answer me! What was she talking about?" He soon did an about-face once Arizona became a part of the conversation. He remembered our abrupt ending.

"What do you care?" I answered shutting the trunk.

"Tell me!" he demanded, but quickly softened. "Please?"

"I waited for you to return," was all I wanted to say, hoping he would let me go without asking any more questions.

"What do you mean you waited for me to return? For how long?"

I stayed silent.

"Damn it, Emily, how long did you wait for me?" His icy demeanor melted as soon as he saw tears well up in my eyes. Though he demanded, he knew he didn't want to know my answer.

"...till it closed," I answered quietly, hoping he wouldn't hear.

"What?" Terror struck him. He understood what he had done. "How could you have waited for me till closing time? Didn't you realize after a while I wasn't coming back? It was freezing that day. You didn't even have a jacket on." His voice began with regret, only to hurt me with his next question. "How stupid can you be?"

How can you be observant enough to notice I didn't have on a jacket that day but not observant enough to know I would be waiting for you? Tears kept surging but I forced them back just long enough.

"Yeah, I was stupid all right." I was angry right back at him.

"Stupid enough to believe you when you said you loved me and wanted to spend the rest of your life with me. Stupid enough to trust your words when you told me you would never let me be alone again. Stupid enough to think that the man I wanted to spend the rest of my life with wouldn't abandon me—that after he calmed down—would come back for me. That's how stupid I was."

He groaned my name in anguish. "I left you by yourself at the Skywalk? You mean you didn't go home with Max?" He really sounded tormented at this point. "I'm sorry, Emily. I didn't mean to leave you there. You know I would never abandon you. I really thought you were with your friends. I can't believe I did that to you. How did you get home? Oh, Emi." He moved closer to embrace me but I pushed him away.

"I don't want your sorry or your pity. My breakup with Max was a walk in the park compared to what you put me through. You made yourself clear by not returning for me, and by not returning any of my messages. I was right to doubt your love. There was no way you could have loved me as much as you said you did!" Tears went everywhere as I fumbled to take off the ring I didn't want to let go. "Here! I don't think this belongs to me anymore." I handed him the ring not so gently as I heard it clang onto the cement and roll down the sidewalk.

I saw a torn look on Jake's face trying to decide whether to chase after the ring or keep an eye on me who was halfway in the cab. He chose the ring.

"JFK" was all I could say to the cab driver before I began hyperventilating.

Chapter 13

Time to Say Good-bye

The flight back home gave me a chance to calm down and think through the conversation I needed to have with Max. I hoped that I wouldn't lose him as a friend after our talk. We were past the point of marrying each other, but he would always be part of my intimate circle of friends.

Once home, I took a last look at my cell phone before shutting it off for good. Fifteen missed calls lit up the screen. Even Jake had called, no doubt feeling guilty about leaving me in Arizona. I chose not to listen or read any of them. Where I was going, there would be no need for a cell phone, and dwelling on my life here would do me no good. I texted back a simple message letting Jane know that I was OK.

Just got home. Thanks for being my friend. Enjoy your dinner. Tell Nick I'm sad I missed it.

She immediately texted back.

I need to talk to you. CALL ME!!!

I ignored the last part. Of course, she called right away, but I declined the call.

One unreturned phone call still haunted me.

"Hi, Max. It's me, Em. I'm sorry it's taken me so long to get back to you. How are you?"

"I'm busy, but doing well. How are you doing?"

"I'm doing ok, I think." I hated lying to people, but lying was the easiest way to get out of drawn-out explanations.

"Are you ready to talk, Em? Can I come over?"

"Yeah, I'm home. Come over if you're not too busy. Or, I can come to you."

"I'll come to you. Have you had dinner?"

"No."

"I'll bring something over. See you soon. Bye."

I sensed a change in Max's tone during this conversation. Peaceful? Yes, he sounded more peaceful talking to me. Perhaps this conversation wasn't going to be as hard as I expected.

Max came over within the hour and we had dinner. We had gone through almost a pot of coffee before I found the courage to bring up the topic of us. In the meantime, we conversed about his school year and all his classes. He told me that he wanted to be a pediatrician, and wanted to eventually go overseas and help children in impoverished countries. I could see that Max had matured since our college days. He knew what he wanted out of life, and he was willing to give more to life than take from it. He had found his peace.

"Max. I'm happy to hear about your plans. When did you decide all this? And what brought on this change?"

"I did some soul searching after Vegas, and realized that I wanted to make use of being a doctor. So many children don't have proper medical care. I want to go and help these kids. My mind is finally settled on what I want to do the rest of my life. The question is, will *you* be there with me?"

"Max. I've been doing a lot of soul searching as well, and let me share my heart with you. That morning on the Skywalk, a lot happened to me after you proposed. Did you know Jake saw you propose to me?"

Max shook his head no.

"Because I turned down his proposal but not yours, he got upset and left me. We are no longer together."

Max looked guilty and surprised.

"Since then, I've been thinking about us and what you mean to me. You know I still love you." This brought a smile to Max's boyish good looks. "I still love you, Max, but not the same way I did back in college. If you think about it, you and I know no other feeling for each other. We saw each other our freshman year, and boom, we were in love. I don't know what it's like not to love you. But, sometime even before I met Jake, my love for you changed. There was no more physical love. I just continued to love you like my family or best friend. You have always been like family and one of my very best friends. That's how I love you and that's the only way I see us staying."

Max looked hurt.

"When I think of the past, I reminisce about us and smile. When I think of the future, the only person I see is Jake. I'm sorry, but I have to say no to your proposal. My big regret is that I didn't tell you this back in Arizona."

"Em, think about it some more. You and I loved each other deeply for four years. It can't be over for us. I know I haven't been fair to you. I understand now what you meant when you told me the other day that you always thought you loved me more than I loved you. I never fully showed you how I felt. I didn't think I needed to. I just assumed you knew. Truly, my love for you was over and abundant. Let me show you this love, now and for the rest of our lives. Please, reconsider."

"Max. Not to make you feel any worse, but I wish you had told me and shown me these feelings when we were in college. I would have been a lot less paranoid." Max gave me a regretful smile. I accepted this as an apology.

"I don't think you love me anymore either, not in that way. Jake brought out a jealous side of you. I was jealous too when I first saw you with Jennifer. It's only natural."

Max tried to argue with me, but I didn't let him continue.

"I think both of us couldn't let go of the thought of being in love with each other. And I'm happy I got to share such a special bond with you. I can't marry you, but I'd still like for us to stay good friends. Would you be OK with that? I really missed you, and I need your friendship more than anything right now."

I moved over and hugged him.

"I don't know, Em. You might have moved on, but I'm still where we left off two years ago. I guess your friendship will do for now. It feels weird to finally have this all out in the open."

"I know, I feel weird too. We finally have closure. We should have done this a long time ago." I sighed.

"Wait, so tell me about Jake. You two aren't together anymore? Why did he leave you stranded in Arizona?"

I didn't really want to relive me and Jake. My head felt battered, and my heart felt bruised.

"I think he got tired of my crazy life. If only I had known sooner he was the only man I loved, I wouldn't be in such a predicament. Only after he left me did I realize this. As for Arizona, he thought I was with you so he didn't come back for me." I didn't know if I truly believed this explanation, but it was the lesser of the two evils—that he didn't return because he didn't care anymore.

"So you haven't spoken with him at all?"

"Well, I actually ran into him in New York this morning. Jane sent me a ticket to come see her, and I left yesterday planning to stay till Monday, until Jake and Nick surprised Jane and showed up at her apartment. We were all in shock. I left, obviously, but got a chance to end everything with Jake in person. He was in a state of shock when I told him that I had waited all day for him. I think he felt really guilty."

"Well, what did he say when you explained everything?"

"I don't know. I got into a cab and left."

"What did you do that for? Weren't you curious to know what was going on in Jake's mind?"

"No, I figured he had moved on with his life. I felt like a stalker with all my texts. A big part of me didn't want to know what he was thinking. It was better not to get hurt again. I'm so done being hurt by you men," I said pointing my finger at Max.

"Oh, Em. Why do I keep doing this to you? I guess I owe you another apology. Not only did I break your heart the first time, I broke it again by making Jake go away. I'm sorry." Max leaned in to hug me, but his hug did little to console me.

"It's not your fault. I created this mess. One good thing came out of this fiasco. Jake's absence forced me to look at my feelings objectively. My head is clear, even if my heart is mangled. I'll be OK."

"Em. I wish I could make everything better for you."

"I know. I know you care and want to help." I forced a smile.

The phone rang, relieving my heart of this awkward conversation. It was Sarah. She sounded ecstatic.

"Emily! You're home! Can Charlie and I come over?"

"Sure. What's going on?"

"We have exciting news. See you soon." She hung up immediately.

"What was that all about?"

"Not quite sure. Sarah is excited about who knows what, and she and Charlie are coming over. Maybe they're finally engaged. Wouldn't that be wonderful?"

That really would be wonderful. Sarah had been looking forward to this day since high school. I hoped this was true for her. I couldn't wish marriage on a better person.

It took no more than ten minutes for Sarah and Charlie to knock on my door. She was bouncing up and down, elated about her engagement to Charlie. She showed me her diamond ring and couldn't wipe the bliss off her face. Her ring reminded me of the engagement ring Jake bought for me in Hawaii. My heart ached, but my faced glowed with joy. My best friend deserved many blessings.

"I'm thrilled for you, Sarah! And Charlie, good job on the ring. How did you keep this from all of us? I surely thought you would need my help pulling off a proposal. So how did you propose?" I asked Charlie.

"Well, we were up in Napa this weekend," said Charlie.

The word Napa made me wince, as I remembered my time up there with Jake. We had made so many indelible memories during our two months together.

Sarah continued the story. "We got on a hot air balloon. The scenery was breathtaking, though I feared we might fall off and die. I also got a bit airsick. I was about to throw up over the balloon when Charlie got down on one knee and proposed. What timing. My body was practically convulsing trying to keep down the upchuck, and he's on his knee asking me to spend the rest of my life with him."

"Oh, Sarah. Ew. It's romantic and gross at the same time. But I'm happy for you. You deserve it." I hugged Sarah and Charlie at the same time. My best friend was getting married.

"Of course, I want you to be my maid of honor."

"I would be honored. So when's the wedding?"

"Memorial Day weekend...this year."

"What? That's four and a half months away. Why so soon?"

"Charlie got a job up north and we'll be separated as of June. I didn't want to plan this wedding without him. We've booked the wedding and reception already. I just need to find a dress, and the rest is easy." Sarah beamed with joy. I felt terrible having to rain on her parade.

"I have some bad news, Sarah." Ugh, what terrible timing. "I'm leaving for Japan in ten days and I don't come back till mid-June. Of course, I'll be back for the wedding, but I can't help you with much of the planning. I'm so sorry. I'd understand if you wanted to ask someone else to take my place in the wedding."

"Why are you going to Japan, and for five months?"

"I applied for a job teaching English last year, and they called me to tell me that there's an opening. I'm going to take a leave of absence at my current school and go abroad for a few months."

"How are you going to be away from all of us for so long? You'll be so lonely. You hate being alone."

"I know. I'm really going to miss you all." I glanced and saw the guilt in Max's eyes. "This isn't your fault. I applied for this position awhile ago, and it's finally happened. It's something I've wanted to do for a while," I explained while putting my arms around him.

Without a word, he left the house. Charlie went after him.

"Emily, does Jake know you're leaving?"

"I just got the call today. You guys are the first to know. I doubt Jake will care that I'm leaving. I don't think he would cut off all ties with me if he still cared."

Another apology was in order for the bride to be. "I'm really sorry I can't be there to help you plan your dream wedding. I feel selfish and guilty for leaving you."

"Don't be ridiculous. You've been nothing but a dear friend. I'm glad you know what you want. Go and get away for a while. Go clear your head and come back rejuvenated. Jake's an idiot for treating you this poorly. How he could ask you to marry him, and then disregard you so easily, is beyond me."

"It hurts to think of it that way, but I don't blame him. I hurt him badly. I was greedy and wanted both men to love me. That wasn't acceptable and I agree with him. I deserve it. I never thought he would cut me off so coldly...he promised me that he wouldn't let me be alone anymore... let's not talk about this."

Sarah agreed. We both said at the same time, "Let's talk wedding."

We talked endlessly about dresses and themes and flowers. As soon as the sun rose, we were going to hit every bridal shop. Sarah was going to be the most beautiful bride. With only one week to help Sarah create her dream wedding, we were determined to get as much of it done as possible.

My principal graciously gave me the second semester off and there was no issue getting a visa on such short notice. I bought my plane ticket and to my good fortune, a businesswoman from India wanted to rent my house immediately till the end of summer. That took care of my worries about having to pay my mortgage out of my savings account. Everything fell into place for me to leave. I was also glad that I got a chance to go visit my parents before leaving for my extended trip. I hoped they weren't too sad at how life turned out for me. I would be OK.

Since all of Jane's messages went unanswered, this was a loose end I needed to tie up before leaving. I knew I was hurting her the same way her brother hurt me, but I couldn't call her. If I called and she asked me not to leave for Japan, there was a good chance I'd listen to her and stay. She was not only my dear friend, but also my closest link to Jake. But, she was not Jake, and I couldn't deviate from my plan. More than anything, I needed to get away and heal myself. Peace became a necessity. Japan would be my place of respite.

It made me sad to leave Jane without a proper explanation, but this was for the best. She would be fine with or without me. She might even be better off if I weren't around. There was no telling what kind of strife I was causing between the siblings. Tomorrow morning, I would tie up the last loose end and leave for my new life.

Unable to get a good night's rest, I rose before the sun, packed the rest of my clothes, and sat down to write Jake's letter. Even though he probably didn't want to hear from me, I wanted to say good-bye.

January 27

Dear Jake,

I'm sorry we had such an abrupt ending in New York, but it makes me happy to know I saw you one last time. You're probably wondering why I'm writing you a letter all of a sudden. With much hesitation, I thought it'd only be proper to say good-bye. Since you don't answer any of my calls, I decided to send you a letter instead.

By the time you get this, I'll be on my way to Japan. I got a wonderful job teaching English in a small village. My principal was kind enough to let me take off the rest of the year.

Please accept my apologies one last time. You were truly the one person who understood me like my mom and dad. I will miss that sense of belonging. Please thank your family for their kindness toward me. For the first time in a very long time, I felt like I was part of a family. I will miss that as well. I hope you found the eternity band. I'm sorry I threw it at you in New York. I'm also sorry I kept it so long. That ring made me feel like I was still a part of your life. I know now it was inappropriate to think this way. Although the band couldn't hold true to its name for us, I hope you will find someone who will wear the ring with confidence, knowing that you two can love each other eternally.
Thank you for loving me. You've touched my heart deeply. I take many beautiful memories of us to a foreign place. Be well.

Fondly,
Emi

With the letter sealed in an envelope, Sarah drove me to the hospital so I could drop it off before leaving for LAX. On the way, I also called Max to say good-bye, and I told him that I would write.

Chief Reid's grin greeted me in the foyer of the hospital. "Emily. What a wonderful surprise!" The chief hugged me.

"Hi, Chief. How have you been?" I asked politely.

"I'm great, now that I see you. Where have you been hiding yourself? I keep asking Jake about you, but he won't give me a straight answer."

"Oh, I've been around, here and there, but nowhere in particular. Could I ask you for a favor, Chief?"

"Sure, anything."

"Could you give this to Jake for me?" I asked handing him the envelope.

"Why don't you come up to OR and hand it to him yourself? He should be out of surgery soon."

"I'm actually going out of town and have a plane to catch. If you could give this to him, I'd be grateful."

"Emily, come on up. Jake has been really upset with me for keeping you two apart, he says. You'd help me get back in favor with him if I brought you up to see him. He will be out any minute now."

Desired. Craved. Longed.

That's what I'd felt since breaking up with Jake. I followed Chief Reid up to OR like a helpless sheep looking for her shepherd. My mind yelled at me to get out of the elevator and to head straight for the airport, but my heart hoped for another chance with Jake. We got off the third floor and the chief had me wait with one of the nurses while he went to find Jake.

Nervously, I stood at the station. I didn't know whether it would be better to see Jake and possibly be rejected again or not to see Jake and never know the answer. From down the hall, I saw him looking at a chart, walking my way. He would reach me in seconds, though he had no idea I was standing there. It took all the strength I had not to throw myself at Jake and beg him to love me again. I thought maybe I could persuade him to reconsider our relationship.

Suddenly, I woke up to the reality of no communication for three weeks and our disastrous meeting in New York. He wouldn't want to see me, and I didn't need another heartbreak. I left the letter at the nurse's desk without any explanation, and ran into an open elevator. As it shut, I caught a glimpse of him looking straight at me and the tears fell without warning. Stupid! Stupid! Stupid! Why had I done this to myself again? Why?

Trying to regain composure, I stayed in the lobby briefly before going out to see Sarah.

"Where were you and who was that?" Sarah questioned.

"That was Jake's uncle. I asked him to give the letter to Jake, but I was stupid enough to follow him to the third floor where Jake would be."

"Did you see him?" Sarah looked happy for me.

"Yeah...but I left before he could see me." I wanted to sound casual though I knew I had failed.

"Emily. Do you want to go back and see Jake before you leave? We have some time before your plane takes off."

Truth be told, I desperately wanted to see Jake one last time. My heart hoped if he saw me, he would welcome me back into his life. Maybe he would even tell me he missed me. I knew I would be crushed when my hope remained only that—a hope.

"No, Sarah. What good will that do? I'd only be hurting myself again. I just wished I knew how much I loved Jake before Max proposed. I didn't realize losing him would be this hard. Let's go."

At the airport, Sarah and I said good-bye and I handed her my contact number.

"This is the phone number to the place where I'm going to stay. I'll call you often to get updates on the wedding. There will be no cell or e-mail access, and when I write letters to people, I'm not sending a return address. Will you promise me you won't tell anyone, not even Charlie, that you have my contact info? Please promise me."

Sarah appeared annoyed with me. "Must you go to this length to forget a man? You're so ridiculous. I have a good mind to call Jake and chew him out for forcing you into solitude. You'll be so lonely there by yourself. Don't do this. You don't have to go."

"Sarah, I want to go," was all I said, walking toward my new life.

Chapter 14
Finding Emily

February 1

Dear Jake,

I'm sure you don't want to hear from me but I thought I should write at least once to tell you that I am doing well. I finally got settled into Mr. and Mrs. Suzuki's home. They have two children named Yuki and Ryu, whom I will be tutoring till June.

When I first got to their house, it made me chuckle to think that their entire house could fit into your bedroom. My room is a quarter the size of your bathroom. I guess everything here is compact.

The village is peaceful. There aren't too many cars here. We either walk from place to place or people scooter around. The school that I work at is nearby. Since all I do is go from school to tutoring, I do a lot of walking.

I hope that you are doing well. Please say hello to your parents and Chief Reid for me. And please apologize to Gram for me. Let her know I really wanted to meet her, and though I'd only spoken with her once, she made a wonderful impression on my heart. Take care.

Emily

February 2

Dear Jane,

Please forgive me for not having called before I left. I couldn't get myself to talk to you after I saw Jake in New York. I'm in Japan right now teaching English. I don't know when I'll come back home. I hope you'll understand when I tell you I want to sever all ties with home for a while.

I've made such a mess of everything. I have so many regrets—turning down your brother's proposal so quickly, not turning down Max's quickly enough, but the biggest regret I have was never having shown Jake how much I loved and appreciated him. I always knew deep inside he was the one for me. Why was I so scared to admit this to anyone?

Even though I didn't get a chance to fully tell him about my love, I hope he got a good sense of it when he read my journal. I gave him my journal as his Christmas present. I hope my writing clearly illustrated these emotions.

Thank you for being such a good friend. When I get strong enough, you will be the first one I send a return address to. Until then, I'll write...you read. Take care.

Emily

February 17

Dear Max,

Hello, dear friend. Hope school is going well. I'm settled here in my new home, and the family that I am staying with is wonderful. It's been a bit difficult since they don't speak much English and I don't speak any Japanese. The children have served as translators.

I've been here almost a month now. Mr. Suzuki, my host, took me on his fishing boat yesterday. We left around 10:00 p.m. and didn't get home till about 4:00 a.m. I have never been so seasick in my life. It didn't dawn on me to take a Dramamine. I threw up many times over the boat.

We, or I should say, Mr. Suzuki and his crew, caught this monstrous tuna. I wish I had my camera on me. When they first caught it, I thought it was a baby whale. I didn't know a tuna was so huge. It's a bit lonely here by myself but I'm doing well and having a great time in Japan. I'll be visiting Tokyo this coming weekend. I'll write again soon.

Em

February 25

Dear Jane,

How are you? Since the last time I wrote, I took the bullet train again and went into Tokyo. What a fun city! I don't remember if I saw a pushpin on Tokyo on your travel board back at home, but if you haven't been, this city is a must.

I woke up early to go see Tsukiji market. They only allow 120 people into the tuna auction so I made sure to get there extra early. It was exhilarating to see how quickly the auction sped by. Everyone was speaking so fast I didn't understand a word. After the auction, I walked into a random stall and had the most amazing sushi. Even though I eat fish almost daily in my village, the fish right at the market is even better. I wonder how this compares to your meal at Masa?

I wrote to Jake once when I first got here. Actually, I write him daily, but end up tearing up every letter. I did mail the first one. Pathetic, huh? I'm such a chicken. Maybe this is why I'm not successful with relationships.

Hope school is going well. You only have a few months left.

See ya.

Emily

March 5

Dear Max,

Sorry it's been awhile since I last wrote. Many more students from my school requested to be tutored so I've been busy making extra money. I guess it's a good thing.

Last weekend, I got to go on a rice picking tour. Our village gets all these Western tourists who come for a day and want to pay money to go rice picking. It's backbreaking work! I couldn't function the next day.

How is school? I assume your semester ends in a couple of months? I'm sure you and Peter are doing fine. How hard can it be?

I miss you and all our friends. As peaceful as this village is, I don't know if I've found my peace yet. I was hoping to mend my broken heart here, but the pain doesn't seem to want to go away. Absence does make the heart grow fonder. Sorry for babbling. I'm sure you aren't thrilled with hearing your ex-girlfriend cry about her ex-boyfriend.

Have you been dating at all? You need to get back out there. You can be pretty irresistible when you want to be. Please tell Peter I said hello. I will write to him soon.

I miss you.

Emily

March 24

Hi, Peter!

How are things in your life? As you know, I'm doing well in Japan. I got to go to Osaka this past weekend to watch a baseball game. A few friends of mine here got tickets to watch the Orix Buffaloes vs. the Hanshin Tigers at the Osaka Dome. It was such a cool stadium.

These fans here are crazy. Did you know that no one gets up to do anything when their home team is up to bat? They don't use the bathroom. The concession lines are empty. It's unbelievable. Every player has his own song that the fans sing during the game. I don't think that we in LA get this excited for anything.

I think this was the best day in Japan thus far. Well, maybe it's right behind visiting and eating at the Tsukiji market. You know I have a weakness for sushi. I'm going to try to visit other stadiums before I get back to the States for Sarah's wedding.

I hope you and Max aren't too stressed out with school. I miss you both. Bye.

Emily

April 3

Dear Max,

I can't believe I've been here two months already. Time goes so fast. I've picked up quite a bit of Japanese during my stay here. Ryu and Yuki have taught me as much as I've taught them.

I really enjoy teaching here in the village. I'm considering staying here another year. When I come back to the States for Sarah and Charlie's wedding, I'm going to make arrangements to come live here at least another year.

I know you're thinking that I'm hiding from my life in LA. I can't say that you're wrong in your thinking. I like it here and it's easier for me not to think about Jake when I know that he's not working a mile from my home.

Sorry it's so short today. Will write again.

Emily

April 12

Dear Nick,

How's school? You're probably studying hard, dying to graduate. I'm sending you pictures of the coolest place I found in Tokyo. Did you know that there is a section of Tokyo that sells all things food, restaurant, and kitchen supply? It's called Kappabashi in the Asakusa district.

I guess it's technically a restaurant wholesale district. The tour books say that it's only a half mile stretch but I spent an entire day here. There are stores that sell only plastic food models. Some stores sell all knives. Some random stores specialize in noren—the curtains that hang outside a door to signal that you're open.

There are little food stalls too, but I didn't eat here. I stopped at a street vendor who sold a variety of donburis. When I went into a general restaurant supply store, I wanted to buy everything. Since I'm thinking of staying here another year, I didn't think it would be wise to collect so much luggage.

I wish you could have been here with me. We would've had a blast. Hope all is well with you. Will write again.

Emily

April 19

Dear Jane,

Have you found a job yet? I'm so sorry to be missing your graduation. I thought I would be there with your brother celebrating your glorious day. I know you will do well in life. You are such an endearing person, and you have been a beloved friend to me.

Please don't be too mad that I still haven't sent a return address. I miss you, Jane. Yes, I miss Jake as well. I still hurt, but I'm feeling more at peace about what's happened between us. I think I've finally accepted my life to go on without Jake and I can say I'm content now.

Perhaps it was a good thing Jake left me. I've become a more independent person. I used to fear being alone. I'd skip meals rather than eat by myself, and spend every weekend with Sarah and Charlie so I'd be among people. Isn't that sad? Now, I am confident enough to walk into a restaurant, be alone, and not feel sorry for myself. Not only that, I travel to different cities and converse with strangers—as everyone is a stranger to me in this country. I just bought my ticket to go visit Hong Kong next weekend. Can you believe how bold I've become?

If I were with Jake I'd probably lean on him, and trust him to take care of all my needs. Though I've taken care of myself since high school, I finally do it with a happy heart and a peace of mind.

There's joy in my heart when I teach, and traveling and exploring a new land, even by myself, is so rewarding and exciting. I finally feel comfortable in my own skin, and it took a huge heartbreak and moving to the other part of the world to figure this out.

I'm sending you an early graduation present. I hope you like the stationery. A man in my village actually makes each one of these sheets. It's painstaking to make artistic paper. I will think twice before ripping up any more of your brother's unmailed letters (or I will just use regular paper instead of these nice ones).

Hope all is well. Study hard, it's almost over.

Emily

May 10

Hello Nick!

I'm so excited for you on your graduation. Aren't you glad to be done with under-grad? Although, I'm sure you'll jump right back into school, as Jake told me that you're the smartest one in the family. If you decide to become a doctor, don't be a cardiac surgeon like your brother. He has no life outside of the hospital. Become a dermatologist—no emergencies—and I can come to you for my Botox shots when I get older (ha ha ha).

Anyhow, you are the first person to enter my mind (well, maybe a very close second?) when I eat yummy food in Japan. Not only are the dishes visually stunning, they also taste just as good as they look. I've been visiting the bigger cities over the weekend and I go in search of noodle, tempura, and oden bars. You and I could have gone on a carb binge. In retrospect, I should've had you meet me one of the weekends I was in Tokyo.

I was so bloated on all the ramen and udon houses I visited. I even went to Masaharu Morimoto's restaurant. It was expensive! I sorely missed your brother funding that eating trip (just kidding).

I'm sending you a foodie picture book as a graduation present. I salivated at each picture. The Japanese know how to make their food look beautiful. Congrats again! Take care.

Emily

May 12

Dear Jake,

Happy birthday! I did my best to have this reach you on your birthday. I hope I was successful. What did you do for your birthday? I guess it's silly to ask since you can't answer back.

I've been doing well here in Japan and my Japanese has improved quite a bit. Have you ever visited Japan? It's absolutely gorgeous here. The food, of course is heavenly. Do you know people here don't eat as much sushi as they do in the States? Though of course, I still eat it a lot.

I hope this has been a wonderful day for you. I'm sure your family has showered you with copious love and attention. This probably wasn't the best idea, but I'm sending you a gift. I found these cufflinks during my trip to Tokyo last week. I was at a department store when I noticed these beautiful pieces with your initials on them. What are the chances of that? I thought these would look nice with that blue shirt you were wearing the night we met at the grocery store. They will both bring out the beautiful blue in your eyes.

If you don't like them, I understand. You've given me so many gifts while we were together, I wanted to reciprocate in a very small way. I'm sorry I was always so selfish. I don't think I ever gave you enough—whether materially or emotionally. I was always on the receiving end. Lucky me!

I wish we had spent more time together before we separated. There aren't enough memories for me to think about when I'm here by myself. I guess we won't be celebrating our birthdays together, huh? I had looked forward to our back-to-back celebrations. It will be difficult to spend those two days without you.

I'm sorry to be rambling about. It's a bit tough being alone tonight. My mom died seven years ago today and I wish I could be with her in Texas right now. I also wish you could be there with me. You always knew the right things to say to comfort me when I thought about my parents. I miss you, Jake.

Maybe when I return in a few years, I'll be lucky enough to run into you, or perhaps fall into you at the grocery store again.

I hope you have a wonderful birthday. Please say hello to your family for me.

Emily

May 14

Dear Peter,

I have to tell you about Akihabara in Tokyo. This is an area dedicated to selling only electronic goods. It's crazy here! You can buy camcorders and computers and even robots.

I saw guys glued to some of the stores playing the latest Nintendo games on large TVs. It reminded me of you guys during undergrad, playing video games till the wee hours of the morning. I'd have to say that you were a borderline addict.

There are many tourists trying to buy camcorders. I see them going from store to store trying to bargain with the shop owners. I'm not quite sure if this place is actually cheaper or if it gives off the appearance of being cheap.

I feel like I'm back in Vegas with all the lights shining in my face at Akihabara. This place is definitely worth a visit for you. I'm sending you some pictures.

Enjoy.

Emily

May 17

Dear Max,

It's a bit surreal that I'll be home in a week. I was finally finding some peace within my heart, and now I fly back to face my reality. Sarah seems to have everything under control, but if you have some time, I'd be grateful if you could help her with anything she needs. I feel so guilty that I can't be there for her.

Since you are done with school, do you get a vacation? I guess I don't understand how med school works. I just know from Jake's schedule that you doctors work a lot. Maybe it's just him?

I hope we can spend some time together—no scratch that. I don't know if I'll be available to spend time with you. I'll see you at the wedding. I'll be the one in that hideous pink dress. I think Sarah purposely put us in those dresses to make herself shine even brighter. Like, she isn't going to be the most beautiful one there.

I've got to go. My students are waiting for me.

See you in a few weeks.

Em

May 20

Dear Jane,

I sent Jake a birthday card and a small present last week. I hope he got it on his birthday. It's only been a month since my declaration of independence to you, and I feel like I've reverted back to the old Emily. Like a fool, I rambled in Jake's letter about how lonely I was, and how I wished he were with me. Why do I do this to myself? I thought I had made peace with my heart. He probably laughed at my letter. Maybe he didn't even read it. (Oh, there go the tears again.)

Did you know Jake and I have almost the same birthday? He was born six years and one day before me. We had promised months ago to celebrate our birthdays for two straight days. I guess that didn't happen this year. I hope he had a good birthday. What am I saying? I'm sure he had a great birthday.

It is nighttime and yesterday and today have been the most difficult days for me since arriving here. I didn't think I'd be alone today, especially not this year. I wished I hadn't trusted all the promises your brother made about our future. It hurts even more when those days come and go without him. I miss you, Jane. I feel so alone today. I tried calling you for the first time, but of course, you weren't home.

By the time you receive this, I will probably be in LA for Sarah and Charlie's wedding. They're getting married this weekend. I assume you are in New York, so I won't bother calling you when I get to the States.

School is almost done here. Do you think you can visit me? I'm finally sending a return address so please write back. I can't wait to hear from you.

Bye.

Emily

Chapter 15

Sarah's Wedding

I walked into LAX, relieved to be surrounded by the familiar sights and sounds of America. It was refreshing to hear English spoken in all corners of the airport. I didn't have to strain to understand what everyone was saying, and I didn't have to translate every word. The clear skies, warm weather, and multiracial faces gave me a warm feeling of home.

Not having driven a car for so long, my legs confused the clutch from the brake to the accelerator—so much for a convertible sports car. The gentleman at the rental agency winced when he heard the car sputter, then peel out of the parking lot. Leaving the airport took a bit longer than expected, so I rushed toward the hotel to check in and then to meet Sarah. We had much to do before tomorrow's wedding. With the top down and the sun beating on my head, I breathed in the LA air—or smog—and drove past the spot that could've been the start of my happily ever after. I couldn't help but stare at the corner of La Cienega and Century Boulevard, where Jake had proposed five months ago. Our indelible memories of love filled my mind. Regret was the only word I could use to describe my feelings right now.

Although my stay would only last till tomorrow night, memories of the last seven months rushed back into my mind. Absent-mindedly, I found myself passing the hotel and going till the end of the freeway toward home. I drove by General Hospital and imagined Jake performing his multiple surgeries. I drove by my house and found my tenant's car in the garage. Eventually, my car ended up in front of Jake's house, idle. I had nowhere else to go. This felt like home. I wanted nothing more than to ring the doorbell and see him smile at me, though this was far from reality.

Hesitant, but desperate to see Jake, I mustered up the courage and walked up his driveway with Sandy and Bobby's gift. I bought a clock from an old gentleman in my village, and knew Sandy would enjoy the story behind the gift. For Bobby, I found an old Japanese doctor's 'manual' from World War II. It contained remedies for all bodily ailments. Of course, I would have to translate it for him. Maybe that could prolong my visit since Jake was probably at work. My legs dragged up the driveway, and my heart weighed heavily upon me. Even with the knowledge that this one visit would undo the months of strengthening myself and my heart, I had a fierce wish for my own undoing.

Feelings of foolishness grew with the number of steps leading to Sandy and Bobby's house. This was my ex-boyfriend's home and I was coming unannounced, bearing gifts. My pride finally protested and made me take a hard look at myself. *You are an idiot, Emily! Nobody welcomes you here anymore. How awkward. What will you say to these people?* Dejected, my body turned itself around.

Walking back to the car, someone honked and waived furiously at me. To my delight, it was Bobby and Sandy. Sandy ran out of the car and hugged me dearly. Her hug jump-started a rush of unwanted emotions. I held back the best I could.

"Emily, when did you get back? I've missed you so much." Bobby came over and hugged me as well.

"I've missed both of you too," I answered weakly.

"Are you back for good?" Bobby asked.

"No, I'm only here till tomorrow. It's my best friend's wedding," I answered both of them while handing them each their gifts. "I stopped by to drop these off."

"That's so sweet of you. Emily, where are you staying tonight? Why don't you stay with us?"

Sandy's mothering plea accelerated my sadness. Both Jake's parents looked shocked to see me cry.

The back of my hand peeled off whatever makeup was left from this morning as I said, "I'm sorry. I didn't mean to startle you. Your kindness reminded me of my mom and dad." I didn't tell them how alone I felt right now. "I should go. Sarah needs me. I just came by to drop these off."

"Emily, wait!" Sandy begged. "Please stay. Remember back on Christmas Day, I asked you to think of me when you needed a mother?"

Tears dropped in unison with my bobbing head.

"Stay with us. Let me take care of you—you look so frail and just as lost as my son." Sandy was the doctor I'd been searching for to heal my wounds, and just possibly, her love could be my panacea. "You and Jake have been in so much pain the last half a year. Let me share your burden and help you resolve this mess."

By this point, there was no stopping the stream pouring from my eyes. I quickly hugged Sandy as tightly as I could, then got in my car and left. The road was a big blur from the dam that flowed out of my eyes.

Trying to push behind the sadness, I sped down the freeway, checked into my room, and then finally went to meet the jubilant bride.

"Emily!" Sarah came running. We held each other, happy to see one another. Charlie came over and gave us a three-way hug.

"Emily." This time Sarah used a disapproving tone. "Why have you lost so much weight again? During all our phone calls, it never dawned on me to ask you if you were taking care of yourself. I should have known."

I shrugged my shoulders and didn't answer her. She would see right through my attempt at a lie, so I decided to change the subject and ask her what I could do to help.

"First off, I want you to go to alterations in the basement and get your dress fixed. There's no way your dress will fit now." Sarah was shaking her head back and forth, critical of my new figure. "Then, I want you to come with me to the salon so we can get a facial. Since the wedding is a noon ceremony, we need to get our faces prepped today. After the facial, we'll have the rehearsal and then we'll have an early dinner."

"OK," was all I could say. Charlie walked me to alteration and got me up to speed on what's been going on in everyone's life.

"Are you really going back tomorrow?" Charlie wanted to know. "You're not going to stick around and hang out with your friends for a while?"

"Charlie. What would I do here if I stayed a few more days? There's no family to visit, no house to stay in, and you and Sarah will be off in Hawaii. What would keep me here?"

"What about Jake?" As soon as he said this, my downcast look made him stop immediately. "All right, Emily. I'll see you tonight at dinner. Bye."

While in Japan, I hadn't noticed much change to my body, but trying on this dress five months later, the mirror displayed an unhealthy figure. As soon as the seamstress finished with me, I headed for the salon and I confessed to Sarah what had happened before coming to the hotel. She shook her head.

"Emily, why? Why do you hurt yourself like this?"

"I don't know, Sarah. I got here and that's where my heart led me. That felt like home." I finished this conversation and started a new one that wouldn't put me in the spotlight.

Standing next to Sarah at the altar during rehearsal reminded me of my emptiness even more. Being back home was more painful than I'd imagined it to be. Of course, a wedding worsened the pain. But, I did my best to focus and know my role as the maid of honor for my best friend. Regardless of my feelings, sadness had no place in this wedding. I would enjoy this day with my dear friends.

Though Sarah and Charlie had only invited immediate family to the rehearsal dinner, greeting all of them and explaining my five-month absence exhausted me. I was hoping to see Max and Peter, but Charlie told me that they were working at the hospital tonight in order to have tomorrow free. Catching up with my dear friends would have to wait until tomorrow.

We all turned in early, as I had the job of picking up the bride at 7:00 a.m. for her makeup and hair appointment at the salon. With a noon wedding, every minute counted and I didn't want to be responsible for making the bride late on her wedding day.

The morning schedule went off without any glitches, and we arrived at the hotel an hour before the ceremony. When I saw Sarah come out of the dressing room ready to walk down the aisle, I went over and carefully hugged her. She shined brighter than the sun.

"Sarah, you are the most beautiful bride!" I declared.

"Thanks, Emily. Thank you for being here. I know it's hard for you right now."

"Sarah, I love you, and I'm so very happy for you. This is your glorious day. Let's not talk about anything else but you and Charlie."

It did make me sad to be here. Seeing Sarah reminded me that this could've been my dream as well. Not wanting to demonstrate any hint of misery, I erased these thoughts and helped Sarah begin her new life.

The minster had the bride and groom say their vows and Charlie happily kissed the bride. We all cheered for the happy couple, and I finally caught a glimpse of Max. As always, he was warmly smiling at me. After pictures were done, we walked into the reception hall and I helped Sarah greet her guests.

After lunch and a long toast by the best man, Sarah and Charlie went out to the dance floor as a couple. They looked blissful together. As their song ended, Max walked over to me, hugged me affectionately, and asked me to dance.

"Hi, Max. It's wonderful to see you."

"Em. It's good to see you too. I've missed you. How have you been?" He held my hand to the dance floor, started asking me about my stay in Japan, and guilted me into telling him the exact location of my whereabouts.

"I can't believe you sent me letters with no return addresses! What was that all about?" He sounded flabbergasted.

I apologized.

"Why would you do this, Em? Didn't you think maybe we'd want to converse with you as well? I had so many things I wanted to tell you. There was no way for any of us to know how you were really doing. I've missed you." Max's worried eyes made me regret not allowing a two-way communication with my friends.

"I've missed you too. Before I leave, I'll write down my address, and you can write to me. Maybe you and Peter can visit me as well."

"How about an e-mail address so we can have faster communication? Or maybe even a cell phone number?" A mocking question, one after another, trailed. "Perhaps we can even text—your *favorite* method of communication?"

"I don't have a computer there nor do I have a cell phone. I could give you the Suzuki's home number but you'll just be better off writing letters. There's something to be said about receiving a letter in the mail—the old-fashioned way." I put an emphasis on the last four words.

"Do you want me to get you a laptop and/or a cell phone before you leave? How can you be so cut off from life? And also, were you serious when you said that you were staying another year?" Once again, there was disapproval in his eyes.

"It's peaceful to be a little backward. Everyone concentrates on what's only in front of them, and we don't worry about keeping up to date with everyone else." Little did Max understand I wanted to cut off every possible way of communicating with Jake. "And yes, I think I will stay in Japan another year. I like it there." This wasn't the whole truth, but it wasn't a complete lie either.

"Em, I need to tell you something," Max turned serious as we continued to dance. "I saw Jake yesterday at the hospital for the first time since Grand Canyon."

My body stopped dancing. My heart stopped beating.

Max led us back to his seat.

I didn't say anything, though I had a million questions I wanted answered. Waiting for Max to continue his thought tested every shred of nonchalance I feigned on the topic of Jake.

"I apologized to him for coming between you two, and he asked me a lot of questions about you. Since you gave me no way of responding to your letters, I told him I knew no more than he did. He looked distraught."

I wondered to myself why he would be distraught. Why would he ask any questions about me? I couldn't give way to hope.

"I hope you don't mind, but I told him you would be here today. He really wanted to come see you. He said that he had to talk to you. He's going to stop by after work." This part of our conversation made me feel distraught.

My heart convulsed and my eyes flushed at the thought of seeing Jake. Hope wanted to resurface, but I had shut the door and thrown away the keys so long ago, it didn't know its way out anymore.

"Are you upset I told Jake you're here?" Max looked hesitant.

"No. It's all right." I put on a brave guise. "He won't care that I'm here. If he cared, he would've done something about it before I left."

"Em, I think he does care. I think there was a big misunderstanding between you two. He still..."

"Max. Please don't. It took me five very long months to accept that we are through. He doesn't care for me anymore." I didn't dare say the word love. "I erased those thoughts a long time ago. Don't say any more. Let's be happy. We're at a wedding." I forced a smile and walked over to help Sarah cut the cake.

Stupidly, but automatically, my eyes looked for Jake. They searched through every guest and scanned each door over and over again, hoping what Max just revealed would come true. The pessimist in me knew Jake wouldn't come looking for me. Not now, not after so many months had passed by. But the optimist in me prayed he would come see me—just once more.

Sarah changed into her going-away outfit, and the last of the dancers lined up to throw rice at the happy bride and groom leaving for their honeymoon.

Before Sarah left, she whispered, "I'm sorry you didn't get a chance to see Jake today. I was hoping Max was right about him."

I forced another smile and wished her a wonderful trip. The happy couple cheerfully left for Hawaii, but my own exit would not be so cheerful now.

"You're leaving already?" Max asked as I walked over to say good-bye. "But Jake's not here yet."

"My flight leaves at nine. I have to go," I answered sadly. Max had no idea the damage he had done by reviving my hope. "Now that you have all my contact info, don't be a stranger. I hope you can visit me one day," I said while hugging him.

"Emily..." Max held onto my hand, "just stay another hour. Have another drink with me, or better yet, eat another meal. Don't they feed you in Japan? Why are you so waif thin?"

"I'm late!" Answering as sternly as possible, I pulled my hand away and waved good-bye.

With longing renewed, I walked through the hotel with my peripheral vision scanning every man fitting Jake's build. Till the very end, I didn't give up hope that Jake would want to come see me tonight. What a fool I was. Even walking on to the airplane, I continued to listen for his tender voice to call my name, like he did back in November when I was leaving for New York. Ugh! Four months of heart mending in Japan obliterated in a matter of a few hours of hope.

Chapter 16

He Loves Me?

I got back Sunday night, and struggled to get my heart back into school the next day. With school letting out in two weeks, we all enjoyed a lighter schedule. Tutoring waned, and I felt free to make plans for the summer. Our principal asked me to teach a summer English course as well as to create the English curriculum for the next school year. With a three-week vacation before summer courses began, I thought about all the places I wanted to visit in Asia during that time. Perhaps Jane could vacation with me? A phone call was in order.

Our school had a holiday on Friday, so I decided to visit Kyoto, and cross off one of my bucket list items and go have a formal *kaiseki* meal. Most people probably wouldn't partake in such a formal meal by themselves but I figured if I didn't go alone now, I may never be able to go. Taking the Shinkansen, Kyoto was not far from my village. I left Thursday after class and promised to free myself of home and all its memories. Home was here now, nowhere else.

Friday morning consisted of a walking tour and a visit to the Nishiki market. Dozens and dozens of shops selling authentic Japanese goods and produce, bustled with customers. I had a small lunch at a famous soba house then visited Tenryu-ji Temple in Arashiyama. Originally built in the 1300's, the temple's stunning greenery and ponds graced a large part of the property. Fully blossomed Sakura trees complemented the famously landscaped garden.

After my walk through the garden, I headed back to the hotel and got dressed for my *kaiseki* meal at Japan's most celebrated *kaiseki* restaurant. The distance between my hotel, Tenryu-ji temple, and the restaurant measured a short triangle. Mr. Suzuki had asked many of his friends and did a lot of research for me before calling in a reservation. Even alone, it was exciting to participate in an activity that had been on my mind for years. I wanted to dress up and look nice for this elegant meal. I couldn't wait!

At first glance, the restaurant was breathtaking. Japanese lanterns in various shapes lined the pebble walkway leading up to what resembled a traditional Japanese house more than a restaurant. When I arrived, it was light enough for me to see the serene landscaping filled with plants and bushes and random bamboo fixtures. The hostess led me to a small room filled with only a tatami mat, a comfortable L-shaped cushion, and a black lacquered dinner table. I waited for the kimono-clad server to start my meal on the beautifully lacquered table. The sounds of the waterfall hummed in tune with chirping birds, and I sat with my back against the door, looking peacefully at the pond. With footsteps coming my way, I eagerly awaited my first course, the *sakizuke* or *amouse bouche*.

My ear listened carefully to what I thought was a familiar voice speaking English. Since there were so many tourists in Arayishima, I assumed it was one of the many coming to eat at the restaurant.

"Finally!" a voice announced, as the door opened. I knew instantly whose voice I'd heard. My head spun around faster than the server could finish opening the door.

Jake. My Jake. My Love.

Tears choked my eyes and my chest writhed in pain. Emotions overtook me. I stared at the handsome face I longed to see for so many months. My heart ached for this moment since I left him standing on a corner in New York. Was this person walking toward me a figment of my imagination? Could I trust my eyes? Even before he took the big step into my room, I wanted to run into his arms. But instead, I turned myself around and contained the hope that wanted to rip out of my heart.

He sat right next to me and whispered, "Hello, Emily." His voice broke as he peered into my eyes. "Very long time no see."

I sensed adoration and relief in his eyes. He probably sensed elation, along with fear in mine. He reached over to embrace me but I jumped back to guard myself from his touch. His face looked hurt. My face probably looked dumbfounded.

"What are you doing here?" I asked, trying to figure out whether this was coincidental or planned. Either way, none of it made sense.

"Why do you think I'm here?" Jake's tone was a bit short with me. Exasperated might be a better word.

"I don't know. Does the emperor need a heart surgeon?" Jake chuckled. I hadn't meant to be funny. I had no other explanation for Jake being in Japan.

"Emily, I'm here to see you. We need to talk. Are you here alone, or are you waiting for someone?"

I heard him ask me a series of questions but I couldn't get beyond the first sentence. *Why are you here to see me? After all these months, what would make you talk to me now?*

"Emily, are you waiting for someone?" he asked again.

"Yes," was all I could answer. *Silly, I've been waiting for you for months now. You're very late, but thank you for coming. I'm so happy to see you.*

"You are? Who are you waiting for? Are you waiting for a guy...? Are you seeing someone already?" Jake looked horrified.

I found his questions absurd. *How could you think I started dating again? Don't you know how much I missed you...how much I love you?*

"Emily!" He tried to snap me out of my glazed look. "I sound like a broken record. Are you seeing someone?"

"Are you?" I didn't mean to aggravate him by answering a question with a question, but I couldn't babble any coherent thoughts.

"Of course not! Do you know how far and wide I searched for you after you left me? Why did you make it so hard for me to find you? Why have you been gone for so long?"

This statement snapped me out of my daze. In a biting tone I answered, "A bit bizarre you would try so hard to find me halfway around the world when you didn't bother looking for me when I was just down the street. And by the way, *you* left *me*."

He had no comeback. My impetuous tone startled Jake. He looked defeated. I was unhappy to see his sad face. I didn't know what possessed me to talk to him in such a manner.

Our second course—*Hassun*, which sets the seasonal theme of the meal—arrived, and I continued eating. Jake paid no attention to his food. "How could you come into town last week and visit my parents, but not me? How could you cut off all communication with me? Didn't you think I would want to see you...that I might worry about you? Didn't you want to see me?"

Of course I wanted to see you. There wasn't a day when I didn't think about you. "How could you accuse *me* of cutting off all communication when you're the one who walked out on me after asking me to marry you? *You're* also the one who didn't communicate with me for weeks. I begged you to talk to me."

He was speechless again. His first and second courses sat. I moved on to eating my third course, *Mukozuke*—a dish of seasonal sushi.

"Emily. Why didn't you send a return address to any of the letters you wrote? Maybe if you did, I could've resolved our issues sooner."

I hesitated giving him an answer. I hesitated not because I didn't have an answer, but because I didn't want to show him how vulnerable I felt. Biding my time, I looked around the table at Jake's uneaten food. Chopsticks lay still, our servers discontinued service, and even the water fountain seemed motionless. The only sound I could hear was my rapid heartbeat, and my heart hollering at me to grab him before he left me again. As his eyes continued to beg for an answer, I eventually gave into his plea. I had no defense to his offense. My weakness was his strength.

After a long sigh I confessed, "I didn't send a return address, because when I didn't get a response from you, I would know it's because you *couldn't* respond to me, and not because you didn't want to respond to me."

My head dropped immediately, sensing the deluge of emotions rushing to my eyes. Tears fell heavier than the water fountain that decorated the lovely garden right outside our room.

Jake appeared encouraged by my meltdown. He leaned over to embrace me again. My body rebuffed his attempts, though a bit more hesitantly this time.

"Emi, can I explain myself now? I'd like to tell you my side of the story."

"Jake, if you came all the way over here to apologize, don't bother. I don't want to hear it. You walked out on me a few days after you said that you wanted to spend the rest of your life with me, and didn't explain yourself for months. How could you not know I would wait for you at the Skywalk? What happened to your promise of not letting me be alone? I have been so alone the last five months without you. I thought you loved me, that you really, truly loved me. Where were you all those days I begged you to talk to me? Why are you here now after all these months?"

At this point, I couldn't contain the sobbing. I could see Jake lifting his arm up and bringing it down several times, wondering whether or not to comfort me. His two failed attempts at embracing me earlier must have deterred his courage. In the end, he kept his hands to himself. Once composed, I finished the words that had burned in my heart for so long. "You can't begin to understand how much you hurt me. I've just begun to piece myself back together again. I don't want my heart broken anymore. You don't owe me any explanation. I have no claim on you. Please just leave."

Defeated, my chest throbbed, feeling beaten and bruised. I wanted to run away and hide in my corner again. My body sat quietly trying to calm my heart that blazed like a fire burning out of control. I knew Jake needed to say his piece. Though I dared not look into his face, pain emanated with his every breath.

Jake cautiously lifted his hand again, and brushed my fallen hair. His fingers traced the side of my temple to my cheekbone then down to my jaw. He held up my face and let his palm rest on my cheek. Very much, I wanted to see what was written in his eyes. My head was up, but my tear-filled eyes stayed down.

"First of all, I'm sorry," he confessed. "I'm sorry I walked away from you that morning, and I can never forgive myself for leaving you stranded. I can't believe I've hurt you so much. You don't know how sorry I am that I left you alone. It was not my intention not to see or talk to you for this long. I came by your house many times trying to reconcile, but couldn't find you. This situation got out of hand." Jake's face actually looked as tormented as my heart felt.

"That morning when you told me about Max, you broke my heart. I have this bad habit of shutting myself down when things go badly. I know it's wrong and I know I've done this to you many times before. I'll work on that. I promise I will. I won't shut down on you or leave you anymore, I promise you."

My heart beat even faster. I was sure Jake could hear the thumping from where he was sitting. Could he actually be trying to make amends with me? The hope within me attempted to break free, believing he might still love me as my tears continued down Jake's hand.

"Anyhow, I initially didn't answer your texts because I was angry with you. Childish, I know, but I couldn't get myself to return your messages. Eventually, I calmed down enough to give you a few days to sort out your feelings and make you want to come back to me and me only. I knew I loved you, but this time I doubted *your* love for me."

This statement angered me again. "Why would I try to communicate with you every day if I didn't want to be with you? I told you in every text I loved you."

"I believed you cared. But you never affirmed to me that I was the only one you wanted. I guess I was looking for affirmation. When I didn't get this, I figured you had chosen Max over me, and I let you go—though only for about half a second—thinking this was the best for you." He actually had the nerve to chuckle.

"Jake!" Frustration colored my face. "Did you read any of my texts? Every day I told you how much I missed you and that I loved you. Did you think it was all a lie?"

"I know. It was stupid of me. I couldn't trust you. I thought maybe you were letting me down easily. Every day I looked forward to your text, but a part of me feared you would eventually tell me you had chosen Max." He frowned at this thought. "When you sent me your last text, I realized I was completely wrong about your feelings. That's when I panicked. I saw these texts from your point of view for the first time. Maybe you still loved me, but my lack of response would make you believe I didn't love you anymore. I couldn't assuage the sick feeling in my stomach. Since I couldn't get a hold of you, my only solution was to see Jane in New York. I hoped she could give me some answers."

Fear entered my heart at this point. If Jake still loved me, could I try again? Desperately wanting to love him again, but scared to be hurt, I listened for more reassurance.

"I came looking for you at your house as soon I received your last text. I wanted to tell you what was in my heart, but you didn't answer the door. Little did I know that I would see you in less than twenty-four hours."

"OK, so you finally saw my point of view, but you still didn't say anything to me in New York to resolve our situation," I freed my face from his hand scared to be held by him—to be hurt by him. "If you still loved me, why did you send me away again? You could've stopped me."

"When I saw you in Jane's apartment, I was dumbfounded. You were the person I most wanted to see, but the last one I expected to see. At first, I said nothing out of shock. Then Nick started talking, Jane started yelling, and the next thing I knew, you were gone. Even before I reached you at the cab, Jane's words about Arizona haunted me. In my mind, I could picture you standing at the Skywalk waiting for me to return. I was angry with myself but took it out on you instead. Please forgive me. All those hurtful words—I meant none of them."

"Jake...I'm too scared to do this again. My heart is beyond repair. Did you have so little faith in me that you would believe one night with Max would lead to something improper? Did you really think so lowly of me? If that wasn't bad enough, you left me without giving me a chance to explain myself. How can I trust you again? All these months, I hurt believing you didn't care anymore—that you coldly cut me off."

The once confident Dr. Jake Reid crumbled with my accusation. My heart broke watching guilt torment him.

"Emily, you must believe me when I tell you I love you! I never stopped loving you. I don't believe I can ever *not* love you. I'm sorry I broke your heart. I'm sorry I abandoned you. I will never do it again. I absolutely cannot live without you. When I read your letter at the hospital, my world collapsed. It was like falling into some dark abyss. I couldn't function for weeks. I took a sick leave and searched for you everywhere. Only when I received your first letter from Japan, did I think that there might be a chance we could meet again. That maybe we would love again. That's when I decided to get my act together, and go back to the hospital and wait for you to return to me."

My head nodded silently. I wasn't sure which statement I was agreeing with—probably all of them.

"I will work to earn your trust again. Just please don't tell me we're over."

At this point, I didn't know what to think or feel. The room spun, as I knew I needed to make a choice.

Love and trust Jake again.

Or, let him go, and regret this decision the rest of my life.

The decision had been made the moment Jake walked into the room. Only I was too afraid to speak it.

"Oh my sweet Emily, how did we go this long, apart? I've missed you so much."

He leaned in and placed his lips gently on mine. I didn't move away this time. I couldn't move away. I felt delirious to his touch. His lips tasted sweeter than I remembered them. During the kiss that I never wanted to end, I began sobbing quietly at the prospect of being with Jake again.

He paused his embrace and looked into my once dejected eyes. My body burned with sensations from affliction, to hope, to elation.

"Emily?" he lovingly called my name. "You still love me, don't you?" his voice unsure, his eyes begging one last time.

I wrapped my arms tightly around him and prayed he would never let go of me again. "Jake, you know I do!" my voice broke. "I never stopped loving you. I'm sorry too for hurting you. This was my fault as well. I've missed you so much!"

Several times the door to our room opened and closed. The fourth *Takiawase* course of simmered meat or fish and vegetables, either sat cold or became overcooked, from the server's many attempts to deliver our meal. My emotions bounced this time from euphoria back to insecurity and then to curiosity.

I broke out of our embrace.

"What's the matter?" Jake asked. "Why do you still look so sad? Don't cry, Love," he said while wiping away my tears with his hands.

"You really still love me?" I had to ask. I couldn't trust reality sitting in front of me.

"Emily, I love you," he reassured with gentle kisses.

"I just can't believe it." The tears wouldn't stop.

"Believe it, Sweetheart. I'm here to be with you, and we are *never* separating again!" he adamantly stated, but it still felt like a dream—possibly a nightmare if it were a dream.

I kissed him one more time. It tasted even sweeter the second time around.

"You're not leaving me anymore?" I whispered meekly, just in case I might be in trouble for doubting again.

"Never," he quietly answered and held me in his arms. Yes, this felt like home again. I was where I belonged—in Jake's arms.

I perked up from Jake's body with a question that nagged since he got here. "How did you find me in Kyoto?"

An agitated grimace colored his face. I knew that I would be in trouble soon. Before he began, our kimono- clad servers found the chance to drop all nine of our dishes that waited while we reconciled. We had everything but the *mizumono*, or dessert. This probably wasn't the correct *kaiseki* protocol, but the servers didn't care. In their own genteel way, they displayed great annoyance with us. Laughter frolicked in our eyes.

"Emily, I wasn't kidding when I said I looked high and low for you. My dad called me the minute he saw you in our driveway. I begged him to keep you there, but when I arrived, you were gone. Then I ran into Max and he told me you would be at the wedding the next day, and when I went to look for you, you had just left. I asked about you at the hotel, but they said you had checked out already. I went to every possible airline that had a flight leaving that night, but I couldn't find you. Ugh! I was *so* frustrated I had lost you again."

His story became even more animated as he flailed his arms up in the air while huffing and puffing. Before any more wrath fell on me, I stole a moment and enveloped my arms into the arch of his body hugging him longingly. Since parting, my body had always felt cold. Finally, Jake filled my body with warmth. He stopped grumbling and just held me.

Contentment.

No other word better described our state of being.

Even with my body in tow, he continued his soliloquy. "Max and Jane both came to me with your address, so I flew here late Thursday, only to find that it was too late to take the train into your village. I waited another day and trekked all the way to your home and of course, you weren't there. Do you see a pattern to this story?" He pulled himself away to look at me while asking that last question.

"I still don't get how you found me here."

"Well, it wasn't easy—like the last five months of our relationship. Your students went back and forth trying to explain who I was and why I was standing at their door pleading for your whereabouts. Thanks for talking about me to your Japanese family," he retorted sarcastically. "Mr. Suzuki thought I was some loony waiting for a chance to kidnap you."

"So how did you get him to divulge my location? Was it your charm or your good looks?" I attempted an impish smile.

"It was Yuki who finally came to my rescue. I've got to remember to buy her a nice gift while we're here. She told her dad that she saw you write me letters daily...then throw them away. How could you send me only one letter when everyone else got copious letters?"

"Jake. One reprimand at a time, please. I can't keep up with all my wrongdoings. Back to Yuki."

"I guess Yuki threw out your trash daily and she told her dad that she saw you cry many times while writing me a letter. She never asked you about it, but she knew I was somebody in your life who made you sad."

I began to tear again. This time more out of relief that I could look back on those days and consider them a sad memory. With his arms around my body, he kissed my forehead apologetically, and empathized with my pain. In every way, they were his pain too.

"At this point, Mrs. Suzuki stepped in, put two and two together, and forced her husband to tell me where you would be today. This is how I got to this restaurant."

"I'm glad you're here," I responded. Are you done or am I still in trouble?"

"I think I'm done...no, I take that back. I'm not done," he continued.

You can really hold a grudge, Dr. Reid. Good thing I didn't say this as Jake's face turned solemn.

"Emily, I need to apologize one more time. I've said so many hurtful things to you. My actions were inexcusable. Please forgive me." With his arms still around my body, I knew in my heart all had been forgiven already.

"Jake, I created this mess. You had no choice but to feel insecure because I wavered. My actions were hurtful as well. I forgive you knowing you've forgiven me as well. Let's not dwell on this anymore."

"I can't let go of the image of you waiting for me at the Skywalk. You've always been so trusting of me to take care of you. All the months we were apart, the thought of you losing faith in me tormented me. It scares me you won't ever completely trust me again."

"Frightened? Yes. But, I don't think I can stay separated from you anymore. Right now, and maybe even forever, my love for you outweighs any fear of getting hurt. I want to trust you again. Just please don't break my heart."

Our lips met once more eagerly. Happiness overcame my many months of anguish and sadness.

"I'll make this up to you the rest of our lives together. Please don't doubt my love for you anymore."

I nodded my head in agreement.

Sitting at a table filled with beautifully decorated but uneaten food, we attempted feverishly to catch up on our five-month absence. There were still too many unanswered questions.

Jake began. "The more I think about it, how could you believe I didn't love you anymore? Didn't I tell you only every day how much I loved you? Do you think I go around asking just any girl to marry me?"

I answered back, "How could *you* go weeks without talking to me, especially when my texts begged you daily for an answer? Do you know how hard it is to send someone a message and to sit around and wait for a response? Plus, do you know how much you hurt me? I had to move to the other part of the world to try to mend my heart. You were the one confused about my feelings for you."

"Could it be any harder than waiting for letters that came to everyone but me? That was really cruel. I pathetically had to read my siblings' letters to find out how you were doing. Don't even get me started on having to ask my girlfriend's ex-boyfriend about what she had written him."

"I sent you a letter. I even sent you a birthday card and a gift." Jake showed me his sleeves. "Oh, you're wearing the cufflinks. They look nice."

"Thank you for your gift. You don't know how much these meant to me."

"Did you have a good birthday?" I'd hoped he did despite our separation.

"How could I have had a good birthday knowing you were alone on yours? Did you celebrate your birthday at all?" he asked, but looked away, not wanting to know the answer.

I shook my head no. "Sarah called me and sent me a gift but that was it."

"Oh, Sweetheart, I'm sorry. Of all the days we were apart, those were the hardest days for me as well. Come here," he pulled me closer to him. "I have your birthday present. I didn't know when I'd be able to give this to you, but I had it made regardless."

Jake brought out of his pocket a stunning piece of jewelry. On a simple white gold chain hung a large, flat heart shaped pendant. What made this pendant so unusual was the stone placed inside a frame of small diamonds.

"Jake, this is beautiful! What kind of stone is this?"

"It's a sapphire cut into a flat piece and then shaped into a heart. My grandfather gave it to Gram on her birthday the first year they were together. Gram sent it to me on my birthday, obviously for me to give to you, and I added the diamonds around the sapphire on your birthday."

"How is Gram doing?" I asked fondly.

"She's healthy but sad to see me so sad. She called weekly to check up on me and to ask about your status. It broke her heart to know we had separated. She was very fond of you as well, and had thought of you as family already."

"I missed her too. We'll have to call her."

Jake put the present around my neck. I admired not just the gift but the meaning behind it.

"Thank you. So am I done being in trouble for not sending you more letters?"

"Not quite," he answered as I laughed. "You know what was almost as difficult as not receiving a letter from you?" He was back to his mini tirade.

"What?" My voice empathetically rose to justify his indignation.

"Whenever you told Jane you had just written me a letter, but had torn it up. That was enormously frustrating. And how deplorable do I look when a seven-year-old-girl tells her dad that my name is synonymous with the word sad?"

It never occurred to me that Yuki saw me cry. I guess I couldn't hide anything in such a small house.

"Yeah, if I had sent you all the letters I'd torn up, you would've gotten several per week. Sorry," I answered, shrugging my shoulders. "But you must have also read in Jane's letters that my feelings for you never changed. They only got stronger while I was away from you."

"That was my only comfort during those long months. It was difficult not knowing when I would see or talk to you again. Jane did her best to keep me patient. She believed you would send her your contact information soon."

"At least you had family and friends to talk to during those days. Do you want to know what was the hardest for me?" I paused wondering whether or not to share this information with Jake. "I had no one to share my feelings with. I hurt alone and that was unbearable. That's probably why I wrote so many letters."

I stopped talking. I felt Jake's heart break.

"Thank you for finding me, Jake. My four months here did nothing to weaken my feelings for you. I think absence does make the heart grow fonder. I didn't want to, but I was going to stay here another year to try to forget you."

"Emily, let's go home. I promised my family I'd bring you back. Can you leave with me tomorrow?"

As much as I wanted to be with Jake, leaving immediately wasn't a possibility. "I need to stay at least till the end of the school year."

His eyes expressed sadness again. He pondered our new dilemma. "When is the school year over?"

"In two weeks. It's not much longer."

"OK. As much as I don't want to leave you, I'm going to allow it on one condition."

"And what would that condition be?" I asked.

"When school is done, pack a bag of clothes, but Fed-Ex the rest of your belongings to Mom's house."

"Why?"

"Because you're going to meet me in Paris. We're going to take that romantic trip you promised me. If you agree to meet me in Paris, then I'll let you finish out the school year."

"And if I don't agree to meet you in Paris?"

"Then, I'll have to lock you up in a tower like Rapunzel and come visit you at night."

I laughed at the thought. "You wouldn't dare."

"Are you going to meet me in Paris or not?"

"Is this a choice that's not really a choice?"

"Yup."

"Well, then Paris it is," I said, thrilled at the thought of spending an entire week with him. It was like a dream come true. No, it was a dream come true.

"Did you end up going to Paris in February?" I remembered we were supposed to be there a few months back.

"Yes, I had to go...*alone*. It was the most depressing trip of my life. I rarely left the hotel. I went from my room to the conference room. It was hard being there without you. The only highlight of the trip was when Gram came to visit me."

I promised, "I'll make it up to you." We both cherished our moment together.

"Also, I have one more request," Jake said. "I'm going to buy you a laptop with a webcam. I can*not* go two weeks without seeing you—not after having endured five months. We will set up a time to talk each day, OK?"

"Is that necessary? It's only twelve days. What a waste of money."

He gave me a stern look that made me cower into his demand.

Jake paid for our beautiful meal that went untouched and we walked through the streets of Kyoto. We couldn't help our fixed smile or our constant touch. We'd been apart for so long. I, more so than Jake, needed a continual reminder of our togetherness. It was amazing how many months of heartbreak could be mended within minutes, with a few magical words. How fickle the heart could be. We sat on a park bench eager to answer more questions and confirm our commitment one last time.

"Emi?"

"Hmm?"

"What happened between you and Max? Max told me at the hospital that you turned down his proposal, but I didn't quite understand why. Believe it or not, it was Max who encouraged me to pursue you when I thought I'd hurt you too much to salvage anything. He strongly believed you still loved me, and left for Japan thinking I didn't love you anymore."

"After seeing you in New York, I called Max, and we finally ended our story. Let me try to explain what got us into this whole mess. When I turned down your proposal, I knew it was temporary. It was just a matter of time before I accepted your offer of marriage. My love for you was already there. I just couldn't take that last leap of faith. Ultimately, I couldn't trust that you wouldn't wake up one morning and stop loving me. As for Max, I knew the moment he proposed, he was not the person I wanted to spend the rest of my life with. You were too deeply imbedded into my heart. No was the correct answer, but I was too much in shock to say anything. And then I saw you running toward me, and I was terrified you might be mad. I froze, not knowing what to do. I hope you can understand these were words I desperately wanted to hear at one point in my life, and I didn't know how to refuse Max but still keep our friendship. Max will always be like family to me, no matter what. Are you OK with that?"

Forming this into a question, I gave Jake a choice. Hopefully, he'd understand my need to keep Max as an important person in my life. Jake looked tentative, but willing to accept my feelings.

"I figured out after you left me that there was nothing wrong with loving Max as a friend, and that turning him down would not end our relationship. Does this make sense? Maybe the better question would be, are you OK with my feelings for Max?"

My answer didn't erase Jake's insecurity. I had to declare my feelings for Jake one more time.

"I love you with all my heart, and I can't imagine my life being void of you anymore. Please don't ever leave me again." This time, my insecurities prevailed.

"Emily, though we were physically apart, I never left you emotionally. You know that, right?"

"I know it now. OK, so I have a question. After New York, why didn't you come talk to me? You knew where I lived."

"I'm glad you asked that because I was curious about something too. First of all, I called you a million times but you never answered."

"Yeah, sorry about that. I turned off my phone after I stopped texting you. With you gone, I had no reason for a phone anymore."

"I tried to call you at your school, but realized I had no idea where you taught. Funny thing how I loved you enough to want to spend the rest of my life with you, but I had no specific details of your life. I didn't know where you taught, or any of your friends' last names. Worst of all, do you know we've *never* taken a picture together? I searched my brain for any stops we made to take a picture, and there were none. What did we do in Hawaii all that time?"

"We, no I, lost a ton of weight from all the exercise you Reids put me through. So you still haven't answered my question. Why didn't you come find me at home?"

"Sorry, got sidetracked. I did come by your house. I came the next day and you weren't home. I stopped by at all hours and you wouldn't answer your door. Then the day after, against my wishes, the chief sent me up to Seattle to co-lead in a heart transplant and I was gone for almost a week. By the time I got back to your door again, someone else answered and said you no longer lived there. I tried to convince this person to give me your contact number, but I think she thought I was some kind of psychopath. She almost called the police on me.

"This is where I'm confused," said Jake. "You hadn't left for Japan yet because I didn't get your letter at the hospital till a week or so later. Where were you all that time?"

"Funny how our lives got so crossed. The day I got home from New York, Max came over and we had our talk. Later that night, Sarah and Charlie came over and shared with us the exciting news of their engagement. With less than two weeks to help Sarah with wedding plans, I went back and forth from my house to Sarah's, trying to help her prepare. Fortunately the house got leased immediately, and that would explain my tenant whom you met."

I felt a sudden panic attack.

"Jake. What am I going to do?"

"Why? What's wrong?"

"I don't have a home to go back to. My tenant is staying in my house till the end of summer."

"Fantastic!" Jake exulted. "Move in with me."

He abruptly corrected himself. "Move into my parents' home with me. You can take up occupancy in the guest room, unless...you get scared on the third floor by yourself and want to sleep in my bed with me."

"You're incorrigible," I said with a huge grin on my face.

I had a list of people to call to share our good news.

"Sarah?"

"Emily? Are you OK? Where are you? Are you back in the States? Whose number is this?"

Of course she would be worried about me. Once I began talking, she would know I would finally be OK.

"I'm fine. How's Hawaii?"

"It's wonderful, but what's wrong?"

"I wanted to let you know that Jake is here with me. He found me here in Kyoto."

"What?" Sarah sounded too shocked to talk. I could hear Charlie ask, "What's wrong? Is Emily OK?" He grabbed the phone from her.

"Emily. What's going on?"

"I'm fine, Charlie. Jake came to me, a bit late, but he's here now."

Sarah got back on the phone and I gave her a quick explanation of what happened. Her tears of joy resonated all the way to Kyoto.

"Emily. Nobody deserves more happiness than you. Tell Jake if he *ever* hurts you again, he'll have to answer to me."

"And me," I heard Charlie yell in the background.

Giggling, I looked at Jake. "My best friend and her husband are threatening your life if you hurt me again."

"You tell the newlyweds there's no chance of that happening. Enjoy your honeymoon," he called into the phone.

"Sarah, I'm leaving here in a couple of weeks and meeting Jake in Paris. I'll see you back at home mid-June. Have a great rest of your honeymoon. I'll call you again."

Jane was next on the list. She, too, was elated to hear that Jake and I were back together, and added to the growing threat on Jake as we put her on speakerphone.

"Jake? Don't screw up this time, OK?"

"I won't. I'm not letting go of Emily ever again." He gazed over at me while talking to his sister.

Our entire make-up story was rehashed in under two minutes but more importantly, I also told Jane how much I missed her. She was the one person besides Jake I most wanted to see.

"When are you coming home, Jane? When can we see each other?"

"I got a job so Manhattan is my home for a while—maybe Thanksgiving at the earliest."

"Jane..." I whined. "Hey, do you want to meet us in Paris?" I thought this was a fantastic idea.

"No way!" Jake yelled at both of us.

Shocked, I stared at him, and Jane laughed.

"Why don't you come see me?" she suggested.

I looked at Jake, hoping he would let me go see her. Neither one of us would want to be apart from each other, but Jane was the sister I never had.

"Can I go visit Jane?" I asked cautiously.

"If she promises not to tag along in Paris," he huffed.

A sour look shrouded my once happy face. Jake softened and offered an alternative. "Why don't we stop by New York after Paris? We can hang with her a few days and then come home."

"Can we really do that?" I asked with excitement.

"Emi, it's your world. We can do whatever you like."

"Jane, I'll call you from Paris and let you know exactly when we're coming. Call Nick and have him join us as well."

"You sound more excited to meet up with my siblings in New York than to meet me in Paris." Jake was pouting again.

"Emily, you better go. Call me later." Jane knew her brother only too well. She probably had a mental picture of his arms crossed and lips protruding like a five-year-old. I turned toward my love, grabbed his face, and kissed him numerous times till I got a smile out of him. His dimpled smile returned, only to be vexed again, as it was time to call Max.

"Hi, Max. It's me, Em."

"I can tell by the tone of your voice that Jake is right there next to you."

"You know me too well." I smiled. "Thank you, Max. You are wonderful to help me find Jake again."

"I'm happy knowing you're happy. I love you, Em. My debt is paid."

Jake took the phone and talked to Max while I pondered my good fortune of having in the present and the past, two wonderful men who taught me to love. They both continued to watch over me.

"Call Gram for me, I want to talk to her," I asked enthusiastically as I handed the phone to Jake.

He did as I asked and handed the phone back to me.

"Hi, Gram!" I started crying again. "How are you? I'm so glad to be talking to you again. I've missed you."

"Emily. Don't cry. I've missed you too. I was very worried when Jake couldn't find you. Hallelujah! This madness is finally over. Is Jake being good to you?"

"Oh, Gram, he's been a dream. I'm sorry we worried you. We won't ever do that to you again."

"Are you going to marry my grandson now?"

"Definitely, Gram! If he asks again, I promise I won't disappoint you."

"Emily, come to London. Let me finally meet you." Her tone, welcoming, I knew I would love her like my own grandmother. "Let me talk to Jake and we'll arrange a visit."

Our last phone call was to Sandy and Bobby, and they were thrilled to hear I would come live with them till the end of summer. Sandy promised to have the guest room ready before we got back from Paris. Jake told them not to bother as he was sure I wouldn't be sleeping there.

Without having eaten much all day, our empty stomachs caught up with us. We walked toward the nearest street vendor.

"By the way, didn't you say that you were waiting for someone back at the restaurant? You made it sound like you were seeing someone already. What was that all about?" Jake questioned. I thought we were done hashing out all of our misunderstandings—apparently not.

"Yes, I said I was waiting for someone, but I never said I was seeing anyone." My ambiguous answer didn't sit well with Jake.

"What does that mean?" I loved that his childlike tone surfaced whenever he didn't get his way. "Have you dated anyone since you got here? Have other men asked you out? If so, how many?

I chose to keep mum. I shut my lips and formed a flat horizontal smile, while eating my udon noodles.

"Emi, aren't you going to answer?" His voice grew impatient while he placed his hands all over my body and tickled me. I laughed, choked on my noodles, and promised to answer without a fight.

"You play dirty," I accused while giving him an evil eye.

"*You*, no, yes, and many."

Jake took my answers and dropped them at the end of each of his questions. He looked upset again.

"I don't understand the first answer."

Staring at him I asked, "Are you really as smart as everyone says you are? You asked me who I was waiting for. I was waiting for *YOU*. I've been waiting for you since you left me last Christmas. Do you get it now?"

"Oh! I get it." He smiled again till he thought through my other answers.

"What do you mean many men have asked you on dates? How many single men could live in that tiny village of yours? And why would they ask you out? Didn't you tell them you were taken?"

"Why on earth would I tell them that? There's no ring on my finger that says I'm taken. And, I didn't stay in the village the whole time. I traveled throughout Japan. You're not the only man to find me attractive."

Jake reached into his pocket and pulled out my beautiful ring. Oh how I had missed that ring. He slowly drew out my left hand and my heart jumped a-flutter.

He was going to propose again!

I definitely knew what my answer would be this time. Jake slid the eternity band on my ring finger and I basked in this tender moment.

To my utter dismay, rather than proposing, he handed me a stern warning. "I don't ever want to see you take this ring off unless I replace with another one, OK?"

"All right..." My lips pouted and my answer sounded sore.

Jake mused at my chagrin. "What's wrong? Were you expecting something else? Do you not like this ring?"

What could I say? *No, I like this ring but I'd like a proposal along with it?* "I love this ring," was all that came out of my mouth.

Night fell upon us and we walked hand in hand back to the hotel.

"Where's your suitcase?" I inquired.

"They're holding it for me here. I haven't had a chance to check in yet."

"Why don't you have them bring up your stuff up to my room?" I didn't have to look in a mirror to know my cheeks had turned bright red. I also didn't have to look at Jake to know his stunned face quickly changed to nirvana. He practically sprinted up to my room.

Walking in, Jake quickly surveyed the double bed. Heaven to hell in sixty seconds, he threw up a prayer. "Love, I've been apart from you for too long to be satisfied sleeping in a bed next to yours."

"Would it satisfy you to sleep in a bed...with me?" I asked sheepishly."

I'd never seen Jake so happy!

We said a quick and sweet good-bye in Kyoto, as we both had to leave for our respective jobs. It pained me to leave him again. I made up twenty different excuses as to why I wanted to go back with him. Every excuse pointed to the fact that we would be apart only twelve days. Then, we would have many joyful days together.

"I don't want you to go. It feels like a dream to be back together with you. I don't want to say good-bye anymore."

"Love, it's only for twelve days. We'll see each other soon. After that, we don't ever have to say good-bye. Make sure you log onto your computer at 9:00 p.m. your time. That will serve as a substitute until Paris."

"OK." I pouted some more. "I'll miss you."

"Me, too, my love. Me too."

I left him standing at the station, knowing that we would soon be together again, and if God was kind to us, we would never have to say good-bye.

Chapter 17

A Proposal in Paris

The plane thumped onto the Charles de Gaulle Airport runway and my heart thumped along with it. Finally, we would reunite. Customs would not be a problem, as I brought only one carry-on suitcase barely filled with clothes and toiletries. Jake arrived earlier this morning and probably already checked into the hotel. What our sleeping arrangements would be like made me curious after what had happened our last night together. It would be an awful waste of money to get two rooms, but I knew that if we only had one room, I would not be able to resist him. We'd been apart for too long. My body now longed for him almost as much as my heart did. My willpower would crumble. I would let him choose what he thought best for us, and I would not fight his decision.

Walking out of customs, I saw the love of my life smiling with his arms wide open. I ran into his arms and hugged him like I hadn't seen him in years. These twelve days felt longer than the five months we were separated. Even with the webcam, I missed him very much. How different it was to feel his secure arms around me.

"Hello, my love. Did you have a good flight over here?" Jake asked.

I looked up at him and responded by pressing my lips against his. I kissed him more longingly than I had ever done. My body desired his touch, his warmth, his passion. Jake appeared to be a bit taken aback, more befuddled than anything else. I'd never displayed such an inappropriate public display of affection. His kiss grew more sensuous as he realized how much I wanted him and our embrace continued. I didn't care that onlookers were gawking. All I wanted was to love Jake.

It was Jake who pulled away for the first time. Caressing the back of my head he chuckled. "Maybe I can undo the second room?"

I didn't quite understand what he was saying but I held his hand out of the airport to a huge limousine that awaited us.

"This is *not* our car, is it? You got us a driver too?" I seriously hoped not.

"Yes, it is, and yes, I did." Jake declared.

"You have got to be kidding me. We cannot ride around Paris in this limo. How embarrassing. We're not rock stars," I complained.

"Get in," he said rolling his eyes.

We got to the Hotel Ritz, and opulent was the only word I could think to describe this hotel. Located on the Place Vendome, in the first arrondissement, Hotel Ritz was surrounded by haute couture. Stores like Christian Dior, Chanel, and Bulgari, surrounded this architectural jewel commissioned by Louis XIV. If I remembered correctly from my last trip here, Palaise de l'Elysee, where the French president resides, was nearby, as well as the Louvre and Jardin des Tuileries. There was only one way in to this exclusive square and one way out. This was definitely not the kind of place Sarah and I had stayed in when we were in Europe.

Extravagant and unnecessary, but a nice way to travel, I had to admit.

Jake had already checked us in and took me up to my room. With a mixture of relief and disappointment, we had two adjoining rooms. Waiting for me in my room was a bathtub filled with rose petals with lavender scented candles lit all around it. Water fell from the mouth of a gold swan as Jake added more hot water to my bath.

"Why don't you unwind a bit and we'll start our trip after your bath," he offered.

"Thank you, Jake. You know, you're spoiling me. I can really get used to this," I answered in a dreamy way.

A girl could really get used to living in such luxury with the man of her dreams.

"It can *all* be yours if you like, my love. No one is stopping you."

While I thought about those words, Jake started toward the door.

"Where are you going?" I asked, waking from my thoughts.

"Um, out to give you some privacy. Do you want me to stay?" he mused.

Tempted, but resisting the urge, I asked, "No, I mean where will you be while I'm taking a bath?"

"I need to stop by Boucheron. I'll be right back."

"What is Boucheron?"

"It's a jewelry shop," he said quickly shutting the door behind him.

Jewelry shop? Why would he be going to a jewelry shop? Maybe he was going to propose to me in Paris? I could only dream, but we had just gotten back together. It was too soon to dream. Having been so adamant about marriage being too soon for us, I probably scared him off that idea.

A proposal—no, two proposals—was what separated us to begin with. I wanted to shoot myself for turning down his proposal the first time.

We would've been engaged or even married by now. Stupid. Stupid. Stupid! Emily, you can be so stupid! But...a jewelry shop? Why? Naw...he already has an engagement ring for me; he wouldn't be going there for that purpose. Great! He's got me all wound up when this bath was supposed to relax me.

The tension only got worse, so with a quick hot shower, Jake's favorite yellow sundress, and a little makeup on the face, I was ready for the day. Comfortable in this lap of luxury, I started flipping through French TV and patiently waited for Jake.

Within minutes of turning on the TV, I heard the door *be-beep* and in walked Jake with a crepe and a cup of coffee.

"Where did you get this? There couldn't be a crepe vendor in this tony neighborhood."

"I stopped by the boulangerie."

"Thank you. I was getting hungry."

He smiled and handed me my snack.

"Emily, tell me some of the things you want to do in Paris. We can go out of Paris as well if you like. Give me your list."

"Well, last time I was here, I never got to go to the Bastille opera house or Palais Garnier and watch an opera. I'd love to do that this time."

"You've been here before? It's not your first time?"

"Sarah and I were in Europe for a month after undergrad. I assume you have been here many times before?" I knew this was an obvious question, as I couldn't imagine the Reids not having traveled to France.

"My mom loves Paris. When we were younger, we used to stay at the Ritz every spring for a month. After we started school, we came during the summertime. Since I was little, they've had the same hotel manager here. I'll introduce you to him when we go to the Escoffier school."

Jake spoke beautiful French to the driver as well as the hotel staff when we first arrived. It only made sense that he lived and perfected his French here.

"Anything else you want to do? I promised you that this week would be your world. Whatever you like, I'll oblige."

"There's not too much else. You know, the usual...the Louvre, Musee d'Orsay, maybe a flea market. You're the expert in this city. You lead, I'll follow."

"I like this attitude," he answered, pleased. "I'll have the concierge send a list of what's playing. Right now, we need to go downstairs. We have an appointment with the chef."

My questions ceased, and as promised, I followed his lead. There was one thing that made me pause. It surprised me that Jake hadn't touched me since I got to Paris. Aside from my attack at the airport, we hadn't embraced. He had been tame for his standards. It made me curious, as well as a bit nervous.

We met Francois Garcon, the general manager of Hotel Ritz, at the Escoffier school. It looked to be a cooking school of some sort but I thought I'd wait for an explanation before asking any questions.

"Bonjour, Monsieur Reid. Ca va?"

"Oui, ca va, Francois."

"Bonjour, Madamoiselle" Francois said turning to me, "Je suis Francois, le directeur de l'hotel. C'est un plaisir de vous rencontrer."

I decided to use my decrepit French and tell Francois that I too was happy to make his acquaintance.

"Bonjour, Je suis Emily Logan. Il est très agréable de vous rencontrer aussi," I proudly uttered.

"Ah, vous parlez Francaises?" Francois asked.

"You speak French?" Jake asked, quite surprised.

"Oui, je parle un peu."

Telling Francois and Jake that I spoke a little was about the extent of our conversation in French. I couldn't keep up with the two of them as they conversed the entire time in French. Here and there, Jake would break the flow of his conversation and ask me what kind of lesson I would prefer. My choices were basic French cooking, pastry making, and even flower arranging. I chose to work with the chef de pâtisserie and learn dessert.

We spent four hours making French baguettes from scratch, croissants, creme brulee, strawberry savarin, mocha pot de creme, apple tarte tatin, lemon souffle, crepes, and even profiteroles. I was so in my element in the kitchen. I loved it, and Jake enjoyed watching me have fun. What was even better than making the desserts was of course eating them. The school set up a table for us in the kitchen and we ate every dessert we made. The pastry chef packed up what we did not finish and we walked out to the square hoping to relieve our distended stomach.

We walked quietly, hand in hand, toward the Tuileries Garden.

Jake turned to me and asked, "What are you thinking right now?"

"I was thinking that our private lesson at the Escoffier was about the coolest thing I've ever done in my life!"

"You liked it that much?" Jake seemed quite surprised that a cooking school would make such an impression on me.

"If life would have turned out differently for me when I was younger, I probably would've gone to cooking school after undergrad. I feel most comfortable in a kitchen. Maybe one day when I'm retired, I'll enroll in a cooking school just for fun. Thanks to you, I've checked off another thing I've always wanted to do. Thank you."

Jake stopped walking and turned to look at me. I saw that same sadness in his eyes again. He was imaging what my life must have been like after I'd lost my parents. He stroked my cheeks with the back of his two fingers and lovingly gazed into my eyes. At first, I was uncomfortable standing so still in the middle of a busy street. But with the touch of his lips, I knew that Jake would make up for me the life that he thought I'd missed.

I broke out of our embrace and asked, "What's next? This is so much fun! I might never want to leave."

Jake laughed and walked me toward Chanel.

"What's at Chanel?"

"We're going to eat at Alain Ducasse's Le Jules Vernes at the Eiffel Tower tonight. You need to pick out a dress."

"What about you?"

"I brought a suit. If you can't find a dress here, we can go to another store."

I couldn't imagine not finding something that I liked at Chanel. The only dilemma I'd foresee was the price tag.

"Jake, I can't buy a dress at Chanel. Let's go somewhere else. This is way out of my comfort zone." Spending an insane amount of money on a dress I'd wear once screamed against my common sense.

"Love, I have one dress picked out for you already. Will you humor me and try it on? I'd like to see what it looks on you." His encouraging words nudged me into an unapproachable shop.

The sales gals led me to a dressing room and had me try on a modern version of Coco Chanel's little black dress. This sleeveless black wool dress was cut above the knee with a simple buttoned belt sewn into the dress. The skirt of the dress had loose pleats that gave it a slightly bouffant feel. The dress was perfect. In addition, the sales lady picked out a pair of muted white patent leather boots with a thin strip of black patent leather at the top that came up about one inch above my knee. Truth be told, I loved the outfit. Minus the sunglasses, pearl choker, and an updo, I felt like Holly Golightly in *Breakfast at Tiffany's*. I stepped out of the dressing room to show Jake.

"You look stunning!" He enunciated each of the three words.

"We'll take the entire outfit," he said to the lady.

Watching Jake pay for the dress—in addition to this entire trip—made me horribly uncomfortable. When this trip was initially planned, details of who would pay for what, never arose, as all I wanted was to be with Jake. Now that this fantasy has come true, I needed to have an awkward conversation with him and tell him I had no financial expectations from him. The Ritz, private cooking lessons, a Chanel dress, and dinner at Alain Ducasse's restaurant did not feel right in my world. I couldn't deny enjoying the indulgence, but the impropriety of delighting in such luxuries made me feel guilty.

As we walked out of the store, Jake immediately sensed the change in my mood.

"Do you not like the dress? Are you upset I didn't give you a choice in this matter? I just thought you looked so stunning..." Jake worried too much about my feelings at times.

"No, no. I love the dress. It's beautiful and practical as well. I can wear it multiple times."

"Then why do you look unhappy?"

"It's just...this trip...we never discussed how we'd pay for it. Please don't feel obligated to provide everything for me. I'd like to pay for something..."

"Emily!" he cut me off before I embarrassed myself any further. "The word obligation does not exist in our relationship. What I do for you stems from love and desire. I don't need or want anything from you but you. What can you possibly buy me that's more precious than you?"

"It's not just the material possessions I'm talking about. You've showered me with love from the start. I didn't actualize or verbalize this love till recently. You've taken me on trips, and brought me gifts and I feel like all I've done was received. I'm ashamed that I've only started reciprocating." As I uttered these words, I realized how true this statement described our relationship.

"Emily. Back in New York, when I was stupid enough to go chasing after your ring rather than stopping you from leaving, then back at home, when you left me nothing but a letter and ran off to Japan, I promised myself that if we ever got a chance to be together again, I would spare nothing of myself. Whether material or emotional, what I have is all yours. And I know that materially, if our situations were reversed, you would do the same for me. So please, let me dote on you the way I've dreamed of for so many months while you were away. OK? What happened to your 'you lead and I'll follow' motto?"

Could I possibly love a better man than this one?

"All right," I answered. "I love you, Jake."

"I love you too. Now let's get ready for dinner."

We got ready in our separate rooms and Jake came over while I was finishing up my makeup. His naughtiness resurfaced when I asked him to help me zip up the rest of my dress. Rather than helping me, he unzipped my dress, and draped his cold hands onto my body. He hands quickly crept up the front side while kissing the back of my neck. I turned to face him and tried to loosen his grip. He had a strong hold on me as he continued to caress my neck with his lips. There was no use fighting this battle, as he was much stronger. Using this as an excuse, I gave into both our desires. His hands traced over my back while his lips traveled to my chin. My hands wrapped around his neck and I brought his head up to join our lips.

Without a fight, my little black dress fell to the ground.

At this point my mind waged war on my body. Should I see this all the way through or should I stop Jake now? My body quivered, "Yes!" My mind retaliated with a "No!" Ugh. What a war this was. I wanted my body to win, but my mind was still stronger. I sighed! I'd been patient up until now, what was a bit longer till I got married? My mind won.

"Jake!" I pleaded. "Jake? Honey? Please, don't." My weak plea did nothing to alter his determination. My body was hoping it wouldn't. Now that the dress was off, his lips and hands ran amok.

I would try once more and figured if this didn't work, I'd concede to both of our desires.

"Jake...I'd really like to honor my mom's wish and stay a virgin till I get married. Please?" I begged one last time.

That stopped him in his tracks. He acquiesced grudgingly. He let me go and walked away while I got back in my dress and finished getting ready.

He muttered something that sounded like, "I gotta get this done soon." He was probably trying to find some other way to woo me into bed.

Dinner at the Eiffel Tower was almost as spectacular as the view. We could see striking views of the city with many impressions of the tower's intricate metal latticework. It was unbelievable to think that three hundred men built this structure in one year.

"Did you know," I said while taking a bite of my grilled sea scallop, "that Sarah and I didn't have time to visit the Eiffel Tower when we were in Paris?"

"Why not?" Jake asked, while enjoying his pan-seared veal with crispy spinach.

"Well, it was our last night in Paris, and we decided to splurge and go have a meal at Guy Savoy. Our meal took almost four hours and by the time we were done, the tower was closed. I'm glad we got to come today. We'll have to take a picture and e-mail it to Sarah."

When we got back in the car the driver took us on a scenic tour of the city. We saw the tower lit up from the ground, and we followed the Seine into the Rive Gauche. Revelers sat outside cafes and brasseries on Boulevard St. Germain des Pres sipping their lattes and grabbing a bite to eat. On the way back, our driver came up the Rive Droit and drove through Champs Elysees again.

"Today was beyond a doubt the most perfect day I could've imagined. I'd be content to go home tomorrow, it was so ideal. Thank you, Jake."

Jake looked satisfied that I was happy.

"So what's on tap for tomorrow?" I asked with a smile. "How could you possibly top today?"

"You start your day with more cooking classes. In fact, there's a cooking class every morning for you at 6:30 a.m. They'll take you through their entire program in the week that we're here."

"Are you serious?" My arms and legs flailed up and down in excitement as we walked back into the hotel. A few hotel guests turned around to see the crazy American.

"If you want to do it, show up at the Escoffier school by 6:30 every morning."

We stood outside my door and I asked Jake what he planned on doing while I was at my cooking class.

"I'll be asleep. You can bring me breakfast every morning when you're done."

"Deal!" I said. "I'm so excited, I won't be able to sleep tonight."

"Glad you like it. Go in and rest. You have an early morning," Jake said kissing my lips.

"Aren't you coming in?"

"I'm only coming in if you let me stay. I won't have the willpower to leave tonight."

My mind fought with my body again. I sighed and let him go.

"Good night," I murmured, while kissing him back.

Today was truly the most magical day, and could have only been better if Jake had proposed. With such a romantic setting as the Eiffel Tower, Jake might have been encouraged to propose again if my first rejection hadn't scared him off. Oh well. I shouldn't dwell on it. I appreciated what I had now.

The alarm went off at 6:00 a.m., and without any struggle, my body gleefully got up and got ready for cooking class. I put on a pair of jeans, a T-shirt, and the Ritz apron I received yesterday. In class, there were two other students ready for our intensive lesson.

Today's lesson: French Sauces: To start, the chef had us make chicken, beef, and veal stock, which would be used today, as well as tomorrow, for our meat course. Once we got all the ingredients in the pot for the stocks, we attempted such sauces as Bearnaise, beurre blanc, and bourdelaise. French cooking definitely wasn't easy. Chef Geurlaine also taught us to make a variety of salad dressings. We packaged all our sauces and dressings, and placed them in the refrigerator ready to be used with the meat courses tomorrow. By the end of class, I had learned a solid foundation in French sauces—another fantastic morning to an already amazing trip.

Tiptoeing into Jake's room, I found him dressed but back asleep on his bed. He looked just as sweet as he did back in Hawaii but this time insecurity didn't creep into my heart. We were meant to be together, and if in the future our relationship didn't work out, I'd be content knowing we had a chance. I placed breakfast on the table and slowly crept into his bed and snuggled into his body. He smiled and cradled his arms around me.

"Hi Beautiful. How was class this morning?" he asked half asleep.

"Excellent," I replied with a jubilant voice. "I have breakfast for you if you like."

"I am hungry…but am enjoying laying here with you in my arms."

"Why are you dressed but asleep?"

"I got an early phone call so I got ready for the day but felt so groggy I decided to go back to sleep. Jet lag must have caught up with me last night."

"Do you want me to leave so you can sleep some more?"

"No." He cut me off and let go of me. "I'm ready to get up. We have an appointment with Henri at Boucheron this morning. We should get going."

Boucheron? Wasn't this the jewelry store Jake visited yesterday? Why would we have an appointment?

Asking Jake what was going on was on the tip of my tongue, but I didn't want to seem presumptuous and I didn't want to pressure him into proposing.

As thoughts of Boucheron wouldn't leave my mind, no different scenarios, aside from a proposal, played in my head. Jake stared at me with a smug gaze. Once again, Jake piqued my curiosity.

We left the hotel and walked to Boucheron. It was excruciating waiting for an explanation that never came. Jake talked about the day and told me that we were going to the Louvre and then to a soccer game after lunch.

"You can't come to Europe and not watch these nationals go crazy over their soccer team. France is playing Italy today. It'll be a great match up. We'll have a car take us to the stadium."

"Will we ever take the Metro here?"

"Why do that when you have a driver at your disposal?"

I let out a chortle and thought what a silly question to ask.

Henri was a delightful elderly gentleman who took us to a small private room upon entering this stunning jewelry shop. I didn't realize regular people actually shopped in stores as glamorous as this one. Gawking around the main room, I looked for movie stars or some famous person, but to my disappointment, there were no sightings. Henri and Jake spoke in French the entire way into our room. They spoke so quickly I couldn't catch any of their conversation. I was rather hoping to figure out why I was here. After a few minutes, I finally got an explanation, but this was not the scenario I had spun out in my head.

After all introductions were made, Jake explained he was here on Gram's request to get her mother's ring reset.

"Oh. How's Gram doing? Can we call her after this errand?" I asked. "I miss her."

"Should we go see her after Paris?"

"I'd love to do that! Do we have time? By the way, do you have a grandfather as well?"

"No he passed away two years ago, and she's been living on her own since. She and Gramps retired in London back in the late nineties."

I wanted to ask more questions, but I thought it rude since Henri was waiting for us.

"So, Gram is about to hand down her mother's diamond to my mom. It was my great grandmother's desire to see this ring handed down from daughter to daughter. Gram wants Henri, our family's favorite jewelry setter, to reset this ring so she can pass it down to her. Neither Gram nor Mom will have anyone touch her jewelry except Henri."

Not the explanation I wanted, but I was still a bit puzzled.

"So I assume the ring is ready and we are here to pick it up?"

"No, it's not ready yet. We need your help."

"What could I do?" I wondered aloud.

"You and Mom have the same ring size and I was wondering if you could try on the ring so we won't have to resize it. Gram thought since we were here in Paris, might as well get it done right."

I kept playing twenty questions hoping for a favorable answer but it never came.

"How do you know your mom and I have the same ring size?" I asked, with a last hope that maybe I might be the beneficiary of good news.

"She was the one who tried on your eternity band. That's how I know," were the final words that made me stop the inquisition.

Jake and Henri looked at each other and said something furtively in French and chuckled. I was obviously missing out on their inside joke.

I abandoned the rest of my theories and waited for the ring. When Henri came back from the safe, he asked me to take off my eternity band and told me he would check it to make sure none of the diamonds were loose and he would clean it as well. I unenthusiastically took off my band while Henri handed the other ring to Jake.

Jake walked over and held out my left hand. His hands trembled and my heart began thumping wildly. He forced a casual smile and slowly pushed an enormous square cut diamond. I felt a chill go down my spine as he placed this dazzling jewel onto my ring finger. I knew it didn't belong to me but the glow on Jake's face suggested this ring was meant to bind us as one. The sheer magnitude and brilliance of the ring made me feel a lump of jealousy as well.

While I reveled in Sandy's borrowed moment, Jake abruptly pulled off the ring and handed it back to Henri.

"Bon! Merci, Henri"

I had to walk out of the room so Jake wouldn't notice the tears in my eyes. I knew the ring wasn't mine, but in my heart, I so intensely wished for a proposal that didn't happen.

Jake walked out after some time and led me outside, and we left, just like that, for the Louvre.

"Jake. What about my ring?" I asked.

"Huh?" His answer was a bit flustered. "How did you...oh! We'll pick up the band before we leave." I was in too much of a haze to comprehend his incoherent thought.

Francois from the hotel had arranged a private tour of the Louvre for us. The docent led us around the entire museum, and even took us into rooms forbidden to the public. The "fix-it" room was the most interesting of these rooms. There were specially trained men and women repairing paintings and sculptures damaged during a move or from natural wear and tear.

Though the Louvre was fascinating, my mind couldn't leave that private room at Boucheron. My thoughts kept drifting back to the ring, Jake's glow when he placed the ring on my finger, and a picture of the ring on my finger. Jake noticed my preoccupation at lunch.

"Emily..."

I heard him call me, but wasn't paying attention.

"Emily!"

"Huh? Yes? Did you need something?" I asked in a fog.

"What's wrong with you? You've been zoned out all morning since Boucheron. Is something wrong?"

Ugh! He noticed.

"No, nothing's wrong," I lied.

"What's on your mind? You haven't been yourself. Your body is here but your mind is somewhere else. You can't even concentrate on your lunch, which is a first."

It was true. Jake brought me to a gorgeous tea salon nestled in an old green very French-looking building in the Saint Germain area of Paris. The server explained to us that this establishment first opened in 1862. This was the type of beautiful but unattainable storefront Sarah and I would visit and purchase a macaron or two. A stunning window display filled with colorful cake plates and fun pastry boxes showcasing cakes and chocolates and tartes greeted us. Inside, a delicious smell of sugar presented in the shape of millefeuilles and éclairs and cream puffs and biscuits, paralyzed me initially.

This place was famous for their pastries, namely my favorite—macarons. These were their "emblem." At around thirty euros for an array of macarons, I should have enjoyed them more than my French Laundry meal but I still couldn't focus. Not my monkfish carpaccio with lemon marmalade or the tray of pastries—just about one of every goody the store had to offer—took me away from that ring.

What to say? Surprisingly, I came up with a legitimate excuse. "I think jet lag caught up with me as well." I lied again.

I couldn't explain the obsession with a ring that didn't belong to me, and a proposal that never transpired.

"OK. You're being awfully strange." Though there was a smirk on his face, I couldn't process beyond our immediate conversation. "You want to go back to the hotel instead of the soccer match?"

"No. I'm fine," I promised. "Let's enjoy our lunch and go watch futbol."

Jake wasn't kidding when he said that Europeans were fanatical about their futbol. We sat with the French nationals and regretted not having worn the French tricolor—blue, white, and red. We saw half-naked men with their national flag painted all over their bodies, and long plastic horns called vuvuzela blew every third second, and the Europeans, too, had a chant or a song for each play. Even with such a spectacle, I couldn't get into the game. I was still in a daze.

Maybe it was because I didn't understand the game.

Maybe it was because the men next to me were drunk and obnoxious.

But, most likely it was because my head was still wrapped around that little, correction—huge—diamond ring.

Who would have thought I'd be so consumed with a ring.

Around midnight, we found ourselves in front of my room, entangled in a kiss good night.

"I guess we have to separate, huh?" I murmured.

"We don't have to. You choose to. Good night, my love," was all he said as he walked into his room.

Today's lesson: Viande et Poisson—Meat and Fish: We used the stock we made yesterday and cooked many classic French fare. Beef Bourguignon, a beef stew, seared Foie Gras, which tasted amazing even at 8:00 a.m., frog legs, Coquilles, and Loup au fenouil, sea bass in a creamy fennel sauce. All of this was a bit overwhelming to taste so early, but again, I enjoyed every moment of the lesson.

Rather than going straight to Jake's room, I headed back to my room to give Sarah a call. We had only spoken once since she got back from her honeymoon and I missed her, and wanted to get an update on married life. It was midnight her time, but I thought I'd give it a try.

"Hello?" answered a sleepy voice.

"Sarah!" I answered back cheerfully.

"Emily. Hi! Are you still in Paris?"

"Yeah, it's our third day here."

"Is life with Jake as wonderful as you dreamed it would be?"

"Yeah, it's been incredible. I'm having so much fun. I'm even taking cooking lessons here at the hotel. Jake's thought of everything for me." My bipolar mood surfaced with each answer.

"That's great, but why do you sound like that? Let me guess…he hasn't popped the question yet."

"No," I moped. "What if he decides he doesn't want to marry me after all?"

"Emily, are you kidding me? This is a man who flew all the way to Japan to reconcile with you. You told me yourself he was miserable without you the past five months. Just be patient and be happy. You're in Paris, the most romantic city in the world! Being with Jake is what you've dreamed of for the last six months. You guys are finally together. Even if a proposal doesn't happen this week, he's not going to let go of you ever again. When the time is right he will ask again." She consoled me the best she could.

"I know. Thanks, Sarah," I tried to say in a more cheery way. "How's married life?"

"Incredible!" she answered.

"You two have dated for nine years. Is it really that much different?"

"Married life is more amazing, more intimate, more…everything!"

"All right, I get the hint. I'm sure I'm interrupting something very important. I'll call when I get back home. Bye."

Sarah started cracking up. "Bye, Emily. Have a great rest of the trip."

We hung up and I promised myself that I would change my attitude. My sour disposition wasn't fair to Jake. *When he's ready, he will ask again.*

Jake caught me as I was about to walk out of my room.

"Why are you here by yourself?" His brows creased with worry. "Is everything all right?"

"It's perfect! I came in to call Sarah. I was just heading your way. Did you get the breakfast I sent over?"

"Yes," he said with a good morning embrace. "Thank you."

"What's on the itinerary today, Dr. Reid? Speaking of, don't you miss being at the hospital?"

"Nope. Not when I'm with you." He smiled. "Today, how about we do a little shopping, and then go to the Opera House? Francois sent over a list of specialty shops. There are two large flea markets we can visit."

"Sounds great!" My chipper face was back on.

Today was a day where I was grateful to have a loaner car and driver from the hotel. At the Saint Ouen flea market in the 18th arrondissement, it took us almost four hours to walk around the entire marketplace. For Sandy, I bought an antique clock, and for Bobby I found an old ink pen. There wasn't anything to my liking for Nick and Jane so we got in the car and visited numerous antique shops, clothes shops, and shoe and accessory stores in Porte de Vanves in the 14th arrondissement. I had better luck there and found a frighteningly racy lingerie for Sarah and Charlie, which Jake begged me to keep for myself, and a cool hat for Jane at a vintage shop.

Next, our driver took us to a most charming group of bookstalls known as Les Bouquinistes. Set against the edge of the River Seine, rows and rows of green metal boites, or boxes, sold old and used books, magazines, prints, posters, and pictures. Over two hundred vendors set up shop across the Seine from the iconic Notre Dame Cathedral.

Upon first glance, every stall looked an identical green color, like the kind one would see in old train cars. We stopped at several bouquinistes before learning that with patience and careful scouring, valuable first edition tomes could be discovered at any random stall. At one particular vendor I found a tattered, leather-bound copy of Charles Dickens' *A Tale of Two Cities* from the early 1900's while Jake chatted with the owner in mellifluous French. I also discovered Julia Child's first cookbook that she wrote while living in Paris, and an architecture book of Paris with schematics of all the historical buildings.

This Dickens' book caused some consternation as I contemplated first, the price, and second, Jake's reaction to the receiver of this gift. Julia Child's cookbook, of course, would make a wonderful gift for Nick; Charlie would love the book of buildings. Knowing I would regret not buying these books I brought all of them up to the owner.

Jake broke from his conversation with the vendor, and placed his arms around me. "Love, are those books for you?"

"Um, no." I dragged my answer.

"Who are you buying them for?"

I gave Jake a timid look. "The cook book is for Nick, the architecture book is for Charlie, and the Dickens' book is for Max."

If I looked tentative, Jake looked unsettled.

"This is Max's favorite book and I'd really love to get his for him," I explained apologetically.

Jake quickly changed his hurt expression to an approving nod. He accepted my desire to include Max in my list of close friends, and even offered to pay for the book.

"Let me get this for him," he said. "I need to thank him for helping us get back together. I might still be looking for you if it weren't for him."

"Jake, that's not necessary. Max helped us both. He'll feel weird if you pay for this. Let me get it for him. You allowing me to do this is appreciation enough from both of us."

We both looked at each other and I hugged him reassuringly.

"You are the only man I love. This will never change, no matter what happens. Now...can we go have lunch? I'm starving!" Hungry from a lack of breakfast and way too much walking—the driver had spoiled me—we stopped in a tourist trap and ate moule et frites. I polished off every last mussel and fry, then asked the driver to take us into Ile Saint-Louis, one of the two islands in the river Seine so we could eat at the most famous ice cream shop. Sarah and I had visited this shop the last time I was here. They made their ice cream only from milk, sugar, cream, and eggs. Any other flavor added to the base was derived from natural sources such as cocoa or vanilla. Two scoops of chocolate chip ice cream later I was content to go back to the hotel. We had accomplished much.

Back at the hotel, the bellhop helped us carry all our presents up to my room. I sorely needed a nap, but instead got changed for dinner and an opera. I dressed as quickly as possible so I would not be in any compromising position like we were the first night. When Jake came in the room, he looked disappointed that I was ready to go. I chuckled to myself.

"Honey, before we leave, I want to give you something," I said.

"Oh?" he asked in a naughty way.

I ignored his comment and said, "Put out your left hand."

I took out a watch from my clutch and placed it on his left wrist.

"What's this?" he asked in a surprised voice.

"I saw this at the jewelry shop and I had to get it for you. It's a vintage Patek Philippe circa 1944. I noticed that you were partial toward Patek Philippes, and I thought it would look nice on you. You like it?"

"Emi." He sounded shocked, appreciative, and above all, touched.

The look on Jake's face stirred another layer of emotion I'd never experienced before with him. Sadly, I'd never really given anything to Jake. I'd always been on the receiving end. How selfish of me. I could see why Jake fancied giving me presents. His expression of love and appreciation gave me goose bumps. The old adage of it's better to give than to receive rang true right now.

"When did you get this? I don't think I ever left your side. Also, this could not have been cheap. Why'd you spend so much money on me?"

He had many more questions but I cut him off and said, "Let's go or we'll be late."

Our dinner was located in the first arrondissement. This two Michelin-starred restaurant was located in an exquisite townhouse of a late duke. This historic location produced the best meal we'd had so far, although it was a quick meal, as we were running late. Our server rushed a rustic risotto with frog's legs that we shared because we were so full from lunch. I deeply regretted having had so many mussels! For our main course, we both ordered the langoustines in an interesting green tea sauce. Both dishes were divine. I could see why they had earned three Michelin stars since 1973 up till recently.

We rushed out of the restaurant and got to the opera house just in time to watch La Donna del Lago. Being in Paris, there were no English supertitles. It was hard to follow. From time to time, Jake leaned over and whispered the plot to me. After the show was over, we walked over to a local bistro to have an espresso and dessert.

"I didn't like this opera as much as *Carmen*. I think I'll have to study some more French when I get back to the States. I couldn't understand anything."

Jake laughed at me. "When did you learn French in the first place?"

"In high school," I answered.

"You really can't fluently learn a language unless you live in that country. You want to live in France for a while?"

What an odd question, I thought. Why would I want to live here while Jake was back in the States?

"No. If I were to live anywhere else for an extended time, I'd like to live back in Japan, maybe this time in Tokyo. But, I don't think I can live too far away from you now so it's a moot point." Jake shook his head and laughed at me again.

<u>Today's Lesson : Legumes—Vegetables:</u> The French made all their food delicious but heavy. My stomach churned at the thought of eating anymore 81 percent pure fat butter. I couldn't intake so much fat this morning. I participated but didn't taste test. An espresso was my breakfast instead.

Jake was ready to go when I got up to his room. He wasn't quite his casual self and seemed a bit on edge. I thought about asking him what was wrong, but instead waited to see what he had planned for the day. All I'd hoped was that we weren't fine dining today. A salad and Perrier for the rest of the day suited me fine.

My body felt nauseous when I saw Jake pick up a picnic basket full of food from the main kitchen. The chef packed enough food to feed an army. We walked toward the Tuileries Garden and found a peaceful spot surrounded by flowers. I guess Jake was checking off another one of my bucket list—picnic in the Tuileries Garden with someone I was madly in love with. Jake definitely qualified. He laid out an unusually large blanket and placed the basket in the middle. I followed his lead and sat on the blanket and waited for him to break his silence. He didn't say a word the whole walk over to the garden.

Finally, I couldn't stand the silence.

"Jake."

No answer.

"Did I do something wrong? You know I don't like it when you turn mute on me. I thought you promised not to do this anymore." I spoke cautiously.

I apparently woke up him up from whatever he was thinking about because all I got was, "Huh? Did you say something?"

"Jake! What is going on? You promised not to go silent on me anymore. You haven't said a word since I got to your room this morning. Last time you did this, I didn't see you for six months." I was a bit frustrated, but more worried than anything else. I didn't understand the sudden change in his mood.

"I'm sorry, Love. I'm just trying to figure out all this stuff that the chef packed. I don't know which is which."

Sounded strange, but I accepted the explanation.

"Jake, I'm sorry but I don't really want to eat any more French food. Can we just skip to dessert?"

Whatever I said brought a frantic look on Jake's face. He began digging through the entire basket and brought out six beautifully packaged small boxes about 1 1/2 x 1 1/2 x 2 inches in size.

"What's in all these fun boxes?" I inquired.

"The chef made petit fours and placed them in here. They go sequentially. Here is the first one. Open it." He finally put a smile on his face when he handed me the first box.

In the first box laid a petit four in the likes of a Captain Crunch cereal box. I shook my head a bit trying to find meaning in this dessert, but was a bit lost. Jake saw my blank expression and began revealing his intention.

"I guess you don't remember how we first met?" He sounded a bit disappointed.

"Oh! Of course. This was the cereal I was reaching for when I bumped into you. Oh, this is so sweet. Do all these boxes contain a memory?"

I took a bite of the dessert and then gave Jake a bite.

"Yum!" we both said.

"It tastes just like Captain Crunch cereal. How fun! OK, I want the next box."

"Demanding," Jake said, while reaching over for the next box. He positioned himself in front of me and handed me the next memory.

I opened this one to find a petit four in the shape of a taco. This represented our first official date at a Mexican restaurant. I took half a bite of the taco and put it back in the box.

"Why are you leaving half the taco in the box, and don't I get a bite?"

"No. Don't you remember? You had to leave halfway through our dinner because you got called away by the hospital. The story of our life!" I huffed, rolling my eyes. "This one doesn't deserve to be eaten beyond the halfway mark. I should've known then you were a workaholic...next!"

Jake just stared at me so I added, "Please?" along with a sweet smile.

The third box was just an ordinary slice of thinly layered chocolate cake.

"No memory on this one?" I inquired.

Then it dawned on me. "Oh, I get it. This is an opera cake. This must symbolize the opera we saw in San Francisco, right?"

"Ding, ding, ding." He rang an invisible bell.

"This is loads of fun!" I exclaimed, while feeding both of us the cake.

I looked no different than a child opening up presents on Christmas morning. Love and satisfaction filled his gaze as I reveled in each gift.

The fourth box was an easy one to figure out. The pastry chef cut the dessert to look like waves in the blue ocean with little orange fish everywhere.

"This must be Hawaii. Too easy. Let's see what this one tastes like." We polished off number four.

The fifth petit four was an intricate Eiffel Tower. It looked too good to eat so we saved it for later—on to the last box.

I was bummed that this was the last one. Jogging through our memories was so much fun.

"Thank you, Jake, for coming up with such an elaborate trip down memory lane. And thank you for crossing off another item on my bucket list. You are just too wonderful."

There didn't seem to be enough adjectives to describe the awe I felt for this man.

"OK, I'm ready for the last one."

Box number six, in my right hand, was quite heavy, so I gathered up the other five into my left hand. Using my hands as a scale, I measured one against the five. This last one was definitely heavier than the other five combined.

"Maybe a pound of butter to symbolize the cooking classes I've been taking?" I guessed.

Jake cracked up, nervously.

As this was the last surprise, I slowly opened the box. Jake was peering into my face as I saw another box inside this box. My heart started racing, as I knew that this was another jewelry box—like the kind a girl received when a man got down on one knee, about to propose to the woman he loved. I tried to tell myself that it could be a pair of earrings just as easily as it could be a ring. Even if it were a ring, there was no guarantee that it was an engagement ring.

Then it dawned on me. Oh. It was my eternity band coming back to me. My heartbeat flat-lined immediately with this revelation. Jake must have picked up the band and was going to place it back on my finger. Bummer! I casually opened the box not putting much thought into it, and to my surprise I found Sandy's ring in there.

I looked at Jake a bit puzzled. "Why is your mom's ring here? Where's my eternity band?"

Jake took the ring out of the box and declared, "Emily, I can't imagine anything I would like more than to spend the rest of my life with you. Will you marry me?" Simple as that, he proposed.

It took me a millisecond to replay what he just said to me. It took me another millisecond to answer, "*YES!*" as I flung my arms around his neck.

Jake hugged me back just as fervently. He eventually tried to pry me off so he could place the ring on my finger but I wouldn't let go.

"Why'd you take so long?" I asked in a petulant and whiny voice. "You know I've been waiting!"

"Have you been waiting? I hadn't noticed." He began laughing. "I rather liked the disappointment on your face each time you thought I might propose but didn't. Your anticipation put me on an emotional roller coaster every time." His laugh turned into a guffaw.

"I can't believe you did that! How mean are you? You knew I was waiting, but you kept it from me purposely and poked fun at me in the meanwhile?" I pulled myself away from him hoping this would serve as retaliation.

"No, of course not...well, kind of." He said, pulling me down onto the blanket for a passionate embrace. Finally letting go, he explained, "Many times I wanted to propose, but I kept thinking of reasons why it wasn't the right moment." Facing each other, head in our hands, he continued, "for instance, I wanted to ask you to marry me at the Japanese restaurant, but it was a bit too soon after we had reconciled. I wasn't sure you were ready, and we still had too many issues to resolve. Then when we were at the park, I thought about proposing with the eternity band, but I knew that if you had said yes, I wouldn't have let you stay in Japan, not even for two weeks."

"Yeah, I probably would've had a hard time leaving you if you had asked that day. But, I was sorely disappointed when you didn't."

"I know. I wish I could have taken a picture of your expression when I put the ring on your finger without much else than a warning for you not to take it off." He fell back on the blanket laughing at the thought of my churlish expression back at the park. "Although I did feel terrible I didn't propose."

"But Tuesday was the most difficult. I desperately wanted to propose to you at Boucheron. The look on your face when I placed this ring on your finger was magical. You absolutely glowed. I used every ounce of self-control not to ask you to marry me that day."

"But why? You could've asked at Boucheron. That's why I was so sad that day. I couldn't get this ring and your would-be proposal off my mind. I was so bummed out. I even called Sarah to grumble."

"I didn't go through with it because I had this picnic in motion already. Also, I didn't want to give you another haphazard proposal like the one in the car on Christmas morning. I planned a deliberate expression of my love and forced myself to wait another few days. I was actually going to wait till tomorrow, but I couldn't hold out any longer."

"I'm glad you didn't wait till the last day. You would've pushed me into depression if this didn't happen soon. As it was, I was giving myself pep talks in the morning."

Jake gently slid the dazzling ring onto my finger. I couldn't believe that we were finally engaged to be married. This elation was far superior to how I imagined I would feel. Our connection was finally complete.

"Wait. Why am I wearing a substitute ring? Did you not bring my ring with you?"

"This is your ring, my love." His face beamed as he said this.

"What do you mean? What about this whole story about your grandma's ring? Did you make it all up?"

"No, it's all true. This ring belonged to my Gram's mother, and she told her to pass it down from daughter to daughter. As you know, my dad does not have any sisters, so there's really no designated heir to this ring. It probably would've gone to my mom and then to Jane. But, Gram offered it to us. When I talked to Gram in Kyoto, she asked me to wait on the proposal till we got to Paris. She wanted you to have this ring. She was most impressed with our love for each other and is elated to welcome you as her granddaughter."

Teardrops percolated. Jake wiped them off and placed his hand on my cheek before kissing me.

"Gram loves you too." He comforted me. "Let's call her. She's been waiting to talk to you. I wouldn't let her talk to you, because I didn't think she could keep my secret."

We sat up and Jake dialed his gram's number and gave her the good news.

"Hi, Gram. I'm calling to let you know that Emily accepted my proposal, and we're getting married." Gram spoke for a long time, and Jake nodded his head to everything she said. "Of course we can. Thank you for everything, Gram. I love you."

He just hung up the phone. "How come I didn't get to talk to her?"

"She wants us to Chunnel into London right now. Do you mind if we cut Paris a day short?"

"Of course not. I can't wait to finally meet Gram." I said. "But, Jake, shouldn't this ring be handed down to a Reid?"

"Sweetheart, you were a Reid the moment I laid eyes on you. You just went about in a circuitous way of becoming one. Mom and Dad have known for a while that Gram had plans to give me this ring. They were pleased it would be handed down to you. And as for Jane, she won't care that she didn't get the ring. Her future husband can buy her a new ring. But...this does mean you need to bear a daughter so you can pass it down to her. Speaking of, how many kids are we going to have?"

"Five."

"Five? I'll be paying college tuition the rest of my life. I'd like to retire one day."

We laughed as we headed back to the hotel to pack up our belongings.

Emily Reid—I reveled in that thought.

Chapter 18

London

We Fed-Exed all the gifts and worn clothes back to Sandy's house and took my small suitcase to London. By the time we were ready to leave, Gram had sent a couple of tickets for us to come visit her. During our two-hour trip on the TGV, I had many more questions for Jake.

"Honey, what kind of ring is this and how big is it?"

"Do I sense a complaint that it's too big?"

"I'm not complaining, though it's a bit...monstrous. How can I go out with such a huge rock on my finger and not have people stare at me? Oh, and where's my eternity band? I really miss it."

"Your band is right here," he said taking it out of his pocket.

"Why'd you make me give this band to Henri?"

"I had to hand it to Henri because we had to fix it a bit."

"What could you possibly fix on this band? It's perfect. I love it."

"It only fits on your ring finger, and you can't wear it there anymore now that you have your engagement ring. So, I had Henri carefully enlarge the ring. This is very difficult to do. Only an expert like Henri can add to an eternity band. Here." He put out his hand asking for my right hand.

He then placed the band on the fourth finger of my right hand.

"Jake, I can NOT wear both these rings at the same time. People will think I'm asking for a mugging. I look so pretentious."

"I think it looks great. Also, your engagement ring is an original Asscher cut diamond. Joseph Asscher patented this cut back in the early 1900's, and my great grandmother bought one of the original cuts before the Nazis came and seized all their diamonds during World War II. The Asscher cuts nowadays have seventy-four facets on the diamond as opposed to the fifty-eight you have on yours. I thought about having the diamond updated with more cuts but I decided to leave it as is. There are very few originals out there."

"So how big is this diamond?"

"It's about six carats."

"Monstrous," I said.

"Gorgeous," he said.

When we arrived in London, Jake's gram sent her driver to pick us up at the station. I guessed this was how the Reids travel in London as well.

"No Underground?"

"No Underground. Get used to it, Mrs. Reid," he answered putting his arms around me. My new title gave me a warm tingle. It sounded delightful.

Gram also stood around five feet seven. She had a pale complexion with bright blue eyes like Jake's, and her face was quite lovely. She was dressed from head to toe in designer clothing. As soon as we arrived, Jake went over to hug his grandmother but she passed right by him and came over to hug me instead.

"Gram, this is my Emily," he attempted to introduce us. No introductions were necessary.

"Emily!" She hugged me like my grandmother used to hug me whenever we hadn't seen each other in a while.

"Hi, Gram." I hugged her just as lovingly. "You're so beautiful! Jake must have been crazy to think I was anywhere as beautiful as you are."

"Welcome to the family!" was my warm invitation from Gram. "Let me look at you. Why are you so thin? Has Jake not been feeding you?"

"Are you kidding me, Gram? She eats like a horse. And, she's got tremendously expensive taste." Jake tried to put his arms around me and pull me away from Gram. They got into a bit of a tug of war. Gram won.

"Gram, thank you for giving us your ring. It's stunning."

"Jakey told me that you refused his first proposal because the two-carat diamond wasn't big enough. He came and begged me for a bigger diamond so I had to pass down my heirloom so you would finally marry my favorite grandson," Gram accused.

My jaw dropped.

I started stammering. "No, Gram. That's not true. Oh my gosh, I can't believe you told her that." My eyes shot daggers. "Gram..." Then I turned to my fiancé, "Jake..."

They both started laughing at me. "Gram's just kidding, Love."

"Oh!" I breathed a sigh of relief. "Funny, Gram." I tried to laugh.

Holding hands, Gram led me to a grand dining hall. She lived in a mansion-like flat with butlers, drivers, and maids. All of her furniture looked to be antiques, and although she lived most of her life in the States, she was born here, so she fancied herself more English than American. I felt like I was having tea with the queen of England.

The maid brought out an elaborate tea with more food than we could consume. There was a variety of scones, biscuits, and pound cakes. I couldn't figure out the variety of creams that accompanied the tea cakes. There were fruits and chocolate and a myriad of teas to choose from. Of course, Jake broke the tradition and asked for coffee. I followed his lead, as hot tea was not my favorite.

"So when's the wedding?" Gram inquired.

"I don't know," I said. "We haven't discussed it."

"How about the fourth of July?" Jake asked.

"Next year, fourth of July?" I questioned.

"No, I mean, July 4th, as in three weeks from now."

"In three weeks?" Gram and I both said, our voices raised.

"Yup!" Jake wasn't fazed at all. He obviously didn't realize that you couldn't put a wedding together in three weeks.

Gram wanted to know, "What's the rush, Jakey? She's agreed to marry you. She's not going anywhere."

"Gram, Emily won't have sex with me till we get married. I need to get married right away."

I just about wanted to die. I hoped that the ground would open up and swallow me whole. I couldn't believe Jake just told his Grandmother about my sexual history, or lack thereof. My face flushed, my head fell to the ground, and I went mute.

"Good for you, Emily. I'm glad to see that my Jakey is marrying someone with virtues." That sounded like a compliment, but I was too embarrassed to thank her.

Jake realized that he would be in trouble once we were alone.

"I'm sorry, Emi," he said trying to snuggle up to me. "It's nothing to be embarrassed about. You see, Gram thinks highly of you for holding out on me."

Nothing he said made me feel any less annoyed with him. If my head were up, I would have shot something even worse than daggers, at Jake.

While Jake tried to make amends, Gram called everyone back in the States. The butler got Jake's parents, Uncle Henry, Aunt Barbara, Jane, and Nick all on conference call. We told them the good news and Jane seemed the most excited as we would become sisters shortly.

Jake announced to the family our plans to get married on the Fourth of July, and I could hear Sandy gasp.

"Mom, consider it a slightly bigger Christmas dinner. Let's have the wedding at the house, and we'll just use all the people you use regularly."

"Emi, do you mind getting married at the house? This idea just came to me. Also, we live so close to the fireworks display, it will be beautiful at night during the reception."

Getting married at the house was a fantastic idea if Sandy didn't mind.

"Mom," I couldn't believe I had a mom again. My heart exulted. "Do you mind if I call you Mom, already?" I asked with hesitation. I wasn't sure Sandy would feel comfortable with me jumping into the family.

"Emily, Bobby and I've loved you since the day we met you in Hawaii, and knew you would be a part of our family. I am thrilled you want to call me mom."

Sandy's answer brought a smile to my lips and a tear to my eye. I felt this weird mixture of sadness and joy, as I no longer had to wish for a family anymore. They were all here on the phone with me. Jake put both his arms around me and kissed my head.

"Thank you, Mom and Dad. I love you too."

"Are you OK with getting married at the house?" Sandy asked.

"If you don't mind…I really like Jake's idea. Could you get the preparations started for me? I'll be back as soon as possible."

"Sandy, Barbara," Gram said. "I'll buy Emily and Jake their dress and tuxedo here. You get started on the reception."

By the end of the conversation, everyone had a to-do list. Once the wedding dress and tuxedo were taken care of here, we'd fly back with Gram and finish up the rest of the wedding preparation.

Gram's driver took us shopping the rest of the day. Gram and I walked into a designer wedding dress shop while she sent Jake over to get fitted for his tuxedo. As soon as we walked in, Gram and I instantly gravitated toward the same wedding dress. The silk organza gown that hung on the first rack called my name. This was the gown for me.

"Emily, go try it on," Gram urged.

The sales lady led me to a suite-sized dressing room and helped me into my dream wedding gown.

The gown fit as though it was made expressly for me. The slightly puffed sleeves naturally fell off my shoulders and the clean bodice hugged my waistline. The skirt was also a clean sheet of pure silk organza. It had no lace, no beading, and no details—just the simplicity I wanted. There was a semi long train and a bow that tied beautifully in the back. I felt like Cinderella going to her ball.

"Gram, I love this dress."

"Emily, I think we are done looking. You look gorgeous," she exclaimed with an approving nod. "Let's buy this dress."

"Gram, Jake and I will pay for this dress. I don't want you to spend any more money on us. Your ring is present enough."

"Nonsense. Don't you know that I'm the richest person in this family?" She probably wasn't kidding.

"Thank you, again, Gram!" I said while hugging her.

"Emily, you've made my favorite grandson a very happy man. I hope you two will love each as much as his grandfather and I loved each other."

"We will," I promised. "We will."

The sales lady agreed to ship the dress to their Los Angeles store overnight, and I would have my final fittings over there. We walked over to Jake, and he was finishing up with the tailor. I was overcome with emotion thinking of Jake standing at the altar. He looked so handsome.

"Why are you back so soon?"

"We're done." I was beaming.

"Jakey, your bride is going to be stunning in her dress!"

"She's always stunning, Gram." He was delighted.

The tailor put the last touches on Jake's tuxedo and we walked to Harvey Nichols Department Store and had a bowl of noodles for dinner. I hoped we were done for the day, but Gram wanted to buy a few more items for the wedding.

"Jakey, you go look around by yourself in the department store and I'm going to take Emily up to lingerie."

My face turned red at the thought of buying lingerie with Jake's grandmother.

"Gram, I'm coming with you," he absolutely insisted. "I should have a say in this. It's really more for me than it is for her."

I was mortified at the thought of both of them arguing over which lingerie would look better on me. I hoped Gram would not allow Jake to follow us. Without a doubt, Jake won this battle. He practically ran to the lingerie department with a silly grin the whole way up. Gram and Jake enjoyed picking out lingerie while I stood there flustered. Jake, of course, picked out the skimpiest outfits. Gram picked out classic and demure ones I felt more comfortable looking at.

Jake feverishly summoned me with a continuous curling of his hand and suggested, "Emily, try these on. I can come in and help you if you like."

Gram and I both slapped him on the arm. Jake was having a ball.

Luckily, Gram didn't make me try on any of the pieces but she purchased them *all*.

"Gram, I don't think I need so many outfits," I said, trying to sway her from buying me too much.

"Emily, a girl can never have too many diamonds or lingerie." With time, I could get used to this adage.

"Amen!" Jake added.

We got back to the flat exhausted. The maid set up our rooms while I helped Gram up to her room. I noticed that she had two twin beds in her room and I asked if I could sleep with her in the unused twin bed.

"Would you mind, Gram? I'd love to hear stories about Jake's grandpa if you're not too tired."

"That would be lovely, Emily. This bed hasn't been used since my husband died two years ago. I'll have the maid get it ready for you."

"Thank you, Gram."

Jake and I got ready for bed, and we said our good nights by his door. He watched me walk up to Gram's room and curiously followed me in. When he realized that we were sleeping in the same room, he insisted on sleeping with us.

I tried to send him away.

"Jake, there's no room in here for you. Where will you sleep?"

"Gram, I can't believe you let Emi in here, but not your favorite grandson. Either I bring my own mattress and sleep between you two or Emi has to move back to the guest room. That's not fair," he whined.

"How old are you? You sound like a five-year-old." I pretended to scold. But, Gram and I both couldn't resist him. We gave in to his tantrum.

Jake and the butler brought in the mattress and the box spring and placed it between Gram and myself.

"What, no bed frame?" I asked.

"I was tempted, but the butler looked annoyed with me so I thought I'd stop here."

So here we were—Gram, Jake, and me sleeping next to one another on three separate beds. It was a Kodak moment.

I asked Gram to tell me stories about Jake's late grandfather, and she started and ended about the same time. She was so exhausted from the day, she fell right asleep. Jake swiftly jumped onto my twin-size mattress and cuddled me.

"I knew this would happen. The minute her head hits the pillow, Gram is out. We finally get some alone time. I don't think I've touched you since we got to London."

"Is this why you wanted to sleep in this room? I'm still upset with you for your indiscrete confession about my lack of experience. I told you I'm not letting you touch me till we get married."

He paid no attention. "We can change..." his lips started on the hollow of my neck, "your lack of experience status..." I became immobilized by his mouth devouring every inch, "right now if you like."

"Are...you...nuts...?" I said talking slowly, breathing heavily. "Gram is five feet away from us." And yet, I didn't refuse him. "You can stay here for a bit but you need to move back down to your bed."

I could hear Jake's silent laugh. He knew I wanted his lips to stay on my body the entire night if possible. I feigned a white flag and allowed Jake to stay with me the rest of the night. I had the best night's rest since we got to Europe.

We left for Heathrow early in the morning but Gram chose not to fly back with us. She had too many loose ends to tie up before coming to the States. She promised to come in two weeks. On our way to the airport, Jake brought up a thought that was on the forefront of my mind.

"Emi? When do you want to go see your parents? Don't you think I should meet them before we get married?"

I instantly started to cry.

"Love, why are you crying?"

"Because I missed them so much when I was in Japan. I almost flew to Texas one of the weekends to apologize to them. Last time I was there, I said a lot of hurtful things and was really mean to them. Those words have haunted me for months."

"What did you say to them?" With his arms around me, I tried to feel comforted.

"I ranted like a child about them being happily together while leaving me by myself, miserable. I apologized in the end, but I'm sure my parents were up in heaven crying with me."

"Let's go make things right, and I need to apologize as well. I'm sure they're not too happy with me since I'm the one who made you cry. Can we postpone New York and stop by Texas instead? From there we will go home."

"Thank you, Jake. I would love that."

"There's nothing to thank me for. Remember, we are a family now. Just like you treat my parents as your own, I will do the same with your parents."

Chapter 19

Texas Revisited

Before we got to the gravesite, we picked up some yellow Gerbera daisies and I prepared my heart to see Mom and Dad again. Coming here always brought joy and sorrow. When I stood before my parents' graves, I could feel their warmth around me. This warmth surrounded me and loved me almost as acutely as if they were standing right next to me. But, after the initial joy, I was all too aware that my parents were not with me anymore, and nothing I did or felt would bring them back. I wondered what it would be like seeing them with Jake—my comfort, my future husband.

"You are in such deep thought. What are you musing over?" We were almost where my parents lay.

"Even with you by my side, I was wondering whether I would still be sad when I saw them."

"Why would you be sad?" Not having lost a parent, this was a part of me Jake could never fully understand.

"I'm usually elated to be with them, but sometime during the visit, I get sad knowing I have to leave them here. They can never go back with me. I can't ever bring them back to life."

A compassionate expression and a loving embrace was his answer to my pain.

"Jake," I turned to him as we stood before my parents, "these are my parents. Mom. Dad. I want to introduce you to Jake. This is the man I want to spend the rest of my life with."

Jake started talking to Mom and Dad, and it looked like he was going to tell them about our entire courtship.

"Hello Mr. and Mrs. Logan. My name is Jake Reid and I am late, but here to ask you for Emily's hand in marriage. I'm sorry I didn't come earlier to ask for your permission. I should have been here back on New Year's Day with Emily but I was a fool. I've hurt Emily a lot since Christmas, but I promise you I will love your daughter as much as you love her if you'll allow me to marry her. I'll take care of her and protect her from any harm. I'll make sure to love her so fully and completely that when she comes to see you in the future, she won't leave sad, missing your love. Thank you for bringing her up so beautifully. Emily has an incredible warmth and sincerity I'm sure she learned from both of you."

Momma. Daddy. Isn't he wonderful? Thank you for helping me get Jake back in my life, and I'm sorry I was so mean to you the last time I was here. You don't know how much I regretted my words. I know you both only want the best for me, and I know it hurts you to see me alone. What do you think of Jake? Isn't he handsome, Momma? I wish you could both be here and experience this joy with me. Oh, Daddy...who will walk me down the aisle?

Jake stopped talking to my parents as soon as he heard me cry.

"What's the matter, Emi?" He hugged me. "I really should carry a pack of tissues around with me. You cry way too easily." He lightly chuckled and kissed my forehead.

"I was just asking my dad who will walk me down the aisle." How ironic that I would feel so sad about walking down the aisle—a walk that would begin my forever with Jake.

"You know my dad would love to walk you down. You can also walk down on your own, and that would make a beautiful statement of how strong you have been, coming this far on your own. We have a few weeks. Let's think about it. You interrupted my conversation with your parents. I finished telling them how we met and I was getting to our botched weekend in Bacara."

He turned to talk to them some more. I heard him talking but went into my own thoughts.

"So, Mom, I was wondering when Emily developed such a foodie taste bud? Has she always liked food this much? I sent her to Le Bernardin when she was in New York, and you wouldn't believe the texts I got from her. She sent me a whole blog of every item she ate."

Do you like him, Momma? After I left you here, I went to Japan and spent four months teaching. Alone but grateful to experience another culture, I traveled throughout the country. Can you believe I did this by myself? I also ate some delicious food. Oh, I didn't tell you. Sarah and Charlie finally got married a few weeks ago. They are in a state of bliss.

"After many months of searching for her," I heard Jake ramble, "I finally got help from Max—yes, Max—and found your daughter hidden away in Japan. She was, of course, at a restaurant ready to eat another ten-plus course meal. I honestly don't know where she hides all those calories. I know the beauty comes from Mom, but where does that metabolism come from?"

I laughed to myself. Jake was sitting right in between both of my parents' graves explaining our entire seventh-month dating / broken-up days.

Almost an hour later, I heard Jake say, "I'm going to assume you love me like my parents love Emily and are giving us your blessing to get married. I know it broke your heart to leave her so early, but I promise to make up for your absence. I will take good care of her. Thank you for Emily, and I love you both."

Are you smiling right now? Only you could send me someone who would try to completely fill your void. From now on, I'll come here happy and leave happy. I'll miss you, but I won't feel alone anymore. Thank you, Momma. Thank you, Daddy. We'll be back often and one day soon, I hope to be back with a baby. Can you believe you'll be grandparents? I love you both.

As soon as I was done, Jake looked at me, and all I could say was, "I'm hungry. Let's go have steak."

He shook his head and laughed.

Chapter 20

Wedding Preparations

It was Sunday afternoon when we arrived at Jake's parents' house. We got a warm welcome home. Jake had me use his room while he took up residence in Nick's room. I unpacked, started laundry, and gave Sandy and Bobby their gifts. My fiancé was fast asleep on Nick's bed when I went to check up on him. Kissing his forehead and placing the blanket on him, I closed the door, wondering what I should do next.

Sleep did not seem to be a part of my plan tonight so I went downstairs to the kitchen and started making croissants for breakfast. Knowing that the dough needed to rise, I started early in order to have it ready for Jake when he left for his 6:00 a.m. surgery. After mixing the dough I let it sit as Sandy came over to the barstool and chatted with me about life in the Reid household during my five-month absence.

"Emily, Bobby, and I are both so relieved you and Jake are back together. I wish I could have videotaped Jake's mood swings while you were gone. It felt like we were living with a depressed teenager." She laughed as she went into specifics about Jake's behavior.

Bobby came over and joined our conversation as Sandy started her lively stories. "Right after you left, Jake was so distraught we didn't know what to do with him. Here was a grown adult suffering like a little child. He disappeared for about a week, and only through Laney did we find out that he was searching for you in Japan. When he returned unsuccessful, he barely spoke to us or anyone else for that matter."

"I'm sorry you had to suffer along with us." I gave them my most apologetic look.

"Well, it got better once he got your letter. He smiled and spoke again like a normal human being. Then came the angst-filled days of waiting for more letters that never came."

"Yeah, it got ugly again when you didn't write to him anymore." Bobby laughed. "Poor Jane and Nick. Jake hounded them daily, asking them if they had received one of your letters. Jane would scan your letter and e-mail it to Jake even before she got a chance to read it."

Sandy chuckled along with Bobby. "What about Nick? Jake forced him to drive your letter over whenever he got one. Oh, and then there was the birthday card and present you sent to our house."

"What happened?" I asked.

"Because he had been so full of melancholy, I threw him a birthday party on the day of his birthday to cheer him up. He protested but seemed to be having a decent time with all his friends and relatives. In the middle of the party, the mailman came with your card and gift. Jake was thrilled!" Sandy started the story, and Bobby chimed in to finish.

"We saw him open the card, but he instantly disappeared. Sandy and I went up to see what he was doing and we found him at his desk crying." This revelation immediately brought tears to my eyes.

Sandy continued, "I hadn't seen him cry since grade school. Jake explained to us about your birthdays, and how it grieved him to think about you being alone on your birthday. He deeply loves you, Emily. I've never seen him so affected by anyone as he has been with you." Sandy had suffered seeing her son so badly hurt.

I hugged Sandy. "I love him with all my heart, too. I promise I'll take good care him."

"Anyhow, the party was pretty much over, and Jake was in a foul mood the rest of the time till he found you again." Bobby finished the story. "Not till you left him, did I realize how much of a sulker my son could be."

"Yeah, I've seen firsthand Jake's childish tantrums when he doesn't get his way. Although, to be honest with you, I find it adorable." A grin marked my face.

"Only you find it cute. The rest of us find him to be a pain." Sandy shook her head. "He was a mess. You need to take him off our hands. We cannot live with Jake, without you now." The three of us shared a hearty laugh.

After our conversation, I went upstairs and checked my e-mail. There were eighty-seven e-mails waiting for my response. Half of them were junk, but the other half I needed to answer immediately. Many of my students from Japan e-mailed telling me how much they missed me, and asked when I would come back and teach them again. The feeling was mutual, but truth be told, I wouldn't trade my life with Jake right now for anything or anybody. While online, Sarah and Max began chatting with me, and we set up a dinner date for tomorrow night.

Looking at the time, I rushed back downstairs and lightly floured the huge marble island. I shaped the dough into a rectangle and covered it with a plastic wrap and placed it back into the fridge. While waiting for the dough to rise again, I surveyed Jake's room and cleaned up all the clutter lying around. I rearranged his closet, refolded his clothes in the dresser drawers, and ironed all the washed, but wrinkled scrubs. Jake had also thrown around his watches in the jewelry drawer so I rolled them back up and put them in their proper place. His cuff links got the same treatment. Color coordinated, the ties hung neatly, and the belts hung right next to them. The men's department at Neiman's didn't look this good. The type A side of me shined tonight. After two hours, I was finally satisfied with the closet makeover.

The dough was probably ready to be laminated so I went back to the kitchen. Unwrapping the dough and placing it back on the floured surface, I rolled it out, folded and refolded with insane amounts of butter. I hoped Sandy wasn't planning on using this butter anytime soon because it was all consumed. I cut the dough into triangles and made a third of them plain, a third had chopped Callebaut dark chocolate, and a third had almond paste and sliced almonds in them. They looked delicious sitting on the baking sheet while the oven warmed to 425 degrees.

Jake ran downstairs in his bathrobe looking a bit frazzled.

"What's the matter?"

"I came looking for you in my bedroom, but you weren't there so I got worried."

"Did you think your bride got cold feet and ran away?" What a ridiculous thought.

Jake's wrinkled face smoothed out as he came over and squeezed his arms around my body.

"Good morning, Beautiful."

"Good morning. You fell asleep at four in the afternoon, yesterday. Are you well rested?"

"Yeah. I feel good. Did you sleep at all last night? I noticed that you ransacked my room, then put it back together in a scary way. Are you normally this neurotic?"

"No. I hope you don't mind. I couldn't sleep so I kept myself busy between your room and these croissants." Though I hated to pull myself away from the love of my life, the croissants were ready to go into the oven. "You have a moment? I need to ask you something."

"OK. Shoot."

"My tenant e-mailed saying that her job will keep her in LA one more year. She wanted to know if she could lease my house during that time. What should we do?"

"If you don't mind her staying another year, we could move into my house in the valley. We'll kick everyone out and refurnish it."

"Well, I was thinking of asking your parents if we could stay here for a year. You know I grew up lonely, and I like the thought of living with your parents. Would you mind?"

"I'm OK, but are you sure? Jane and Nick might move back in for a while too."

"I'd love nothing more than a big family."

Jake smiled and hugged me again, partly because he appreciated my love for his family, and partly because he felt sad when I talked about loneliness. I hugged him back.

"Go change. I'll have breakfast ready for you." I sent him back upstairs and began laying out my spread.

The Sub-Zero fridge had a variety of vegetables so breakfast included a veggie omelet in addition to the croissants. Jake came down in his scrubs, ready for work. He sat on the bar stool around the island and I handed him the veggie omelet, a variety of croissants, and French pressed coffee. Moving into Bobby and Sandy's home was most definitely a good idea. We felt like a married couple already.

As Jake ate, we heard the door open, and Nick's voice boomed across the large living room and into the dining room. "What is this delicious smell?"

"Nick," I exclaimed, walking over to hug him.

"Hi, Sis. How was your trip? You've gotten prettier since I last saw you in New York!"

"You're such a charmer. I guess when personality genes were handed out, they all went to you?"

"Not just personality, looks and brain as well. I don't know what my siblings got. I obviously got all the best." All three of us laughed at his humor.

"What are you doing here so early in the morning?" we both asked.

"I'm off on a camping trip, and I needed my hiking boots. I see I came at the right time. These croissants are delicious." He took another mouth full.

"Emily baked these just now," Jake proudly declared.

"No way, from scratch? How long did this take you?" Nick seemed pleased to have another cook in the house.

"I've been working on them since yesterday. Take some for your trip. I'll pack them up for you. Do you want some coffee as well?"

"You're the best, Sis. I think I'll move back in the house if you're cooking."

Nick's loud voice woke up Bobby and Sandy and they, too, raved about the croissants. Sandy and Bobby relived many more Jake, while Emily was in Japan stories, and we had a very early but entertaining breakfast. We, in this case, did not include Jake. He didn't find any of these stories as comical as we did.

Sandy and Bobby were more than thrilled with the news of us living with them for a year, and Nick said he might move back into the house as well since school was done.

We walked hand in hand to Jake's car and dark clouds grew bigger with each step. With a huge sigh, I stepped into his open arms and dreaded our separation. It reminded me of my empty days in Japan.

"I'm sad to see you go," I whimpered. "How am I going to go the whole day without you? When will you come home?"

"Probably not till late—maybe sometime after midnight. I'll know better as the day progresses."

"Midnight?" My whine became even more pronounced.

"The chief told me I've got a tough three weeks before the wedding. You're OK taking care of this wedding without me?"

"Yeah, I'll be fine. I'll just miss you!"

"I know, Love. I'll miss you too." He kissed me a long good-bye and unwillingly we parted. I, too, had a long day of wedding preparations.

Bobby, Sandy, and I left the house early with the intent of getting everything started today. Our first stop was to the print shop to pick out wedding invitations. We thought these should go out immediately since many guests may go out of town on a holiday weekend. Sandy had already contacted all the family members to let them know of the impending wedding. I didn't have much of an opinion on the invitation and Sandy had such impeccable taste, I let her make most of the decisions. I would only assert myself if I really didn't like something she picked out. The designer would send a proof via -mail later today, and they promised to print all the invites as soon as we accepted the copy. Sandy and I, in turn, promised to send addresses so they could label and mail our invitations for us. Our first stop was successful.

From here, we went to the florist. This was really Sandy's area of expertise. The florist had worked on the house before, so she already had a layout of what she wanted to do. We explained that we wanted to get married inside the house and then hold the reception in a tent out in the vast backyard. The floral designer named off all the flowers that she would use in different parts of the house, and Bobby and I just listened, as botany was never my strong suit. My job from here was to e-mail a picture of my wedding gown, as well as the bridesmaids' dresses, and she would e-mail back sketches of bouquets. E-mail was a wonderful invention. It saved so much time for everyone.

Next we headed to the department store to pick out bridesmaids' dresses. Both Sarah and Jane would stand as my maiden and maid of honor. I thought picking out a dress from a large department store would be easy for Jane since she could pop into the Manhattan one for a fitting. Sandy and I easily found a cute green summer dress, formal but not so formal where they couldn't wear it again. I took a picture of the dress and sent it to Jane and Sarah. They both gave it a thumbs-up so we bought two dresses, one here and one in Manhattan.

Not having consumed anything since six in the morning, the three of us were ravenous. Lunch was next on the list before another fitting at the bridal shop.

Finally, Jake called.

"Hi, Honey!" My voice bubbled with enthusiasm.

"Hello, my love. What are you and my parents up to right now?"

Even with Sandy and Bobby by my side, I felt such a void without Jake.

"We are eating a grilled veggie salad, and after lunch, we're going to the dress shop for another fitting. Your tuxedo is here and they want you to come in for another fitting as well."

"I probably won't get there till the week of the wedding."

"OK, I'll stop by the store and let them know."

I proceeded to tell Jake all that had been accomplished today, and he told me about his day thus far. I excused myself from the table and went outside briefly to finish our conversation.

"Jake?" I bemoaned.

"Yes, Love. What's the matter?" he asked in a comforting voice.

"I really miss you. Can't you come home any earlier than midnight?"

I could almost hear his smile over the phone as he said, "I miss you too. I'll be home as soon as I can, but don't wait up for me. It will probably be very late."

I told Jake how difficult it had been today without him by my side. He had spoiled me the last week with his constant attention. Who would have believed that I had spent five months apart from him by the sound of my wimpy confession? Of course, I heard the pager go off and we said good-bye. I went in to finish my lunch.

The fitting went well, and Sandy and Bobby both loved the wedding dress.

"Emily, you will be the most beautiful bride," Bobby said.

"Thank you," I answered, embarrassed by the compliment.

Our stop at the caterer took the longest of all of our stops. The caterer would not only take care of the food and beverages, but they would also provide all the rentals—tent, tables, chairs, linen, and of course the cake. We tried many flavors and since we were going to have a four-tiered cake, each one of us chose a flavor. I chose one for Jake in his absence. The caterer would send linens over to the house tomorrow morning so we could pick out color schemes.

The three of us had accomplished much today with the time allotted. Sandy and Bobby dropped me off at the restaurant just in time for my dinner with Sarah, Charlie, Peter, and Max.

"Thank you for all your help, Mom and Dad. I'm honored to be joining your family," I said, giving each of them a hug and a kiss on the cheek.

"We're really happy to welcome you into our family as well," Bobby and Sandy agreed with a hug and kiss in return.

We parted and I walked into the restaurant bearing gifts for my closest friends.

"Em, over here," Max said, as I searched for them. They were hidden away in a corner table.

I ran over to them and gave them all a big hug.

"Let's see the ring," Sarah exclaimed. "OMG! Why is it so big?"

"I know, I said the same thing to Jake when he gave it to me. It's almost embarrassing to wear this ring, especially with the band on the other hand. Jake says I have to wear both, and I told him I'm asking for a mugging."

They all laughed.

"Hey, where's Peter?" I asked surveying the dining hall.

"We have this tough doctor who's been working all the students. Peter got called in right as we were headed out the door," Max explained. "He should be at General Hospital by now."

"That's where Jake is today. Maybe they'll run into each other." Of course my face lit up talking about my fiancé. I didn't want to appear too giddy, so I turned to all of my friends and announced, "Presents!"

Sarah opened her gift and her face immediately turned red.

"You like?" I asked.

"I really like!" Charlie affirmed.

Charlie thought his architecture book paled in comparison to the lingerie gift that was more for him than for her.

"Max, this is for you," I said handing him his gift.

He opened it and flipped through the book realizing that it was Charles Dickens' *A Tale of Two Cities* from 1918. He read my inscription on the second page.

Thank you, from the bottom of my heart, for giving me four wonderful years of your life. You challenged me to grow as a person, and I hope I made you as happy as you made me. I will never forget your love. You will always hold a special place in my heart.

Love,
Em

Max turned and hugged me. I knew he understood how much he meant and still means to me.

During dinner, I told everyone about Paris and how Jake proposed. Max showed a sadness that made me conscious of my glow. Rather than continue with wedding talk, I turned the conversation on my dear friends and asked them about their lives. "What are you and Peter doing during your summer vacation?" I asked.

"What summer vacation? Only the teachers get time off. We are in the hospital working every day. In fact, I have to go in for a midnight to 6:00am shift."

"What a bummer. I thought that everyone was off during the summertime."

"No. I wish. I'll probably see Jake if he's at GH the whole time. I'm sure they'll send me up to the OR at some point."

Charlie talked about the newest house that he was designing. It was for a big movie star whose name he couldn't reveal. We all begged for a hint. Even Sarah had no idea who he was working with.

Sarah's advertising firm kept her busy all the time. I seemed to be the only one with not much to do on a daily basis.

"Oh, Sarah, I brought your dress." I interrupted Charlie's flow. "The hostess is holding it for me in the front so you need to take it with you, OK? Also, can you come by Jake's parents' house? I want to show you where the wedding will take place."

"I can come by after work," she answered.

As soon as dinner was done, my head started nodding and I kept apologizing to my friends for falling asleep on them. We decided to part and Max drove me home before his midnight shift.

"Thanks for the book, Em. I really love it."

"You're welcome. Jake actually wanted to buy the book for you, but I didn't let him. I wanted it to be a gift from me."

"Tell Jake I said thanks, as well."

"You tell him if you see him tonight. Also, if you see him, tell him that I'm pining away for him at home."

That probably wasn't the most sensitive thing to ask my ex-boyfriend to tell my fiancé.

"Sorry. TMI, huh?"

"It's OK," he said with an attempt to laugh it off.

It saddened me to see Max so down. I knew Max was happy for me, but I sensed that he hadn't gotten over me rejecting his proposal. I hoped our encounter in Arizona would become a distant memory and that he would find his happiness soon.

"I guess I'll see you at your wedding."

I hated it when his face turned somber, and he couldn't look me in the eye. I smiled, hugging him, and answered, "We'll definitely see each other before then. Bye." I gave him a quick peck on the cheek and walked toward the house.

It was near eleven o'clock when I got home and washed up for bed. Pulling an all-nighter last night made me extremely sleepy, but I tried my hardest to stay up and wait for Jake. My head bobbed up and down trying to watch whatever was on the television. Instinctually, I jerked awake at the sound of the garage door opening and closing. My legs took me as fast as they could downstairs in my pajamas, excited to see Jake. As he opened the door, I surprised him and jumped into his arms, almost knocking us both down.

He dropped whatever was in his hands, picked me up, and started embracing me. I didn't think twice about the fact that he was carrying me, kissing me, and walking up a flight of stairs. What was the worst that could happen? We would fall and break his surgeon hands? We got to his bedroom and lay on our bed. We made out like two hormonal teenagers. For the first time, I didn't stop him or push him away. I responded to his every move. I let him explore with his hands, his mouth, his tongue and soon my pajama top came undone. As my body continued to reciprocate, Jake paused and stared at me.

"Aren't you going to stop me?" he questioned. "This is unusual that you haven't said no yet."

"Um, I wasn't ready to stop, but I guess we should, huh? Sorry I got carried away." I giggled.

"You've got to be kidding me. I stopped us?" He had this incredulous look on his handsome face. "I can't win."

"Yup, I guess I have you trained better than I thought." I giggled even harder.

Jake groaned and walked in to take a shower.

I must have fallen asleep while Jake showered because when my eyes opened, I was alone nicely tucked away in his bed. It was 4:00 a.m. and sleep was done for the night. I was tempted to crawl into bed with Jake in Nick's room, but I thought I should be good. There were only a few more weeks left for us to be apart. Instead, I drove downtown to the fish market and bought a variety of fish to make sushi today.

The fish market was bustling with vendors and chefs. It was tiny compared to the Tsukiji fish market in Tokyo, but the fish and seafood smelled fresh and delicious memories of Japan paraded through my morning. Mr. Yamaguchi's suggestions for the day were tuna, salmon, yellowtail, halibut, sweet shrimp, and uni. This would absolutely make a nice lunch for the whole family. Maybe I would surprise Jake and bring him lunch at the hospital.

Once home, I put all the fish away and started making a batter for crepes. All the necessary ingredients for my own version of the Ritz Hotel crepes were found in the pantry. I chopped up bananas, strawberries, and peanuts and whipped up some heavy cream with vanilla and confectioners' sugar. Sandy and Bobby cheerfully walked from their room, ready to be my chauffeur and wedding planner again. Though today, we needed to stay home and work with all the vendors who wanted to come see the layout of the house. Samples of linen would be sent to the house by 8:00 a.m., and Aunt Barbara, the chief's wife, offered to be our interior and exterior designer for the wedding. Since I didn't have much of an eye for design, I was glad she volunteered to help.

Good morning. I have strawberries and whipped cream crepes or Nutella, peanuts, and banana crepes. What can I get you?" I offered.

"Good morning, Emily. I'll take one of each," Bobby said. "I really enjoy your breakfast in the mornings. I feel like I'm at a bed and breakfast."

"Emily, dear, you know that you don't have to make us breakfast every morning, right?" Sandy looked worried.

"Oh, I know. It's not a have to, it's a want to. Cooking is something I love to do. Plus, I can't sleep beyond 4:00 a.m., so I might as well be useful. Don't get too used to it, though. Jake will tell you I'm not much of a morning person. Breakfast may soon be a thing of the past so enjoy it while it lasts."

I went to work on my new electric crepe maker that I picked up yesterday while registering for my wedding gifts. The first few crepes turned out too thick so I threw them out, but after that, I got the hang of using the wooden rabot and perfected the spreading technique. Each crepe after the first few came out perfectly. Aunt Barbara and the chief came over and I made them each a couple of crepes. The kitchen island simulated a diner and I felt like a short order cook. It was fun.

"How do you take your coffee?" I asked both of them.

"Emily," Aunt Barbara said, "I'll get our coffee. Why don't you sit down and eat with us?"

"I'll wait till Jake comes down. Oh...speaking of, there he is." My mouth grinned from ear to ear.

I heard Barbara turn to Sandy and whisper, "Look at how her face lights up at the sight of him."

Sandy in turn said, "You think that's bad; my son's a hundred times worse!"

Jake ambled into the kitchen and our eyes locked immediately. With his back to the family, he grabbed me and devoured my lips. A bit friskier than I would've liked with an audience, I turned crimson, but didn't pull away. I was learning to cherish every touch without being so self-conscious about what others might think. Brazen? Bold? Audacious? Whatever it was, I was enjoying it too much to stop.

"Hi, Beautiful. Did you sleep well?" Jake asked with an adoring look.

"I slept very well, all four hours of it."

"You got up at four this morning?"

"Yeah, I couldn't go back to sleep."

"You could've come into bed with me." He looked vexed I didn't.

"The thought did cross my mind," I mused.

As we tried to continue our conversation, Aunt Barbara and the chief began clearing their throats.

"Ahem! Hello, nephew. Don't I get a good morning kiss?" the chief asked facetiously.

Startled, Jake turned his body around. "What are you doing here, Chief? Hi, Aunt Babs. Good to see you." He tried to hold me with both arms while leaning over the island to give his aunt a kiss on the cheek.

"I need a ride to the hospital with you this morning. Your aunt and I have a dinner to attend, and she's going to come pick me up later," the chief explained.

I told Jake that Aunt Barbara was here to help us with wedding decorations. Whether or not he was interested, we three gave him a rundown of all the vendors coming to the house and what would be accomplished today. While I gave more wedding details, Jake jerked his head up and startled me.

"Emi!"

I jumped and answered, "Yes?"

"I forgot to tell you, you need to stop by the bank today. The manager is expecting you."

"Why?"

"I sent in the paperwork yesterday to add your name to all my accounts. I was supposed to tell you to stop by the bank yesterday, but I forgot.

"OK," I answered.

He reached in his pocket and took out a card for me. "Here's your ATM card. You need to activate it."

I sheepishly smiled reading the ATM card. Below the sixteen-digit punched card, I saw in bold print, EMILY REID. I whispered the name aloud. It sounded even better than I imagined. I saw Jake grinning from the corner of my eyes.

"Also can you deposit my paychecks into our checking account while you're at the bank?"

The words *our account* sounded so wonderful they gave me goose bumps. I knew it was silly to be so animated over the obvious joining of names and official documents, but those chosen words made everything sound so much more real.

Without thinking, I opened up Jake's paychecks, shocked to find how many digits were in the dollar box. I turned to Jake with eyes wide open and said a little too loudly, "Do you really get paid this much? Is this a monthly or every other monthly paycheck?"

I could hear all the chuckles coming from the left side of the island.

"Emi, this is a two-week paycheck," Jake answered back in a somewhat offensive tone. "You do know that I save lives by operating on hearts, daily. Sometimes it's multiple hearts."

"Well, you do know that I save lives by teaching children their fundamentals before they can get to their higher medical learning, but my paycheck looks nothing like yours. I probably need six paychecks to equal one of yours," I responded back.

He chuckled and added, "We need my paychecks if we're going to enjoy trips like Paris. We probably spent at least one paycheck in Paris."

"Are you kidding me? We spent that much money there? We cannot vacation like that anymore. What a ludicrous amount of money we spent."

"Well, it shouldn't be as bad next time since we won't have to get two rooms," he answered, reaching over to kiss me again.

The words two rooms seem to be of interest to everyone else at the island. Aunt Barbara was the first to ask, "Why did you have two rooms at the Ritz?"

Jake rolled his eyes and answered, "Don't ask. I got into big trouble for telling Gram that Emily's a virgin."

My head automatically dropped into my hands and Jake realized his big mistake, again. My cheeks turned bright red and once again, I was hoping to be swallowed up by the floor. My lips were shut tight, my eyes squinted and my head came up just long enough to give Jake a *you are in big trouble* look.

The conversation that ensued troubled me even more than the topic of my virginity.

"You mean you're not pregnant? That's not why we're having this shotgun wedding?" the chief bellowed.

My head jerked up at the word pregnant. I stared and processed in my head what he just said, and what the rest of the family members might have thought about us. It never occurred to me everyone would think that we were rushing into marriage because I might be pregnant.

Mortified. Horrified. Aghast.

I felt all of the above.

Jake almost fell off his barstool howling in laughter. The rest of the family looked at me apologetically for jumping to this conclusion, and embarrassed for putting me in such an awkward situation.

If I wanted the ground to swallow me up earlier, now I wanted to stay there till after the wedding. How would I face every guest who would be thinking what my immediate family members thought?

Jake finally calmed down enough to pull me to his lap and comfort me. He knew the scenario I had conjured up in my head.

"Don't worry. When everyone sees us at Christmas minus a big belly, they will realize that you and I did not have a shotgun wedding. That is... unless you want to be pregnant right away. Then we can start trying even today." Jake somehow turned this situation even worse.

I turned to Bobby and Sandy, hoping someone would be on my side. "Mom, Dad, did you also think I was pregnant?

"Sweetheart, we're sorry! We did think it was odd you and Jake wanted to get married so quickly. Most couples don't have three-week engagements. The thought did cross our minds." They looked as mortified as I felt.

"Let's go up to our room," Jake said trying to break my flabbergasted glower. "Let me give you all the bank account numbers," he added, pulling me off the stool, and pulling my hand toward his room.

We got away from the family and Jake stopped and looked concerned. "You OK?"

After thinking about it, I let it go. I had overreacted. It would only be natural for people to assume we wanted to get married right away before my stomach popped.

"I'm fine." I looked into his sparkling blue eyes and felt protected. Once again, I couldn't imagine being in a better place with a better man.

"I'm guessing you won't let me finish where we left off last night?" he suggested, pushing me against the wall, mouth nibbling on my ear.

"You're guessing correctly!" I said, attempting to pull away. "Jake?"

"Hmm?" His lips traveled to the neck while the hands rummaged under my shirt.

"Can I come visit you at the hospital and have lunch with you today?"

Delighted, Jake's head popped up.

"I'd love that, Emi. My colleagues keep asking when you're going to stop by. When do you want to come?"

"Maybe around 1:00 p.m.? Will you be done with your morning surgery? I'll make you something yummy for lunch."

"I should be. If I'm not done, wait for me in my office and I'll meet you there."

Uncle Henry's loud voice bellowed up the stairs. "Dr. Reid, we've got a patient in OR waiting for us. You can work on that baby later."

We both shook our heads and laughed.

"See you later. I'm excited you're coming by. I love you."

"I love you too," were my last words, as I let Jake go save more lives.

Once Jake left, it was back to wedding preparations. Sandy and Barbara simultaneously agreed on linen colors as well the China pattern for the tables. They leaned toward a classic look for the wedding and I agreed with their every suggestion. The only area of interest for me was the dinner menu. I would voice my opinion when the caterer stopped by with her suggestions for the meal.

Midmorning, I made the sushi rice, filleted the fish, and cut them up into sushi and sashimi slices. I also put the rest of the frozen croissants in the oven for the nurses at the hospital. Aunt Barbara, Sandy, and Bobby sat down to lunch while I began working on a bento box for Jake, the chief, and myself.

While in Japan, I found these beautiful round bento boxes during my visit to Kappabashi, the restaurant supply district. I placed a large green leaf in each of the five boxes and began assembling the sushi pieces. The bottom layer contained sliced-up pineapples, strawberries, blueberries, and oranges with whipped cream in a separated container. A nigiri sushi sat on the second tier. There was toro, hamachi, kinmedai, hirame, sake, uni, and amaebi. In the third box, I arranged sashimi pieces on top of shredded daikon radishes, just like they did at sushi bars. In the fourth, partitioned box, I placed a salad and little pickled side dishes I purchased at the fish market. The top box had all the shrimp and veggie tempura. I wrapped the bento box in a large silk scarf, put the miso soup with amaebi heads in a thermos, and the necessary utensils in another carrying case, and I left for the hospital.

Walking into the hospital, I looked no different than a pizza delivery boy. Bearing an armful of food, I asked the receptionist for directions to Dr. Jake Reid's office. Her answer made me laugh.

"You take the elevator up to the third floor, turn left, and follow the yellow line into the Reid Wing. His office will be a few doors down on the right."

Of course, his office was located in the Reid Wing. Jake's late grandfather spent his money generously. If I were ever to get ill, I would be well taken care of at this hospital. Jake's office resembled an office cubicle. It was also as messy as the closet in his bedroom. This room needed my housekeeping services right away. Bookmarkers were placed in opened books and stacked on his desk and neat piles of patient files were made from the folders strewn about the desk and sofa. I made a mental note to myself to bring some flowers to brighten up his dreary office next time.

Once I finished straightening up, the couch looked inviting as sleep overpowered me. I curled up on the sofa and dozed off, only happy to find Jake's soft lips awaken me. He was kneeling on the ground, staring at my sleeping face. I grabbed his face and pulled it harder on my lips, not wanting to stop the embrace. Jake responded as he usually does with more passion than I was ready for. I pulled away and sat up.

"I hate it when you pull away," he complained.

"Believe it or not, I hate it even more," I confessed. "Can you call Uncle Henry? I have lunch for all of us."

Jake introduced me to his nursing staff at the front station, and many welcomed me, while a few evil eyes didn't. I dropped off a box of croissants for the staff, which seemed to win over the opposition.

Many of Jake's colleagues also stopped and congratulated us on our way to the Reid cafeteria. Most of the doctors I met in this department were men, but there were a few women, who also weren't pleased to meet me. We walked into the cafeteria and sat with the chief.

I looked at both men and commented a bit sarcastically, "Don't you find it weird to work in the Reid Wing and have lunch in the Reid Cafeteria?"

"No," they both answered matter-of-factly.

What could I say to that? I opened the bento boxes, passed out plates, utensils, and soups. Then we started eating.

The chief looked impressed.

"Emily, did you make all this?" he asked. "If your meals look like this, I'm coming over every day for a meal." He sounded completely serious.

"No you're not," Jake retorted. "My bride is not your personal chef. I don't want her working any harder than she wants to. Although, I must say, you outdid yourself with this meal. Thank you, Sweetheart."

Jake smacked his lips on mine, and suddenly his blue eyes sparkled even brighter.

"Emi, have you thought of what you want to do after the wedding?"

"What do you mean? I'll enjoy married life till school begins, mid-August."

"Would you consider quitting work and going to culinary school? We have a top-notch culinary academy five minutes from our home. Why don't you enroll there in the fall?"

That idea made me pause for a moment. Would I want to stop teaching and go to culinary school? This wouldn't be any ordinary school with books I'd memorize just for exams and forget the next day. This would be all hands-on training. A dream I thought I would live later in life presented itself today as a reality.

"I don't know if I'm cut out for the Culinary Institute. I'm not that good and it's expensive. Plus, I don't want to work in a restaurant, and I don't want to become a professional chef. I just want to be a home chef."

"Love, first of all, you said yourself you've always wanted to go to cooking school. Here's your chance before we have kids. As for expenses, did you not take a good look at my paycheck? I can afford to send you to cooking school. In fact, we will have a plethora of extra money living at my parents' home. Both our mortgages are covered by rent, and we can mooch off my parents as long as we like. Lastly, you don't have to become a professional chef. Just go to school for the fun of it. Our livelihood won't depend on your success at school. You have some time so think about it. I'd love to do this for you."

We all continued to eat as I thought about how much fun it would be to go and learn to cook. This was definitely a viable and exciting option. The two doctors began talking about their afternoon rounds and I looked at Uncle Henry, hoping this lunch put me in his good graces and could get some time off for my fiancé.

"Uncle Henry," I asked in the most polite voice.

"Yes, soon-to-be niece?"

"Any chance Jake could get off at a decent hour so we can spend some time together tonight? As you know, we don't spend any time together deep into the night so our evenings are cut real short if he comes home at midnight."

The chief snickered at Jake, Jake grinned at me, and I stared hopefully at the chief.

"Sorry, Emily. He's been on vacation for a week and he'll be off for two more soon. The other doctors will accuse me of nepotism if I don't work your fiancé. I promise you, though, I'll lighten his schedule after you get married. We're in the process of hiring another surgeon."

I sighed, "Ok," for the first half of his explanation, but mouthed a "thank you," with a sigh of relief, for the latter part of his explanation. Chief Reid hugged and kissed me as he left to go back to his office.

"I tried," I said, shrugging my shoulders.

"I know. I'll try to leave the hospital as early as possible," Jake promised. "You want to come back at dinnertime?" Jake was the hopeful one this time.

"No. The ladies here aren't too friendly. I don't think they want to see me and my massive engagement ring twice in one day. You have quite a fan club here," I said bitingly.

"You can be so silly at times," he answered with a guffaw. "See you at home."

I packed up all my belongings and left the hospital.

When I got back home, nothing had changed. It was if the two ladies hadn't moved all afternoon. They were sitting in the same position from hours ago. They sat on the couch deciding which floral arrangement would look best on the table with the linen they chose earlier. They looked to me to be the tie breaker and realized that my only desire was to say, "I do," and be Mrs. Jake Reid. Fortunately, they were more than happy to fill in for my mental absence and continued on without me.

I walked into my / Jake's room and called my soon-to-be-sister.

"Hello, Sis. What are you up to right now?"

"Emily. Hi. How are you? I'm swamped with work. All the senior partners are dumping their busy work on me. I get in by six in the morning and don't leave till close to midnight. I eat all three meals at the firm."

She sounded terribly unhappy.

"Your work schedule sounds like your brother's. I can't see him unless I go to the hospital."

I, too, wasn't happy with his schedule.

"How are the wedding preparations going? What's been done?"

"Honestly, I'm not quite sure. Mom and Aunt Barbara are downstairs making all the decisions. I'm happy to just show up on the day of and say, 'I do.'"

"I talked to Mom briefly today, and she and Aunt Babs were really happy being your wedding planners. They're living their vicarious wedding dreams through you. Are you OK with all of their decisions?"

"Yeah, they both have exquisite taste. I do hold veto power so if something isn't to my liking, I'll let them know. Anyhow, when can you come home? I miss you."

"I know, I miss you and the whole family. I hear you've been quite the Martha Stewart every morning."

"My eyes open at 4:00 a.m., and I have nothing else to do but cook. So, can you make it home this weekend?"

"I begged my boss so we'll see. I won't know till the last minute. I'll call as soon as I know. Emily, my boss is calling. I have to go. Bye."

"Bye, take care."

I missed Jane and was hoping to catch up with her, but her new job kept her extremely busy. I milled around the room contemplating a nap when Sandy called me down.

"Emily, Sarah's here."

Excellent. It would give us a chance to catch up.

I gave Sarah a tour of the house and showed her where the wedding and reception would take place. Sandy and Barbara were more than happy to show her all that they accomplished today, and Sarah in turn was more than happy to give opinions of what she liked and didn't like about their choices. I took Sarah up to my room when the two ladies were done with her.

"This room is almost as big as your engagement ring," she commented.

After appraising the room, she added, "I think this room is actually bigger than the apartment Charlie and I are living in right now."

"I know. All the rooms are big in this house. I guess it's only fitting since the house is so big. So, tell me what's been going on. We haven't talked in months."

"Well, Charlie and I are now transferring next spring so I'll be around a bit longer."

"Yay! You have to give me pointers on married life."

"Are you excited that you'll finally have sex? Or, maybe I should ask, are you scared?"

"Sarah!"

"Well, it's a reasonable question."

I was quite scared about my wedding night, but I tried not to think about it. It's not like I didn't know about the birds and the bees. I knew what would happen, but that didn't discount the butterflies that fluttered in my stomach every time I thought about the topic.

Sarah continued her inquisition.

"Are you prepared?"

"What do you mean prepared?" I asked.

"Do you have lingerie?"

"Yeah, Gram bought me many in London." I felt my cheeks flush as I thought of all the lingerie that sat in Jake's closet right now.

"What about birth control?"

"Huh? I haven't really thought about that," I confessed.

"Are you planning on having kids right away?"

"No." We hadn't discussed this, but Jake probably didn't want kids right away either.

"Then you better decide what you want to do about birth control. Go see your doctor immediately and get on something."

"OK," I answered. "I guess I should've thought of this earlier, but I kept pushing it off. I'll talk to Jake when he gets home. How are you and Charlie doing?" I asked, trying to change the subject.

"It's been heavenly. Married life is definitely better than dating life. There's more work and compromise, but the love and commitment we feel toward one another is absolutely at its highest level."

This was wonderful to hear that married life would be an even greater extension of what Jake and I had right now. I didn't know how I could possibly love him more, but I looked forward to finding out.

Sarah also carefully brought up the subject of Max during her stay. I knew that this was inevitable, as he did not seem happy when I saw him at dinner.

"Emily, did Max say anything to you when he drove you home?"

"No, but he didn't seem happy. What's going on with him?"

"He's happy for you, but not happy for himself, is the best explanation I can think of. He thinks of you as the one who got away. He still believes that if he proposed on graduation night, you'd be his bride and not Jake's."

My heart broke for Max. What he was thinking could have been true, but it wasn't, and there was no point in beating himself over what could've been.

"Did you try to knock some sense into him?" My voice turned irritated. "What's the point in thinking about what could've been?"

"I know…Charlie and I have had many conversations with him but he can't shake off what's in his heart."

"Wait, wasn't he the one who led Jake back into my life? Jake told me that Max encouraged him to pursue me again. Why did he do that if he felt this way?"

Absolutely, I was forever grateful that Max helped me find Jake again.

"Emily, don't you see? Max loves you. He always has. He loves you enough to let you go to the man you love. That's what bothers him more than anything—the fact that you love Jake and not him. Know that he's happy that you're happy—that you've found your true love. He just wishes it were him."

I exhaled an uncomfortable breath. I thought Max was in a good place and now I felt this burden to make sure he would be OK.

"Let me think about this, Sarah. I don't know what I should do."

"There's not much for you to do. He'll get over it."

Sarah looked at her watch and it was already 8:00 p.m.

"I gotta go. Charlie's waiting for me at home."

"Thanks for coming by." We walked toward the front door together. "I'll come by and visit you at work again so we can have lunch."

I opened the front door to let Sarah out and simultaneously, Jake walked in and surprised us.

"Jake, you're home early!" My heart and face beamed.

"Hi, Jake," Sarah said. "Look at your fiancée's ridiculous grin." Sarah giggled and rolled her eyes.

"Hey, Sarah," Jake said, giving her a hug and a peck on the cheek. "You're leaving already? Stick around."

"Look at Emily. Does she look like she wants me to stick around? I have to go. My hubby is waiting for me." Her face glowed talking about Charlie, but it couldn't rival my delight. "See you soon."

"Bye," we both said.

We entered the house and Jake picked me up again and repeated last night's steps. We kissed all the way up in one piece, but did not make it to the bed as I wriggled down and pulled Jake to the couch. I had much to discuss with him.

"How'd you get home so early?"

"Your lunch must have put the chief in a good mood. As he was leaving, he told me that I could leave if there wasn't much going on. So, after checking on all the patients, I bolted."

"I'm glad you're home early," I uttered, making another mental note to be even nicer to the chief.

"Me too," he said between kisses.

I pushed Jake away so that we could talk over more wedding details, as well as a few other matters that he may not care to talk about. He sat on one end of the couch and I moved to the other end, with my legs stretched out and my feet on his thigh. He started massaging my feet.

"We need to talk wedding."

"OK. I thought I deferred all decisions to you." I could tell he too just wanted to say "I do," without any of this fuss.

"You did, and I gave your mom our proxy, but there are a few matters I'd like for us to decide. First, where are we going for our honeymoon?"

Jake's face pondered that question for a long time. Neither of us had a preference as long as we were together.

"Do you want to go more toward an island honeymoon or a city honeymoon?" I added to help in the decision-making process.

"I don't care. What do you prefer?"

"I don't really care either, but I don't want to spend the entire time at a beach, plus we were in Hawaii not too long ago. I think it might be boring. I don't know if I want to go back to Europe since we were just there as well. Honestly, we could just stay home all day for two weeks, and I'd be OK with that." Anywhere with Jake sounded heavenly.

"How about we go to an island in Southeast Asia for about five days and stay in one of those huts you mentioned on your list? I have to keep pecking away at your list. Then, let's go to Japan for the rest of the honeymoon. You can eat a formal *kaiseki* meal this time without any tears, and even take some cooking classes. I'd love to get a better sense of where you lived. There are many hot springs we can visit and we can also stay in Tokyo and enjoy the city life."

"That's a fantastic idea! My students would love to meet you. I'll call the travel agent and make all the necessary arrangements."

"OK, what's next?" he asked, trying to get up from his corner to come toward my corner. I stopped him and told him we needed to finish our discussion first.

"Dinner menu. What do you want to eat? I'm not crazy about the usual steak and potato meal, but I also don't want to have all fish just in case our guests may not like fish."

Jake had no problem coming up with an answer for this quandary.

"Emily, that one is easy. Let's not do a sit-down dinner. Let's have different food stations and hire local restaurant chefs. For example, we can call your dream sushi chef—you know the one who studied under Masa—and have his crew come and do a sushi and sashimi station. We can also have a pizza station, and a tapas station. I'll have Dad call his connections, and there will be a nice steak and veggie station. Oh, we should also call Gram's favorite Italian restaurant and have the chef come over and do a pasta station."

Jake's idea sounded divine. I could only think of two problems. First, could the chefs commit at the last hour and second, the cost. We were looking to have at least five of LA's best chefs come and cater our wedding. As much as I liked the idea, I didn't think it was realistic.

Jake saw the doubtful look on my face.

"What's the matter now?" The foot massage stopped.

"Do you think we can get all these chefs to cater our wedding on such short notice?"

"Fourth of July is on a Sunday, and most of these chefs don't work on Sundays. I'll have my dad, the chief, and Gram call all of them. They won't be able to refuse. If they themselves can't come, they can always send sous chefs." He seemed quite sure of himself, so I decided to trust him on this one. "What else?"

This last point I didn't know if I should bring up. I knew that Jake didn't like me talking about money.

"Well...what about the cost? The chefs and sous chefs alone will be a fortune, plus you're talking sushi and Wagyu beef."

"Emily, you really worry too much about how much things cost. We're only having seventy-five guests. Let's splurge on the food. I thought you'd be ecstatic with this idea. You're the foodie."

"I am excited! This is probably the best idea I've heard all week but..."

"No, buts. It's decided. Are we done?" He came toward me with a naughty grin.

"No." I pushed him back to his original corner. "Just a little more and we'll be done.

Jake obediently sat back in his seat, waiting for me to continue so he can go on with his agenda for the evening.

"What shall we do about...?" I couldn't bring up this topic. It was so embarrassing. Maybe I would just talk to Mom and not include Jake. But, then again, he was the other half of a baby so it would be wise to include him in this discussion.

"About what?"

"Never mind." I changed my mind. I couldn't do it. "I'll talk to Mom tomorrow about it."

"Emily. Speak now or we're done talking for the night. I didn't come home early just to talk. We, no I, have more urgent needs."

"OK. What do we do about birth control? Do you want to have a baby right away?"

"Are we actually talking sex?" Indubitably, his face lit up.

"Yes, we're talking about sex. What do you want to do?"

"That's up to you. What do you want to do? I'm OK with trying to make a baby tonight if you agree to it," he shined a devious grin, "or we can wait till whenever you are ready. Do you want to come see Carole at the hospital? She's an OB/GYN."

"You're OK with whatever I decide? Maybe I'll go on the pill. I don't know. Can you make an appointment for me so I can go in and see the doctor?"

"Sure. Are we finally done?" Jake was agitated now.

"Just one more topic. I need to talk to you about Max."

Jake looked perplexed and tentative when he heard Max's name. We still couldn't seem to talk about my ex without any tension.

"What about him? I actually saw Max and Peter at the hospital today."

"Oh?"

"They were on their rounds with Dr. Carter, and we said hello but not much else." Jake began to chuckle, "Carter runs a tight ship with these students, and he wouldn't let either of them stop to talk to me."

I sighed deeply before continuing my story.

Jake's chuckle turned into a frown as soon as he heard my sigh. He nudged my feet down and pulled my body over to him. We sat next to one another, my head on his chest, both his arms wrapped tightly around me.

"OK. Shoot."

"Sarah told me today that Max is unhappy."

Jake dropped his arms and pushed himself back to look at me.

"Why?"

"How can I explain this? He's happy to see me happy with the man that I love…"

"But unhappy that *he* is not the man that you love?" Jake finished my sentence.

"Yeah, I guess you can put it that way. Sarah says that he feels that I'm the one who got away. He regrets not having proposed on graduation night."

"I don't! Emily, Max will be fine. He will eventually find another woman and forget you ever existed." Jake grinned and searched for an annoyed look I refused to show.

"He can't ever forget me!" I retorted, but regretted saying as soon as the words left my mouth.

"Does that mean you can't ever forget him as well?" Jake's voice accused with a mock-menacing arching eyebrow.

"No," I stammered. "It just means that…well, you should know… it's not easy to forget me." I laughed.

Jake suddenly forced his body onto mine. Conversation was done for the night.

The rest of the week went no differently than the first few days. I saw Jake first thing in the morning before he left for the hospital. I fixed us breakfast, and he didn't come back home till I was asleep. I spent my waking hours registering for gifts, picking the dinner menu, and giving my seal of approval on all of Sandy's picks. Aunt Barbara spent most of her waking hours at our home as well. She figured since the chief was working all the time, she would stay busy with us.

Friday night, I tried my hardest to stay up and see Jake. I was annoyed that we saw each other no more than thirty minutes a day. I texted, I called. Rarely did I get more than a minute conversation before he got paged to another patient. Once again, my eyes failed me, and I couldn't stay up any longer. I sent one last text.

I cannot believe I have seen you no more than an hour in the last three days. It is one thirty a.m. My eyes are closing. Wake me when you get home. Good night.

Was this how it was going to be the rest of our married life? Ugh, I hoped not.

I was startled awake with a heavy arm on my body. Jake was fast asleep in our bed. I slowly got up to shower, but woke Jake up in the process.

"Don't go," he whispered.

I listened and stayed in bed with him a bit longer.

"What time did you get home?"

"About an hour ago." His voice sounded like he was in a sleep coma.

"You mean you worked twenty-four hours yesterday? What happened?"

"Lots of emergencies. I am so tired!"

"I'll let you sleep. We'll talk later." I kissed his forehead and left the room. Exhausted, he didn't put up a fight. His arm thumped on the bed as I dropped it from my body. Once downstairs, I turned on both ovens and put in the croissant bread pudding and brown sugar-glazed apple wood smoked bacon. Water for the french press began boiling as Sandy and Bobby trickled downstairs.

To my surprise, Nick came into the kitchen with Jane.

"Jane!" I ran to give her a welcoming hug. "What are you doing here?"

"What about me, Sis?" Nick opened his arms. We shared a three-way hug.

"My boss decided late yesterday to give me this weekend off so I flew in this morning. I thought I'd come and help you with wedding prep."

"Mom's done just about everything so there's not much to do, but I'm super happy you're here."

"Where's Jake?" Jane wondered.

"He ambled into my room about an hour ago and I haven't seen him since," Nick answered.

"Oh, he's sleeping in his bed right now," I said.

"I'm up," was all I heard as I walked into the breakfast room with all the food.

I was surprised to see Jake up and dressed already.

"Why are you up? You should sleep some more."

Jake came over and kissed me passionately in front of his whole family. Jane and Nick started gagging and Bobby and Sandy laughed.

"Are they like this all the time, Mom?" Nick questioned.

"All. The. Time!" Sandy answered.

"Sorry," was all I could say in between the onslaught of kisses.

We all sat down for breakfast and Jane and Nick both had great news.

"Mom, would it be OK if I moved back in for a year?" she asked. "My firm wants me to work in the LA office starting this fall. It would be too much of a hassle to find an apartment, so I thought I'd move back home."

"You too?" Nick said. "I need to move back in for a year as well. I'm going to defer med school and go do some research at the VA, over by enemy territory." This of course was his affectionate term for my alma mater.

"Jane. Nick. That's fantastic news. Do you know that your brother and I are going to live here for a year as well?" I shared our great news. Nick of course knew we were living here, but Jane didn't take it as happily as I thought she would.

"Why?" she asked. "I don't know if I want to be living under the same roof as you two lovebirds. You'll probably be worse than you are now. Eew!" To show her disgust, Jane stuck her index finger in her mouth and pretended to gag again.

Sandy turned to Bobby, who was taking a bite of his bacon, and exclaimed, "Bobby, let's charge rent. We can make a fortune off of these three. Finally. No more freeloading."

"Mom!" Jane and Nick complained loudly enough that Sandy backed down from her landlord-tenant idea.

I smiled, watching my new family talk, argue, and love each other. From the corner of my eyes I saw Jake watching me revel in his family's banter. He reached over and squeezed my hand.

"Emily, what's on the agenda for today? I am here to help with whatever you need." Jane looked eager to start her day with me.

"I'll help too," Nick added.

I turned to Jake to see what his schedule would be like, hoping the four of us could hang out today. Jake read my mind before I spoke. "I have to go back in this morning but I should be done sometime in the afternoon. I'll call and see where you three will be and join you."

He then turned to me and continued our discussion about cooking school. "Have you thought some more about enrolling in the CIA this fall?"

Nick loved this idea.

"I think I'm going to continue teaching this year. I don't want to go to school anymore. Even though it's cooking school, I don't want the pressure, and I'm sure the instructor and students won't like it if I'm there just for the fun of it."

Jake tried to convince me otherwise until I told him about my alternate plan.

"But, I think I'll continue taking informal cooking classes. It's more casual and I can pick and choose what I want to learn. Depending upon your schedule," I said to Jake, "I'll go and take evening courses. I will drive you and myself crazy if I'm home every night with nothing to do, but wait for you."

All of a sudden, I had a fantastic idea.

"Nick, you want to take these classes with me? I'll find classes over by the VA and you can join me after work. We can go eat at new restaurants before or after class."

Nick loved this idea even more. "Cool! Will Jake be paying for all my classes?" He sniggered over to Jake.

"I will treat you, but I expect payback when you become a doctor, OK?" Nick heartily agreed to this deal and we finished our breakfast.

Jake got up to clear our dishes when Nick stopped him with a request.

"Hey, Jake?"

"Yeah?"

"Are you ever going to make up for that botched Masa meal?"

"What do you mean, 'botched Masa meal'? What happened?"

"After you left Jake standing on a street corner in New York," Nick started laughing at his brother, "he was in such a foul mood he canceled our dinner. He actually paid the entire cancellation fee instead of allowing us to go and have our meal." Nick rolled his eyes at his brother and waited for an answer.

"I'll call that Urasawa and see if they can seat us tonight. I doubt that he will have four seats at the bar on such short notice." Jake walked into the next room to make his call.

Urasawa was one of LA's premier Japanese restaurants. It had earned two Michelin stars, and was the closest thing to a Japanese *kaiseki* meal in America. Hiro trained under Masa and bought the restaurant from him years ago.

"Nick, you're in luck. An entire group of eight canceled just now. I reserved all eight seats for us at 6:00 p.m. Don't eat lunch today." Nick's face lit up. My face lit up. We gave each other a high-five. We were each other's biggest food allies.

"Emi, have you been to Urasawa before?" Jake turned to ask me.

"No. We can't afford meals like that on a teacher's salary." I joked. "Why did you reserve all eight seats? Mom and Dad are going to a dinner function tonight with Uncle Henry and Aunt Barbara."

"I thought we'd take Sarah, Charlie, Peter and Max."

I gave Jake an appreciative look and called Sarah immediately. We had plans to spend Saturday together, so she was more than happy when I told her about Urasawa. I then called Max's apartment and Peter picked up the line.

"Hi, Peter. Are you still sleeping?" He sounded very groggy.

"Yeah. We got in a couple of hours ago."

"Are you on the same schedule as Jake? He too got in this morning."

"We may be on the same schedule but definitely not on the same pay scale. What's up? You need to talk to Max?"

"No, I called to see if you and Max wanted to have dinner with us tonight. We have reservations at Urasawa at six."

Peter salivated at the thought of eating at such a luxurious restaurant, but was unsure that they could get the night off. Listening to our conversation, Jake got on the line.

"Peter, I'll talk to Carter and make sure that you and Max get a free night. I know he's been working you. There's a chance that he may want you to come in this morning instead so be ready."

Jake got off the phone and jumped off his seat when he realized that he was going to be late. I walked out with him to say good-bye rather than grossing out Jane and Nick.

"I'll see you tonight at six," Jake said between kisses.

"You can't join us any earlier?" I frowned at another day without Jake. "Are you always going to be this busy? I might go get a night job too if you're going to come home in the wee hours of the morning all the time. It's lonely without you."

"I'm sorry, Emi. It should get better when the chief hires a new surgeon. Just think, in a couple of weeks, we'll be off on our honeymoon and we'll be together twenty-four hours a day for fourteen days. And finally, I won't get kicked out of my own bed."

We said another round of good-byes, and Jake left.

I finished getting ready and Nick, Jane, and I met Sarah at the department store for a final dress fitting for the ladies. We then walked a few blocks over and fit Nick in his groomsman's tuxedo. When Nick walked out of the dressing room, all three of us ahh'ed.

"Nick, you look almost as handsome as your brother," I gushed.

"Only in your eyes, Sis. I'm definitely the handsome one in the family," Nick joked.

After Nick's fitting, I finished registering for our wedding gifts. We made a pit stop at the dress shop so I could show Sarah and Jane the wedding dress. I felt like a princess again when they opened the curtain to show the bride.

"Oh, Emily. You look gorgeous! Has Jake seen you yet?" Jane asked in awe.

"No, he hasn't. He won't see me till the wedding day."

"He's going to go berserk when he sees you in this gown. As it is, he can't keep his hands and lips off of you. Yuck! I shudder at the thought." Jane literally shuddered at the thought. It was funny.

We had some time to kill so we walked into random shops and looked around. Without my knowledge, Jane and Nick had purchased a whole luggage set for us as a wedding gift. Since Nick was unemployed, Jane most likely paid for most of it. I was grateful for their generosity and love.

"Thank you both," I said from the bottom of my heart. "I couldn't ask for a better brother and sister."

"We love you too, Emily. I'm glad that my brother found such a cool wife. You're a great addition to our family," Nick uttered while giving me a hug.

Going from an adult orphan to a big happy family, my less than stellar luck with family finally reversed itself.

With six o'clock fast approaching, we put half the suitcases in Jane's car and the other half in Sarah's car. They barely fit, but we got them all stored away before we walked to dinner.

We walked through the sliding wooden door into Urasawa and found Jake waiting for us at the sushi bar. There were only ten seats at the sushi bar and one table of four at this restaurant. The chef and owner would serve anywhere from twenty-five to forty courses during this one seating.

My walk hastened to a sprint toward Jake in this tiny restaurant. We embraced and I sat right next to him, holding his hand.

"Geez!" Jane and Nick commented on our affectionate hug. I could feel their eyes rolling without actually seeing them. Within minutes, Charlie walked in and he and Sarah had a similar exchange. Peter and Max were the last to walk in. We all sat, Charlie, Jake, myself, Sarah, Jane, Max, Peter, and Nick. Hiro started with the appetizer courses, and we all broke into our own conversations.

Charlie spoke about his movie star architectural project, but still wouldn't give us a name. Jake, being an architecture buff, enjoyed listening to Charlie. Though the two of us didn't talk much tonight, any time we weren't eating, Jake held my hand or caressed my back to acknowledge my presence. Sarah and I discussed wedding details. Peter and Nick mainly talked about med school and college life. Those two were in the same fraternity so they had lots of mutual friends. Surprisingly, Jane and Max appeared quite engrossed in whatever conversation they were having. They didn't look away from each other unless one of us spoke to them. Sarah and I looked at each other with raised eyebrows.

"What's going on over there?" Sarah whispered.

"I don't know." I had to admit I was slightly perturbed at his attentiveness toward Jane. Obviously, he wasn't that afflicted that I was getting married. What happened to his love for me—the one who got away?

"They look like they are smitten with one another, don't they?" Sarah continued to stare at them.

"I guess," I answered curtly.

Sarah looked at my face and laughed. She read my annoyance immediately.

"Be nice. You did turn him down and accept another man's proposal. Let him move on."

"I never said he couldn't move on," I answered most defensively. I couldn't look Sarah in the eye. It was a strange feeling, Max showing interest in another woman. I knew I was being childish and unfair since it couldn't be easy for him to watch Jake doting on me. All the same, I wasn't used to him giving another girl so much attention. My feelings were unjustified.

Dinner lasted four hours. After seven *kaiseki* courses and twenty-five sushi courses, our chef graciously bowed and inquired about my favorite dish of the evening. Among the thirty-two courses I could pick out my favorite instantly.

"From the *kaiseki* menu, I loved the shabu shabu trio of scallop, goose foie gras, and Wagyu beef. And from the nigiri menu, it's a tie between the Otoro and seared Kama toro. I love the way Otoro melted in my mouth, and the meaty, creamy charredness of the Kama toro stayed on my taste buds for a long while. I can still taste it." Even after thirty-two courses my mouth watered just thinking about our meal. I added one more comment. "I think I could eat the tamago as a dessert rather than a nigiri. I'd love to learn how to make this savory sweet sponge cake."

Both chuckled at my dinner nostalgia.

"Dr. Reid, you're going to have to perform many surgeries to keep up with your future wife's palate," the chef teased.

"That's why I work such long hours," Jake poked fun at me as well. I pretended to put on a sour face.

After dessert and tea, Nick and Peter got up to leave for a frat party.

"Aren't you a bit old for this, Peter?" I asked.

"No way. This is how I keep myself young."

We waved good-bye and the rest of us finished dessert. Jake took care of the bill and we confirmed our wedding menu with the chef as the others went to the garage to retrieve all of our cars. Charlie hitched a ride with Peter and Max, so he got into Sarah's car. The valet brought up Jake's car and to only my surprise, he'd brought his two-seater.

"Jake, how am I supposed to go home with you if you bring a two-seater?" Jane let out a weak complaint. We all caught a glimpse of their— Max and Jane's—giddy mugs. Annoyance clouded my perfect evening.

Our car scenario played out like a bad TV movie. Jake and I were paired, Charlie and Sarah were together, and guess who had to ride home with each other? Max and Jane. Sarah got into her car quickly before busting up with laughter. I gave Sarah a cross look. Jake quickly got me into his car, and we left as well. Once we were out of the garage, Jake, too, started laughing.

"What are you laughing at?" I asked, irked.

"You sound a bit agitated," he answered and started to howl.

"What?" I asked.

"Well, I don't think that you have to worry about Max. He obviously isn't as devastated as you think he is about losing you. But, I worry about you, as your ego appears quite deflated." Jake's smug face continued to snigger.

I stayed silent the rest of the ride home.

When we got home, I furtively surveyed the house for Jane. Jake carried me upstairs and whispered in my ears, "She's not home yet. We don't do bed checks in this house."

Perturbed, I got down and walked into my room with Jake in tow. We got ready for bed and he jumped into my bed before I got there, but I was too disturbed to be torn about whether or not to hop into bed with him. I grabbed my pillow and opted for the guest room.

"Emi!" Jake protested. "Don't be mad. I thought this whole night with Max and Jane was comical—weird, but comical. I don't know why you are so upset by this situation. Are you jealous?" Jake's mocking voice disturbed me even more. "You're making me jealous and insecure now." His roar continued.

I left my, his, our bedroom and walked up another flight of stairs to the guest bedroom. Right now, I was more agitated with myself than with the situation. Why was I acting so foolishly about Max and Jane? It wasn't as though they were getting married tomorrow. They hadn't even started dating. Plus, it was none of my business that my ex-boyfriend might like my future sister-in-law. Ugh. I was still annoyed.

Jake's run up the stairs forced me to close my eyes and pretend to sleep. The fact that I pulled the comforter over my head didn't stop him from picking me up off the bed, flinging me over his shoulder, and flopping me onto our bed. He didn't mock, he didn't laugh. He did what he does best. His mouth pounced on mine and rummaged all he wanted. His lips, his tongue, ran over my body as if it were a map he needed to read. I shivered in delight, but shuddered at the thought of reigning in my self-control to stop him. Self-control waned as the wedding date got closer.

"Jake?" My voice was weak.

"Hmm?" His voice, suggestive.

"If you are planning on sleeping here tonight with me, you need to behave," I spoke, unconvincingly.

"Can I sleep here?" His face lit up.

"You can if you promise to behave. My wall of defense is crumbling by the day. *You* need to help *me* at this point. OK?"

"OK," he said casually, knowing that he had the upper hand now. He stopped his adventure quest on my body, content just to hold me close. I fell asleep in his arms, but woke up to find Jake's lips and hands grazing liberally. I softly moaned and went back to sleep.

Sunday was glorious for many reasons. Finally, I had slept soundly with Jake lying right next to me for the first time since we got back home. My eyes didn't automatically open at 4:00 a.m., and I wasn't cold at any point in the night. Also, Jake had the entire day off. We didn't get out of bed till it was almost lunchtime. We had both slept the morning away. When we finally awoke, Jake went downstairs to fix us something to eat and brought it up to our room. We ate, watched TV, checked e-mail and happily spent a lazy morning in our room.

The front doorbell finally coerced me out of the bedroom. Sarah and Charlie came by to drop off the suitcases that were left in her car last night. I invited them upstairs and we hung out for a while.

"Wow, this house is huge," was Charlie's first comment upon entering.

"Wait till you see Emily and Jake's bedroom," Sarah commented.

We walked into our room and immediately Charlie and Jake started playing video games on the giant TV. Sarah and I sat next to the boys.

"Hey, where's Jane?" I asked. "Shouldn't we take her to the airport?

"Jane left already," Jake answered with his eyes glued to the game. "Mom said her boss called last night and wanted her to come in to work today. She left this morning."

"How'd she get to the airport? I feel bad. I would've taken her."

Jake cautiously answered, "Um...maybe she had a car service pick her up."

"And maybe they have a driver named Max," Charlie added, and all three busted up laughing.

They immediately stopped laughing once they saw that I found no humor in his comment.

"Lighten up, Emily," Charlie quipped. "You broke the guy's heart. Let him mend it with someone else. Who better than your future sister-in-law? Maybe you two will finally end up as family, though I'm sure this is not the way you or Max envisioned it to be."

Jake only exacerbated the situation by adding, "Emi, will you be upset if you see Max and Jane coming down to breakfast together once she moves back home?"

"Ugh!" I stared at Jake dumbfounded. "Are you kidding me?" was all I could ask as they broke into a guffaw at my expense again. Annoyed, I walked out of the room to grab some drinks. When I got back, Charlie and Jake were having another disturbing conversation.

"So, Jake, have you and Emily started living together?"

"Seriously? Have Sarah and Max never told you about my fiancée?"

"I know the deal, but I thought maybe since you're almost married, and since she's living in your house, she might..."

"Charlie. Let's not go there," I warned.

Jake complained to both my friends. "I sleep in Nick's room while she stays here. I'm counting down the days till I don't get kicked out of my own bed."

This conversation made me uncomfortable so I looked over to Sarah for a little help. She jumped in and asked if we wanted to join them for a movie and dinner.

I answered, "We would love to," and kicked them out of the house.

After they left, I turned to Jake and said, "I can't believe you and Charlie today."

"He asked," Jake said defensively. "Are you mad? I didn't tell him about last night." His face was too smug. I had created a monster.

"Well since Nick is back at his apartment, you can go back to his room till we get married."

"Aw come on, Emily. Last night was fantastic, wasn't it? Didn't I behave?" Jake's face was pleading for another hall pass for tonight.

"Don't think I didn't notice your hands and lips all over me in the middle of the night."

Jake shot back at me. "And don't think I didn't notice you *enjoying* my hands and lips all over you in the middle of the night."

I ran up the stairs trying to hold my lips together from breaking into a smile.

Chapter 21

The Rehearsal

The next week and a half were a blur, as so many people came in and out of the house. Gram finally arrived from London and stayed in the guest suite up on the third floor. I thought she might have a difficult time getting up there, but soon found that the house was equipped with an elevator for her. My job was to keep Gram entertained while Sandy and Barbara finished up all the details of the wedding.

Jane came home on Friday and all the out-of-town guests started arriving as well. Jake and I had our final fittings and thanks to Aunt Barbara, Jake started his vacation as of Friday. We decided to have our dress rehearsal on Friday instead of Saturday, just in case there were any last-minute changes. We rehearsed at the house and then went to the chief's house for dinner.

Aunt Barbara set up her backyard to look like a Moroccan Riad, or garden. She replicated a riad by placing a fountain as the focal point in the middle of the tent. Hovering over the fountain stood a large open tent with rich fabric graciously draping over each pole. Lemon and lime trees stood near these drapes, while rugs simulating zellige tiles covered the entire grassy area. We sat on pillows on the ground and dined on couscous with vegetables, pastille—a squab meat pie, lamb tajine—a stew, and Zaalouk salad with eggplant and tomatoes.

During the meal, musicians playing the lute, drums, tambourine, and fiddle circled the tent, and we all clapped in awe when the belly dancers strutted among the guests. They tried to get me and Jake up to belly dance with them, but neither one of us was keen on making a fool of ourselves at our own rehearsal dinner. Charlie, Uncle Henry, and Doug got up to dance with all the ladies. Aunt Barbara was a good sport and she tried her best to keep up with the hip-swinging ladies.

With dinner and entertainment finished, Uncle Henry stood in the middle of the tent and thanked everyone for joining us. To my surprise, he called up Jake to continue a family tradition.

Looking at a crowd of thirty or so cousins, aunts, and uncles, Jake addressed our loved ones. "Most of us in this tent know that we Reids have a tradition at our dress rehearsal dinner. This tradition is started by the first child of his generation to get married and all the other children in that generation must follow the same tradition he chooses. Since I am the first among the cousins to get married, you all must follow my lead when you get married."

Many whispered, "I hope he chooses something cheap." I wasn't quite sure what they meant by this statement.

"The chief says that I need to pick from one of the wedding traditions of something old, something new, something borrowed, or something blue. Gramps apparently chose something old and gave Gram a pearl necklace that his mother wore on her wedding day. Gram?" We saw him circling around the tent looking for his grandmother. "Will you be giving this pearl necklace to my Emily as well?"

This question brought on a holler of boos from all the cousins. Again, I wasn't sure what they were unhappy about as opposition mounted.

First one to oppose was Doug, the chief's oldest son. "Gram, I demand a recount. Who voted to give Jake the six-carat diamond ring?" A round of "yeah's!" came from the other cousins. Most of the aunts and uncles found this dissention hilarious, and some of the aunts joined in with the protestors.

Oh, so that's what everyone was booing about. I, too, found the family ribbing comical.

"Doug, sit down!" Jake ordered. "I have the mic. Anyhow, before I was so rudely interrupted," my fiancé continued, "the chief continued the tradition by picking something blue, and he gave his bride a measly blue garter. All of his brothers had to do the same for their brides as a wedding gift. Now I must say, that's a crappy wedding gift."

All four aunts and Mom stood and gave Jake a standing ovation. We were rolling in laughter.

"Now it's my turn, and I pick something old and something new."

"Show off!" Cousin Glen yelled.

"The only way to outdo a *six-carat Asscher cut diamond ring*," he emphasized and enunciated each of those words while a hiss rang through the tent, "is to shower my bride with more diamonds."

At this point, every cousin paraded his and her strong opinion. The girls hailed Jake as a hero. They jumped up and down with animated faces, knowing that their future fiancés would be subject to the same tradition. They danced around like they'd just found a pot of gold at the end of the rainbow, and made the aunts' standing ovation look tame. The men, on the other hand, jumped up to the imaginary podium where Jake stood and put him in a head lock, pretending to assault him. The rest of us broke into every kind of laughter in the dictionary—a chortle, a cackle, a guffaw. My belly never hurt so badly from laughing as it did tonight.

When everyone settled down, Jake came over to me and walked me up to his stage. His eyes only on me, he uttered, "Emily, I don't think I ever told you this, but when I first saw you at the supermarket, I followed you around the store like a lost puppy."

"Stalker!" I heard one of the cousins yell out. The audience, myself included, found the comment hilarious.

"I was more than happy to help you after you fell. I told all the doctors and staff in ER to slow down your treatment so I could spend more time with you."

"Malpractice!" was the next shout we got from a different cousin. While we all laughed, Jake sent out a lighthearted threat to the hecklers.

"Just remember that you all are getting married after me. That means that you will all be up here at some point, and I don't forgive or forget easily." Jake attempted an evil eye. Nobody was scared.

Some yelled back," Oooh!" The others sarcastically called out, "Scary!" Jake continued with his story.

"After our first date, I knew that you would be the girl I would marry. What I didn't know was how deeply I would fall in love with you, and still I grow to love you more each day. I cherish your warmth, your honesty, and the way you trust me to take care of you. In turn, I strive to be your shield and protector and make you the happiest woman in the world. In short, my life is only complete because you are here with me. I love you."

There was not a dry eye in the tent. All the women cried. I too became overwhelmed with emotion and cried in Jake's arms. For a change, they were tears of joy. While I pulled myself back together, Jake excused himself and went over to his mother and embraced her. Though I couldn't hear their exchange, I was sure he was thanking his mother—his first true love.

Jake came back to me and held out a small jewelry box—yes, like the kind a girl received when a man got down on one knee about to propose to the woman he loves. Since that was already done, twice, I wondered what this could be. I thought I'd add some humor to this situation and put up both my ring-bearing hands and told Jake, "I don't have any fingers left to wear another diamond ring."

Jake found this statement funny as he opened up the box. I found a big diamond stud earring. I looked at the stud, looked at his face and looked back at the stud. Everyone in the room, including me, wondered why there was only one stud.

"Jake, this is gorgeous, but how does it become something old and something new and why is there only one?"

"Well, for those of you who don't know the story, I first proposed to Emily back in December, and she turned me down."

Everyone in the tent booed, even Gram. I hung my head low to the ground till Jake brought my chin up with a tender kiss.

"So this diamond," he continued the story, "is the first diamond I bought for her seven months ago, that I decided to turn into an earring since I got a new diamond from my favorite grandma." He waved my ring finger to the crowd for one more razzing.

"The other diamond," Jake pulled out another jewelry box, "is a new one that I picked up at Boucheron in Paris. So here you go my love, something old and something new." He handed me both boxes, and I thought it only appropriate to put them both on immediately. This time, I wrapped my arms around my love and embraced him passionately. It was only when Gram started clearing her throat we released one another.

"Thank you, Sweetheart. They're beautiful," I crooned.

Jake and I thanked Uncle Henry and Aunt Barbara for our special evening.

"Aunt Barbara, you throw the most exciting theme party I've ever attended. I can't wait to see what Thanksgiving looks like at your house. Thank you from the bottom of my heart." I gushed, giving both my aunt and uncle a hug.

"Now Jake, don't forget we have one more rule that starts tonight," warned Aunt Barbara.

I looked to Jake for an explanation and he hesitated.

"Aw, Aunt Babs, can't we forgo that tradition?"

"Nope."

"How about starting tomorrow night like customary?"

"See you at the wedding, Nephew." She walked away and I turned for an explanation.

"Well, you see…there's another tradition where they keep the bride and groom away from each other after the rehearsal dinner. Since we had our dinner a day early, you and I will be separated from tonight till Sunday evening. The guys usually spend the night together at one of the homes, which I think it's the chief's this time, and the ladies will all be at our house. I think Aunt Babs is enforcing this policy even more harshly to get back at me for taking the diamond." Jake found this thought comical.

I found nothing comical about being separated for two days. My lips must have formed into a pout.

"Love, it's only two more days," he consoled me. "After that, I won't let anything or anybody separate us again, OK?" He lifted up my sullen face. "I'll see you at the altar." Jake leaned in and placed his lips on my forehead.

This was the last time I saw Jake till I walked down the aisle.

Saturday morning we all slept in. We consisted of Mom, me, four aunts, eleven female cousins, Gram and her staff. Even with our huge house, everyone jostled for space. No one wanted to spend the night in our room, as all the ladies thought it would be weird to spend the night in what they termed, "the honeymoon suite." As much as I liked company, I was happy to be by myself while everyone crowded in the extra bedrooms. I heard a light knock on the door and I knew alone time was over.

Laney, the chief's daughter, walked in. "Can I use your shower? It's crazy how all ten showers can be taken at the same time. Do you need to use it?"

"I think Gram is taking all of us to the spa today as my bachelorette party/bridal shower. I'm probably going to go use the shower there after my treatments."

"Oh, well if that's the case, I guess I'll do the same. Can I hang out here with you for a while?"

"Of course." I was only too happy to get to know more family members.

Laney sat on the couch and proceeded to tell me a fascinating story.

"Did you know that you and I were in Japan at the same time?"

"No way!" I answered, coming off the bed and sitting on the couch with her. "When were you there?"

"All last year. I participated in a student exchange program and did my sophomore year at Tokyo University."

"Oh, I wish we had met earlier, Laney. We could've been friends in Japan. It was lonely living there without a friend. I took the bullet train many times into the city. What fun that was." Memories of Tokyo flooded my mind.

"Jake was so frantic when you left for Japan. He was such a mess. He flew to Japan and we looked for you, but it was too difficult to figure out where you were staying. Eventually, he went back home, but called me daily asking me to help him find you. It makes me want to cry when I think about him searching for you. He was *really* devastated." Her pretty face turned dour.

It made me want to cry as well. Those were not the happiest days, but I guess it solidified our feelings for each other. Those days also made me a stronger person knowing that I could live alone—lonely, but alone.

"So where exactly were you staying? I tried to help, but it was too random looking for you in every village." Laney's shoulders slightly shrugged and she looked apologetic.

We talked about where we lived in Japan and all the fun places we had visited. Not surprisingly, our paths crossed many times even in such a big country. Laney had even visited our village after I had left. I enjoyed my talk with her.

Spa time provided more revelations about Jake during our separation. Gram treated all the ladies to a full day at the spa. Because of the enormity of our group, the spa separated us into three groups of six. Mom and the aunts chaperoned Gram through all of their treatments. Jane, Sarah, Laney, and I hung with Uncle Billy's two daughters. We started with a body wrap in the mud room, and ended with a Shiatsu massage before meeting up with our group for lunch.

We sat in our private patio and Aunt Barbara asked Gram the question that apparently was on everyone's mind.

"Estelle," Barbara spoke. It never occurred to me that Gram had a name. "What finally convinced you to give up your most treasured ring? I thought you weren't going to let go of it till you passed away. We were all curious as to who it would be passed down to, although we figured it would be Sandy."

I never realized the importance of this ring to the family. Envy was not the motive for their curiosity, as each aunt could purchase one for herself if she so desired.

"This ring does mean a lot to me. My father bought it for my mother as a present after she had me, her firstborn. My dad loved my mother more than all nine of us combined. All I remember from my youth till the day my parents died was how they put each other high above everything and everyone else. When Jakey first told me about Emily, I thought it was a passing phase. He spoke so ardently about a girl he'd just met. Then when Emily left for Japan, I'd never seen Jake so distraught. I had dinner with him in Paris in February and he grieved for this girl who was alone in the world. He believed it was entirely his fault that she had left. There was nothing anyone could do to comfort him. That was when I knew he truly loved her and would do anything to be with her again."

Sandy put her hand over mine, knowing how sad I was hearing about Jake's pain.

"Eventually, he found her, and she breathed life back into my grandson. He came to see me before proposing to Emily in Paris, and he told me about every date they'd ever had. More than any of my own children, Jakey's love for Emily reminded me of my dad and my beloved husband. His love for a girl he's known less than a year was more passionate than any I have seen. He didn't ask me for the ring. I offered the ring to him. His passion earned him the ring, not his pleading."

Gram looked at me and lovingly encouraged, "You and Jake are perfect for each other. You complement each other well. Love him as much as he loves you, and you two will live a happy life together."

"Thank you, Gram. We will work hard to live up to your parents' legacy."

After ordering every treatment on the menu, we all had a light dinner and went home. I was sure there were many missed calls from Jake, but my phone got confiscated by Aunt Deborah early in the day, so I had no way of communicating with my groom. As soon as I got to our room, I texted Jake, hoping he could get away to call me.

Just got home. If you are able, call directly to our room. Missed you very much. Can't wait to become Mrs. Reid. Love you even more.

As soon as I pushed the send button, the phone rang immediately.

"Hi, Honey. How was your day?"

"Hi, Beautiful. I had a fun but lonesome day today without you."

"Where are you and what did you do all day?" I too felt alone.

"We're about an hour north of home and we're up at someone's ranch, pheasant, quail, and chukar hunting. I shot a Reid record ten, beating the chief's old record by two." Haughty was not a word I associated with Jake, but he always enjoyed beating Uncle Henry.

"That's great but what's a chukar?"

"It's a type of bird in the pheasant family. What did you do all day, my love?"

"We went to the spa and enjoyed every treatment thanks to Gram, but I really missed you."

"I missed you too."

As soon as he let these words out, I heard many unfamiliar voices making fun of my fiancé.

"Who are all those people in the background?"

"My college and med school buddies along with the rest of the family. You'll meet them tomorrow."

"When do you get back home?"

"I think we're spending the night up here and then we have appointments at the spa tomorrow. I don't exactly know. No one will give me a clear answer for fear that I may bolt on them. They're all seeking revenge because I gave you diamonds for your wedding present."

"Oh, I see. What would they do if I came to see you?" It was a tempting thought to drive over and see my soon to be husband.

"I wouldn't be surprised if Jane is guarding your door right now." We both laughed. "I guess I'll see you at the wedding."

"Yes, you will, Dr. Reid."

"Good night, my love. Sweet dreams."

"I love you. Good night."

Chapter 22

Our Happily Ever After

Sunday was the most beautiful day of the year. The weather was a perfect eighty degrees, and everyone arrived at the crack of dawn. Because of the perfect weather, Sandy and Barbara decided to hold the wedding outside, so it was chaotic for a while getting everything moved out of the ballroom and into the backyard.

I woke up and watched all the hustle and bustle outside, but decided not to leave my room. I liked being alone, giving myself some time to think about the magnitude of today and the joy that awaited us. Surprisingly, my nerves didn't rattle me. I only reveled in the happiness of becoming Mrs. Reid by the end of the day. My face couldn't keep from smiling as I watched all the workers transform the backyard into my dream.

Though it was early, I called Jake to see what he was up to. With so many men in one place, there would be no way he would still be sleeping.

My groom answered the phone on the first ring.

"Good morning, Handsome." I sounded even sappier than usual.

"Hello, my beautiful bride. You're up early. Did you sleep well last night?"

"No. I can't wait to have you in bed with me." It was my wedding day. I figured I could sound as brazen as I liked.

"Aw, Sis! I don't need to hear this kind of stuff so early in the morning. It's making me nauseous."

Normally I would have died of embarrassment at Nick having heard our conversation but today, nothing bothered me.

"Nick, go find something else to do. Don't listen in on a soon-to-be newlywed's conversation. What did you expect?"

"We're driving and you're on speaker so we're going to have to keep this conversation G rated, although I like the way you're thinking." Jake grinned through the phone.

"Where are you off to so early in the morning?"

"We're coming home briefly to pick up our tuxes, and then we have to meet everyone at the spa for haircuts and grooming."

I jumped out of bed excited that I might spend the morning with my groom.

"Does that mean we can see each other this morning?" I sounded much too hopeful.

"I will try to sneak into our room, but Nick is supposed to be my guard. He promised the chief to keep me away from you."

Quickly, a suitable bribe for Nick popped into my head.

"Nick, if you give me thirty minutes with your brother, I promise you a meal at Masa when we get back from our honeymoon. What do you think?"

Nick wouldn't budge.

"Sis, if I let Jake see you, the chief promised to torture me on my wedding day. He threatened many times."

"Nick, we won't tell him. I promise!"

"They'll read it on Jake's face. He'll have a stupid grin instead of this scowl he's had since Friday night."

We both pleaded and bribed, but to no avail. Jake took me off speaker phone and promised to try to come see me when he got home.

Aunt Barbara sent Laney to tell me to shower, but to stay in my robe. The esthetician would be arriving within half an hour and I would be the first one to receive treatment. After all the treatments yesterday it seemed unnecessary, but obviously Aunt Barbara thought otherwise. They converted Nick's room into the facial / makeup area, and Jane's room became the hair salon. We were all on a tight schedule, and we were warned not to miss our appointments. Jane was in charge of getting all of us to the right place at the right time.

I continued to watch the workers outside, while waiting for Jake and the esthetician to arrive. I saw that the rental company placed two rectangular rows of chairs on both sides of the grassy aisle. Over the chairs they draped white tulle, loosely pinned together with yellow and off-white roses in the back. They then set up thin trellises all along the outside of the ceremony area. Initially it looked like the trellises made a bracket on either side of the chairs without enclosing the walkway, or where we would stand.

The florists feverishly worked to cover all the trellises with mossy vines and every flower that bloomed in July. I recognized various lilies, jasmine, daisies, dahlias and freesias. There were many beautiful flowers that I didn't recognize, but enjoyed my leisurely gazing. By the end of their labor, they had created a huge flower tent loosely covering our ceremony. I had never seen such a sight. Then, I saw the florist cover the aisle with hundreds, maybe thousands of white rose petals. What the florist created looked prettier than any picture in a wedding magazine. Once again, I felt a surge of emotions—happy, blessed, and thankful to name a few.

While continuing to look out the window, I heard much commotion right outside my door and knew that Jake was trying to come see me. Laney frantically called for her mom and both Aunt Barbara and Gram came to stop him from walking into our room. Lane slightly opened the door and squeezed in to grab Jake's tux and quickly shut the door before we could see each other.

Jake was begging both ladies to allow him to see his bride, but neither budged. Jake hollered through the door. "Emi, I'm off to the barber. I'll see you tonight, Sweetheart. I love you."

"I love you too. I feel like a prisoner in my own house," I yelled back.

The esthetician began work on my face while I followed Jane's every instruction. Facial first, then a light breakfast, then sit and watch a movie, while all the cousins and aunts got both their hair and makeup done. My makeup session would be the last one.

Two more tents went up during the tedious hours of waiting. The first tent resembled a night club. The rental company set up a sleek lounge for what I assumed would be the cocktail and drink hour. Maybe we would dance in there as well, since a wooden dance floor was placed before the tent went up. Stark white lounge chairs and sofas with tons of white pillows were carried in one by one. Some sofas looked like shortened sectionals, and some were large round ottomans. Old chandeliers dimly lit the tent. The only dark furniture pieces in the tent were bar tables and an eight-foot table where probably a DJ would be spinning his tunes.

The other tent that went up next to the lounge tent looked stunning—similar to the wedding trellis with poles outlining the outside of the dinner tables. There was a beam on top with two triangular beams on the top sides. These all connected to rectangular beams to resemble the skeleton of a house. Then large swags of white mesh fabric hung from the top beam and draped along the sides of the horizontal poles. About six or seven of these swags fell from the top to loosely form a tent. Because no one drape fell right next to each other, the tent felt airy and open. We would be able to see the sky between each swag.

Three romantic chandeliers hung on the top beam to light the evening as well as hundreds of candles on the table. There was a mix of round tables with silk taupe linen, and rectangular tables with a rich mossy green silk tablecloth, decorated with a paisley-like crewel embroidery. The florist placed more white flowers all over the dinner tables. I assumed that the chairs in the wedding area would be transported to the dinner tent when the ceremony was over.

Finally, the hair and makeup artists came into my room and began working on me. Butterflies flitting around in my stomach signaled that my trip down the aisle was near. Both artists worked meticulously. The hair stylist decided to put my hair in a classic updo. The makeup artist chose not to put too much makeup on my face, as she thought that the warm weather might smudge the makeup. When they were done, the tailor helped me into my dress, and I was ready to commit my life to Jake. I would finally marry the love of my life.

Gram, Sandy, and Jane gathered around me to complete the last of the old wedding tradition.

Gram was the first to talk. "I'm delighted to give you something borrowed. Here is a pearl necklace my mom gave me when I got married. It's simple enough to complement your gown. I won't say much more since I don't want either of us to start tearing. We welcome you into the family." Gram put the necklace on me and I hugged my new grandmother.

Sandy came over next and gave me something blue. She continued her generation's tradition and bought me a blue garter. "Here is something blue. Your father and I love you as though you have been a part of our family from the very beginning."

"Thank you, Mom, for accepting me into your family. I can't begin to express the love and gratitude I feel toward the Reid family. My parents might have left early, but they definitely watched over me and steered me toward a new perfect family. I'm proud to become a Reid today." I too had to stop talking as tears hovered.

Jane told me that we still had an hour before the ceremony would begin. Mom left to go check on last-minute details and I looked out the window again to see what else had been accomplished since my time away.

Musicians began situating themselves toward the front of the ceremony area and by the time everyone sat in their place, it was a large orchestra. They tuned their instruments and began playing even before a single person sat down. Perceptively, Jane opened some windows assuming the free-flowing music might calm my nerves.

I also saw the florist moving a couple of eight-foot tables toward the front of the dinner tent. Sods of grass with white and yellow Gerbera daisies decorated this table. I smiled, thinking of my mom. On top of the grass sat white dinner place cards with thin light green ribbon on top, and what looked to be a small white daisy glued to the side of each card. The garden theme flowed through every detail of the wedding. Sandy and Barbara had outdone themselves.

With the hour looming, I missed Jake dearly. We'd been out of touch since early this morning.

"Jane, can I talk to your brother? Can you call him for me?" I begged.

"Oh, all right. You have less than an hour till you see him," she sounded annoyed. She dialed Jake's number and handed the phone over to me.

"Hi, Honey."

"Emi!" Jake sounded so excited to hear my voice. It was like we'd been separated for weeks. "Hi, Love. My gosh, I've missed you. Can you believe we're finally getting married?"

"I'm so excited," I gushed. "Are you home? Do you see how incredible the house looks?"

"Yeah, I'm home, but they won't let me outside because they see you watching from our room. This has gotten ridiculous. But it's almost over. I'll see you soon."

My eyes started to well up and Jane quickly took the phone from me.

"Sorry, Jake, time's up. She's starting to tear. See ya later." She hung up on him without any other warning.

"Emily, you've got to get a hold of yourself!" Jane chastised. "Sarah, you and I will have to carry a handkerchief just in case Emily starts to bawl during the wedding. Jake wasn't exaggerating when he said you cry easily."

After what seemed like hours, I saw guests begin to take their seats. If the butterflies were flitting around before, now they were demanding to be let loose. Jane and Sarah helped me get up and the artists touched up my hair and makeup one last time. I concentrated on getting down the stairs without tripping. My left hand tightly gripped the railing, and Sarah firmly held my right hand. Right as we got to the bottom step, "Pachelbel's Canon in D" began and Gram, Sandy, and Bobby took their seats.

Sarah and Jane walked me to the French doors that led to the backyard, but made me stand behind the door away from the wedding guests. Jane walked down the aisle first and before Sarah took her step she whispered, "Jake is looking for you."

Sarah stood between me and my future husband so a glimpse of him wasn't possible for a few more minutes. My best friend fixed my veil one last time, and told me to keep my head down till I heard Wagner's march and left me to face the audience alone. I chose to walk down the aisle by myself even though Bobby and Uncle Henry both offered to be by my side.

There it was. Wagner's wedding march. My time had finally arrived. I walked toward the door and saw the feet of every guest stand and turn my way. My head stayed down for a few more seconds to make sure that my heels were not caught on my dress, and to make positively sure my stance was solid. What a nightmare it would be to trip. Hundreds, maybe thousands of rose petals lay on the grass as an aisle for me to walk down.

As my head lifted, I searched only for Jake. Overwhelmed with emotion, our eyes locked. He lovingly held my gaze all the way down the aisle. The walk made me think about my parents. They would be proud of me. They would also love Jake as Sandy and Bobby loved me. It made me sad to wish that they could've been here today to witness our union in love. We would have all rejoiced together. But now, there was Jake and the Reid family, who compensated a thousandfold for all my lonely days.

When I got to the altar, Jake stepped out and held my hand over toward the minister. He pushed back my veil and whispered, "You look beautiful" and unorthodoxly kissed my lips even before the ceremony began. Our guests chuckled, and the minister proceeded. We exchanged rings and said our vows, and promised to love another for as long as we both shall live. I proudly got through the entire ceremony without a tear. When the minister told Jake that he may now kiss the bride, he held me tight but kissed me gently. We both rejoiced that we were finally husband and wife.

Hand in hand, we walked back down the aisle, kissing a few more times before we got back into the house. Jake picked me up and spun me around.

Elation. Felicity. Bliss.

Just a few of the many words to describe what we both felt. Two, finally became one. There truly were no words to describe this joy, this feeling of total happiness.

Jane rushed over with the makeup artist and had her reapply my makeup before we all went out to take family pictures. On our way out, I greeted many guests, but with some difficulty, as Jake refused to let go of me. With a newfound appreciation for his possessiveness, I knew that he would not ever let go again.

With joy cascading, I told Jake, "I can't believe we're finally married!"

"I know, Mrs. Reid. I didn't think that I could be this happy. I love you, Sweetheart."

"I love you too," I answered. We tried to kiss again, but Jane came between us and stopped Jake from ruining my makeup. She called us to the photographer and we obliged by taking copious pictures with family and friends.

The reception was in full swing when we arrived, and our guests immensely enjoyed the dinner spread. We first walked into the lounge tent where everyone comfortably sat around the chaise lounge and ottomans happily eating their appetizers. There were three bars with three bartenders, each serving every possible cocktail invented. The first station near the bar prepared Mediterranean Tapas as appetizers. Guest noshed on bacon-wrapped dates filled with parmesan cheese, chicken liver crostini with pancetta, and jamon Serrano.

A few yards away from them, Sandy had rented an outdoor pizza oven and this staff busily popped out pizzas and antipasti. My favorite bianca pizza with sage and fennel sausage was on the menu, as well as Jake's favorite funghi pizza. We also asked the staff to prepare fried squash blossoms with ricotta and brussels sprouts with prosciutto breadcrumbs. My mouth watered watching everyone eat. Jane wouldn't let me eat yet for fear of ruining my wedding dress. The DJ began spinning his tunes while we waited for the dinner tent to open.

Over by the dinner tent, I saw the sushi chef and his staff of three in a large area to themselves. He had laid the stunning ice sculpture I saw him carving this morning, out in the middle of the table. About a dozen variety of sashimi graced the table. From a quick glance, I spotted three kinds of tuna—toro, hon maguro, and albacore; salmon, yellowtail, shrimp, several snappers and tamago, along with grated wasabi root. His sushi chefs also used this same fish and assembled a large variety of nigiri sushi.

Near the sushi table was the pasta station. This staff of four cooked our favorites from seafood risotto, gimelli pasta with shrimp and tomato, and a spinach lasagna. Across the way from these two was our most famous California chef, preparing Japanese and American Wagyu steaks, along with onion rings, Matsutake mushrooms, roasted carrots, and Jerusalem artichokes. My mouth watered again smelling all the food in the air. When the dinner tent opened many guests flocked over and grazed these marvelous food stations.

Our four-layered cake, covered in a mossy green fondant with flowers sitting on all four layers, sat next to darling petit fours with caricatures of both of our faces. This was a tribute to our Paris trip I wanted to include in our wedding. We went over to see ourselves emblazoned on a piece of dessert. I snacked on a caricature of Jake before sitting down for dinner.

All our guests happily noshed on dinner and sat in the large open tent with the orchestra playing all our favorite music. Jake and I walked over to our table to finally have a bite to eat before beginning our festivities. Jane and Sarah continually came by to see if they could help with anything, and Jake eventually told them to leave us alone.

We saw Nick go up to the podium, ready to give a heartfelt best man speech toward the end of dinner.

"Jake and Emily are the only married couple I know who were broken up longer than they were together. I think they technically dated less than three months. Due to my brother's stupidity, Emily left him for Japan for four months and they finally reunited with the help of Emily's ex-boyfriend, of all people." This got a few howls from the audience. Nick continued to tell of our disastrous reunion in New York and our fateful one in Kyoto. He also explained our trip to Paris, and why there were so many petit fours on the dessert table. "I'd like for you all to help me cheer my brother and sister, Dr. and Mrs. Jake Reid." The crowd rejoiced while Nick came and hugged us both.

Jane signaled for us to come cut the cake, and I heard her warn her brother not to get any cake on my face or dress. But just in case, the makeup artist followed us to the cake table. I chuckled to myself. Jane obviously didn't trust her brother to fear her threat. We sliced the cake, with a paparazzi of photographers marking our every move. Jake carefully fed me the first slice and though he had a devilish look on his face, he was an absolute gentleman.

I, on the other hand, was not a lady. With an extra-large helping of cake in my hand, I couldn't help but mash it on his face. All of the cousins loved this and gave me a standing ovation. Jake retaliated with a ferocious kiss. I hoped the photographers captured those moments as well.

With dinner and dessert about done, the orchestra died down, and we all moved back into the lounge tent, as the DJ came back to life. He called us out for our first dance. Without my knowledge, Jake had chosen an Elvis Costello song that reminded him most of me and our relationship, and we happily glided to the song. Thanks to Jake crossing off another line on my to-do list, I could dance in front of people without tripping over my own feet. We squeezed in ballroom dancing lessons during our few free days and became decent enough to dance the night away.

"Honey, do you know that by the end of our honeymoon, you will have crossed off half my bucket list already?" I commented while dancing.

"My goal is to cross them all off for you, although I don't think I can send you on a trip with some random man. Maybe I can somehow arrange for you to have a meal with him when we visit New York."

"Do you know that you are the most amazing man?"

"That's why I'm married to the most amazing woman."

Everyone joined us on the dance floor but Jake and I might as well have been in a room by ourselves. We noticed no one. We broke into another one of our endless embraces and didn't notice Max attempting to dance with me. We had tuned everyone out.

"Excuse me, may I cut in?" I heard but didn't pay attention.

A little louder the voice repeated, "Excuse me, may I cut in?"

Our lips parted, annoyed. It was Max chuckling at our annoyance and smug that he finally got our attention.

Jake hesitated and warned, "Briefly. I'll be right back to claim my wife." He winked and tried to walk away but I quickly whispered a favor in his ear.

"As if it isn't bad enough that I have to watch you make out in front of me, must you whisper to one another while I'm standing right here?" Max jokingly complained. "Em, you look gorgeous!" he added with his boyish grin.

"Thanks, Max. I'm happy to see you here."

"I'm glad to be here and thrilled to see you so happy. Is this what you imagined married life to be?"

"It's better than anything I've ever imagined. Thank you. I owe a lot of this to you. I thank you for loving me for four wonderful years. Much of who I am is thanks to our relationship. I learned so much from you. I truly wish you the same kind of joy."

Max leaned closer and hugged me. "You know I'll always love you, Em."

I wanted to reciprocate, but saw Jake return with his sister. I turned to Jane. "Um, Jane? Do you mind changing partners with me? I'd like to be back in my husband's arms." With this, I leaned over and kissed Max on the cheek and whispered, "I love you too, Max. Debt repaid."

I fell back into Jake's arms and watched the happily surprised Max and Jane dance with one another. Jake looked at me with an appreciative smile.

"You are the most incredible woman in the entire world!" Jake exuded with joy. "Thank you for putting a smile on my sister's face."

The evening wore on, and we finally got to my wedding gift for my husband—the fireworks. Everyone sat in chairs laid out on the grassy field. The DJ announced to everyone to look out for Jake's wedding gift during the fireworks display. Jake kept distracting me with his lips and I had to force him to watch the show.

"Honey, your wedding present is coming up. You need to pay attention or you'll miss it."

"What does that mean?"

I gave him a stern look and pointed to the fireworks display.

Toward the end of the display, I saw a happy face light up and this was my cue to have Jake watch his present on display.

"Here it comes," I announced to everyone with excitement.

There lit the letter I,

Then came the shape of a heart,

Then the letter U,

Then they spelled out JAKE one by one.

Afterward, they shot off many more hearts and big explosions to end the display.

Our guests all clapped and cheered for us. Jake had an incredulous look on his face. This time, I leaned over and kissed his shocked lips and declared, "I love you, Jake."

"How did you do that? That was the coolest present ever!" Jake said, as his family members gathered around us.

"It wasn't easy. Once I got the name of the company in charge of the display, and after numerous calls, I finally got the name of the owner of the company. I called and begged him daily, asking him to add this to his show. He refused me for two straight weeks. Eventually, I wore him down and he agreed to do this for me under a few conditions:

I am to never call him again, and

I am to never give his information out to anyone."

I also told Jake, "I also promised him excellent heart care if he ever needed it. I promised him just about everything, but our first child." Everyone chuckled at this last comment and we all went out to the dance floor again.

By 10:00 p.m., Jake badgered me to leave the reception so we could get on to more pressing matters.

"Jake, we're not leaving already. I'm only getting married once. This reception is amazing. I don't want it to end yet."

"Then, can we go upstairs to our bedroom for a little bit and come back and rejoin the party?" He looked like a child begging for candy. I waited for the "please, please, please" to happen.

"No. I can't exactly get in and out of this dress easily. You'll have to wait. What are a few more hours? We'll be together for a lifetime."

He let go of me and walked away pouting. I grabbed Nick and Doug and danced with them instead.

"What's with Jake?" they both wondered.

"Oh, he wants to move on to the next portion of our wedding," I answered giggling.

They both understood a little too well what I conveyed. By the end of our dance, all the cousins played keep the bride away from Jake the rest of the night. Everyone, man, woman, and child, wanted to dance with me to keep us from leaving for our wedding night. The aunts and female cousins also did a good job keeping Jake occupied.

By 3:00 a.m., I wanted to leave. Pretending to give into Jake's pleas I whispered in his ear, "I'm ready." He was more than ready.

Most of our guest started eating and drinking again. The party continued as Nick put our suitcase in Jake's car and we showed our appreciation to Jake's parents and Aunt Barbara.

"I don't know how to thank you for this amazing wedding and reception. You two could go into the wedding business. We'll make sure to bring back a huge gift for both of you from our honeymoon." We kissed all three of them and sprinted from our house to the car without getting too much rice in our hair. I chose to stay in my wedding dress even though Gram brought me a trousseau from London. We hugged everyone goodbye and left for our hotel near the airport.

During the ride over to the hotel, Jake couldn't stop talking about our wedding night.

"Which negligee did you bring?" Jake asked with a puppy dog look.

I decided to be coy and not give him any straight answers. "Oh my gosh! I forgot to pack the negligees. I only brought my flannel pajamas," I answered nonchalantly. I also yawned and said, "I'm exhausted. I couldn't sleep a wink last night. Aren't you tired?"

Jake gave me a *you can't be serious* look.

I turned my head toward the window and held back a laugh.

"You can sleep on the plane all you want tomorrow." Jake's voice sounded like a pleading.

"Will you allow me to sleep on the plane tomorrow, or will you be making out with me again in front of ten strangers? I tell you what. I'll give you a choice. You can have your way with me tonight in private with my full participation, or you can try to have your way with me tomorrow on the plane, with me fighting you the whole way. Your choice." I knew the obvious answer but I thought I'd put it out there and hear his response.

"I pick tonight! So answer me, which negligee? Is it that red one that I picked out in London? It's not that boring white one Gram picked out, is it?"

Jake kept bobbing his head from me to the road often enough to make me nervous so I gave in.

"I'll give you two clues. Tonight's outfit was not purchased in London, but you've seen it before."

It took him all of two seconds to figure it out.

With way too much enthusiasm he shouted, "You kept that one from Paris? The one that was supposed to go to Sarah?" His grin was from ear to ear.

"Possibly," was my only answer.

I looked out the window reveling in our conversation and thinking how just a few weeks ago, I was alone in Japan. Funny how life had a way of untangling itself for the best.

Jake reached over to hold my hand and asked what I was thinking.

"Are you OK? Am I making you nervous about tonight?" He, himself, sounded nervous.

"I'm fine—a bit scared, but happy to be here with you." I leaned over to kiss his cheek. I knew that this was where I belonged, as Mrs. Jake Reid.

"Sweetheart, you have nothing to be afraid of. Although it was frustrating at times, I'm thrilled you have been with no one else. I consider it a real honor to be your first and only man." He held my hand till we got to the hotel.

With some difficulty getting out of the car in a wedding dress, I surfaced to a throng of cheers from hotel guests. Jake checked us into the honeymoon suite and we walked hand in hand up to our room. When we arrived, Jake stopped me right outside the door as he opened it with his keycard. He grabbed the Do Not Disturb sign and hung it on the doorknob with a heavenly grin. He lifted me up and carried me over the threshold. We gazed into each other's eyes knowing this was just the beginning of our happily ever after.

Thank you for reading *Indelible Love—Emily's Story*. This is my first self-published novel and I had so much fun dreaming up the Reid family. If you enjoyed this love story, I would be most grateful if you could write a kind review on Amazon or Goodreads. Word of mouth, and a good review for self-published authors like me, help tremendously. If you'd like to write to me personally, here are all the ways to contact me.

www.dwcee.com
www.facebook.com/DWCee
www.twitter.com/DWCee_

I'd love to hear from you and I'll try my best to answer all your questions.

The following is a taste of *Indelible Love—Jake's Story*. Hear his version, starting from the moment they meet to the family they create after the wedding. The first chapter is included. Also included are *Entwined*, a stand-alone novel, and *Indelible Lovin'—Max & Jane's Story*, the continuation of the Reid family story.

But, before you read the latest excerpts, there are deleted/rewritten chapters of this story I thought you might be interested in reading. Here is what originally happened at Sarah's Wedding.

Chapter 17

Sarah's Wedding

When I saw Sarah come out of the dressing room ready to walk down the aisle, I went over and carefully hugged her. I was thrilled for her.

"Sarah, you are the most beautiful bride!" I declared.

"Thanks, Emily. Thank you for being here. I know it's hard for you right now."

"Sarah, you're being ridiculous. I'm here for you. Let's not talk about anything else but you and Charlie today."

It did make me sad to be here. Seeing Sarah reminded me that this could've been my dream as well. I didn't want to appear down today so I erased these thoughts and helped Sarah begin her new life.

The minster had the bride and groom say their vows and Charlie happily kissed the bride. We all cheered for the happy couple and I caught a glimpse of Max smiling at me. After pictures were done, we walked into the reception hall and I helped Sarah greet her guests.

After dinner and a long toast by the best man, Sarah and Charlie went out to the dance floor as a couple. They looked blissful together. As their song ended, Max walked over to me and asked me to dance. He held my hand to the dance floor, he started asking me about my stay in Japan, and he guilted me into telling him the exact location of my whereabouts.

"I can't believe that you sent me letters with no return address! What was that all about?" He pretended to be flabbergasted.

"I'm sorry. I'll leave you my address before I leave."

"Why would you do this?" As I was about to answer, I saw someone stand directly behind Max tapping him on the shoulder. A strangely familiar voice said, "May I cut in?" I knew this voice. How could I forget it? But, it must have been my imagination because there was no reason for this voice to be here at this wedding. My heart leaped with hope.

Max turned around and I stared at the handsome face I longed to see. My heart ached for this moment since I left him standing on a corner in New York. I couldn't believe he was standing in front of me about to hold me in his arms again. I gave Max an incredulous look and he leaned in to kiss my forehead. He whispered in my ear, "My debt is paid. I love you, Em."

Before Max left, he turned to Jake and said, "We're all keeping an eye on you. Don't hurt her and don't make her cry. We are at a wedding."

"I can guarantee you the former but I can't promise the latter. She can be a bit of a leaky faucet." Jake mused.

"Don't I know it!" Max laughed.

This conversation was even more unbelievable. Jake and Max were both making fun of me. When did they become friends?

Jake shook Max's hand and said, "Thank you." Max walked off.

My bewildered look amused Jake and he quickly put his arms around me, and we began our dance. I didn't know whether to speak, ask questions, or just wait for an explanation.

"Do you know that you are the most beautiful woman here tonight?" Jake declared.

"Do you know that it's blasphemous to consider anyone more beautiful than the bride on her wedding day?" I chided.

"I guess I've just committed blasphemy." He smiled and held me even closer. I cherished this smile. "Hello, Emily." His voice broke as he peered into my eyes. "Very long time no see."

I could sense adoration and relief in his eyes as I'm sure he could sense tears and hope in mine.

"Hi," I whispered back.

I felt a rush of emotion all at once.

Desire.

Hope.

Love.

Anger.

But above them all...

Pain.

"What are you doing here?" I asked weakly. "Did Sarah and Charlie invite you?"

"No, I'm rudely crashing their wedding. I did send a nice gift ahead of time so I'm sure I'll be forgiven," he claimed nonchalantly.

I looked over at Sarah on the dance floor and she beamed my way. She gave me a look of encouragement and confidence that I did not share.

"Seriously," I said. "Why are you here?"

"Why do you think I'm here?" Jake's tone was a bit short with me this time.

"If I knew, I wouldn't keep asking." I said exasperated.

I noticed that the music changed to a fast-paced one but we were still slow dancing to the last tune. Everyone pushed us out of the way, and Jake let go of me just enough for me to start walking away from him.

"Where are you going?" Jake asked, pulling me back to him. "We're not done talking."

"I thought since you weren't answering my question, we were done." I tried to push his hands away.

"OK. I'll talk," he said, looking forlorn. "I came to dance with the maid of honor. Max told me that you were going to be here tonight."

I wanted to ask Jake more questions but I thought I'd let it go. What would be the purpose in reacquainting myself with heartache? Maybe Sarah did invite Jake to the wedding without telling me. I wouldn't make a scene at her wedding.

I walked over to help Sarah with her dress as she went to cut the cake. Jake closely followed. When it was time to toss the bouquet and garter, I quietly disappeared into a crowd of onlookers so I wouldn't have to stand in that awkward mass of single women. Jake stood right next to me and goaded me to go into the center of the circle.

"Why aren't you standing with all the other single ladies? Who knows? You might be the next one married." He gave me a most playful grin.

I felt my face scrunching into an unattractive scowl. For a man who went out of his way to ignore me, he surely wasn't lacking any words tonight.

"Emily. When did you get back to the States?"

"Yesterday morning."

"When do you go back to Japan?"

"Tomorrow." I curtly replied.

"Of course, you do!" He sounded angry. He had the scowl on his face now. "You leave no room for any chances of error. Who flies overseas on a Friday and goes back on a Sunday?"

"Excuse me?" I asked him.

"Why do you make it so hard for me to be with you? Why were you gone for so long? Do you know how far and wide I searched for you after you left me?"

"A bit bizarre that you would try so hard to find me halfway around the world, when you didn't bother looking for me when I was just across town. And by the way, you left me." My tone was biting. He had no comeback.

"Can we talk?"

"Jake, I don't know when we would talk. I leave tomorrow morning and I don't want to create any unhappiness here. I need to stay till the very end."

"Can we talk after the wedding? I'll stay with you till the end."

That promise you already broke. I didn't want the miserable pain that ripped my heart again but I wasn't ready to let him go. Even in torment, I preferred Jake next to me than away from me.

"Jake. Why now? Why after so many months do you want to talk now?"

"You really didn't give me much chance to explain myself before fleeing the country." His mood stayed humorous, though I found no humor in this conversation.

"You're kidding, right? All those unanswered texts? New York? Let's stop here. I should go help Sarah change."

I walked away from Jake, and I saw him walk toward Max. Evidently they formed some kind of a friendship while I was gone. How this could've happened, I did not know.

The last of the dancers lined up to throw rice at the happy bride and groom leaving for their honeymoon. Before Sarah left, she whispered a last word of encouragement. "Just hear him out." was all she said. They cheerfully left for Hawaii. It was one o'clock in the morning and I wanted nothing but to go to bed and get ready to leave early in the morning. I went to grab my purse and my shadow followed close behind.

"Can we talk now?" he asked impatiently.

"Jake, if I said no, what are you going to do? If I told you that I was tired, and that I haven't really slept in forty-eight hours, will you make me go and talk with you? I flew in yesterday morning, gladly fulfilled all my maid of honor duties, and would love nothing more than to sleep right now before getting on a flight in seven hours. If I said all this to you, will you let me go?"

My impetuous approach startled Jake. He looked defeated. I was unhappy to see his sad face. I didn't know what possessed me to talk like that to him.

He thought about it for a while and finally relented. This was not the response I wanted but I guess I asked for it.

"If you really don't want to talk to me, I'll walk you back to your room and leave you alone. I was hoping to apologize and straighten out our misunderstandings before you left. I've been waiting for this day for a long time. I thought that you'd be here a bit longer." His voice trailed sadly.

"But, can I ask you something, Emily?"

I stared at him neither answering yes or no. He must have found encouragement in my silence, as he continued his query.

"How come you cut off all communications? Didn't you know that your friends would worry about you?"

I became defensive.

"I wrote weekly. All my friends knew that I was doing well."

"I don't remember weekly letters. I believe you sent me one, but who's counting? Only through Jane, Max, and Nick did I know what you were up to. I can't believe you sent Nick more letters than you sent me!"

I laughed to myself. I did only send him one.

"With you...I purposely only sent one."

"Why?"

"Maybe I didn't consider you a friend! Maybe I didn't think you wanted to hear from me. As it was, I thought I was pushing my luck sending you any form of communication. Aren't you the one who told Jane that we were no longer together? Why waste my efforts on someone who's moved on?" My heart began twisting into knots. I started walking toward the elevator.

Jake followed.

"Well, if you were willing to communicate via letters, why didn't you send a return address so we could communicate back with you? Maybe I could've resolved our issues sooner if I knew how to get a hold of you.

I hesitated giving him an answer. I hesitated not because I didn't have an answer, but because I didn't want to show him how vulnerable I felt.

"Please, can you let me know why there was no return address?" His eyes begged for an answer.

I gave into his plea, as I knew that I would. I had no defense to his offense. My weakness was his strength.

After sighing I confessed, "I didn't send a return address, because when I didn't get a response from you, I would know that it was because you couldn't respond to me and not because you didn't want to respond to me." That did it. My heart let go and the tears flowed. I felt mad and embarrassed that I showed so much weakness. I revealed my deepest insecurities to a man who had moved on with his life. I couldn't stop crying. I fumbled for my key card, so I could go to my room. I couldn't wait to go back to Japan and away from my reality.

Jake appeared encouraged by my meltdown. He smile and tried to grab me by my arm and pull me to him, but I pushed him away and ran toward the elevator. He followed me into the elevator.

"Emi. Please give me a chance to talk. I want to explain myself. Don't I get to defend my actions?"

"What's there to explain?" I bawled. "You walked out on me a few days after you said that you wanted to spend the rest of your life with me and didn't explain yourself for months. What happened to your promise of 'I won't ever let you be alone again?' I thought you loved me, that you really, truly loved me. Why are you trying now? You don't owe me any explanation. You're free to do whatever you like. I have no claim on you."

My words weakened, and I sobbed even harder as I hurried to my room. I knew that at some point I would have to give Jake time to say his piece, if I wanted to leave town today. In my mind, I'd already agreed to give Jake a chance to redeem himself as I let him follow me into my room.

We got into the room and I saw Jake find himself a chair. I went into the bathroom, changed my clothes, and washed my face, trying to put on a brave guise. I waited for my heartbeat to settle before walking outside.

"OK. You win." I answered. "Explain yourself and then leave. I need to rest."

"First of all, I'm sorry. I'm sorry I walked out on you that night, and I'm sorry I hurt you. You don't know how sorry I am that I left you alone again. It was not my intention to not see or talk to you for this long. This situation clearly got out of hand." Jake's face actually looked as tormented as my heart felt. "The night you came back from Vegas, you broke my heart. I have this bad habit of shutting myself down when things go badly. I know it's wrong, and I know I hurt you the first time I did it on the way home from Hawaii. I'll work on that. I promise I will. I won't shut down on you anymore, I swear to you."

My heart started beating a mile a minute. I was sure that Jake could hear the thumping from where he was sitting. Could he actually be trying to make amends with me? I tried not to hope that he might still love me.

"Anyhow, I initially didn't answer your texts because I didn't know what to think. I knew that I loved you, but I wasn't sure that you loved me back. After a few days, I thought that maybe I would give you a chance to sort out your feelings and make you want to come back to me and me only."

This statement flamed my ire. "Why would I text you every day if I didn't want to be with you?"

"I believed that you cared. But you never affirmed to me that I was the only one you wanted. I guess I was looking for affirmation. When I didn't get this, I figured you had chosen Max over me and I let you go thinking this was the best for you."

"Jake!" Frustration colored my face. "Did you read any of my texts? Do you think I have some sadistic side in me where I would send you messages every day even though I loved another man?"

"I know. It was stupid of me. I basically gave myself a pity party." He frowned at this thought. "I realized when you sent me your last text, that I might have been wrong about your feelings. That's when I panicked. I saw these texts from your point of view for the first time. Maybe you still loved me but my lack of response would make you believe that I didn't love you anymore. I couldn't assuage the sick feeling in my stomach. That's when I decided to go see Jane in New York. I hoped she could relieve my frustration." My heart began to hope that there might be a light at the end of my dark tunnel. "I came looking for you at your house as soon I received your last text. I left the hospital midshift and wanted to tell you what was on my heart, but you didn't answer the door. Little did I know that I would see you in less than twenty-four hours."

"OK, so you finally saw my point of view but you still didn't say anything to me in New York," I charged. "If you still loved me, why did you send me away again when I saw you? You could've stopped me."

"When I first saw you in Jane's apartment, I was dumbfounded. You were the one person I most wanted to see, but the last one I expected to see. At first I said nothing out of shock. When I tried to speak, Jane started yelling at me, and you left so quickly. When I reached you at the cab, I wanted to hear what you had to say. I wanted to be sure that you still wanted me."

"Didn't you hear me tell you that I love you? I spoke in the present tense. Not the past, purposely hoping to evoke some feelings, some response, but I got nothing out of you."

"When you said, 'I love you,' it took me a second to process that you were talking in present tense. I replayed it several times in my head to be sure. When my head cleared and I tried to tell you that I loved you too, you were gone again. I flagged down another cab and tried to follow you but you were too far gone."

I felt weak at this point from having expended so much emotion into this conversation. I went and sat on the edge of the bed. I thought I might collapse. Jake followed me to the bed and sat in front of me, his knees on the ground, between my feet. He put both his hands on mine. The room spun as I imagined two scenarios that would result from this conversation.

Jake still loves me and we would be back together.

Jake did not love me anymore and this conversation would negate my four months of heart mending in Japan.

I hoped and believed it would be the former. With my luck in life, it would be the latter.

"Jake," I said, "can we stop for a while? I'm really tired. I just want to rest."

He looked up at me, and I knew he needed to continue, but my heart hurt too much to listen.

"Please? Can we stop?" I begged, voice sounding weak.

His hand pushed back the hair that fell onto my face and he brushed my cheeks. He listened to my plea.

"Go ahead and lay down. I won't bother you. But, can I stay here with you?"

"OK," I answered.

Jake sat on the bed and laid my head on his lap. He continually caressed my hair. I purposely closed my eyes and turned my face away from him so that he would not see the anguish in my eyes. I was afraid to go on with this conversation. I wanted so badly to believe that Jake wanted me back, but I feared that this hope would mar me if it were only a hope.

Within minutes, he called my name.

"Emily, are you sleeping?"

"No." I answered.

"Would it be OK if I just told you a few more things? I don't think I can live with myself if I don't get all this off my chest. After I tell you everything, if you ask me to leave, I'll go."

How could he possibly believe that I wanted him to leave after everything I confessed to him tonight? Couldn't he sense my desperate heart begging him to love me again? He must know that I loved him more now than I'd ever loved him.

He started talking, knowing that my silence gave him the green light.

"Emily, before I go on any further, I need you to know. I love you. I never stopped loving you. I don't believe I can ever not love you."

I began sobbing quietly at the prospect of being with Jake again. He sat me up to look into my once dejected eyes. Forcefully he pulled me onto his body and held me. My heart pleaded that he wouldn't let go of me anymore. My body burned with the sensation of affliction, turned to hope, ending in elation.

"I'm sorry that I broke your heart. I'm sorry that I abandoned you. I will never do it again. I absolutely cannot live without you. When I read your letter at the hospital, my world collapsed. It was like I fell into some dark abyss. I couldn't function for weeks. I took a sick leave and searched for you everywhere. Only when I received your first letter from Japan, did I think that there might be a chance we could meet again. That maybe we would love again. That's when I decided to get my act together and go back to the hospital and wait for you to return to me."

"Emily?" He lovingly called my name. "Do you still love me?" His eyes begged.

I gave in to my true feelings. "Jake. Of course I love you. I never stopped loving you. I was stupid to realize this so late. This is all my fault. I love you so much!"

He held my soggy face in both his hands and kissed me tenderly. We held each other the rest of the night, grateful to be together again.

Chapter 18

A New Day

When I woke up, Jake was sitting at the desk finishing up a phone call.

"Good morning, Beautiful. How do you feel?"

"What time is it?" I asked in a groggy state of mind.

"I think it's around 10:00 a.m."

"Oh my gosh." I jumped out of bed. "I missed my flight. What am I going to do?" I ran to the bathroom, brushed my teeth, washed my face, and started throwing clothes into the suitcase.

Jake chuckled at my plight. He pulled me to toward him and sat me on his lap. It took me a moment to realize that we were back together again. I couldn't believe that Jake was here holding me.

After a long kiss, he said, "Calm down. You can leave a little later. I have a few more questions. Let's talk again."

"No! I'm tired of depressing conversations with you. Didn't we work everything out last night?" I protested.

"Yes but we still need to talk. Now that we are together, do you need to go back to Japan? I don't want to be separated from you anymore. I missed you terribly." His eyes expressed sadness again.

I had to think about that. It was true. I didn't want to leave Jake. But I made a commitment and I didn't want to let my students down.

"Honey, I have to go back. I made a commitment."

He closed his eyes and pondered for a while. I could tell he was trying to find a solution to our new dilemma. "When is the school year over?"

"In two weeks."

"OK. As much as I don't want to let you go, I'm going to send you on one condition."

"And what would that condition be?" I asked.

"When school is done, pack a bag of clothes but Fed-ex the rest of your belongings to my mom's house."

"Why?"

314

"Because you're going to meet me in Paris. We're going to take that romantic trip you promised me. If you agree to meet me in Paris, then I'll let you go back and finish out the school year."

"And if I don't agree to meet you in Paris?"

"Then, I'll have to lock you up in a tower like Rapunzel and come visit you at nights."

I laughed at the thought. "You wouldn't dare."

"Are you going to meet me in Paris or not?"

"Is this a choice that's not really a choice?"

"Yup."

"Well, then Paris it is," I said, thrilled at the thought of spending an entire week with him. It was like a dream come true. No, it was a dream come true.

"Did you end up going to Paris in February?" I remembered that we were supposed to be there a few months back.

"Yes, I had to go. It was the most depressing trip of my life. I didn't leave the hotel. I went from my room to the conference room. It was hard being there without you."

I promised, "I'll make it up to you." We both cherished our moment together.

"Also, I have one more request." Jake said. "I'm going to buy you a laptop with a webcam. I canNOT go two weeks without seeing you—not after having endured four months. We will set up a time to talk to each other and you need to check in with me daily, OK?"

"Is that necessary? It's only twelve days. What a waste of money."

He gave me a stern look that made me cower into his demand.

"All right, but what about my flight?"

"I took care of it. I just bought you an LA to Tokyo then back to LA ticket. I'll call back and add Paris to the itinerary."

"What time do I leave?"

"Midnight. This will buy us some more time together. By the way, you want to change into what you're going to wear on the plane, so we can go and eat? I'm starving."

"Can't I wear these sweats on the plane? It's a long flight."

"I don't think they allow sweats in first class."

"Jake," I objected. "It's expensive flying first class, especially international first class."

"I'm horrified at the thought of you sitting in coach for twelve hours. Stop complaining. I've had no reason to spend any money since you left me. Let me splurge a little."

"Correction...since you left me. I was forced to leave after that."

"Whatever," he said, rolling his eyes. "Let's go eat and buy you a computer."

We hung up the phone and got seated for brunch. Jake sat very close to me in our booth and was back to his old self. He was actually worse. He couldn't keep his hands and lips off of me.

"Jake, we are in public. You can't keep touching and kissing me like that. It's making everyone feel uncomfortable."

"I'll stop if you'll agree to go home with me after breakfast and give me a couple of hours of private time with you. We need to make up for lost time." His face looked dangerous.

"Only a couple of hours?" I asked devilishly. "I was thinking maybe the rest of the day till I had to catch my flight." I started to laugh.

"Let's go right now. Forget breakfast." He tried to hurry out of the booth but I begged, "I'm hungry."

"Sit down. I really do need to eat something, and I have a few questions that weren't answered last night," I said.

"Shoot. I'll answer everything."

"First of all, how are you going to get so much time off? Did you get fired?" I sounded horrified.

"Oh, I forgot to tell you. I started lecturing at the medical school this semester. Chief saw that I was not in the right state of mind to be performing several operations a day so he recommended that I teach three days a week and come in the other three days to see patients. I think he felt guilty, because I pleaded with him not send me up to Seattle after I saw you in New York. Once he realized that you left, he became a lot nicer to me. The semester ended on Friday, and summer session doesn't begin till mid-July. I have a lot of time now.

We should go see the chief before you leave. He'll be relieved to see you. This is also how I met up with Max. He enrolled in my class and we became friends. You weren't kidding about him being smart. I think he knew the curriculum better than I did."

We both laughed.

"It was Max who told me that you were coming back into town, and it was Max who told me how you turned down his proposal. He encouraged me to pursue you when I thought I'd hurt you too much to salvage anything. He strongly believed that you still loved me and left for Japan thinking that I didn't love you anymore. I'm genuinely sorry, Emily. But, I do have a question that wasn't quite cleared up. Do you think I can ask you this question?" Jake said this with too much caution. I feared what this question might be.

"Um...OK. I hope I can answer it," I responded with hesitation.

"I'm still a bit unsure as to why you couldn't say no to Max back in Vegas. Why did it take you so long to turn down his proposal when you were able to turn me down so easily?"

A slight frown painted my face. I could see Jake still felt insecure. I needed to erase this immediately.

I leaned over and kissed him before giving him my answer. "When I turned down your proposal, I knew that it was temporary. It was only a matter of time till I would trust you enough to want to marry you. My love for you was already there. I couldn't make that last leap of faith so soon. I believed that you would wait. Although, you gave me a good scare when you went silent on me during the ride home from LAX. Can you promise never to do this to me again? You can't understand how much I fear your silence."

"I think your absence cured me of that bad habit. I promise I won't ever go mute on you anymore. We'll talk through any issues we may have." Jake's lips reached for mine again. I happily accepted.

I encouraged Jake to eat while I explained the rest of my answer. "As for Max, I knew the moment he proposed that he was not the person I wanted to spend the rest of my life with. You were too deeply imbedded into my heart. But, I didn't say no immediately, because I thought that my refusal would completely end everything, even our friendship. You know that I think of Max as family, even now?"

I formed this into a question, hoping that Jake would understand my need to keep Max as an important person in my life. Jake looked tentative, but willing to accept my feelings.

"I figured out after you left me that there was nothing wrong with loving Max as a friend, and that turning him down would not end our connection. Does this make sense? Maybe the better question would be, are you OK with my love for Max as a friend?"

My answer didn't erase Jake's insecurity. I declared my feelings for Jake one more time.

"I love you with all my heart and I can't imagine my life being void of you anymore. Please don't leave me again." This time, I was the one who sounded insecure.

"Emily, though we were physically apart, I never left you emotionally. You know that, right?"

"I know it now. OK, so I have a question. After New York, how come you didn't come find me? You knew where I lived."

"I'm glad you asked that because I was curious about something too. First of all, I called you a million times but you never answered."

"Yeah, sorry about that. I turned off my cell phone after I stopped texting you."

"I tried to call you at your school but realized that I had no idea where you taught. Funny thing how I loved you enough to want to spend the rest of my life with you but I had no fine details on your life. I didn't know where you taught. I didn't know any of your friends' last names. Worst of all, do you know that we've never taken a picture together? I searched my brain for any stops we made to take a picture and there were none. What did we do in Hawaii all that time?"

"We, no I, lost a ton of weight from all the exercise you Reids put me through. So you still haven't answered my question. Why didn't you come find me at home?"

"Oh. Sorry, got sidetracked. I did come by your house. I came the next day and you weren't home. I stopped by at all hours and you wouldn't answer your door. Then the very next day, the chief sent me up to Seattle to co-lead in a heart transplant and I was gone for almost a week. By the time I got back to your door again, someone else answered and said that you no longer lived there. I tried to convince this person to give me your contact number, but I think she thought I was some psychopath. She almost called the police on me."

"This is where I'm confused," said Jake. "You hadn't left for Japan yet because I didn't get your letter at the hospital till a week or so later. Where were you all that time?"

"Funny how our lives got so crossed. The day I got home from New York, Max came over and we had our talk. Later that night, Sarah and Charlie came over and shared with us their exciting news of marriage. I told Sarah that I only had two weeks left in the States, and we decided that I should stay with her so I could help her prepare for the wedding. I was fortunate enough to lease my house immediately and that would explain my tenant whom you met. I lived with Sarah till I left."

As we hashed out all the questions, I felt this panic overcome me again.

"Jake. What am I going to do?"

"What do you mean? What's wrong?"

"I don't have a home to come back to. My tenant is staying in my house till the end of summer."

"Fantastic!" Jake exulted. "Move in with me."

He abruptly corrected himself. "Move into my parents' home. Of course, you can take up occupancy in the guest room, unless...you get scared on the third floor by yourself and want to sleep in my bed with me."

"You're incorrigible," I said with a huge grin on my face.

"If you're done, let's go. My promised my parents that I'd bring you home today. They, especially my mom, are ecstatic that you're here."

After brunch, we stopped by the Apple store and Jake bought me a laptop to take back to Japan. Then we stopped by Chief Reid's house to say hello.

"Emily! Welcome back." The chief hugged me, a little too tight.

"Hi, Chief."

"Can you call me Uncle Henry instead? Everybody calls me chief."

"OK, Uncle Henry." I smiled at him.

"Thank God you're back. Jake here has been a basket case since you've been gone. I assume you are both back together and all lovey-dovey again? I need him back at the hospital to perform more surgeries. I've had to step in and do many of his operations." He guffawed.

"Did Jake tell you that after you left, he was so distraught that I kicked him out of the operating room? He could've killed someone with his lack of concentration."

"Aw, Chief, it wasn't that bad."

"Yeah, it was. Don't kid yourself. When are you coming back to the hospital full time? Don't you miss those fat paychecks? Lecturing doesn't exactly pay the bills."

"Well, I've committed to teaching the summer courses, and then I'll be back maybe three to four days at the hospital. I still want to teach one day a week at the school. I don't want to work six or seven days a week anymore, Chief. You've got to cut me some slack."

"Uncle Henry, I'd be grateful too if you didn't work Jake so hard. We never get to see each other once he's at the hospital." I pleaded my case along with Jake's. I saw Jake smile.

"I'll think about it. He's the best heart surgeon at the hospital, aside from me, of course." We laughed for a while then left for Sandy and Bobby's house.

I received another gracious welcome from Jake's parents as they gave me their warm Reid hug. Sandy actually cried when she saw me and thanked me for the beautiful clock.

"I'm so glad I'm getting a chance to thank you for the most wonderful Mother's Day gift. We were in New York that week for Jane's graduation. I found your gift waiting for me when we arrived home on Sunday. I was so touched. None of my kids got me anything this year." All three of us stared at Jake.

"Jake, how can you not get your mother something for Mother's Day?" I gave him a horrified look. Sandy looked pleased that I was scolding her son.

"I was preoccupied with your homecoming. I couldn't think of much other than that. Sorry, Mom."

"That's a terrible excuse," I said while Sandy's head nodded.

"I'll make it up to you next year, Mom." Jake won her over with his pleasing tone of voice.

They asked me questions about my stay in Japan and told me how much they missed me. Sandy started telling all kinds of what she called Jake's "moody" stories during my absence from his life. Embarrassed, Jake attempted to steer me away from his parents.

"I have something for you in my room. Let's go upstairs," he whispered.

"I don't believe you," I whispered back. "You're just trying to get me in bed. I think I'll stay right here."

"Mom," Jake interrupted, "Emily and I have some business to take care of up in my room."

Jake pulled me off the couch and forced me up the stairs.

"Jake. That was so embarrassing. I can't believe you said that."

"My parents don't care. They're probably laughing about it right now. Anyhow, I really do have something for you in my room."

When we got to his room, Jake felt the need to hash out our separation a bit more. He initially complained about my lack of trust in him.

"The more I think about it, how could you believe that I didn't love you anymore? Do you think I go around asking just any girl to marry me?"

I answered, "How could you go three weeks without talking to me—especially when my texts begged for an answer? That was really mean. You were the one confused about my feelings for you. Do you know how hard it is to send someone a message and to sit around and wait for a response?"

"Could it be any harder than waiting for letters that came to everyone but me? That was really cruel. I pathetically had to read my siblings' letters to find out what you were up to. Don't even get me started on having to ask my girlfriend's ex-boyfriend about what she had written him. I bet you he secretly gloated whenever he got a letter from you. Plus, how come everyone in my family got a gift but me?"

I sat on the large couch and watched Jake go into his mini tantrum. I took it all in knowing that he hurt as much as I did.

"You know what was even worse?" he asked with a frown on his face.

"What?" My voice empathetically rose to justify his indignation.

"Whenever you told Jane that you had just written me a letter but tore it up. That was enormously frustrating."

"Yeah, if I had sent you all the letters that I tore up, you would've gotten several per week. Sorry." I answered shrugging my shoulder. "But you must have also read in Jane's letters that my feelings for you never changed. They only got stronger while I was away from you."

"That was my only comfort during those long months."

"At least you had family and friends to talk to during those days. Do you want to know what was the hardest for me?" I paused wondering whether to share this information with Jake. "I had no one to share my feelings with. I hurt alone, and that was unbearable. I guess that's why I wrote so many letters."

I stopped talking. I could feel Jake's heart break.

Jake walked over to his desk and pulled something out of his drawer. He walked back to me and tenderly drew out my left hand. His look of love made my heart jump-a-flutter thinking that he was going to propose again. I definitely knew what my answer would be this time.

Jake slid the eternity band on my ring finger and I basked in this tender moment. But to my utter dismay, rather than proposing, he warned, "I don't ever want to see you take this ring off unless I replace with another one, OK?"

"All right." My answer sounded sore.

Jake mused at my chagrin and asked, "What's wrong? Were you expecting something else? Do you not like this ring?"

What could I say? No, I like this ring but I'd like a proposal along with it.

"I love this ring," was all that came out of my mouth.

We said a quick but sweet good-bye at the airport. It pained me to leave him again. I made up twenty different excuses as to why I couldn't go back. Every excuse pointed to the fact that we would be apart only twelve days. Then, we would have many joyful days together.

"I don't want to go," I whined like a young child. "It feels like a dream to be back together with you. I don't want to say good-bye anymore."

"Love, it's only for twelve days. We'll see each other soon. After that, we won't ever have to say good-bye. Make sure you log onto your computer at 5:00 p.m. your time. That will serve as a substitute until Paris.

"OK." I pouted some more. "I'll miss you."

"Me, too, my love. Me too."

I left him standing at the gate knowing that we would soon be together again and if God was kind to us, we would never say good-bye.

Indelible Love
Jake's Story

a novel by d.w.cee

Chapter 1

Chance Encounter

Exhausted! That was the only word that came to my mind after working an eighteen-hour shift. I was sure it was illegal for anyone to work so much, but in these life-and-death situations, I suppose I had no choice. This was the life I had chosen as a heart surgeon. Though, I probably would have been better off working at a different hospital. The chief purposely worked me harder to prove to others that he was not showing any favoritism to his nephew.

Hungry. That was another word that never left my mind when working so much. My stomach grumbled from a lack of food, as I've had one meal all day and it was almost midnight. What were my options? Drive home and stop by a fast-food joint on the way? If I hit the freeway now, I should be able to reach my house in the Valley in twenty minutes. Or, go to Mom's down the street and hope that she had food in the fridge? I decided to forgo both options and stop by the market to pick up a protein shake before heading home.

Walking into the store, the most beautiful woman walked by and I couldn't help but follow her from afar. She turned into one of the aisles and started looking for cereal. I paused to stare. She was gazing intently at the boxes in a peculiar way. It was comical how serious this decision was for her. Her long brown hair was pulled back into a ponytail and her porcelain skin would put dermatologists all out of business.

There was something about the way she looked—Innocent? Angelic? Scared? She intrigued me. I decided to stand next to her pretending to buy cereal as well. She had no clue anyone was watching her even though I stood two feet away. Closer up, she was even more stunning.

What was wrong with me? I was staring at a stranger in the market at midnight. As drawn as I was to her I decided to go get my protein shake and come back later. It would give me some time to muster up the courage to ask for her number. It had been a few months since I'd been on a date. It'd be nice to meet someone new.

Walking past her, I noticed she had precariously stepped on the bottom shelf to reach for the Captain Crunch box located on the top shelf.

I thought about getting it for her when she suddenly fell and knocked us down to the ground. She was embarrassed. I was grateful for the opportunity.

"I'm so sorry!" Her voice sounded almost as sweet as her face. "Are you all right?"

"I'm fine. Are you OK?" Hopefully, she had broken something so I could take her to the hospital.

"I think I'm OK. My ankle feels a little weird but I'm sure it's nothing."

Yes! Here was my chance. I would force her to go with me to the hospital regardless of how minor the injury might be.

"Do you want to try to get up?" I asked while holding her hand and helping her to her feet. Giddy, I felt like a boy holding a girl's hand for the first time. Her fingers were soft.

"Ouch!" She almost fell back to the floor and I couldn't believe my luck tonight. "I guess it hurts a bit more than I thought it might. It's OK. I'll be all right." She pulled her fingers away while finishing her sentence and tried to walk down the aisle. I didn't know where she thought she was going without me.

"Wait. Let me help you." In two steps I reached her five hobbling steps. "Let me take you to my hospital just down the street and let's x-ray your ankle."

"No, that's so not necessary. I'll just go home and rest it. I knew I shouldn't have been out here this late." It was cute the way she was scolding herself. She was right, though. What was she thinking coming out here at this hour?

"Please, let me help you. By the way, my name is Jake, Jake Reid."

"Hi, I'm Emily Logan." Her lips curled up into the most beguiling smile, sucking me into her world. Where had this girl been all my life? Being a cardiac surgeon I knew a thing or two about hearts but I couldn't explain what was going on in my own. My pulse beat faster, my blood rushed, and my excitement level shot through the roof. We'd barely spoken and I felt like this was the girl of my dreams—the one I would love the rest of my life. Perhaps I'd lost my mind.

Ignoring her scared look, I forced her to General Hospital and wheeled her into ER.

"Will you be OK waiting for me here while I get some paperwork filled out?"

She nodded yes like a young schoolgirl. Oddly, I sensed through her wide brown eyes that she trusted me to take care of her. My entire being felt this wonderful burden—a loving responsibility—to make sure that this Emily Logan would be OK. I had never felt such a strong desire to take care of someone like I did right now for his girl.

Practically waltzing into the front office, I had to figure out a plan to ask this girl to go out with me.

"Dr. Reid, what are you doing back? Aren't you done for the night?" Linda, the head nurse, asked.

"Yeah. I came back in with a patient. She might have sprained her ankle."

I saw all the residents heading my way.

"Who's that hottie you just walked in with?" asked one of the residents.

"Who she is does not concern you. If any of you as much as talk to her, I will make sure you're doing midnight shifts in ER the rest of your stay here at our hospital."

"Oooh! You're so scary, Dr. Reid." Jeffery, our youngest intern, at age twenty, attempted a joke. I gave him a be scared of me look and he backed off.

"I'm going to go back out and stay with her. Take your time calling her in. Treat her like any other patient who comes into this ER. I don't want to be out of here any time soon." I gave them all my most serious doctor look. I didn't think any of them bought it. Laughter erupted behind me, and I followed suit.

"What's so funny?" she asked with curious enthusiasm.

"Um...those residents were harassing me." I smiled at my inside joke. Placing myself as close to Emily as possible, I gingerly elevated her legs and hoped for hours of uninterrupted conversation.

"Do you work here?" Her trusting eyes made me want to tell her my whole life story. "Are you a doctor or a nurse?"

I guess I had forgotten to explain to her who I was. "I'm a doctor here. I work up in the cardiac department."

"Are you working right now? If you're busy, I can stay here by myself. Please don't let me keep you from your job."

I thought to myself, are you kidding me? You would need a crowbar to pry me away from you right now.

"No, I just got off at midnight and I was at the market hoping to pick up a bite to eat when you fell."

"I'm so embarrassed. I can't believe I did that. I'm very sorry." I took a snapshot of her beautiful smile and saved it in my memory. "I feel bad you haven't had dinner yet. You must be starving. Please go and get something to eat."

"I'm all right. I'm sure we won't be here long. I told the ER doctors to take good care of you."

"That was really kind of you. I would feel much better if you went and ate something, though."

"Would you like to grab a bite to eat with me, later?"

"Um…" I heard the hesitation I feared. Before she could answer, those pesky residents called Emily's name already. We had been there less than ten minutes. This had to have been an ER record.

I wheeled Emily into ER and saw a guffaw in each one of their eyes. There were two residents, one intern and one nurse waiting to attend to Emily and waiting to see my reaction. The staff was having a good time at my expense.

"Ms. Logan? How does this feel?" Michael began feeling her ankle.

"It doesn't really hurt there…ow!…that's where it hurts." Tears dotted her eyes as Michael poked into a tender spot. She looked childlike when she hurt. Instinctively my arms went around her shoulders and gave her a light squeeze.

She looked up at me surprised, and I retracted my arms. I could see the staff wanting to howl at my faux pas.

"So, Ms. Logan? How old are you?" Jeffery the intern asked.

"Twenty-four."

"I'm twenty!" I don't know why he sounded so excited revealing his age to Emily.

"Aren't you a bit young to be a doctor?" Emily asked in amazement. Her interest spurred him to continue.

"I'm what you call a genius. I graduated from medical school last year and this is my first year in residency." He had a smug look on his face. I tried to give Jeffery a back-off look but he purposely avoided my eyes. "Ms. Logan, do you want to go out on a date with me?"

Emily and I both looked at him shocked! I vowed to make Jeffery's life miserable when he got to my department. The other two residents had made a wise choice not to say anything.

"I don't think it's a good idea for us to go out." Thank God she was turning him down.

"Why not?" he persisted.

"You're really cute but I don't think it will be possible with our age difference and all."

"We're only four years apart."

"Well you're too young to even go and have a glass of wine with me. Plus, my ego couldn't take people carding me all the time while you got a pass for the next decade."

We all roared in laughter. She had a good sense of humor. I liked that.

"What about me, Ms. Logan? Would you be willing to go on a date with me? I'm off in thirty minutes and we can go grab a burger and a beer."

"Wow...tempting but I don't drink beer. Sorry!" She gave him an apologetic puppy dog look. Enamored with her, I couldn't even get mad at Al for trying.

All of us stared at Michael to see if he would try.

"I guess I have to throw my name in the hat as well even though I have a girlfriend," Michael decided.

"Ms. Logan, I'd be honored if you'd like to go out on a date with me." That two-timing jerk!

"Sorry, I definitely don't date two-timers."

"Yes!" I thought. That's exactly what I was thinking.

"Thank you all for your kind offers. I haven't had a date in almost a year and a half. Go figure, I should have hung out in ER more often." She shrugged her shoulders and her eyebrows arched up. "But, if you don't mind, I think I need my ankle examined more than I need a date right now."

Fed up and shaking her head, Linda came over and offered to put her in a private room while waiting for the attending doctor to come and take care of her ankle. I was grateful for her help.

"My apologies for those silly doctors. They're here late all the time and they try to find humor in every situation," she explained.

"No apologies necessary. It was all in fun. I'm flattered more than anything." She was as gracious as she was beautiful. Emily Logan...truly, where have you been all my life?

Linda put us in a nice room and her eyes signaled a good luck sign. I mouthed a thank you. Emily comfortably rested in the hospital bed and I sat in the recliner next to her.

"So sorry about all those guys..."

She cracked up. "I hope I didn't sound too mean to any of them. You have a bunch of cute young doctors here in ER. Are all the other departments this fun and lively?"

"No, the rest of us are old and boring."

We laughed together this time.

"So..." I asked nonchalantly, "you really haven't had a date in a year and a half?"

"Uh-huh."

"It's hard for me to believe no man has asked you out. Have you been hiding under a rock all this time?"

She stared at me, probably wondering why I cared. "Well, I've been asked out but I haven't gone out with anyone."

"May I ask why?" I asked cautiously again. I didn't want to appear too nosy.

"Um...I'm a one-man kind of girl, and I haven't found the guy I want to date. Dating around is not my thing." She hesitated then explained a lot more about herself than I expected to hear. "I was in a serious relationship for four years—all throughout undergrad, and my boyfriend dumped me on the day of our graduation."

I felt bad for her and angry toward this guy as tears flickered in her eyes again. Whoever he was, she must have loved him deeply if she was still hurting.

"Is he why you haven't dated in so long?"

"Um...I don't know if I'd say it was because of Max. It's really more because I haven't met anyone that I'd like get to know. Sorry. You look so tired. Details of my life must be boring you to death." Her eyes perked up again and tried to make humor out of her sadness.

She hadn't responded to my dinner request and I was just about to repeat myself when Linda came back in the room.

"Ms. Logan, I'm sorry but the attending doctor got called away. You'll be in here a bit longer."

"OK, thank you."

"Jake?" Her voice sounded like it was dipped in sugar.

"Yes?"

"Do I really need to stay here? I feel horrible you've been here so long with me and I'm really tired."

"You should be examined by a doctor." I wasn't ready to let go of her.

"Aren't you a doctor? Do you not know about ankles? Is it too minor of a body part for you?" With almost a coquettish grin she was coaxing me and teasing me at the same time.

Chuckling at her humor, I saw the exhaustion in her eyes and had to give in.

"Why didn't I think of helping you earlier? Let me take you to x-ray, then bandage you up if nothing is wrong."

"Would you? Thank you." Her weary eyes filled with relief.

Silently kicking and screaming I got someone to x-ray her ankle and confirming my initial theory that nothing was wrong, I wrapped her ankle with a bandage. I hope she didn't wonder why I hadn't done this the moment we walked into ER. All the residents came by one last time as I wheeled her to my car.

"Bye, Ms. Logan! Let us know if you change your mind." They all chorused in unison.

Emily turned to me as I helped her into the car and shuddered. "That was creepy. Please don't bring me back here ever again."

I couldn't help but laugh one more time. I hadn't had this much fun in a long while.

"Do you want me to drive you home?"

"No, I need to go pick up my car. I'll be OK."

We got to her car and I hated the thought of letting her go. Perhaps it was wishful thinking but as tired as she looked, there seemed to be a part of her that was comfortable with me—that liked being here with me.

"Jake?"

"Yes?" Subtlety not being my forte, I answered her question too quickly.

"Would it be OK if we went to dinner another time? I don't think I can sit through a meal right now."

My heart performed a loop de loop in response to what she said.

As casual as I could be, I answered, "Sure." But of course, much too quickly I added, "How about tomorrow night?"

I saw her hold back a laugh. She leaned over and gave me a light peck on the cheek. Like a schoolboy kissed for the very first time, her lips sent me over the moon.

"Thank you for all your help tonight." With that she hobbled out of the car. Frozen from her embrace, I stupidly let her limp to her car. Running toward her, I encircled my arms around her body and carried her off her feet. In turn, her arms folded around my neck and momentarily, I hoped time could stand still. Bodies close, face to face, I struggled not lock her lips with mine. As I couldn't help staring, she looked away abashed.

"Were you planning on running away without giving me your phone number?" I slowly let her go when her body pushed away.

"Oh, I guess you need that, huh? I have to warn you…I only have a cell phone and I'm not good about answering it. I respond better to texts."

She proceeded to rummage through her purse and jotted down ten digits onto a piece of paper.

"Good night or morning." She waved as she closed her car and left the parking lot.

My eyes finally blinked long after her car drove out of sight.

entwined

CAN LOVE REALLY CONQUER ALL?

DW CEE

OLIVIA 2010

"Olivia!" Shocked would be an understatement for what I felt right then watching Jamie approach me. "Oh my gosh! What are you doing here? I mean, it's great to see you again." He grabbed me, hugged me, and wouldn't let go. I felt like I was breathing again for the first time in many years. "God, I've missed you," he breathed, still holding onto me.

It had been a long and hard six years without him. Last we saw each other, he asked me to leave his life once and for all and never to contact him again. I choked at this memory and worked to control thinking about that night. All those times I needed him while raising Ollie. All those days I missed being loved by him. I shook my head and rid myself of these thoughts. After all, I should consider him no different than any other acquaintance—except for the fact that Oliver bound us for life.

My heart pained at his release. "Hello?" Jamie waved his hand over my face. "Are you there?"

"Sorry. I'm surprised to see you again. How are you? What brings you to New York and Central Park of all places?"

"I was going to ask you the same thing. I've been so stressed out with work. With it being tax season and all, I've been running during my lunch breaks."

"Are you here on business?"

"No. I live in Manhattan now. I moved a few years ago."

Here he was, in a neighboring state, and we run into each other at the park of all places with Ollie just a few steps away.

"What are you doing at a kiddie play area and in New York of all places?"

"I live in Jersey. We moved here five years ago."

Jamie's face looked like I just solved a riddle for him. "So that's where you went. I went looking for you at your house after we last spoke and I couldn't find you. Did you come here to be near your mom?"

"Yes." My voice struggled to find a monotone. I wanted to hide my true feelings of love, desire and yearning, even now, so many years later. "It was nice seeing you again, Jamie, but I have to go." I wanted to get away before he saw Ollie. Though I wasn't as anxious as I thought I would be, I wasn't ready for him to meet our son.

"Wait!" Do you have a number or an e-mail address? Can I contact you?" There was some desperation in his voice—maybe that was more my wishful thinking.

I probably gave a half smile wondering why he wanted my info. He was happily married with at least a couple of kids by now. His first child would be just a month or two younger than our Ollie. I didn't need to complicate his life with our presence.

"I don't think that would be a good idea. I really have to go." Walking away, my heart broke as he let me get away from him again so easily. Deep down, I wanted him to beg me for a number. It wasn't right of me to desire a married man. My pace hastened.

"Mommy," Ollie called me over. "Can you push me on the swing?"

"Sure. Let's go."

I picked up our son and plopped him on the swing and pushed him gently.

"Mommy, that's not high enough!" Ollie yelled. "Higher...Faster!" he yelled even louder.

I did as I was told and my son's cackles of delight echoed through the park. I kept my head down not looking back at where I was just a minute ago. He had most likely left. There was no need to check. Jamie was not mine anymore. He had made himself clear the last time we spoke.

"I'm hungry. Can we eat, Mommy?"

Slowing down the swing, I picked up Ollie and left the sand area. "What shall we eat?"

"How about pizza?" My four-year-old could eat pizza every day if I let him.

"Again?" I kissed his nose. "All right. Let's go eat pizza again for the third time this week."

I looked up from Ollie's smiling face and nearly had a heart attack when I bumped into Jamie again.

"Hey," he called hesitantly.

"Hey," I called back.

"Who's this?" Jamie asked both of us.

I had no idea how I was going to explain Ollie to his father.

"I'm Oliver and I'm four, almost five. I was thwee a long time ago." My explanation wasn't necessary. Our loquacious four-year-old introduced himself to his daddy without missing a beat.

"Hi, Oliver. I'm Jamie. What a great name. My middle name is Oliver."

Ollie stared at this stranger who should have been his closest friend. "Who's this, Mommy?"

I saw the surprised look in Jamie's eyes. I knew what he was thinking.

"Mommy?" Both Hutchison boys asked simultaneously—one out of shock, one out of curiosity.

"He's an old friend of Mommy's. I knew him when Dani and I used to live in Los Angeles."

Ollie leaned over and whispered in my ear. "Could he be my daddy? Is he the one?"

Tears formed unwillingly. Lately, Ollie had been asking more frequently about his father. His father stood just a step away and I couldn't tell him the truth.

"Olivia, I thought you couldn't have...Are you married?"

Words halted, his eyes immediately darted to my ring finger. What were the chances that he'd recognize this antique gold band on my ring finger to be the one he gave me? It was scratched up and worn through since I never took it off. Though our relationship broke, the ring stayed on my finger to keep other men from paying any attention to me...or so that was the reason I gave myself and to those around me. Painfully I had to acknowledge now that I wore this ring as a constant reminder of what I once had with Jamie.

"I'm hungry, Mommy."

"Ok, sweetheart. We'll go now." I stepped around Jamie without answering his question. "Good seeing you," I said walking away.

"Wait, can I join you?"

Before I could answer no, Ollie spoke for me again. "Sure, Mr.... What do I call him, Mommy?"

"My name is Jamie Oliver Hutchison. You can call me Jamie."

"Hey, that's my name!" My heart skipped several beats. Ollie knew that his last name was Hutchison but I had told my son many times he could never tell anyone this information. He usually told people his name was Oliver Maize.

"I told you we had the same Oliver name." Jamie put out his hands ready to shake Ollie's. Instead, Ollie gave him a high-five. "Where are we going for lunch?"

"We're having pizza!" Ollie shouted into the air and ran off ahead of us.

"What happened? I mean, how did Oliver happen? Didn't the doctor tell us you couldn't have kids? Isn't that why we had to break up? And when did you get married?" Jamie sounded anxious for an explanation. I wanted to tell him that it wasn't me who ultimately broke off the relationship. It was him who didn't want to see me anymore. He chose having kids and living a life with Melinda, his ex-girlfriend, over me.

More than anything I wanted to tell him the truth about Oliver but disrupting his idyllic life would be selfish.

"Ollie's adopted." The words just popped out of my mouth. Why had I said this? What a mistake.

"Huh? That doesn't make sense. Why? How random. Ollie seems wonderful, but you never mentioned wanting to adopt. What happened?" He sounded frustrated now.

"I wasn't looking for Ollie. He came looking for me. It's a long story, Jamie. Maybe one day when we're in a different place I'll explain it to you."

Dumbfounded. That's how Jamie appeared.

"Liv, he looks just like you. And, where did the name Oliver come from?"

I chuckled at the inside joke. Only if you could see that your son is a mirror image of you. From the day he was born, I understood I would never forget your face.

"I guess we've lived together long enough to start looking alike," I answered with a slight laugh. "As for his name...he came with the name." I was on a roll with these lies.

Jamie looked to be buying every misinformation. We stopped talking as we sat in a booth with pizza in hand.

"Ollie, what's your favorite food?"

"Pizza."

"What about your favorite toy?"

"Firetwucks," he answered with his mouth full.

"Are you in school yet?"

"I'm going to start kindergarten soon, Mommy says. Right, Mommy?"

"Yes, sweetheart," I answered wiping down his mouth.

"Any favorite places you like to visit?"

"The zoo—that's my favorite place in the whole wide world. I like sleeping in my mommy's bed a lot too. That's my favorite place but I can only do that on special days, Mommy says."

Jamie and Ollie looked smitten with one another. Blood was thicker than water.

"I used to love the zoo when I was little. That was my favorite place, too. Maybe we can visit the zoo in Central Park? Would you want to do that with me, Ollie?"

Our son looked up at me with expectant eyes. He wanted to go but didn't know if I'd let him. My silence kept Ollie quiet as well.

"Oliver, if you are almost five, when is your birthday?"

"Tomowow."

"Tomorrow? Happy birthday. I'll have to get you a present. What would you like?"

"To see my daddy. Mommy says I'll see him one day. I hope it's tomowow."

Ollie's request left us both speechless. I pulled our son from his chair and brought him onto my lap.

Hugging him, I reassured, "Ollie, your daddy is missing you too. You will see him soon. If you're done, let's say thank you to Mr. Hutchison and go home. It's time for a nap."

"Thank you, Mr. Hutchison." He yawned and was ready for a long nap. I picked him up and carried him out the door.

"Thanks for lunch, Jamie." Without saying much else, I walked toward the subway. I felt Jamie walk behind us but neither of us uttered a sound. As I shifted Ollie's drowsy body Jamie came up from behind and carried our child to the subway. Silently we waited for the train to approach.

"Olivia, can we go somewhere and talk? I have so many questions for you. Like...where you've been the last six years. Why you've never tried to contact me. Did our relationship mean so little to you that you could abandon it after one argument? And, where's your husband? Did you two separate?"

"You told me never to call you again," I whispered.

"I was mad," he answered, frustrated. "You left behind a terse message saying you were giving me time to think through our relationship, before flying off early to Africa. Then you went AWOL on me for two months. Not one e-mail, call, letter—not one word—for two whole months. What did you expect?" Now he was angry.

"I came back and told you why I did that and how sorry I was. You were the one who said you couldn't forgive me."

"I'm sorry. I was an idiot. I couldn't see past the anger for a long time. Once I did, I came back looking for you but I couldn't find you again."

"It doesn't matter now," I responded with deep sadness. He was married and he thought I was married as well.

"Are you going to disappear again without a trace? Will you at least take my number and call me? I've missed you. It's been so long...too long."

He laid a heavy burden on my heart. I wanted his number, his heart, his commitment to me and Ollie. This could never be.

I took Ollie from his father and stepped into the train.

"Wait!" He held my arm. He slipped his business card into my purse and said, "Please call me. We need to talk." He sounded desperate now.

"You made yourself clear to me the last time we spoke. I don't want to be your 'burden.' Hope Melinda is well."

With perfect timing the door shut and I sat with my back against Jamie's face. I heard the banging on the window but my crying eyes didn't turn around. Hugging our son tightly to my chest I cried all the way home.

Carrying Ollie from the station to my mom's house, I was lost in my own thoughts of what had transpired today.

"Olivia!" My mother yelled. "Wait up." I turned to see her hastily walking toward us. "Have you been walking with Oliver this whole time? Here, give him to me."

My mom looked up at me in fright. "What happened to you? Why have you been crying?"

"Ollie and I ran into Jamie at the park today. What am I going to do, Mom?" The tears fell even heavier.

BLOG STYLE

Indelible Lovin'

Max & Jane's story

d. w. cee

December 4, 2012 A Harley Man?

I looked out my window as a loud roar of pipes rolled up the driveway. Max pulled up on a sleek new motorcycle. At least I thought it was new. I hadn't seen Max in about six months so I couldn't be sure when he got the bike.

Max was *so* not the Harley type of guy. He was the straight-laced, straight-A, straight-shooting type. The boy next door, as my sister-in-law, Emily, described him. Those monikers, as well as Max's ex-girlfriend, and my new sister, Emily, were the reasons why we took a break for a while.

I stared at the good-looking brown-haired, brown-eyed guy. With more ease than I preferred, he gave Emily a hug and a kiss.

"Max! What a wonderful surprise. What are you doing here…and so early in the morning?" Emily greeted.

"Hi, Em. I see motherhood agrees with you. You look beautiful even at this early hour." *Really???* Did he always need to find her so enchanting?

"Hey!" Of course, where Emily was, my brother wasn't far behind. "Get your hands and lips off my wife!" he demanded.

"Lighten up, Dr. Reid. I was just saying hello to my beautiful ex-girlfriend."

"Must you always bring up the fact that you and my wife once dated?"

"We didn't just once date; we were together twice the length of time you and she have been together."

The irritation in Jake's eyes was cracking me up. He was so easily riled. Though, the conversation outside was making me feel a little snarky, myself. *Relax…*My new mantra as we were going to try again. I needed to get over my "hang-ups," as Max called them.

"Cut it out, both of you," Emily warned while giving her husband a loving embrace. "Good Morning." Now she was only addressing Jake. "I brought the kids out so they wouldn't wake you. You got in so late last night from the hospital."

"It was lonely in bed without you," Jake announced loudly, so the whole neighborhood could hear. "I wanted to be out here with my family." My brother's voice got louder with each word, but not as loud as his twin son and daughter—Elizabeth and James.

"Da! Da! Da!" The twins screeched. The four of them made a gorgeous family and the smile on Max's face warmed my heart. For a change, he didn't look like he was still in love with Emily, but instead, he looked like he was in love with the idea of a happy family.

Time to make my grand entrance!

"Hey," I greeted.

"Hey..." His voice was soft as he locked eyes with me. Had he thought about me in the past six months? Had he missed me? Had he been dating around? Would we be able to make it work this time?
"Is this what you meant when you said you wanted to go for a ride?"

"I thought we'd ride up the coast for a while.?"

"OK, I guess..." What would happen today? Things had ended so abruptly between us. One day we were, then the next day we weren't.

"I can't wait to spend the day with you. I've been looking forward to it all week."

Really?

He somehow heard the doubting Thomas question in my head.

"Hey." He gently tugged my chin up with this thumb and forefinger. "I guess you haven't missed me as much as I've missed you.? Can we try this again and see where it takes us?"

Twenty-plus words were all it took to melt away the bitterness of the past year and make me want to start again. I smiled. *Pushover!* Yeah...pushed-over and falling again. I was such a LOSER.

"Don't let go of another good one!" my brother sarcastically yelled as Max tried to muffle his words with the roar of the bike.

"Hold on tight!"

Ominous and yet very promising words…

December 9, 2012 Well...That Didn't Go So Well...

"You're back!" My sister-in-law smiled with more enthusiasm than totally necessary. "You spent the night?"

"No," I cut her off, "I mean yes, but no."

"Explain, Sister." The thing about Emily—as sweet as she is, she's ruthless when she wants something from you. Whether it's the dazzling smile she throws your way, or her sweet innocent pleading look, you can't say no. Does this woman have any negatives in that beautiful frame of hers? I love her, but *ugh*!

"We rode up to Santa Barbara and were having brunch at the Four Seasons when everything went downhill."

Emily didn't need to know that the ride sucked. There was too much wind, the seat was uncomfortable, it was cold, and we didn't say one word to each other for an hour and a half, but did I complain? No! I was accommodating—as accommodating as Jane Sydney Reid was ever going to be.

"And..?"

"Max's cell phone kept ringing. After about the fifth ring, I kinda yelled at him to pick up the phone, and guess who was calling him?"

"Who?" Emily's big brown eyes were bugging out. It was cute, in a freakishly bugging sort of way.

"Some *GIRL*! He was so uncomfortable talking to her and he couldn't—no, he wouldn't tell her that he was out with me. I was so pissed, I felt like walking out on him but I sat through his awkward conversation to get some answers."

While I was pining away for him the last half of the year, apparently, this jerk was dating around.

"He explained that he had 'group-dated' this girl, another doctor at his hospital, briefly." Emily's mouth opened but I didn't give her a chance to start.

I had too many things to say. "And though it bothered me, all would have been OK except...his last date with her was just 'a few days ago.'"

Those were the jerk's words, verbatim! What kind of man tells one woman that he misses her and would like to try for a relationship with her one day, then goes out with a totally different woman the next day? Am I wrong to want someone to love me and me only? Forget love—way too soon for that concept. I just want someone to want me and me only. Maybe it's an LA thing? Perhaps I should move back to New York and work a hundred hours a week and be on track to become the youngest partner at our firm.

"No!" Emily was horrified, then mad. She pulled out her cell phone and before she could call Max, I took it away from her. "Let me call him and yell at him. He can't treat you like that! Oh, Jane..." Then, she hugged me. I think she was more hurt than I was. No matter what I thought or said about my sister, I loved her and she genuinely loved me. The rivalry was only on my part and solely in my head. "So where were you all yesterday?"

"I left Max, got myself a room, then a rental car. After calling around, I got a hold of my girlfriend, Hilary, and we hung out the whole day. The thought of sitting in the hotel room and gorging on ice cream was tempting, but I spent a boatload of money on clothes and shoes instead."

"Oh, sweet Jane! Your knight in shining armor will come around. Max just needs to sort out his life and grow up some more."

At this point, Max ≠ a knight in shining armor. Well...back to the drawing board!

December 13, 2013 Another date...And His Initials Aren't M.D.

This was the text that greeted my morning.

Can we meet for a quick lunch? You need to give me a chance to explain.
I *need* to give you a chance?
OK, sorry. Not the right thing to say. A lunch for a chance to grovel?

That made me laugh. Since I left without hearing the full explanation, I suppose I needed to give him a chance. Ha! It was more like I was dying to know who this Joyce girl was that he had been dating. From what my brother Jake told me, she was this brilliant doctor from Stanford who had been after Max for a while. When I asked what she looked like, he shrugged, saying that he hasn't paid attention to another woman's looks since he met Emily. Whatever...*Dork!*

OK but you've gotta come my way cuz I only have 30 min.
Perfect. See you soon.

The morning flew by between meetings and prep work for a case I was assisting.

"Jane, you have a moment?"

"Um, sure."

Donovan, the head lawyer in mergers and acquisitions, waited for me to get up from my seat and practically held my hand into his office.

"What's up?"

He handed me an envelope and gestured for me to open it.

"I just got these tickets to a Laker game and I was wondering if you wanted to go with me?"

"Like...as in a date?" I sounded so sophomoric, or better yet, so moronic asking this in a high-pitched voice.

"Yes, as in a date. Dinner at the Palm, floor seats to watch Kobe, Pau, and Howard in action? Unfortunately your favorite player is still injured."

Damn!
Double Damn!

Floor seats, Laker game, hot successful lawyer…Why couldn't he have asked me out just a few days ago? Do I go? Do I need to explain about Max? What would I say? *Um…I'm kinda re-seeing this guy who had been dating around while I thought about him constantly?*

"Hello. Earth to Jane?"

"Wait, how'd you know Steve Nash was my favorite player?"

"I heard you mention it the other day and bought these tickets with you in mind."

A man who listens to what I have to say even when I wasn't talking to him? Was he for real? Was I an idiot for letting this one go?

"Sure. I'd like that."

"Great! We'll take the company shuttle. I'll pick you up at six?"

A goofy smile crossed my lips. "See you at six."

That high didn't last long as the speakerphone buzzed. "A Max Davis waiting for you in the lobby…"

Triple Damn!

Printed in Great Britain
by Amazon.co.uk, Ltd.,
Marston Gate.